CONSUMED

CONSUMED

A novel by Michael W. Bugni

ARCHWAY
PUBLISHING

Cover Design by Maureen Hoffmann, Kunstdame

Jacket Photographs:
Face © kwasny221/Thinkstock Images
Fire © DVARG/Shutterstock Images
Concrete © Reinhold Leitner/Shutterstock Images

CONSUMED is a work of fiction. Names, characters, and incidents are products of the author's imagination or are used fictitiously. Any resemblance to actual events or persons is entirely coincidental.

Archway Publishing books may be ordered through booksellers or by contacting:

Archway Publishing
1663 Liberty Drive
Bloomington, IN 47403
www.archwaypublishing.com
1-(888)-242-5904

ISBN: 978-1-4808-0620-7 (sc)
ISBN: 978-1-4808-0622-1 (hc)
ISBN: 978-1-4808-0621-4 (e)

Library of Congress Control Number: 2014903757

Printed in the United States of America

Archway Publishing rev. date: 3/19/2014

This book is dedicated to the many worthy advocates serving in the battlegrounds of family law. Standing for the welfare of others in their time of grief and loss is a noble calling.

Some secrets must be shackled
and sentenced to the grave.
For they defy belief.
They haunt the souls who bear them.
They cry out to be known,
but they are mute.

-Anonymous

PROLOGUE

HARVEY FIELD — SNOHOMISH, WASHINGTON

Just beyond the tarmac, headlights pierced the fog. From behind its filtered beams a silver BMW edged past a stable of modest hangars. As the sound of gravel grew still beneath its tires, the driver killed his lights. A figure emerged from the passenger side and picked the lock beneath a sign that read, FOLLOW THE SUN. A mercury-vapor lamp stood guard, the lone sentry protecting an idle row of single-engine planes.

Once inside the hangar, two men quietly hoisted their dangerous cargo, exchanging it with a normal tank from the bin marked Sunday. But theirs had been sealed with faulty welds. Inside a receiver-detonator, armed to ignite a few deadly ounces of C-4 explosive, began to blink. The propane had been laced with liquid hydrogen, and at 250 psi it was groaning to escape.

They left in silence, one of them attending to his laptop. The other was set to return in twenty-four hours, armed with three five-gallon drums and a siphoning hose.

SEA-TAC INTERNATIONAL

Forty miles to the south another pair of headlights pierced the fog as JA Flight 1206 approached on final descent. A man's worried face peered out. His trip to Seattle, arranged in haste, was supposedly a secret. He entered the terminal walking briskly, his eyes to the ground. His bodyguard remained with the crowd, twenty paces back. Despite being no bigger than his boss, he could kill a man barehanded.

The conveyor awoke and eventually surrendered the traveler's nameless bag. His companion pulled to the curb in a gleaming rental, obtained with his boss's ID. As the weary passenger settled in the back, he gave his driver an approving nod. Only one of them knew that death was coming.

KIRKLAND, WASHINGTON

At the first hint of light, the fog clung even tighter to the murky windows of the modest condominium. In his makeshift office a lone figure sat hunched over his keyboard, his face bathed in a reflective cobalt glow as he typed feverishly. The screen flashed the words: *Installation Complete. Logging into Vortex (E7 restricted).*

He glanced at his watch and slid a finger across its crystal, before donning a headset that molded to his face. The translucent visor bisected his sightline from temple to temple and earphones dangled from each end piece. He inserted the earphones, turning his head to one side and then the other. Lowering the mic, he held his index finger to his left temple as a faint green light glowed from within the visor.

He slipped on a pair of thin-sheathed wired gloves and reached for a sawed-off broomstick. His foot depressed a floor switch as a desk fan spun to life. Tapping each wrist, his fingertips glowed green. He touched his temple again as the visor turned black.

Standing at attention, he began moving his right hand in patterns as if conducting a symphony. In response, his watch confirmed his login to a classified server deep within the Vortex. He grasped the broomstick firmly between both hands.

On a stunningly clear morning, he found himself perched atop St. Petersburg's most illustrious cathedral. Peering at the rushing cars below, he felt the wind and heard the fabric of his hang glider flapping with the breeze. He steadied himself. Poised to soar above the ancient city, he turned to the second spire and gave his companion a hearty thumbs-up.

"Perfect timing," his partner said. "You ready to roll?"

"*Budem zdorovy,*" he replied, then whispered to himself, "Game on," as the two stepped off in flight.

PART ONE

CHAPTER ONE

"*Budem zdorovy,*" muttered Les to himself while launching his query into legal cyberspace. His mind was on Byron, downing a vodka, spouting off some Russian salute.

The late day sun was slipping away though he barely noticed. A frown appeared as he considered the document flickering on his tablet: *Wells vs. Wells—Wife's Trial Brief.* Beverly, Marcia's best friend and his one-time college tease, was smack in the middle of a high-stakes, take-no-prisoners divorce. And it had fallen on him to break the grip of an ironclad prenuptial. If only she'd listened.

A decade earlier he'd urged her, "Bev, I'm telling you this as a friend, not as your lawyer. Don't sign it. He's still going to marry you, prenup or not."

"Leslie," she'd insisted, "I know what I'm doing. His parents are behind it. Trust me, as soon as it's signed it'll be forgotten."

Her words, spoken during what seemed like some other life, now ran like fingernails across a distant chalkboard. He wondered, was it really the prenup or her marriage he'd hoped to stop? He glanced at his arsenal of income tax returns, bank statements, and deposition transcripts piled high on Marcia's most recent acquisition, a handcrafted beech-wood deck table. It had been designed by pygmies, and at six feet four he was forced to play contortionist every time he squeezed onto the bench. He should have persuaded her to keep his ancient wicker rocker. But she'd sweetly insisted, and he now owned a houseful of chicly understated Hasaku furniture.

Their long-anticipated move to Queens Gate had landed them in debt, thanks to a housing market no longer on life support. But how could he complain? He had the house, the gift-wrapped wife, and a nine-year-old for whom he would gladly give his life.

To the amazement of his friends, he even loved his work, though at times he wondered why. In the course of an average week, Les McKee might experience enough greed and duplicity to fuel a third world coup. Broken and battered clients drifted in and out of his understated Park Place office in a sad parade that never seemed to end. Here it was a Sunday, but was he shooting hoops?

Occasionally it depressed him the way things fell apart. Even the smallest wave could sink a buoyant marriage—along with the helpless children left floundering in the wake. Not him, he vowed. An odd fringe benefit from his daily sorties into the minefields of the heart was the lessons he learned and used to strengthen his own time-tested marriage.

He wished he could say the same for Byron, the wormy little bastard. Just months before, with Beverly's mental stability collapsing at the seams, Les had tried to reason with him at a Super Bowl party they both attended. While a crazed Seattle was in the midst of celebrating its first title, Les was busy pleading her case with Byron: would he at least consider counseling? He could still see the disgust in the pit of Byron's black, steely eyes, staring back at him with utter incredulity. *"Budem zdorovy"* was all he said, as he tipped back his head, finished off his drink and walked away.

Les had to admit that by the end he was glad to see them split. At the trial he was going to make a spectacle of Byron Wells.

With disconcerting satisfaction, Byron seemed to relish any chance to slice at his opponents with the sharp edge of his biting tongue. When it came to Les he employed particular spite, his wilting affect as razor thin as the touch-screen technology he'd perfected for Digitron during one of his week-long obsessive-compulsive benders.

Cheating spouses were commonplace for Les, though in the case of Beverly and Byron's marriage it was not another woman, but the intoxicating power of an online world gone mad. Aware of the irony, he focused on his tablet, which happened to be chock-full of Digitron software, as his query brought up a dozen out-of-state-cases on the issue of debunking a prenuptial.

A strange, distant hissing made him stop. He looked out at the field behind his house but couldn't find the source. The hissing burst again, this time more abruptly, then rumbled low like steam. He turned his head up sharply, shielding his eyes from the sun's glare. The mammoth object passing overhead was so close it startled him at first—a hot-air balloon, descending gracefully toward the bright green field beyond his deck. Its giant torch fired on and off as it gently nudged its way toward earth.

"Marcia, check this out." When she didn't answer, he reached for his jacket, fumbled for his cell phone, and toggled it to video. By the time he'd framed his subject, the huge yellow sphere had drifted past him and dropped almost even with his deck, less than a quarter mile out. Its gondola dipped below the tree line as he started to record. He could faintly hear their voices.

While directing his camera phone with two hands, his eye caught another splash of yellow moving slowly to his left. A sports car crept toward him down the narrow service road that wound past his house, through the trees and toward the massive turf farm below. He could see it was a newer anniversary Corvette, so he stopped recording and zoomed in on it for a still shot. It seemed to glow even brighter than the quarry it was tracking.

Turning back to the horizon, he framed the balloonists, toggled to wide-angle and snapped two more stills as they passed directly in front of Mount Rainier. "Perfect," he said aloud. Pale pink and shining, the mountain silently agreed. They seemed close enough to touch. Zooming partway in on the six passengers staring out, he snapped a close-up.

The pilot appeared to be orchestrating a skillful descent toward their apparent landing site in the next field over. The tops of a poplar grove appeared in Les's frame. He toggled back to video and began to record again. The approaching row of trees, rising like stout sentries, had been planted decades earlier to deflect the wind from structures long since demolished. Today they were the only remnants of an era when the valley had been dotted with working farms.

The green expanse was still a farm, more than five hundred acres of lawns-to-be, fertilized and harvested year-round. The landscapers would soon descend, roll up their crop, and cart it off to the far-flung outposts of King County's suburban sprawl. Then it would begin again.

The road behind his house was rarely traveled, except by the flatbed crews that passed by every few days, toting the lush instant lawns that dominated the fertile floor of the Sammamish River Valley.

While tracing the balloon, his mind drifted to childhood summers in suburban Chicago where he and his brother would ride their bikes to the

Cook County Fairgrounds in August, hoping to catch a glimpse of the great round wonders of flight as they came to rest. He would email this clip to his mom as she'd been pestering him to send her pictures of their brand-new house with its panoramic view.

The hot-air balloons had become a fixture of the Eastside skyline, home to Seattle's high-tech corridor and luxury hybrids. But he'd never seen one come this close. He kept filming as one of the passengers drew a phone to his ear. Another was waving toward the chase car. He zoomed in all the way as one of them suddenly lost his balance and grabbed for the wicker railing. They'd clipped the top of a poplar tree.

Without warning a horrific flash, followed by an explosion, engulfed them in a cloud of fire. Time stood still as the fireball filled his frame and an abrupt concussion of heated air rushed past. He kept his camera steady as the raging ball of black and orange billowed skyward, then disappeared. Scorched debris fanned out like fireworks. He gaped in disbelief as the reverberation of the sickening blast echoed down the valley. The orphaned balloon, its gondola shorn free, floated and bobbed with its cables dangling helplessly. It too was burning.

He stopped recording. Clouds of smoke rose from a tall patch of dying weeds near the base of the trees. He could see their bodies lying motionless in the inferno of burning fuel and dry grass. God help them, he thought. The top of the tree they'd clipped was wrapped in flames. Nausea gripped him, then panic. The chase car had disappeared through the bordering grove of poplars. He looked at his phone and dialed 911.

"What was that?" exclaimed Marcia, running onto the deck. Confusion and fright spread across her delicate features.

"A hot-air balloon. They hit the treetops and exploded," he said, pointing toward the crash site, his phone clamped to his ear. He looked over at her and thought he could see his own horror mirrored in her pale face. "Don't let Bree out here," he called to her.

The dispatcher finally answered. "This is 911 Police, Fire and Medical. What are you reporting?"

Marcia was clearly in fight or flight mode. "She's in the van. Didn't you hear me? We need to leave," she said.

"I've got 911." He tapped his lips to let her know he couldn't talk.

"Sir?" The dispatcher seemed impatient. "What are you reporting?"

"I'm outside my house, about a mile east of Kirkland. A hot-air balloon was about to land on the turf farm by the slough when they hit a tree and exploded. Six men on board."

He watched as Marcia stepped to the rail for a closer look and heard her gasp as even more color drained from her dusky complexion. Her face looked ghostly against her chestnut hair.

"Are there survivors, sir? Can you get to them?"

"Not really. The hill running down from here is steep thicket and there's a grass fire where they crashed. They need firefighters and medics. You can't miss the smoke."

"Sir, what is your address?"

"One-three-five-seven-two Willows Road," Les said as Breanna emerged from the kitchen. "Hold it, sweetie."

"Pardon me?" the dispatcher asked.

"Sorry. My daughter—"

"Please hold, sir." She didn't wait for him to answer.

"Bree, come here," he said. Carefree as ever, she slid into his arms as he walked her back inside, waiting for the dispatcher to return. She took notice of the smoke and turned a worried face to her parents.

"Bree, honey?" Marcia closed the sliding door to bar her daughter from the deck. "Get back in the van. We can't be late for your recital."

"We can't leave now."

"But Daddy, Tiff and I need to practice, remember?"

"Les, we are going," Marcia said. Her eyes were telling him that home was the last place they needed to be just then. Minutes seemed like hours while he waited.

"Sir?" The dispatcher returned. "We're receiving other calls on this and we have units responding. Can you remain on the line?" It was more of a command than a question.

He checked his phone's display—5:42 p.m. The auditorium was a twenty-minute drive, but Bree's performance didn't start until 7:00. He looked at his wife and daughter. "You two go ahead."

"Les," Marcia pleaded. But he was back on the deck, his eyes glued to the scene, his phone pressed to an ear.

"Did you see it?" He looked up to find their new neighbor standing on the deck next to his. She'd come running out to see what it was that had rocked her plate glass windows.

"I'm calling it in," he told her. "I filmed it." He nodded toward the phone he held to his ear. "Is there a trail down, or just the road?"

"No trail—just thorns and fences. But look, here comes someone now."

He decided to end the call. He set the phone down on his tablet, while scoping for a path through the underbrush, and spotted the Corvette. It had come to a halt on the side of the road. An irrigation ditch prevented the driver from getting any closer to the fire. The door flung open and a woman emerged. She ran across the field, extinguisher in hand, dashing from body to body, dousing the flames as best she could.

Les and his neighbor looked on in helpless shock as the woman's small red canister emptied itself and went silent. Sirens wailed from a distance. A bright yellow van pulling a trailer was bouncing toward the crash site from the east. A small crowd of onlookers had gathered at the top of the ridge while a few brave neighbors started jogging down the road. The spent balloon was enshrouding a web of poplar branches half a mile away. The staffer at the scene was screaming hysterically.

When he heard Marcia honk the horn, he wondered how long it had been since he'd told them to go ahead. He was glad she'd stood her ground. "I have to leave," he told his neighbor, who returned a curious glance.

As they pulled away, Marcia said, "Breanna, did you remember your slippers?"

"Yes, Mama."

"Your headband. Where's your headband?"

"I'm wearing it," she said and giggled.

"Well, I know we've forgotten something. Les, call Bev and let her know we're running late."

"My phone," he said, "I left it on the deck." He was halfway into a U-turn.

"For God's sake, use mine," she sighed, rifling through her purse. "Don't you dare turn back."

He thought about his video, but decided to drop the subject and take her phone instead. He called Beverly and left her a voice mail, then slipped Marcia's phone inside his jacket. As he resumed his course on Willows Road, an ambulance raced by them.

Breanna's voice was almost a whisper as she surprised him with her next question. "Daddy, did all the people die?"

"Maybe not," he answered. "Try not to worry, okay kiddo?"

"Turn on the radio," said Marcia.

He complied but cranked down the volume. Straining to hear, he could just make out the words: "It apparently struck a tree or a power line while attempting to land and burst into flames. We have no word yet as to any casualties, but *News Radio's* Dale Rodriguez is en route to the scene to bring us a live report."

"Hurry," Marcia murmured.

He wasn't sure if she meant him or the reporter. Traffic was sluggish for a Sunday. In the back, Breanna nervously fingered the bows of her ballet slippers. Her lavender eyes—inherited from her mother—were dark with worry.

"It's okay, sweetheart," he told her. "We'll get you there on time." Through the rearview mirror he managed a smile that looked more like a grimace.

CHAPTER TWO

Regent Hall was a madhouse by the time the McKees arrived. Breanna's teacher, Melissa Peters, or "Mrs. Peters" as the children called her, hustled her into the dressing room while Les and Marcia paced the foyer, visibly distraught. With only twenty-five minutes until curtain, Breanna's dancing partner, nine-year-old Tiffany Wells, had not arrived.

"I'll try her house," he said.

"How's Breanna supposed to dance a *pas de deux* by herself?" was all that Marcia could offer in response.

As the young ballerinas filed out from their dressing room for one last backstage rehearsal, he waved at Breanna and mouthed, "She'll be here! Don't worry." He was relieved to see that Breanna, flushed with excitement, did not look worried at all. It was her mother who was buckling under.

"She's like the bad sister—always late."

Not *always*, he thought, privately ashamed. He knew more about his client than he should, though it had been nearly two decades since their passionate but short-lived romance. Still, he felt flushed when he thought back to Beverly Blake. They'd barely gotten started before she decided to move on. Yet in an epic twist of fate, she'd introduced him to her closest high school friend before passing on Les to play the college field.

He recalled his first date with Marcia, sitting in the darkened theater, studying her classic profile and holding her slender hand. By the time the credits rolled, he knew she was the one he'd marry. And after seventeen years together, they were still very much in love.

Beverly, on the other hand, had been widowed once and was currently slogging her way through her second divorce. He had managed to represent her both times. Her current divorce was the largest estate he'd ever handled, thanks to Byron's holdings.

"She's such a flake," Marcia complained. "A shopping trip? And she leaves Tiff with Byron's parents?"

"Where'd she go?" he asked.

"Down the coast, supposedly with a girlfriend. I should've known she wouldn't make it back in time."

"So the grandparents are bringing Tiff?"

"They were going to come together."

"Even Super Dad? He's not with them, is he?"

"God only knows," Marcia started to say as Mrs. Peters approached.

"Everything is under control," she announced. "Breanna will solo."

"Wonderful!" Marcia exclaimed, as she hurried off to find Breanna, her camcorder at the ready.

Les returned to the auditorium to reclaim their front row seats. Breanna was part of the opening routine, so he decided to use the camera phone in his pocket to record some footage of his own.

Halfway through the number, Marcia caught his eye from behind the curtain. She was trembling and looked horror-stricken and on the verge of tears.

"What is it?" he mouthed, as she motioned him to join her backstage. As the second number started, he found her hunched against the railing, sheltering her eyes as she stifled back tears.

"I'm afraid it's bad," said Mrs. Peters, who was attending to Marcia. Her expression betrayed the gravity of the words that tumbled from her mouth. "Tiffany's grandmother just called. They won't be coming because there's been an accident. Tiffany's father was killed this evening in some kind of crash."

Marcia looked at Les, not knowing what to say. She grew pale and sank all the way down on the stairs as Melissa tried to place a reassuring hand on her shoulder.

He thought only of the next notch of hell that Beverly's life had just become. Her nightmare had started a year before when Digitron abruptly fired Byron for allegedly selling company secrets. He countered by filing suit for Wrongful Termination. Soon after that he walked out on Bev, calling her a "luxury tax." Corporate scandal, divorce, and now he was dead?

"My God," he whispered. "Did she say what happened?"

"I could barely understand her. But I think she said he was riding in a hot-air balloon that went down."

He turned sharply toward Marcia, who had already made the connection and was keeping it to herself. He started to explain when Marcia interrupted. "Where is she now?"

"With her in-laws," Melissa offered. "The grandmother said you two would probably want to come."

"Of course," she replied, steeling herself for the task ahead.

"What about Breanna?" he asked.

"Let her stay and dance her solo," suggested Melissa. "Leave your camcorder with me and I'll have someone tape it for you. I've already spoken with Marlys Scott. They've offered to take her home and have you pick her up there later. We shouldn't say anything to her about this yet."

Numbly, Les nodded. He caught Marcia's arm and led her out of the building.

CHAPTER THREE

Byron's parents lived in a sprawling Spanish-style mansion poised high above the twinkling waterfront of Maydenbauer Bay. Marcia had been there before, but this was a first for Les. It was 7:50 p.m. by the time they pulled into the wide, circular drive.

"Impressive," he muttered. "Daddy sacrificed some trees to pay for this." Byron's father, the grandson of a Polish immigrant named Ivan Velski, had amassed a fortune in Northwest timber long before his son struck it rich with Digitron.

"Oh great, look who just arrived," said Les.

David Dietrich stepped briskly from the sedan parked in front them. He was Byron's friend and former colleague at Digitron. He looked fit and handsome though artificially tanned for Seattle. His curling blond hair was cut short, his square jawline softened by a dimpled cleft in the center of his chin.

Dietrich was busy texting. As Les stepped to the curb and walked to Marcia's side of the car, Dietrich turned and almost collided with him. He tried to catch his eye, but Dietrich was hotfooting it impatiently toward the mansion's grand entrance, appropriately garbed in an Italian leather jacket. Les found him intimidating, notwithstanding his own physique.

Dietrich and Byron had been fired on the same day for allegedly conspiring to sell classified source code to an undisclosed competitor. It had been headline news. They were now co-plaintiffs in a widely publicized lawsuit for Wrongful Termination. Their trial was less than two months away. And although it wasn't Les's case, the outcome would bear heavily on Beverly's divorce.

What divorce? In the blink of an eye she was not his client any more. Her highly anticipated multi-million dollar settlement had just gone up in smoke, though it meant her custody case was over too. She was a widow for the second time.

Inside the mansion the mood was morbidly subdued. In the formal room beyond the massive entryway, Les spotted Beverly, sobbing quietly at the dark cherry table. Her hair was the shortest he'd ever seen it: styled in a posh bob. She had her arm around Tiffany, who was curled up against her mother's shoulder, half hidden beneath her pink tutu.

Even at a distance, he could see the pain etched on her face. Tears formed behind his own eyes—not for Byron, but for the confusion and agony he could see was gripping Bev. Her skin, usually colored with a healthy glow, looked pale and lifeless in the light from the chandelier. Several women hovered around her, trying to help her shoulder the unbearable.

"I should be with her," said Marcia. "Why don't you find the Wellses?" He nodded as she drifted through a gathering throng of stunned but silent mourners and searched for Byron's parents. He wondered what sort of people could have raised such a heartless predator as Byron Wells.

Byron had risen swiftly within Digitron's inner circle—until they canned him. His company stock at the time he was fired was worth almost fifty million dollars. He had another fifty million in stock options, not yet vested, with a market on the rebound. Not bad for a thirty-eight-year-old. Married or divorced, he might have kept it all, thanks to his parents and an airtight prenuptial.

Les still rued the day, but who in God's name could have stopped her from signing it? Beverly did as Beverly pleased. She was an enigma with an uncanny knack for playing the victim while she controlled her men, at least those unlucky enough to stray within her orbit. Years after he'd seemingly been released by her, he could still feel her pull—the way she spoke to him in her low, breathy voice. Even now her presence in the room was palpable. So how could she have been so horribly misguided when it came to choosing husbands?

In seventeen years of marriage, Marcia never once asked Les if he'd slept with her in college. Perhaps she knew they'd never gone that far, or maybe she didn't care. It was Les who couldn't shake it, try as he might.

Through the years, as the two women drifted in and out of each other's lives, Beverly stayed stubbornly present in some unswept corner of Les's mind. He hated it, but the more he couldn't have her, the more it tore at him that he'd almost had her. And when it came to be that Byron got her, only to dump her—well, no doubt it was the reason he took her case again.

Les's obsession with Beverly and her marriage problems had started within two years of his graduation from law school. Until then she was just an ex who doubled as his wife's high school and college friend. She was one of the first in their college circle to be married, to the quarterback no less, an Indiana farm boy named Tyler Pruitt.

Les knew it was probably jealousy that brought these memories and regrets to mind. Maybe he'd hoped she would never marry well—that she was somehow saving herself for him. Pruitt played briefly in the NFL, two uneventful seasons, never rising above a third-string backup for the New Orleans Saints. He overdosed on cocaine and died before his twenty-fifth birthday, just three weeks after the Saints had cut him at the start of his third season.

Shortly after Pruitt died, Les remembered an email from Bev to Marcia, disclosing that she'd received half a million dollars from his insurance. Yet within a year of being widowed, she remarried a sleazy New Orleans nightclub owner, ten years her senior, by the name of Victor Garving. As soon as Victor got her money, he started to abuse her. But that was just the start of the ugliest chapter in Les's life.

CHAPTER FOUR

He felt alone in a house of faceless mourners, Seattle's upper crust. He did not belong, but neither did she. Her flawless looks could not conceal her troubled soul. His mind kept drifting through the depressing saga of Beverly's tumultuous life. Time and again she'd ensnared him in her woes. Twelve years earlier she'd almost been his undoing. The thing that ate at him the most, more than her union with Byron, was her marriage to Victor Garving. How could someone so perfectly sensual end up wasting it all on such an old and hopeless loser?

The McKees had been settled in Seattle for almost two years when Beverly resurfaced in their lives. She was fresh out of rehab, with little more than the clothes on her back. What she needed was a divorce. Les, a second-year associate in a downtown firm, was eager to build a practice, so he readily took her case.

Victor Garving, he learned from Beverly, was a lowlife drug-pusher. She claimed his New Orleans nightclub was little more than a clearing house for a staggering narcotics trade. According to her, his patrons included "A-list" professional athletes, and he kept ties with certain mobsters in the city. Her fear of the man was evident.

She said Victor had coerced her into investing her life insurance proceeds in his club. Around the restaurant he would introduce her as his partner, but in the privacy of their home he'd beaten her more times than she could count. Before long he had her hooked on crack cocaine. And then one day she decided to escape. She grabbed what cash she could, caught a plane for Seattle, and entered rehab.

From the moment she cleaned herself up and stepped back into their lives, Les had vowed to bring Victor down. He started by threatening him with criminal prosecution unless he gave her back the money. And though it bordered on extortion, he could live with that. After several trips to New Orleans, he'd gathered enough dirt on Victor's operation to guarantee a conviction for any prosecutor who would listen. But Les wasn't after a conviction.

His words back then sounded so inane today. "Victor, you're one call away from a law school buddy of mine who prosecutes for the D.E.A."

Victor accused Les of circling for the kill though he was the one behaving like a predator. He pointed out that he had no lawyer of his own and claimed that certain gangsters in the city would kill him if Les brought in the feds. The only way to get out from under his debts and return Bevy's money would be to torch his club and collect on the insurance. Les thought he was bluffing, but Victor kept on. Les could see his mind was set, though he wondered why he was confiding in his wife's divorce attorney.

At the time Victor claimed he was telling him so *Bevy* could decide for herself. "All I need from you and Bevy," Victor said, "is a small bit of help with my alibi. Nothing illegal. I want you to schedule my deposition in Seattle for a date to be announced. In exchange for a subpoena, which you will insist was filed by you on your timing and yours alone, Bevy will end up with her dough, followed by her divorce."

It would be years before Les could face the truth: that his age and inexperience, together with his obvious obsession over Beverly, made him an easy target. In retrospect he knew he should have gone to the police. But the prospect of recovering her money, even some of it, with no significant risk was too strong a temptation. He never even told her what he was doing; if he had, she might have warned him he was in too deep.

Unbeknownst to Les, Victor later claimed he'd conscripted Sonny Lile to set the fire. Sonny was a Seattle private eye whom Les employed from time to time in connection with his divorce-related investigations. Like everyone else, he'd heard the long-standing rumors of Sonny's penchant for sidestepping the law and for manufacturing evidence, though he'd never observed it for himself.

In retrospect, the plan made perfect sense. Victor would need an out-of-towner to set the fire. And he'd need some form of leverage to make certain that Les and *Bevy* kept quiet should things go bad. Had he used a native son, the New Orleans mob would have found him out and blackmailed him with the crime.

Sonny never spoke about the fire nor did he admit involvement. But Victor managed to convince Les that Sonny had served as his accomplice. He was a natural for the job—a Navy man with twenty years on the Seattle Arson Squad. He testified frequently in court, touting his C.F.I. credentials. As a successful arson-buster before his retirement, he was revered by some and considered infamous by others.

Les had to admit he looked more like an arsonist than a firefighter, with his unshaven face, oily hair, and a cigarette always dangling from his lip. One of his hands was badly scarred from burns. But he was likable and unpretentious. To this day, Les still used him for minor investigations.

Victor never shared any details with Les, but two months to the day from when he'd announced his diabolical plans for arson, he was sitting in Les's office, providing a deposition, when the call came through about the fire. Les would never forget the look on Victor's face, so smug in his silk suit, fingering his moustache and twisting the gilded chains around his wrist.

The deposition was suspended as Victor rushed back to Bourbon Street. But as he departed Les's office, he'd whispered something only Les could hear. "I'll be in touch, fire-boy." Then he turned and left.

The divorce dragged on, stalled by an investigation into the suspicious nature of the nightclub fire. When the insurance company finally cried foul, Victor dragged Les in deeper. He told him Sonny set the fire. He threatened, "If I go down, McKee, then so will you and Bevy. I'll tell them how you lined me up with Sonny Lile."

Les had been too petrified to ask Sonny what he knew. Victor insisted that Les would file a lawsuit on behalf of the Garvings against their insurer, to help him prove it wasn't arson. He announced that Sonny would be their expert. After that, Les never wanted to know the truth.

"What's it feel like having to sweat prosecution?" Victor asked, using the same words Les had used on him shortly before the fire.

Although Les had done nothing illegal, Victor had managed to entangle him as an unwitting accomplice in his fraud. He would never forgive himself for becoming so ensnared. He was forced to tell Beverly he suspected arson. Reluctantly, she agreed to go along with Victor's plan. They put their divorce on hold while he moved to Seattle for marriage counseling. Les represented them as a couple in a lawsuit filed in federal court against the club's insurer.

The case eventually turned on Sonny's discovery of a faulty fuse box from the scene. Les figured it was Sonny's plant.

The insurance company ultimately settled, paying out a million and a half. Sonny collected thirty thousand dollars in expert fees. Beverly netted $460,000. Victor paid the last of his debts and pocketed the balance. After signing Les's uncontested divorce papers, he quietly disappeared.

For a time it had seemed as if his troubles were over. It had been the perfect crime of sorts—that is, until a year after the fire when Victor reappeared in Les's office. After telling Les he was broke and his suppliers were after him again, he demanded a hundred grand from the recently remarried "Bevy," or he'd be going to the police to expose their collective fraud. He must have read in the papers that she had finally married into money.

"Either way I'm a dead man," Victor told him.

When Les told Beverly, she wept in his arms. She and Byron were newlyweds, and she was pregnant with Tiffany. Suddenly Victor was threatening to destroy her hard-earned happiness. Les and Beverly held several secret meetings. At one point she suggested killing Victor.

"You can't be serious," Les replied, brushing it off with a nervous laugh.

On another occasion, while he and Beverly were huddled behind closed doors, puzzling over what to do, Marcia dropped by the office. Afterwards she asked him, "Are you and Beverly having an affair?"

"God no," he swore. He saw the disbelief in her fiery gaze and couldn't blame her. Beverly crowded his thoughts by day and his dreams by night. There was no escaping her.

As for Victor Garving, she managed to escape him on her own, for the second time, and without any help from Les. "I paid him off," was all she ever said. The two of them never spoke of it again.

More than a decade later the statute of limitations for arson had run in Louisiana, and he finally felt safe from Victor Garving. No one had seen or heard from Victor since his nefarious reappearance in Les's office. But he thought of him often and vowed never again to cross the line. This time he would divorce her by the book.

As for Sonny, perhaps he just felt safer keeping tabs on him. Maybe, by continuing to send him work, he was letting him know that his loyalty was worth a price. Over time they had almost become friends, yet not once had either man discussed the Garving fire.

As for his colleagues at the bar, Les had been toiling since the fire to earn a decent reputation as an honest family law attorney. Some even called him the Gentle Giant and not just because of his imposing height. He liked to settle more than he liked to fight. But who could have known that he was only doing penance?

CHAPTER FIVE

Emerging from his unpleasant reverie, Les walked to the granite fireplace and picked up a framed photograph of Byron. His perplexity over Beverly returned. She was a train wreck when it came to marriage. Byron Wells was the polar opposite of Victor Garving, yet in some ways even darker. How could such a geeky, uninspiring presence harbor so much revenge? As if destroying his marquee marriage weren't enough, he stood accused of high-level corporate espionage.

Byron and Dietrich had been fired ten months earlier with almost no explanation from their employer. But starting on the day after they were dumped, *The Seattle Times* ignited a firestorm of controversy with a series of articles about two of Digitron's "finest." The story claimed they were suspected of selling source code, military technology to be exact, though very few details were provided. The two had been working on "undisclosed research" within Digitron's black-box Virtual Reality division. They'd been "in the box" for over two years, working on a new form of heads-up display technology for the Air Force, specifically for fighter pilots. From there they'd branched into military training games, eventually pushing the frontiers of VR spectography into the paramilitary gaming franchises of *Call to Battle*, *Black-Ops Modern Warfare*, and *Armored Assault Horizon*.

The news stories speculated that Byron and Dietrich had turned traitors when Digitron failed to credit them for a recent breakthrough. Allegedly they'd opted to offload their success to a more appreciative competitor. Further details were scanty; the *Times* either wouldn't say or didn't know what the technology entailed. For their part Byron and Dietrich denied the charges and filed suit together.

Two months later Byron filed for divorce. He was seeking custody of Tiffany, declaring Beverly to be unstable. He refused to look for work, taking the position that in addition to being "Mr. Mom," his new job was fighting Digitron for his old job back. In the course of staying home and enjoying equal time with Tiff, he'd become obsessed with building his case for Father of the Year.

Staring at the photo he remembered his last public confrontation with the deceased. They were arguing in Family Court as Byron stood beside his silk-stockinged mouthpiece, Milton James. "Your Honor," Les recalled telling the judge, "Mr. Wells may be brilliant when it comes to virtual worlds, but he's not even online when it comes to parenting a third-grader—"

"Cute, Les," Byron interrupted, to the stunned silence of everyone in court, including his attorney. "Almost as cute as you boning my wife—"

Crack! It was the judge's gavel.

He almost dropped the photo as he recalled the gavel cracking. Byron left him red-faced and speechless in open court, looking as if the allegation were true.

Now he was dead . . . and Les had watched him die.

"Les? Mr. McKee?"

He felt a strong hand on his shoulder and turned to face a stately, gray-haired man almost as tall as himself.

"I'm Fred Wells," he offered. His extended hand trembled slightly before making contact with a solid grip. "You're Beverly's attorney, right?"

He nodded.

"I know your wife and Bev are friends. We love her like a daughter. She was good to Byron, not to mention she's the mother of our only granddaughter—and family is all we have. I don't mean to trouble you, but can you tell me briefly what will happen to their divorce, seeing it never went through?"

The elderly man's compassion for her seemed real, though at times Bev had led him to believe that Byron's parents were applauding their son's divorce. "It'll be as if he never filed," he answered. "I'll notify the court this week. Will you and Mrs. Wells be okay with that?"

"As far as we're concerned, the less said about divorce the better for Tiffany's sake. Did Beverly tell you they were talking about calling the whole thing off?"

"Yes, and she was the happiest I've seen her in a long time. She never wanted the divorce." He wasn't certain if his last comment was true, but he wasn't about to speculate otherwise in front of Byron's father. Throughout much of the case it had seemed as if Beverly was consumed with rage toward Byron. She told Les, "I want you to clean his clock." Then recently she'd announced a possible reconciliation and she still wore her ring.

"As for the Digitron matter," he continued, "there's no reason Milton James can't continue on as the lawyer for your son's estate—assuming Beverly will have him." Milton James, a legend in Seattle legal circles, was representing Byron in both his divorce and Wrongful Termination cases and Beverly despised him.

"Les," Wells said, "you obviously haven't heard. Milton James was on the balloon with Byron. He's dead." He looked stricken.

Les felt more gnawing pain in the center of his abdomen. "I'm sorry, Fred. I had no idea. What were they doing in a balloon together? They weren't that close socially, were they?"

"No, but with the trial coming up . . . I take it you haven't heard who else was with them?"

"No," he said, wondering what was next.

"The authorities just informed us. It'll be on the news tonight once they release the names. There were six victims in all. Two were crew, then Byron, his attorney, and another lawyer by the name of Sutherland. But the last victim is the one who will make headlines . . . Akira Nakamura."

Les leaned forward as if he'd misunderstood. Akira Nakamura was the kiss of death to Byron's suit for Wrongful Termination. He was a lead engineer for the Japanese-based corporate giant, VVG, or Vortex Video Games, a household name in children's entertainment. He was the "buyer" who the early tabloids claimed had paid Wells and Dietrich untold sums to give him cloud technology from Digitron.

When Nakamura's name first surfaced, both sides denied having any knowledge of the other. VVG was still standing by their man, and no proof had ever come to light of any money changing hands.

"They claim Sutherland was Nakamura's lawyer," added Wells.

Byron's firing went national once the mainstream press confirmed that he was linked to Akira Nakamura. Before then the press had provided few if any clues as to what secrets had been stolen or to whom they might have been sold. Digitron still wasn't talking about the case.

The *Times* series joined the fray six months after Byron's firing, reporting on a large-scale corporate defection impending at VVG. Nakamura and his team of researchers had supposedly developed an enhanced and integrative graphic accelerator, a 4G signal amplifier, able to provide smartphones and the 4G consoles of VVG's competitors with VG access to platforms like the Vortex.

Still in development, the Vortex was the most widely anticipated and sophisticated gaming platform ever conceived by VVG. Cloud-based, it was not beholden to expensive discs. It was monetized instead by subscription packages, including a lease (not ownership) of the Vortex *VVViron*, VVG's high-speed portal to its virtual world of amazing real-time graphics.

Gamers would gather worldwide inside the Vortex, where they could choose from an unlimited menu of the company's top-rated games, to play whenever and for as long as desired. Vortex players could earn subscription discounts and cash rewards. The best could earn significant taxable income for their exploits. There were legendary Vortex "ninjas" who were reportedly earning six-figure incomes for their masterful skills and swagger.

VVG had long derived its success not only from its software, but from its hardware's ability to enhance conventional broadband speeds while communicating with the company's mega servers. Its subscription model, with annual upgrades, included wireless controllers, two head-mounted devices (or HMDs) and the VVViron console. It was marketed as the "Triple V Package" (for *Virtual Vortex enVironment*). VVG was predicting the Triple V would soon become as commonplace in homes and college dorms as HD flat screens and tablets.

The superiority of the Vortex platform was threatening to bury every competitor in the space, including Digitron. Only the VVViron could enhance broadband capability to the speeds required for communicating with Vortex-level servers. Even VVG's competitors had started referring to its graphic-hogging signal accelerator as "VG speed."

But according to the press, Nakamura was out to change all that. A series of undercover reports and insider interviews claimed that Nakamura was about to alter the paradigm of the gaming world forever. He was warning VVG to "evolve with the times" or fall victim to natural selection. The reports claimed that Nakamura was on a personal quest to break VVG's monopoly over VG access to Vortex-level platforms. He believed the next great technology wave, granting cell devices full access to the Vortex or its equivalent, had become bottlenecked at VVG. He proposed that Vortex-level platforms be opened to smartphone and tablet devices of every type.

Nakamura was pushing VVG to throw its support behind his latest microchip, integrating the company's proprietary signal amplification with any 4G device. Insiders were claiming he wanted VVG to grant public domain rights to the Vortex, allowing it to become the world's premier online gaming environment for the next ten years.

His microprocessor was supposedly half the size of a flash drive. In addition to gaming in the Vortex, it enabled flawless streaming of live HD broadcasts and movies over 4G networks. And while VVG might still retain a marketing edge by way of its Vortex-enabled mega games, consumers would no longer need the VVViron or VVG games alone to play inside the Vortex. Competitors could license their games as part of the Triple V or other subscription plans. A patent was reportedly imminent, though VVG was under fire over reports they were going to bury it as soon as it was granted. The concern on the company's part was that Nakamura's chip might only serve to put its competitors back in business.

In an exclusive the *Times* claimed that Nakamura was prepared to go "head-to-head" with VVG and co-opt the server assets of its competitors if needed. He was being touted as "a consumer's hero." No doubt massive litigation would erupt over rights to his chip, but if he prevailed his team of renegades was threatening to break VVG's grip over the fast-approaching promised land of real-time virtual worlds.

Both Nakamura and VVG denied the reports concerning trouble at VVG. The company would reveal precious little except to say their chip was still in prototype. Unlike Wells and Dietrich, Nakamura had not been fired when the story broke. But the press would not give up. The fact that Digitron had fired two of its top engineers for selling secrets to someone was only pumping fuel to the fire. And tonight Seattle was about to learn that Wells and Nakamura were together when they died.

Nakamura and five other executives from VVG were slated to testify in the Digitron case later that same week. Their depositions were being taken in Kyoto. All six witnesses were supposedly going to affirm that no one at VVG, including Nakamura, had ever been involved with Byron Wells or David Dietrich. But things had been heating up, and there were rumors flying that at least one witness was getting ready to change his story.

Les had arranged for a representative of his own, a lawyer from Kyoto, to attend the depositions as his co-counsel in the divorce, seeing that Beverly's property settlement would be so closely linked to the outcome of the Digitron fiasco. Suddenly the plaintiffs' key witness, Nakamura, was dead—possibly murdered—on the eve of his critical performance.

"This changes everything," said Les. "Has anyone told Bev?"

Since the scandal broke, Beverly had scoffed at the notion of her husband selling secrets. She claimed he got fired on purpose, as a part of his self-concocted scam to cheat her in their divorce. She wagered he'd be rehired once their divorce was final, as part of a settlement with the software giant. Knowing Byron as he did, Les agreed. From the standpoint of their divorce, his untimely firing was a brilliant move.

"She couldn't believe it when we told her," Wells replied. "Arlene and I were shocked as well. Byron swore to us he'd never met the man."

"I see Dave Dietrich is here," said Les. "I wonder what he thinks about it."

Wells shook his head. "I haven't spoken to him yet. This doesn't look good, does it?"

He tried to sound ambivalent. "At least they were up there with their lawyers. Maybe they were meeting about the depositions in Kyoto. That's why I'd love to know what Dietrich has to say."

"He'd say that only a scumbag divorce lawyer would think to judge a dead man guilty, simply by his associations."

Les wheeled in surprise as Dietrich met his gaze with an angry sneer. He imagined taking him on in a not-so-friendly game of half-court.

"Fred," Dietrich continued, as he laid an arm on the elder Wells's shoulder, "I only wish Byron could be here now to defend himself. I rushed over as soon as I heard. You know how close we were. I'm sorry for your loss. It's a horrible time for all of us, so you'll have to excuse my being rude to Mr. McKee, though I happen to know exactly what your son thought of his wife's divorce attorney."

Turning to Les, Dietrich said, "I'm surprised you had the balls to show." And with that he returned to filling up his plate.

"Ignore him," Wells said. "You're welcome here, Les. In fact, your wife was the first person Beverly asked for. Frankly, I don't see how Byron's legal troubles matter anymore."

He was surprised at the older man's naiveté. "Byron had two years left until his massive tranche of options vested—meaning there's another fifty million at stake, so long as we can prove that he was fired without cause. His options, if not forfeited by means of a lawful termination, would become part of his estate, or Beverly's estate to be correct. According to his contract, stock options granted but not vested at the time of his death would not be lost. In fact, in the event of his death they fully vest."

"Is that standard?"

"No. He negotiated for that, though I'm sure he never planned on getting fired before he died. If his termination was legit then his estate will have to forfeit all those options."

"Who can we get to take over?" Wells asked.

"Good question. Milton was a sole practitioner."

"Can you look into it for me? I'm concerned for her. It's probably the farthest thing from her mind right now."

"Of course," he answered. "I'll find a probate lawyer for her too. Not to mention, she and Tiffany have a case for Wrongful Death. Did they say what happened? Can a hot-air balloon just explode like that?"

"They said a fuel tank ruptured, though there's still a lot to sift through. Apparently the blast was heard for miles."

"I know. I heard it," Les said. "It happened near my house as we were getting ready for the recital. I mean I actually saw them. I was outside on my deck, watching it land, though I had no idea that Byron was in the group. I was in the middle of filming their landing when they crashed. Marcia was loading Bree in the car when they were first passing over." He thought of the camera phone in his pocket but decided not to mention it.

"My God, Les . . . how bizarre."

"They were trying to land in the field behind my house when it seemed like they came in too fast, too low, and glanced off a tree. Then it just exploded."

"What did you do? Did they—"

"I'm sure they died instantly," he offered quickly. "They had crew on the ground right away and the paramedics arrived within minutes. So we left because we had no idea who was involved. What time did they finally call you?"

Wells hesitated. "A little after six. Beverly was running late. She had just pulled up and we were loading the car when we got the call. She took it very hard. I've called my doctor. He's prescribed sedatives for her to take before we go to the morgue to identify his body."

Les was only half listening. He looked toward the formal room, hoping to spot Marcia. He was beginning to worry about Breanna. As they moved toward the large dining table, he went to Beverly first. She sat holding her sleeping daughter as she dabbed at her eyes with a handkerchief. "Leslie," she said in a hushed voice. She reached for his hand and gripped it with a strength he hadn't expected.

"God, I'm sorry," he told her.

"Me too." Looking up at him, her eyes were glazed with tears. Mascara spread like a bruise across her face, yet despite the ravages of shock and grief, she was beautiful. Her new cut suited her, emphasizing her high cheekbones and slender neck. She dropped her handkerchief.

As he knelt to retrieve it, he couldn't help noticing her long, shapely legs. His gaze wandered the sleek landscape of her body. Beneath her sheer chiffon blouse he could detect the curve and rise of her generous figure, though he averted his eyes, ashamed of himself.

"Beverly, please. Let me help," he said, handing her the handkerchief. "Anything you need, just ask."

She smiled wanly through a veil of tears. "I loved him," she choked. "Remember how I told you, I chased him? You looked at me like I was crazy. And maybe I was, but I loved him."

He nodded and left her to her sorrow.

"Les?" Marcia caught his hand. "I should go with her to the morgue. Can you pick up Breanna and put her to bed? I may need to spend the night, which means you'll have to get her off to school in the morning."

He nodded and brushed a kiss across her cool brow before he took off through the crowd. At the door he looked back, hoping to catch her eye and mouth "good night." But she'd already turned away.

CHAPTER SIX

As he walked from the house, adrenaline started surging through him in yet another rush of panic. Several car alarms were sounding and one was his. His headlights were flashing as he arrived and saw that his passenger window had been smashed. Frantically he checked his surroundings. Two cars behind his had been vandalized as well. He quickly searched inside though he'd left no valuables. Their camcorder was with Mrs. Peters. His stereo was untouched.

He returned to the mansion.

"I'm afraid some gangbangers have vandalized a couple cars out front," he announced. Fred Wells came to his aid and helped him clean the shattered glass from his seats. He gave him duct tape and a roll of heavy plastic from the garage as Les did his best to seal out the elements.

As he drove away he dialed 911 to report the crime. The dispatcher said it would take at least an hour to respond and advised him to file a report at the Bellevue precinct in the morning. One more errand, he thought irritably. He realized he would have to tell Breanna about Tiffany's father. She had never experienced a death before.

"Sweetheart," he began while tucking her snugly into the back seat. "Mommy and I were with Tiffany and her mom and her grandparents tonight. They didn't make it to the recital because of all those fire trucks and ambulances we saw. Her daddy was in that accident."

"Did he die?"

"Yes," he said, fighting back tears. His own mortality flashed across his daughter's upturned face, and she clung to him tightly.

"I feel so sad," she whispered. They held each other for a time. He stayed and let her weep until she finally fell asleep.

It was pitch black by the time he pulled into his driveway. He was not yet well enough acquainted with his new neighborhood to notice that the silver BMW parked just beyond his house did not belong there.

He carried his daughter through the garage. Normally Marcia would have left some lights on, but things had been far from normal when they'd departed. Still, something felt odd. There was a draft. Then he saw it, and panic hit him for the third time that night. His back door was ajar! In their rush to leave, he might have forgotten to lock it but he would never have left it open. Someone was in their house or had just run out.

Breanna was still asleep. Gently, he laid her back in the van and backed it up the street. Sitting behind the wheel he started dialing 911 again, then halted.

What if Breanna left it open?

He had to know. Locking the van he re-entered the house and ran upstairs to the master bedroom where he kept a loaded .44 Auto Mag, inherited from his father, locked inside its case. He threw on the lights and started searching room by room. Nothing. Dead silence. He made enough noise so the intruder, if there was an intruder, could still escape without a confrontation.

He saw the first signs of invasion as he walked back down the stairs. He must have startled whoever was rifling through a basket of Marcia's video cassettes, DVDs and flash-drives. She kept them in the family room with her endless album and editing projects, photographs and media. She was a one-woman paparazzi. Les surmised that someone had been looking for his video, first in his van and then in his house. But Byron's father was the only person he'd told about the film.

A footstep fell behind him. Wheeling in horror, he aimed at the lighted doorway to the kitchen as he saw a figure's silhouette. He almost pulled the trigger but was stopped short by a woman's gasp.

"For God's sake it's me." He didn't lower the gun. As his eyes adjusted he recognized the pleasing and familiar features of his next door neighbor. They'd spoken for the first time that afternoon. She was trim and attractive though he still didn't know her name.

"What are you doing here?" he asked, his pulse still exploding. "You startled me half to death."

"I saw you drive up," she answered. "I've been waiting for you, though I didn't expect this kind of greeting. Do you mind?"

He was still menacing her with his gun. Awkwardly he joined her in the kitchen and placed it on the counter.

"It's been a madhouse around here," she said. "Your back door was open, so I tried to get your attention, but you didn't answer. I guess we haven't met, officially."

"I'm sorry," he managed. "I'm Leslie McKee. Please call me Les." Oddly, she didn't seem menaced at all. She extended a slender hand and squeezed gently as he offered his in return. She kept her other hand behind her back.

"I'm Virginia . . . Dwyer, your new neighbor. My friends call me Ginny. Anyway, why did you take off in such a hurry? You missed all the excitement."

"I feel silly about this and I apologize," he said, nodding toward his gun. "My van was broken into and then my house. I thought maybe you were the prowler."

"Your wife must be waiting in the car?"

"No, but my daughter is. I have to get her."

"So soon?" she replied as she removed a wine bottle and two glasses from behind her back and set them on the counter. "Your Christmas Fund just matured. A band of reporters has been swarming the neighborhood tonight. Every Tom, Dick and Harry wants to pay you for your pictures."

"What pictures?" He did a double take toward the wine, furled his brow, and then motioned her with a nod to follow him to his van.

"I'll wait," she replied, causing him to hesitate. But he thought of the prowler and his plastic car window held by duct tape and made a beeline to the van.

"Come here, sweetheart, everything is fine," he said, panting from the run. Breanna moaned as he picked her up and fell back asleep. He carried her inside.

"This is my daughter, Breanna. She's nine. So how do you know about my pictures?"

"You told me, remember? When we were on our decks. You said you'd filmed it, but then you took off. Since then I've been approached by every affiliate in town, wanting to know where in the hell you went. The *Times* would like a copy for the morning front page though you need to call them tonight. And the stations are bidding, starting at eight thousand dollars.

I think we should celebrate." She nodded toward the bottle of Merlot, wrapped in a scarlet bow.

He shook his head in disbelief.

"Housewarming," she said coyly and followed Les as he carried Breanna up the stairs and down the hallway to her room, where he laid her gently on the bed.

"Why so much fuss over my video?" he asked, deciding not to mention it was just a camera phone.

"Haven't you heard? There were corporate big shots on board. It's breaking news," she answered cheerfully.

Suddenly, it made sense. She'd been drinking and had probably called the press herself. "Virginia," he said sharply, "did you see anyone enter through my back door tonight? Looking for a videotape, or my camcorder?"

"They're offering you big money, Les, but only if they can see it right away. I couldn't tell them when you'd be back. They knew your door was unlocked because they'd tried it. They said I could go in as your neighbor and that way you'd have a check waiting for you when you got back."

"They had you walk in here, looking for what exactly?"

"I was only trying to help. Reporters are like piranhas."

"I wouldn't call it help, Virginia. More like unlawful entry and theft. Not exactly a housewarming. Did you forget to close the door? Because it was ajar when I got home."

"I closed it. I've been watching and nobody came to your front door that I could see, though you've certainly had enough strangers around your house tonight."

"Were you the one sifting through my drives and discs?"

She looked vaguely contrite. "When I told them I couldn't find your camera, they asked me about tapes or DVDs. I showed them your basket, but then I put it back exactly how I found it, I swear."

"Great. That means somebody else has been in here. You could've locked up. That would have been the neighborly thing to do."

"It's up to ten thousand dollars, Les. If you act fast. News today isn't news tomorrow. You're certainly big enough to handle a pesky reporter or two. At least have some wine and we'll call it square. Where is your camera, anyway?"

"You mean this?" he asked, as he pulled a cell phone from his pocket and set it down by her wine bottle.

"A phone . . . of course. So let's have a look."

"I have no intention of giving this to the press."

"Suit yourself. The cops will take it as soon as they get here, so don't you think you should collect while you can? A lady from *KOMO* said if it's digital she can copy or email it to herself in seconds and be on her way. I've got her card, so pour some wine and I'll tell you which affiliate is offering what."

Her logic had an odd appeal, but he had no need of an agent, especially one hooked on red wine and the *Real Housewives*. As he uncorked her bottle, he wondered what other offers were on her mind.

"A guy from *Dateline* was here an hour ago. When I told him what KOMO was willing to pay us, sight unseen, he offered the ten grand, provided he can see it by 6:00 a.m." She toasted him and sipped greedily.

"I'm not following the *us*, Virginia. You're talking as if we were partners."

"Neighbors, partners—who knows where this could lead?" Her laugh was more disturbing than her comment as he nearly choked on his wine.

"I'm not interested in your help," he managed.

"Take their cards," she said. "I promised them you'd call." As she held out the cards, her fingers brushed his hand. She was wearing a thin silk blouse.

"Let's have a look," she said seductively. She reached for his phone and giggled when he covered it with his hand. She playfully slapped her hand against his and let it rest there. In that moment, with the wine, his empty stomach, and the softness of her hand, he was teetering on the edge of a cliff.

"You've had too much to drink," he muttered, removing his hand and sliding his phone along the counter until it stopped against his gun, just beyond her reach. "I think you should leave." Instead, she edged closer to him.

"Come on, Les, just a little look."

"I said I think you should leave," he responded with surprising firmness as he nodded toward the door.

"Suit yourself," she replied. "I guess we'll have to finish your housewarming some other time." Without looking back she said peevishly, "I hope you have a permit for that .44."

He tried not to dwell on the rhythmic sway of her hips as he watched her leave. Mercifully the phone rang. He dashed upstairs to the den. It was a reporter. He hung up on her and unplugged their only landline, then went down the hall to check on Breanna. Returning to the den he forwarded through nearly a dozen recorded messages from the local press, wanting to know if he'd actually filmed the crash.

One of the callers, Brenden Fosse from *Dateline*, urged him to "Call at any hour. We might go as high as fifteen grand, cash tonight, if what you've got is decent."

Fat chance, he thought, deleting the message. The next was from Detective Rick Gaitano, King County Homicide. Les scribbled down his number. He noticed it was 11:03 and turned on the news just in time for the report of the hot-air balloon crash:

"Also on tonight's newscast . . . as a follow-up to this afternoon's devastating crash in Kirkland: HOT AIR BALLOONS—are they safe? And could this happen again?"

Now there's a lawsuit, he thought. He'd send Sonny to the crash site first thing in the morning. Maybe it was time to adopt the opinions of Marcia's parents and leave divorce law altogether. He fumbled in his jacket for his phone. Not there. He could imagine the re-enactment. He'd show the jury what he'd filmed himself.

As he headed downstairs to retrieve his phone, he was startled by a helpless cry coming from down the hall. He could tell Breanna wanted her mother.

CHAPTER SEVEN

He felt a hand touch his cheek and jumped, then through squinted eyes he saw it was Breanna. He heard the television blaring down the hall. They'd fallen asleep together, Breanna crying, Les comforting. No Marcia. Not even a wake-up call. Then he remembered he'd unplugged their phone and wondered where he'd left his cell. He checked his jacket, which he was wearing from the night before, but there was no phone in his pocket. "Breanna, get dressed!" He squinted at his watch and saw it was 7:40. Her bus arrived at 7:45 and she was going to be late for school.

"I'm dressed," she said sarcastically. But she hadn't packed her notebooks and she still needed a lunch.

"I'll drive you, sweetheart." He hastily assembled what would have to pass for a lunch that day as they flew into the garage. Then he froze. His garage door was open and his van was missing. Someone had stolen it! He paused until he recalled that he'd parked it up the street. Then he remembered the intruder. Where was his phone?

He darted back inside, recalling he'd left it on the counter, next to his loaded gun. He saw the wine bottle and the half-empty glasses . . . but no phone. No gun. He commenced a frantic search of the kitchen, wondering if his neighbor had returned. Or the prowler! Something felt horribly amiss. His neck and face were hot and prickling with panic.

"Daddy?" It was Breanna from the garage. "We've got to go."

"Coming dear," he answered, trying to stay calm. He would have to deal with this later.

By the time he left Breanna's school and proceeded to his office, it was 8:50 a.m. He encountered a court reporter in the lobby and remembered that he'd scheduled a deposition to start at nine. He had no time to think let alone worry about how he looked. He felt his face and realized he hadn't shaved or bothered to wear a tie.

"Ms. Whitson is in the conference room with her client," his receptionist whispered. "Mr. Van Parys has been here since 8:15. He's waiting for you in the small conference room. Did you forget? And did you hear about Byron Wells?"

"Tell them I'm running late, Janie. Is that this morning's paper?"

She folded the *Times* like a guilty schoolgirl and handed it to him as he strode past. He closed the door of his teakwood corner suite, a sign he was not to be disturbed. Behind his high-back leather chair was a bookshelf laden with casebooks and treatises on everything from domestic violence to sexual assault hysteria. And in the center of it all was a photo of Les and Marcia, taken on their wedding day.

The crash was front-page news though the picture they'd used was second rate. The balloon company was disclaiming negligence, insisting it was a bomb. The F.A.A., the A.T.F. and the police were all investigating. Scenarios for "foul play" were being spun as to all four noted victims. But the hardest hitting probe was two pages in—an editorial that raised damning assumptions about the Wells and Nakamura connection. After that came a smaller inset, describing how hot-air balloons had been known to catch on fire and explode. Always the lawyer he took it to his assistant.

"Peggy, call Sonny and get him out there. This sounds like *res ipsa* to me."

Res ipsa loquitor was Latin for, "the thing speaks for itself." That is, "they take you for a joy ride and they return you looking more like toast, somebody's gonna pay." At least that's how Sonny would have defined it.

"I'll call him," she said. "You'd better get in there. Oh and here," she said as she passed him a handful of message slips. It meant his voice mail was full. Two of them caught his eye. The first was from Detective Gaitano/ King County Police, with a note printed in red ink: "Says it's urgent." The other was from Brenden Fosse of *NBC Dateline* offering fifteen grand "if it's decent." But he wasn't about to discuss his video until he could get back home and find it.

"Peggy," he said, "schedule this detective for tomorrow morning."

"No problem," she replied, as he went in to greet his client.

⇀ | ↽

By the time he'd finished his dep another dozen message slips had gathered at Janie's desk. Four were from attorney Mike Farrago, David Dietrich's lawyer. Each read, "Urgent re: Thursday's depositions."

He dialed Farrago and received an earful.

"I assume you'll be taking over as plaintiff's counsel," Farrago said, "at least for the depositions? My flight leaves tonight so we should coordinate as far as which of us will be handling which witness. James and I had divvied them up, and I'd like to stick with that if possible."

"Are you crazy?" Les responded. "The funeral for your client's best friend is Thursday. Your key witness at VVG is dead. We'll have to put these deps on hold for now. The entire case is in serious trouble."

"Excuse me, counselor, but my case is doing fine. My client never so much as met or spoke with Akira Nakamura. As for Byron, who can say what they were doing up there in that balloon? For all we know it was their first meeting. And Dietrich isn't going to Japan, which means he'll be at Byron's funeral."

"Don't you want a continuance?"

"Do you have any idea how hard it was to set this up? My client isn't rich like Byron Wells. He needs a verdict and his trial is in seven weeks."

"No way," argued Les. "We can't go to trial in June. Wells and James are *dead*. I can't take this over. I'm a divorce lawyer for God's sake. My client will need new counsel if she's even got a case after what happened yesterday."

"We're talking *fifty mill*, McKee. His options vested in the event of his death. All you have to prove is that Digitron lacked any grounds for firing him, which should be easy."

"You don't think my chances are looking pretty bleak?"

"If so that would be where our respective clients part company," he replied. "Maybe Byron was in bed with Nakamura. We'll never know. But my guy sure as hell had nothing to do with Vortex Video Games or with selling any secrets period. Thanks to life insurance your client may have the luxury of postponing her fight for Byron's extra fifty mill, but my client is unemployed. And he wants his goddamn job back—yesterday."

"Look, McKee," Farrago continued. "Either you're coming to Kyoto or

I'll handle the deps myself. I wouldn't mind except I'm not prepared for two of them. Milton's files are now the property of your client, Byron's widow. Go get them.

"These deponents are heavy hitters. They'll make or break our case depending on what they say. If I go it alone I can't promise I'll be looking out for her interests. My client pretty much holds her fucked-up husband responsible for this mess. And if you want to know the truth, he's pissed as hell that his co-plaintiff was *caught dead* with Nakamura if you catch my drift."

"All right," said Les, relenting. If he could establish Beverly's innocence at the very least, Digitron might still settle with the grieving spouse. It wouldn't look good for the trillion-dollar software giant to leave a company widow penniless due to her dead husband's failed duplicity.

He'd arranged for a bilingual attorney to attend and represent him at the deps. His Japanese co-counsel, Masao Shimizu, could help him prepare for some questioning of his own.

"You take Watanabe and Yamamoto," Farrago instructed. "I've got Sugiyama and the others. He's the whale."

"Roger," Les agreed. "I guess I'll go get those files."

He buzzed Peggy. "Book me on the next available flight to Kyoto, Peg. Tomorrow afternoon."

On his screen he noticed she'd scheduled Gaitano for noon the next day. His mind returned to the crash as he clicked backwards through his calendar, to where he'd started entering notes at the beginning of the year. He typed, "DOA 4/13" on the January page. To him it meant *date of accident*, though he paused and shuddered at its other meaning. He wondered how badly they'd suffered as his thoughts seized on his pictures.

With a sickening churn he remembered he still didn't have his phone. He picked up his handset and dialed the house. He was caught off guard when Beverly answered.

"McKee residence," she said in that low throaty voice that brought him to his knees. Something about her always left him feeling tongue-tied and awkward. It seemed as if their every encounter gave way to a baser instinct he'd determined to hold captive. He often wondered if anything similar was ever stirring inside of her.

"Beverly, is that you? Are you okay?"

"I'm doing better, Leslie, thanks. Marcia took Breanna to her lesson.

She's invited Tiffany and me to stay with you for a few days until the funeral. I hope that's okay. She thinks we should get away after that, so she's offered us your cabin for the weekend."

"That sounds like a good idea." He hesitated. "I won't be going to the funeral, Bev." He outlined his trip to Japan and how it would benefit her in the long run.

"I'd be lost without you, Leslie."

He doubted that.

"So, was there a message for Marcia?" she asked helpfully.

"Actually, yes. Can you ask her to look around for my cell phone?"

"The police have it," she replied.

"Are you sure? How did that happen?" Marcia didn't even know he'd filmed it.

"A detective Gaitano came by here about half an hour ago, asking for it. He said your neighbor has been telling anyone who will listen that you have footage of the crash. Leslie, that's too unreal. You watched him die?"

"Have you seen where they crashed?"

"Yes," she answered, almost in a whisper.

"I was outside as they passed over. I started filming, thinking it was so picturesque. I told your father-in-law last night. He didn't say anything?"

"No, he didn't. It's just so strange. It's like this isn't happening."

"So where was my phone? I couldn't find it this morning."

"It was on the kitchen counter. Detective Gaitano said he needs it for evidence. Leslie, was this something more than an accident? The news reports are speculating that a fuel tank exploded."

"No one knows what happened yet," he replied. "But I have to ask you something different—and this is awkward. I keep a gun in the house and I left it sitting on the counter by my phone. Did you see it when you found my phone?"

"No, there was no gun, Leslie." She sounded worried. "Why would you keep a gun in plain view with a child in the house? Was it loaded?"

"Did Gaitano show you his badge? I'm sorry, Bev, but the paparazzi would do just about anything to get their hands on my footage."

"Yes, he had a badge. When I told him who I was he seemed taken aback that I was here. Do they think there was foul play?"

"It hasn't been ruled a homicide yet," he answered, "if that's what you mean. It may still end up as an accident investigation. They need to piece together what happened and maybe my pictures will help. If it was a defective tank or pilot error then you should file for Wrongful Death, at least on Tiffany's behalf." He paused. "Are you really going to be okay?"

"I'll live," she said, as if she weren't okay at all. "Leslie? I'd better go."

He could still hear her voice, muffled by tears, long after he hung up the phone.

CHAPTER EIGHT

As he approached Seattle, the sixty-story Ventnor Tower rose sharply against the city's skyline. The palatial law office of Milton James was on the 44th floor of Seattle's newest skyscraper. The Tower was home to more lawyers than the entire nation of Japan, according to urban legend as nurtured by lawyer-bashers.

Soon he'd be rubbing shoulders with the Japanese legal system for himself. Finding a Kyoto lawyer licensed to conduct depositions had not been easy. It had taken him several weeks to secure Masao Shimizu for the deps.

When he called ahead, James's assistant cautioned him that their office had gone paperless. He said, "In that case I expect you to print every scrap of data on your server or in the cloud that relates in any way to Wells vs. Digitron. I'm taking over and I've got to get up to speed." Thirteen boxes worth of printed materials, along with the corresponding discs, were waiting for him in James's upscale lobby. The staff was attempting without much success to cope with the sudden shock of their prominent boss's death. Les found the mood as morbid as the night before at the senior Wellses.

He arrived home feeling famished, but the only sign of dinner was a pizza flyer on the counter. Breanna was pounding away at the piano. It was the usual din of after-school energy, compounded by the presence of Beverly and her daughter.

"Were you here when the police came by?" he asked Marcia, giving her a hug and kiss.

"I was running Bree to her lesson. You never told me you filmed it." She seemed annoyed with him, but he brushed it off. He wondered whether Beverly had mentioned his missing gun.

"You know they're talking foul play," he said.

"I can't deal with that now, so don't bring it up at dinner. We need to be here for Bev and leave the rest to the police. That same detective called and he wants you to call him back. He said it's something about your phone."

He looked at his watch and decided it was too late. He was skeptical of law enforcement, but at least his pictures were safely with the cops. For the moment he had a more fascinating investigation of his own awaiting. He excused himself and went to the den to pore over his new-found treasure, the files of Milton James.

For Les the intrigue was palpable as he sorted through box after box filled with business records, inter-office memos, email, software coding logs, legal pleadings, deposition transcripts and more. It was a strange sensation, having total access to the files of his opponent. A day before it would have been unethical if not illegal for him to have these files. Tonight it was his job to digest them inside out.

In their grief and shock, and without their skipper at the helm, Milton's staff had printed everything, perhaps secrets and confidences they didn't even realize they were holding. As he began to dig, he wasn't sure where to find the records on the men he'd be deposing, let alone any meaningful details revealing why their testimony mattered, or exactly who they were. He would need to learn at least that much before framing any intelligent questions of his own.

Fortunately, the boxes were highly organized. James's staff had prepared a dossier on each deponent. A chart showed their names, together with their photographs, on the VVG corporate ladder. He faced a monumental task of reading and organizing, but was well on his way when he heard the doorbell ring, signaling that dinner had arrived.

After a quiet meal, Breanna led a subdued Tiffany upstairs as the conversation at the table turned to Byron's death.

"Before he left I used to pay the bills," Beverly said, "but that's about it. He shared almost nothing with me about our investments or our debts. Neither of us was any good with money."

Les could attest to that. In the divorce Byron and his attorney had consistently ignored or delayed the exchange of financial information. On the afternoon of Byron's death he'd been working on a "motion to compel discovery."

"I did bring these." She handed him their mutual wills, signed shortly after Tiffany's birth. "The lawyer who prepared them for us told me there were never any updates."

He studied them and realized the surviving spouse inherited all, fifty million in stock, maybe more if they could settle with Digitron. In typical fashion, Byron had forgotten to change his will when he filed for divorce. As Les turned through the pages, Beverly pulled her chair in close. Marcia, who'd been sitting across the table from them, rose and poured him a fresh cup of coffee. She came and stood between them, setting down the cup with a touch of force.

"This is incredible," he said, while casting a curious glance toward Marcia. "I would have expected him to change this as soon as he filed. It trumps the prenup. A divorce would have voided the will, but as it stands you could inherit a hundred mill."

"What if he changed it with a different lawyer?" she asked, scooting her chair to the left.

"We'll proceed as if this is the only one and wait to see if his parents come forward with another. I doubt they would, even if one exists."

It was eleven by the time he'd answered all her questions. He rather enjoyed the way she suddenly needed him. She made it clear she didn't want him handing her matters off to other lawyers. The prospect of spending more time with her made him feel both anxious and prematurely guilty.

Although he had more work to do on Byron's files, he went upstairs to be with Marcia. Closing the door behind them, she said, "You were impressive tonight, the way you helped her with her questions. You shouldn't be afraid to stay with all her cases: Digitron, Byron's probate, the balloonists."

"I don't know, Marsh. She's behind on her bill."

Marcia looked thoughtful. "Now that her divorce is cancelled, can't she sell as much of Byron's stock as she wants?"

"That's a good point," he answered.

Until now, the parties had been forbidden by a restraining order from selling any Digitron stock. Les had threatened to file in court for an exception, just to cover her unpaid child support and attorney fees, but James had argued that any sale, no matter the reason, might weaken Byron's case for Wrongful Termination. Les wanted to proceed, but Beverly refused to appear desperate for Byron's money. She claimed to have money of her own, though he observed no willingness on her part to spend it.

"You're right," he said, stroking the curve of Marcia's cheekbone. "Milton isn't calling the shots any more, is he?" He took her in his arms and pulled her toward the bed. She seemed delighted with his warm embrace and his long, affectionate kiss. He moved very close to her, but it was intimacy not sex that each was craving.

"I love you, Marsh," he said, looking straight into her eyes. She cradled the back of his head and pressed her cheek to his.

"If I lost you, Les, I don't know what I'd do."

He felt her tremble as the events of the past twenty-four hours rippled through her body. He said nothing for several seconds as he continued to hold her tightly. "I'm not going anywhere," he whispered.

"Except Japan," she said, smiling. "You need to go back to work, don't you?"

It was rare that he received her blessing to keep working after hours, but for now she seemed content with his affections, which was why the edge in her next comment took him totally by surprise.

"I'm sure Beverly appreciates what you're doing." He looked at her quizzically. Her words were ordinary enough, but Les suspected they were meant for harm, like the time a decade before when she'd accused him of having an affair with Beverly. Both women were pregnant at the time, and Marcia had actually asked him whose baby Bev was carrying. That absurd question still lingered and bore a ghostly presence in their marriage.

"Marsh," he said firmly, but with tenderness, "Beverly is a client—and your best friend. You have no reason to be jealous." It was true. In all his married life Bev hadn't once come onto him. Les was the guilty party, but only in his mind.

She smiled. "Thank you, darling."

"Can you remember to wake me in the morning?"

"Yes," she said. "It'll be chaos with Bev and Tiffany here."

"I think it's great you had them stay."

"I didn't ask her to stay," she said. "She told me *you* did when you called here this morning."

"Well, it isn't true. Maybe she was too embarrassed to invite herself, but it wasn't me, I swear."

"Who did you have wine with last night?"

"What? Oh that. Our neighbor introduced herself and proposed to toast me for selling my footage to the press. I told her *no way*."

"*Her*? How did she know you filmed it?"

"She was on her deck when it happened. Her name is Ginny. I guess she saw me filming."

"You had wine with her? That's weird, Les. Just go downstairs."

He didn't know how to read her. He felt sick as he recalled his missing gun, though he didn't dare mention it, at least not yet. She detested the fact that he kept one in the house at all.

He tied his terry cloth robe and left. When Beverly appeared outside the guest room, he felt like he was awakening from a daze. Clad only in her sheer nightgown, she seemed to shiver in the chilly air. He averted his gaze from her fully outlined breasts. Barelegged, she looked vulnerable and inviting. He dutifully suppressed the urge to reach out and trace the curve of her satin-covered nipple. Twenty years of inner conflict loomed there in the silent hall. He despised himself for wanting to stay.

She seemed to linger for just a moment, almost as if displaying herself. Then she stiffened in awkward recognition that she was very thinly clad. "Have a safe trip," she said. "And thank you, Leslie, for everything." She gave him a polite hug.

Through the crème-colored satin of her nightgown, he felt her skin grow warm beneath his touch. Her look was that same knowing gaze that had long ago besieged his soul. It wasn't so much a look of shared desire as of a destiny not yet revealed. He'd known that look since her first divorce, since before she'd married Victor.

They parted, but electricity was still surging through his body. As the sparks disbursed he kept thinking of what had just occurred. But he shook it off and headed for the den. He would escape, once more, into the law.

CHAPTER NINE

He normally left for work by 7:50, trailing the exhaust of Breanna's bus, but today he hung around, discreetly searching for his gun and watching the local networks for updates on the story. The press was positively mesmerized by the coincidence of Beverly's divorce attorney having filmed the crash, though no one had actually seen his footage. He could not be reached for comment, but his pictures were reportedly in police custody.

While Les was in the shower, Detective Gaitano called with instructions for him to buy a replacement phone, but leave his existing number attached to his old phone. Marcia took the message. He said Les was not to cancel or change his account and he wanted to speak with him before their meeting at the office.

"It can wait," he told Marcia. "You know the press has a right to see my pictures. Gaitano can make all the copies he wants, but I expect him to return my phone. *Dateline* is offering me fifteen grand for an exclusive."

"How could you even think of profiting from his death?"

"She owes twice that on her bill."

"Quit obsessing about her bill and get to work. I'll pick up a new phone for you and drop it by the office. You'll need one for your trip." She was speaking in hushed tones as Beverly was in the kitchen, fixing Tiffany's breakfast.

Les was sick with worry at the thought of either child finding his loaded gun, but for reasons he couldn't explain he kept quiet about it. "Okay," he said, lightly kissing the nape of Marcia's neck. "Be sure you write down my new number."

➤ | ↢

He arrived at his office at 8:45 with his bags packed and was greeted by a fistful of new messages. After tossing out the media calls, he started returning the others. He was putting out fires in preparation for his unexpected absence when Janie buzzed him.

"Mr. McKee, there's a Mr. Fosse here to see you."

He groaned. "He doesn't have an appointment so tell him no." Glancing at his watch he added, "Marcia should be here soon. Can you send her back when she arrives?"

At 10:07 Janie buzzed again.

"She's here and she's bringing you a phone."

"Thanks for doing this," he said as he ushered Marcia into his inner sanctum.

"It took forever, and now I'm late for my aerobics class. Is that Detective Gaitano in the lobby?"

"No, why?"

"He won't stop calling. He wanted to come by the house before coming here. He said there aren't any pictures of the crash on your phone and he wanted to look around to see if you used a different camera. I told him I was leaving."

"That's impossible, Marcia. I know I filmed it and that I used my phone. I'll straighten this out with him as soon as he gets here."

As he walked her out, he tried to ignore the stranger on the sofa but to no avail. The guy was a reporter after all. The man jumped up. "Mr. McKee, Brenden Fosse with Dateline NBC."

Silencing him, Les tugged Marcia toward the door.

"What's going on?" she demanded, "You didn't tell me he was some smarmy reporter."

"He doesn't have an appointment," whispered Les.

"Isn't he the guy who wants to pay you for your pictures? Where are they? Do you have a second camera, Les?"

"Honey," he said, trying to maintain some semblance of composure. "The police have my only phone. I have nothing going on with this reporter."

"Well, I don't want you talking to him. Can't you see what this publicity thing is doing to you? What time is your appointment with Gaitano?"

"Noon," he answered, realizing for the first time that he'd be on his way to Sea-Tac.

"You have a flight. You made the police wait until you were gone, but you let a reporter in here instead?"

"Peggy must have scheduled Gaitano before she booked my flight." He wanted to kiss her good-bye, but she was already out the door. Turning back to the reporter he snapped, "I'm not giving any statements."

"It's about your video, Mr. McKee. Your neighbor, Ms. Dwyer, says she saw you filming with a camera phone. She told me—"

Les didn't let him finish. "Whatever she told you it didn't come from me. This matter is now in the hands of the police."

"Has someone offered you more? Because if that's it—"

"That's not it."

"Is it missing, Mr. McKee? I couldn't help but overhear—"

"I don't have time for this," he barked. "I'm on a short line to the airport so you'll have to excuse me."

"Japan? Is your trip related to Wells and Nakamura?"

Les impatiently waved him out the door and turned to Peggy. "Cancel Gaitano. Tell him I had to make an emergency business trip to Kyoto and that I'll call him just as soon as I get back. Have you managed to reach Sonny?"

"Yes, he's seen the papers. He says he'll get right out there."

"Thanks, Peg. *Sayonara*."

CHAPTER TEN

He'd immersed himself in the Digitron files before his 747 left the ground. He started with a research and development disc on Digitron's answer to the Vortex. He'd stumbled across it the night before, buried among dozens of hastily labeled CD cases. He wondered whether James had even seen it.

He loaded the disc on his office laptop so he could use its search capacity. To his amazement he found evidence of private correspondence between Akira Nakamura and Byron Wells, mostly emails, peppered throughout some eight hundred pages of scanned documents. They'd been encrypted when they were sent, but Byron had provided his attorney with the key. Here was damning evidence that no one else had yet unearthed. One email, less than six months old, leapt off the page:

Byron. I've attached my latest schematic for the embedded micro mirrors. Infrared is safe. It has extensive testing in Germany by MSB and is in use already by hospitals. The color specs from RV were very good. We can program drivers in straight-forward C++ (see attached non-formatted trial).

I think we finish on schedule. For now I calling the prototype "Galileo." Sugiyama and Yamamoto are having success with investors. Maybe we launch INTERACT sooner than expect. This is a breakthrough of my life. Greetings, Akira

He opened the attachments though the algorithms they revealed made no sense. One schematic, annotated in Japanese characters, included hand-drawn sketches of a futuristic HMD, thin and light across the eyes, allowing for normal vision. Like Google Glass, it included an integrated webcam, earphones, heads-up display and a built-in mic. But unlike any next-generation Google Glass, it provided an immersive 360-degree environment, or *VR Universe*, and took up half the footprint of anything on the market. A second sketch showed a contact lens with embedded circuitry. In the margin Akira had printed GALILEO in English with an arrow pointing to his sketches.

Several emails mentioned Sugiyama and Yamamoto, who were clearly co-conspirators. Both were on the list for the Kyoto depositions. They were VVG directors, supposedly loyal to the company. It was obvious that VVG was in serious peril.

Kotaro Sugiyama, Farrago's witness, was mentioned most. According to James's chart, as VVG's senior vice president, Sugiyama was in charge of *New Markets* and *Research Capital*. Funding for the company's first 128-megabit Virtual Vortex project had been his baby. Les now had proof that Sugiyama was a major player in Nakamura's secret scheme to destroy VVG.

With the company's conversion to the 256-megabit VVViron, nearly a decade before, the 128-megabit Virtual Vortex had long since become a cast-off. VVG was counting on its next generation cloud-streaming VVViron, a sporty console boasting three separate coprocessors, to keep it on top of the server-based video game world for the next five years. But Nakamura had a microchip in development on a parallel track that would link the Vortex to smartphones and other 4G devices, including Digitron's Xterminator. So much for VVG's twenty-five-year history of proprietary hardware. Sale order on VVG stock, Les told himself.

Nakamura's processor, referred to as the *GC Quantum*, was actually striking fear in the heart of VVG's strategists. It was essentially an add-on for smartphone motherboards. Nakamura called it a "ventriloquist" or a "voice-thrower," as it was designed to fool cell tower voice algorithms into aggregating and multiplexing voice channels into a single device. With the GC Quantum 4G devices could summon the bandwidth strength of multi-channel sessions. It was burstable, meaning cell devices could access bandwidth in a way that was expandable on demand. Gamers would no longer require wireless access or a hardwired VVViron to play inside the

Vortex. Once the GC Quantum hit the market VVG might be relegated to selling software only.

But the Quantum paled in comparison to the Galileo, an experimental VR device completely foreign to VVG. The Galileo surpassed the next generation of HD spectography like nothing he'd ever seen. Nakamura's email included a sample press release highlighting its extraordinary functions:

> Byron, With some English help I've been playing on ideas for media splash:

> *The INTERACT Galileo—a VRD (or Virtual Retinal Device) — is best described as a retinal projection scanner. Through the use of completely safe and medically approved infrared technology, a low energy light source is projected directly onto the human retina. Instead of looking at a screen, players focus their vision through the Galileo. Its vibrant crystal clear image, with insanely sharp definition, is transmitted directly onto the retina, using the same focusing process as occurs inside a plasma screen. The interpretive neurons of the occipital lobe will be unable to distinguish between the Galileo's infrared transmission—and reality.*

> Tinker with this and let me know. Greetings, Akira

An endeavor this huge would require millions for R & D, not to mention FDA approval. Nakamura had delegated his venture capital needs to Kotaro Sugiyama. There would almost certainly be litigation over patent rights to the GC Quantum and the Galileo, which meant their scheme could only prevail with megabucks behind it.

Nakamura had conceived the birth of a corporate hybrid that he and Byron referred to often and affectionately as INTERACT. INTERACT would develop and market the GC Quantum, the Galileo and the web-streaming server technology needed to bring Vortex-level gaming platforms into the public domain. If VVG remained unwilling to share its super-server source code with the open market, Nakamura was prepared to launch a web-streaming server environment of his own, which he'd appropriately named the Matrix.

It was for this purpose that he needed Byron Wells. The firepower necessary to launch such a scheme had required a dual piracy of the highest order—namely that of Wells and Nakamura. These discs and documents contained the lethal blow to Byron's case. Les was holding irrefutable proof that Byron had been conspiring with one of Digitron's fiercest competitors for nearly two years. He and Nakamura were breaking the law and deserved to be thrown in prison. Perhaps VVG or even Digitron had taken matters into their own hands.

Les was amazed the termination case had survived this long at all. Byron had been keeping it alive by withholding critical documents, like these, from the Digitron lawyers and from Beverly in their divorce. How had they planned to pull it off? Was Byron to remain a silent partner? He needed two more years to vest his second fifty mill, provided he could get his job back.

Their scheme was more than a case of corporate spying; it was a game of lethal sabotage played on a massive scale. And now that he knew what they were up to, Les was faced with a dilemma. Wells and Nakamura were dead. Either one of their employers had the motive to make it happen. Should he turn these files over and decimate Beverly's shot at options that had vested overnight? Or assuming it was a case of corporate murder, should he just keep quiet and let the jury decide whether Byron had been fired for cause or not?

He thought it odd that Dietrich's name appeared nowhere in these discs. He recalled Farrago's fevered pitch for his client's innocence. Why had Dietrich been drawn in at all?

And there was something else. Digitron, not VVG, had uncovered the plot that resulted in the instant firing of its top two VR engineers. At the time, the software giant either didn't know or wasn't saying who it thought Byron's buyer was. The conspiracy luring Byron and Dietrich had been born and bred in corporate Japan. So what essential contribution did they require from the Americans? It was more than source code, which is bought and sold by traitors all the time.

And what about the rumors that Byron's defection hadn't been uncovered by Digitron at all? Supposedly the *Times* broke the story based on a tip. If true, it was a monumental embarrassment to the internal security apparatus at Digitron.

Les could not believe a scandal of this magnitude could be leaked to the press before Digitron found out. He wondered if Byron had leaked it himself, as Beverly maintained, just to foil her in their divorce. Maybe he *intended* to be fired. So long as he could conceal his tie to Nakamura, he could join forces with him later.

He probably filed suit to prolong his unemployment in the divorce, thinking he would settle later, maybe get his job back, maybe not. In any event the piracy scandal was real, and enough of it had been leaked to insure his termination.

No doubt Byron was keeping his options open. The chain of email revealed that Nakamura was planning to go public with his defection from VVG in May, at the international "Virtual World's Consortium" in Seattle. If Byron could settle with Digitron before the trial in June, he would wait and join forces with Nakamura in two years.

But he was equally prepared to lose at trial, in which case he'd remain unemployed while appealing his adverse verdict. Once the divorce was behind him, and with INTERACT operational, he would liquidate his holdings, whether fifty million or a hundred, and buy in with Nakamura. Either way, Beverly would come up short. She'd receive no part of Byron's separate property, thanks to the prenup, and share none of the upside to his post-divorce new venture.

Had Byron waited until after he left Bev to quit, the Family Law Commissioner might have clobbered him with imputed income. But by getting himself fired *before* they split, he'd preempted any claim of intentional unemployment. As it stood, she was getting zero in spousal maintenance.

As for his options, maybe he didn't care if ultimately they vanished. Digitron's stock was going to plummet once INTERACT went IPO. It appeared his plan was seamless. So what went wrong? How had the press uncovered his link to Nakamura? And why such a risky meeting in Seattle on the weekend before the deps?

Hoping to roll boxcars, he turned from his laptop to a hard file labeled *Outlook correspondence for Kyoto depositions*. Perhaps Farrago had been duped but not Milton James. Somehow Milton was privy to their plot. It made sense to assume he would have received some kind of notice that Nakamura was coming to Seattle.

As if on cue, he caught sight of a letter-sized envelope, sitting loose in the file of printed email. Its contents were still inside. A note was scribbled on the outside in Byron's hand: "CONFIDENTIAL: Hand-deliver to

Milton James." He removed an email from Nakamura dated April 1. At the top was a note to James: "Milt, this sounds urgent. I couldn't risk leaving it on the server, encrypted or not."

> Byron. We are losing Sugiyama, and just a month before Consortium. He blames you for leaks. As you know, the press enticed a traitor here who may soon go public with what he knows. Harsh measures are in store. I am ready to take on VVG and even Sugiyama if I must. He says Digitron will file in U.S. District Court to restrain us at Consortium. He says to cut you out and bury INTERACT for one more year, but I wish to proceed. We simply keep denying any tie—and what can they prove?
>
> Several of us are to be deposed, but before that we talk. I shall come to Seattle and have my Mr. Sullivan arrange for time and place to meet you and Mr. James. Also I wish to accept your invitation for balloon excursion. I feel certain we can preserve our plans and win back Sugiyama. Greetings, Akira.

His heart was pounding above the dull roar of the jet engines. He flushed as he looked around. This was too sensitive to be reading among strangers in close quarters.

The setting for Les was as surreal as Nakamura's Galileo. At 30,000 feet there was nowhere he could run and no one he could tell. Byron, the renegade, had leaked too much in his effort to cheat his wife. It had cost him his life.

Nakamura and his co-conspirators were prepared to battle VVG over patents, but they weren't prepared to take on Digitron over stolen code. Byron had committed theft, an act that would put both men out of business and in prison if proven. Nakamura was willing to take the risk and keep his ties with Byron. Sugiyama was not.

The purpose of the meeting was to salvage their conspiracy. Les understood why they'd been extinguished, but not at the hands of either corporate giant. They'd been shut down by their fellow racketeers. He was sure who'd ordered it, and in a few short hours he would be squaring off with Kotaro Sugiyama.

CHAPTER ELEVEN

Kotaro Sugiyama entered the room flanked by his attorneys, his presence dark and heavy. He was the fourth deponent of the day. The first three deps had been a farce. VVG execs who'd previously defended Nakamura were abruptly turning coat. Witness number one, Tadashi Yonekawa, director of personnel, had the power to fire Nakamura when the scandal broke but didn't. Witness number two, Yasuo Iwaguchi, had launched the company's internal investigation, which at one point had completely exonerated their favorite son.

Les had questioned witness number three, Kenjiro Watanabe, a high-level VVG software engineer. Watanabe was clearly the "traitor" referred to in Nakamura's final email. In a recent turnaround, he'd been the first at VVG to publicly acknowledge the existence of a plot. Initially he'd implicated both Nakamura and Sugiyama, but in his deposition he turned against Nakamura only, perhaps to avoid ending up dead himself. He was clearly afraid of Sugiyama. It was obvious to Les that Sugiyama, not Nakamura, had been running the show from behind the scenes.

The Japanese media had penned its English-language version of the crash as follows:

NAKAMURA KILLED IN SEATTLE—
EXPLOSION OR "EXPOSE-ION?"

Prior to the *expose-ion*, each of the first three execs to testify had defended Nakamura. Now they claimed either that they'd suspected or had known of his secret dealings all along. To a man they claimed any prior statements in support of Nakamura were intended only to divert the press, while the company investigated.

Les wondered what would become of their master plan so carefully devised. It must still be alive, or why kill Nakamura just to keep it quiet? How soon until it surfaced? Was Dietrich in on it and if so was he in danger too?

Like the first three witnesses who went before him, Sugiyama denied any personal involvement in a scheme to steal source code. But he went further than the rest in outright condemning Nakamura. He claimed he had irrefutable proof of Nakamura's guilt and produced the same "encrypted" email that Les had discovered on his flight, only Sugiyama's version had been purged of any references to himself or Takeo Yamamoto.

Les could hear the screams of the dead men rising from their fiery graves. He could have proven Sugiyama's perjury then and there, with the correspondence in his briefcase. But at what cost? He might not leave Kyoto alive if he nailed Sugiyama. He wished to keep his exits open.

These men were cowards who had turned on their own. They cared only for their jobs and for saving face. Any one of them was capable of murder. They'd collapsed as a band of raiders, and whatever remained of their corporate coup d'état was clearly in limbo for now. The press had been getting too close, forcing them to crawl back underground.

Sugiyama seemed especially monstrous and his excessive weight only added to his formidable presence. Les tried not to meet his hooded scowl. He just wanted to go home. He wondered what he'd filmed that they were all so worried about.

Farrago was livid. Instead of helping his case, these witnesses were turning on Nakamura, yet because none had implicated Dietrich, he continued to lay it on. It was laborious, with each question and answer passing through an interpreter. As Farrago droned on for hours, it was obvious to everyone but him that he was weakening his case with every question.

"Give it up, Mike," Les whispered to him at a break. But Farrago kept slogging away. After fourteen hours of grueling testimony, he returned to his room at the Hotel of the Pacific and collapsed. At some point during the night he awoke with a start in his pitch-black room. It was his cell phone and it took several rings before he found it. By then he'd figured out it was his wife.

"Hi, honey," she said. "What time is it there?"

"Hi you. I was asleep but it's great to hear from you. How are you and Breanna?"

"We're fine . . . we're getting ready for the cabin. How's Kyoto?"

"My room looks out at the Kiomizu Temple, which is built into the eastern slope that overlooks the city. It's amazing, but honestly I've barely glimpsed Kyoto. And the deps are going lousy. Byron's case has major problems. We weren't able to finish today, which means I've got to squeeze in one more dep in the morning before I fly home. How was the funeral?"

"It was awful, Les. Just awful. Beverly fell apart. I'm sorry we parted on bad terms and that I gave you such a hard time about your video."

"It's okay, honey. Any news about my phone?"

"Gaitano was upset that you left before he got there. He says there are no pictures on your phone, except for a few seconds from Breanna's recital."

"Bree didn't delete them, did she?"

"I don't think so. The recital pics weren't selfies—so they weren't hers to delete. Someone else took them."

"I took them after I filmed the crash. I'm too tired to think now, Marsh. Ask Bree if she's been fooling with my phone. We need to buy her one of her own."

"He sounds suspicious, Les. He said you need to get back here."

"Well, I agree there's not much I can do for him from here. I'll call him as soon as I get back. I promise. We'll figure this out, don't worry."

CHAPTER TWELVE

Les had returned to a sound sleep when he was startled by another piercing ring—the hotel phone. On the other end was his co-counsel, Masao Shimizu, who was calling him from the lobby.

He dressed and quickly packed. As he hurried downstairs, he thought of his favorite motto: that people hate lawyers but cling to their own. Its truth had been borne out by his experience in Kyoto. Farrago, the Digitron lawyers, and the VVG in-house counsel seemed cold, calculating, and poisoned by their own venom. But Masao had been a different story altogether. From the start he'd been incredibly helpful—a perfect gentleman and host. Their ride through downtown Kyoto to the site of the depositions was no exception.

"I ask in lobby for American breakfast food. So strange—they tell me either Danish or French toast. Here . . . for you." He handed him a sweet roll and a coffee.

Les ate while Masao drove.

"Takeo Yamamoto is someone I have had prior dealings with. He is not in the technology but the finance. There is rumor he has connections with the Yakuza."

Les had done his homework on Yamamoto. He was a notch above Sugiyama on the VVG corporate ladder. The two were among the most powerful on the board. Yamamoto was a multinational financier, in charge of VVG's investments. Fifteen years earlier he'd single-handedly orchestrated the VVG IPO, still the largest in the history of the Japanese exchange. He continued to court VVG's whale investors. Whereas Sugiyama would raise the capital for new ventures, Yamamoto managed VVG's overall financial empire. For some reason the two had failed in their efforts to convert the rest of the board into supporting Nakamura. So they were going to resign and break away—until something went wrong.

Les and Masao arrived at the deposition to find Yamamoto and his lawyers waiting. After polite introductions, the questioning began. Yamamoto turned out to be as unpleasant and overbearing as Sugiyama. But as chance would have it, like Nakamura, he spoke fluent English.

"Mr. Yamamoto," Les began, "I'm sure you recall your statement to the press, shortly after Akira Nakamura was implicated in the Digitron scandal. Showing you what's been marked Exhibit A, an article from *Newsweek Magazine* dated January 7 of this year, you said, and I quote, 'a scheme such as this would have required massive venture capital. Had anything been afoot, I would have known about it,' close quote. In the next sentence, you say, quote, 'I'm convinced Akira is nothing but a scapegoat for the American press.' Sir, as you sit here today, do you stand by your prior statements?"

Yamamoto glanced at his attorney, who was about to object to the compound nature of Les's question. But without hesitating further he turned and abruptly answered, "I no longer stand by my prior statements."

"Big surprise," Les heard Masao whisper before turning to Yamamoto. "Are you admitting you knew a conspiracy was afoot, or are you saying you've since changed your mind regarding Akira's innocence?"

Yamamoto looked bewildered by the question. He leaned over to confer with his attorneys. As they were rereading Exhibit A, Masao seized the moment to conduct a private sidebar with Les in the corner of the room. To that point he'd revealed precious little of his impressions as an outsider to the case. But he surprised Les by whispering, "I'm intrigued always by your English language. Virtual Reality—what does this mean, really? I have researched it for a translation. Virtual means among other things implied. I think that's an excellent assessment of these so called witnesses—an implied reality. Not actually real at all, but . . . manufactured." His big grin said the rest. For Les it was like a shot of Starbucks' best espresso.

Back at the conference table Yamamoto stiffened as he prepared to answer. "I no longer believe Akira was innocent."

"But your statement implies that he couldn't have pulled this off this without your help, am I correct?"

"What I trying to say at the time was that I thought he was incapable of treason. It turns out he was quite . . . capable."

"Then why refer to him as a scapegoat? Scapegoats are by definition innocent, correct?"

"The evidence was not all in. We wanted to believe the best about Akira."

"But privately you were concerned, am I right?"

"Yes, we were concerned."

"I'm sure you were. And when you say we, Mr. Yamamoto, I assume you mean yourself and your billionaire venture capitalists, whose money he would have needed to pull this off?"

"I suppose I mean everyone here at VVG was concerned. None of us wanted to believe—and why do you keep using the term 'pull this off'?"

"I'm referring to the emergency investors' meeting you assembled in Kyoto on April 1, barely two weeks ago today. Was that when you decided to dump Akira and Mr. Wells from INTERACT, on account of growing press leaks in Seattle? Who actually made the final decision to have them killed? Was it you or Mr. Sugiyama?"

In that instant the room fell to a deafening silence as everyone sat transfixed by the look of utter horror on Yamamoto's ashen face. He couldn't turn his gaze away from the Les, who held him fiercely in the grip of truth.

Without blinking, Les started speaking to the court reporter. "Let the record reflect that Mr. Yamamoto, who speaks perfect English, hasn't been able to force a single word from his gaping mouth in over thirty seconds now and counting."

"I object," Yamamoto's lead attorney barked. "Counsel, you can't testify as to what my client looks like. I move to strike."

"Can we go off the record for a goddamn minute," Farrago interrupted. "McKee, I want to speak with you outside."

It was perfect, Les thought. A stab in the dark or at the dark. Perhaps he shouldn't have cut the wire, as he'd triggered a bomb of his own. But that was his nature and he couldn't help himself. The commotion he'd created in the enemy camp was worth his airfare over. They were guilty and everyone here knew it, except Farrago. He was clueless. The term INTERACT meant nothing to him. As for an alleged investors' meeting on

April 1st, that too was a wild guess by Les, based on the date of Nakamura's email. *April Fools.*

Out in the hall, Farrago collared him. "You idiot! How dare you suggest he was involved in a nonexistent conspiracy. And then you call the man a killer? Who in the hell are you working for, you asshole?"

"Mike," said Les, "Every one of those so-called witnesses was in on this to some extent. That's probably why you took their depositions. You thought they would continue lying for your client."

"You're insane, McKee," Farrago spat out. "Fucking insane. You just cost your client fifty mill. I'm sure your malpractice limits aren't worth a fraction of that, you moron. I may sue you myself for fucking up my case. Now when we get back in there—"

"He's yours," Les interrupted. "I've got a plane to catch. I'm not sure what to think of Dietrich, but it's clear that Byron's case was a sham from the day he filed. I just hope you're getting paid. I'll catch you back in Seattle."

CHAPTER THIRTEEN

Les's heart didn't slow until his plane was twenty-five thousand feet above the ocean. His initial rush of exhilaration was being replaced by anxiety and remorse. Too much bravado, he thought. Though he was convinced he'd exposed the killers, not much proof would emerge from the printed page. And what if Yamamoto's surprised reaction had an alternate explanation?

It didn't matter, he told himself. He would be getting out. Let someone else dig up the proof. He'd seen enough. Farrago was not worth losing any sleep over.

His exhilaration returned as he pictured Yamamoto delicately removing his soiled underwear in the men's room down the hall. He was not afraid of Sugiyama as he and his cronies could only make things worse for themselves by harming Les.

He pondered something Masao had mentioned earlier in the deps—that the Japanese authorities were investigating the mysterious disappearance of Nakamura's bodyguard, Minoru Kawashima, whose family had reported him as missing. He was last seen in Kyoto on April 10. The authorities weren't sure if he'd accompanied Nakamura on April 11, though it seemed likely. Several witnesses claimed that Nakamura did not come to Seattle by himself. Kawashima was suspected of having played a role in killing the man he was employed to protect. The "accident" was obviously an inside job.

For his long flight home he settled in with an airport novel about a divorce lawyer who fell for his client. By the epilogue the protagonist had managed to get himself disbarred, divorced, then killed. Byron would have called it a happy ending.

His plane touched down at 4:40 a.m. It was Saturday morning and the freeways felt abandoned. As he pulled into his driveway, his thoughts returned to Sunday's prowler. Had there been one or had he imagined it? His gun was missing. If he didn't find it soon, he would have to report it stolen.

In the kitchen he found a note from Marcia tacked to the microwave with crumpled masking tape:

> Les— Hope you got home safe. We're off to the cabin and staying through Monday to avoid the ferry lines. It's Spring Break—remember? Breanna thinks we're taking her to the coast on Wednesday, but you're probably swamped, so maybe we'll go with Bev & Tiff instead. See you Monday.
> —Marcia

After a weekend of catching up on work he entered his office late on Monday morning, feeling no closer to the truth than when he'd left for Japan. Peggy looked up at him as he passed her desk. "Les," she said in a low voice, "I just listened to a voice mail from Sunday. It's that detective who dropped by here after you left. He said you gave him Marcia's phone by mistake. He said he checked the number and it's hers. He says he's coming to get yours. And the reporters are still calling." She looked at him wide-eyed and inquisitive, as though to ask "what's wrong?"

If she only knew, he thought. His mind started reeling with flashbacks of his frantic search for the phone and the gun on the morning after Byron's death. It was bothering him how Beverly had managed to find it so easily and give it to the police. Now it seemed she'd given them Marcia's phone instead. So where was his? And why hadn't Marcia mentioned that hers was missing? She was on it all the time.

With a start he remembered that she'd given him hers on their way to the recital to call Beverly. He'd left his on the deck after calling 911. That was more than a week ago. Someone had surely found it by now—or could it still be outside after all this time? He shrugged Peggy off and closed his office door. Something was bothering him about Beverly's access to their house. He decided to go home and take a look outside on his deck. He hadn't been back there since the crash, though Beverly had. She'd told him so.

He rushed out of his office. As he emerged from the building, a car door slammed and he looked up. *Damn!* he thought. *He's here.* Averting his eyes he made a beeline for his Saab.

"McKee," a voice called out. "Where are you off to in such a hurry?"

Feeling caught he briefly pondered how the man knew his name, then went over to shake the hand of Detective Rick Gaitano, who was wearing a tie, a jacket and a raincoat. "Just running an errand," he said sarcastically, having dealt with his share of cops before, mainly in the course of representing their wives. The law enforcement industry was a prime employer of family law attorneys.

He could tell as he sized Gaitano up that this was not a pleasure visit. Nor was Gaitano what he expected, aside from being Hispanic. He was young and handsome for a cop, athletic, with an innocence about him. His eyes were steely black and disarmingly intense. He had jet-black wavy hair and a cop's standard-issue mustache. He was almost certainly a zealot, fueled by his idealism. He'd probably always wanted to be a cop. And this, six murder victims on his hands, was no doubt the biggest investigation of his young career.

"You must be Detective Gaitano. May I call you Rick? I apologize for standing you up on Tuesday. I had to rush off overseas."

"Can we step inside?" Gaitano asked, as if Les was going to chew the fat with him right there.

"Janie, hold my calls," he said as they walked through the lobby.

"Mr. McKee," Gaitano began, once they were behind closed doors, "I'll get right to the point. We're investigating the crash as a multiple homicide. If you'll cooperate and there are no more delays, your involvement will be short and sweet. We'd like to see what you filmed as soon as possible, but it turns out this is your wife's phone, not yours."

He set Marcia's smartphone on the desk.

"Homicide? Do you have any suspects yet?"

"Counselor, you'd have to agree that it would be pretty damn hard to conceive of two dead lawyers and no suspects?"

Les didn't smile.

"We're also looking at who might've wanted to kill your client's husband. So, here's the deal. Hand over your phone and we'll make sure you get a copy. You can sell your footage to whomever you please. I'm sure you've already secured the book and movie rights for this."

"This has nothing to do with money," he replied. "I haven't seen my phone since the night of the crash. I thought you had it. Are you certain this is my wife's?"

"Dial her." Gaitano pointed to the phone on Les's desk.

He picked up his handset and dialed Marcia's number as cell on his desk began to vibrate.

"How is it a week goes by, yet neither of you has figured out your phones are gone?"

Panic and confusion settled over Les. His flashbacks were pouring in—images of his phone on the picnic table, wanting to turn back while en route to the recital, calling Beverly twice on Marcia's phone instead.

"Go ahead." Gaitano gestured toward the phone. "I've looked for pictures on there a hundred times. There's nothing from April 13 except for a short clip of your daughter's recital."

"Look, Rick, I'm sorry. I just got back."

"Counselor, I take it you've never been in the middle of a murder investigation before?"

"No," he said, feeling like a wayward teen in Juvie.

"Well, the first forty-eight hours are the most important. The killer's trail is growing cold while we sit here making chitchat. Now where is your phone?"

"I think I left it outside on my deck that afternoon, after calling 911. We were late for the recital. My wife gave me hers to use on the way. It looks like mine."

"We figured as much," he replied. "We pulled your carrier's records. They show you called 911 at 5:36 p.m. from your phone. Then you called your client from your wife's phone about fifteen minutes later. I listened to the voice mail you left her. A little later you called your client's house but left no message, then you made another call to 911 to report a car prowl—all from your wife's phone, not yours.

"There have been no more calls to or from either of your phones since then. No texts, emails, uploads or downloads. But why would you call your client within minutes of her husband's murder?"

The question wrenched at his throat. Gaitano was taking the offensive.

"Our daughters were dancing in the recital and we were running late. You heard my message. I had no idea when I placed that call that Byron was involved."

"Seems odd," was the only response the detective offered.

"I've been trying to call your phone. It goes straight to voice mail which means it's off. But you didn't turn it off that afternoon, did you?"

"No, but the battery would have drained by now. When you stopped me outside, I was on my way to look for it on my deck."

"We looked. It's not there." He shifted in his seat. "But it's still got battery."

"How do you know?"

"Because somebody turned it on for forty-seven minutes yesterday. We got a warrant on Friday that allows your carrier to trace and report its signal if one shows up. About 8:15 this morning it came on again. We know its exact location. In fact, we were waiting for it to come back on so we could hack in and transfer your pictures, but whoever turned it on turned it right back off. It's like they knew we were watching.

"That's when I decided to pay you a visit. Is it common that you show up for work and dash right off? You just got here, now you're going home? I've been trying to interview you for a week. So who do you think started turning it on and off over the last two days?"

"I have no idea. But since you know its location, why don't you go and get it?"

"We'll get there in a minute, counselor. First, your neighbor tells me that on the night of the crash you were worried about prowlers. She claims you drew a gun on her because you were convinced that someone had broken in your house, looking for your video."

"She walked in uninvited," he retorted. "She's the one who summoned the reporters. She was searching inside for my camera or for my pictures while we were at the recital."

"Mr. McKee. May I call you, Les?"

He nodded.

"Les, if a reporter or even an amateur somehow managed to steal your video, or had someone like Ms. Dwyer track it down for them, don't you think we'd be watching it on YouTube by now?"

"I never thought to look for it on my deck."

"Well it's not there," he replied. "How about Mrs. Wells? She was out there where you say you left it, right?"

"Beverly? How would I know?" he answered wryly. They'd tapped his phone!

"How about we take a ride on the Reading?" he quipped, motioning toward his car. "Maybe we can lift a set of her prints from the railing. By the way, she's with your wife right now, correct?"

"Something tells me you know her whereabouts."

"Maybe. We think she's been on San Juan Island with Marcia. Funny thing, that's where your phone came to life yesterday and again today. What do you think of that?"

Les didn't know what to think. Their drive to his house was awkward and silent. He was troubled. As they came to a stop, he led Gaitano around back and up the stairs to his deck. Staring out at the area of scorched field below, he noticed a team of investigators was still combing through the scene. Gaitano was on his phone, calling for a couple of them to come up and dust for prints. A quick search of his family room revealed that his tablet and case files had been moved inside the house. Gaitano commented that his tablet would be easy to dust for prints.

He led Gaitano back to the deck. "This is where I stood," he said, as if to bolster his credibility.

Gaitano offered him a curious expression as he looked around. "Do you remember where you set it down?" he asked. "The phone, I mean."

"Right there, on the table, on top of my tablet."

"You never turned it off?"

"No."

"How about the tablet. Who turned it off?"

"I have no idea," said Les.

"Interesting," said Gaitano. As they walked back in he powered up the tablet. "Somebody must have turned it off 'cause there's still a charge on here. You mean you didn't clean up? After you threw your neighbor out? Or are you accustomed to leaving your electronics and case files in the weather? In April?"

"Rick, I was a wreck that night. Marcia must have cleaned it up. Maybe that's why she has my phone."

"Or the victim's wife could have found it, right? Who told her you'd filmed the crash?"

"Nobody. She learned about it when you came by, asking for my phone," he said, wondering if he was offering up too much. Attempting to change the subject he asked, "Did you tell my wife you have her phone . . . and that mine is still missing?"

"She doesn't like me. We asked your carrier if she'd reported hers as missing but they said no. How does somebody go a week without their phone? You mean to say she said nothing to you about it?"

"We haven't talked much since the accident," said Les.

"She hasn't been much help to me either. I called her, but I have to admit I didn't think to ask her if you owned identical phones. Most people customize them, you know. Regardless, I just received a text that she's on her way here now. ETA five minutes. I think maybe we should both ask them together—Beverly and Marcia—what's going on. But if you know, Les, tell me." He glared at him as if preparing to make an arrest.

"You're the one holding back," said Les.

"Okay," conceded Gaitano. "If Mrs. Wells was on San Juan Island with your wife, then why would she place a call to your wife's missing phone this morning?"

He felt his heart race as Gaitano showed him the display on Marcia's phone. It revealed the last incoming call, prior to the one just made by Les, had come from Beverly.

"I let it go to voice mail," Gaitano said, "but she left no message."

"What are you getting at? If she didn't leave a message then how can you be certain it was her? Why not call that number back?"

"Good question. We know it was her. See, we're monitoring her phone too—with a warrant. She's made three calls so far today. This one to your wife's phone, no message, then two calls to yours, one while your phone was on, though she left no message. Les, she thinks I have your phone, the one with the pictures, so why would she be calling it?"

"You just said that the phone with my pictures is with them. You know they're together because you've been tracing both signals."

"Maybe you should call Beverly," Gaitano suggested, "to confirm that she's with your wife and not just her phone." He held out Marcia's phone for him to dial. "She'll pick it up if she thinks your wife is calling."

"There's got to be an explanation." Les took the phone but he wasn't about to assist Gaitano with an investigation of his client.

"Cell phones solve more crimes for us than fingerprints, Les." Gaitano nodded toward the uniforms on the deck, dusting for prints, and let the silence hang between them.

"We know that somebody turned off your phone, here at the house. It happened the day after the crash, in the afternoon, after your client gave me the wrong phone. She found the right one on your deck, looked at your pictures, then shut it off. And it stayed off until yesterday, when it came back on for forty-seven minutes at your cabin, then for another short time this morning."

"What am I supposed to say? You have all the answers." He heard the automatic garage door opener revving into action, as if on cue. "Look, that must be Marcia. She'll be able to tell us what's going on."

"Surprise . . . we've got company," Les said as Marcia and Breanna came in through the garage. He gave Marcia a nervous hug, as if the stranger beside him wasn't there. Breanna came skipping in behind her and flew into his arms. He hugged her briefly, then walked her halfway up the stairs.

"Hello, Detective," said Marcia.

"I guess you two have met."

"Only by phone," she said. "I'm pretty sure I know why he's here." She looked at Gaitano.

"He's here because Beverly gave him your phone instead of mine. Did you even know that yours was missing?"

"Not until this morning. I thought it was in my purse. It was off. I never used it. You were gone and we were at the cabin, where it never works anyway. But it turns out I had yours, right? The girls took it out to play games and take pictures with it yesterday. They turned it off when they brought it back because they said the battery was low. At that point I still thought it was mine."

He saw Gaitano perk up as he realized they'd simply swapped their phones. It meant Beverly hadn't taken his at all.

"We were on a walk into town for coffee this morning when I turned it on to see if I could get reception. That's when I realized it wasn't mine."

The mystery was solved.

"But there's a problem." She looked chagrined. "Now I can't find it. I've checked my purse, the car . . . everywhere." She was visibly perplexed. "I think I left it at the cabin."

"Slow down, Mrs. McKee." Gaitano interrupted. "Let's take this from the top. How did you end up with your husband's phone?"

"I don't know. It was in my purse."

"Who brought my tablet and case files in?" asked Les.

"I had Breanna bring them in when she got home from school on Monday."

"So how and when did you realize that the phone in your purse was actually your husband's?"

"Well, Detective, if it wasn't mine then it had to be his. It was just sitting there until I turned it on this morning. Bev had reception, so she dialed him and it rang."

"If you knew you had the phone with the pictures, why didn't you look at them?" asked Les.

"I realized it was evidence and it was almost out of power, so I just shut it off."

"Then you promptly lost it?" Gaitano was in furious disbelief. Les felt flushed and clammy.

"I swear I dropped it back in my purse. After coffee we walked home and started packing. Somehow, it got left behind. I realized it as we drove off the ferry because I was going to check it for reception. But it was gone.

"Bev thought maybe the girls had been playing with it on the boat. They said no, but she used her phone to dial Les again, just in case someone had turned it on. We were hoping it would ring inside the van, or if it was on the boat, that somebody might hear it and pick it up."

"And?" Gaitano was now fully engaged.

"Straight to voice mail, meaning it was off."

"Marsh," Les interrupted, "you should have checked it for the pictures. That's all he cares about."

"Bev said to leave it for the police. I didn't really want to go there, Les. Can you imagine if she saw it?"

"Did she try dialing *your* phone . . . around the time she dialed Les's?" asked Gaitano.

"Yes. She tried mine first. When the phone in my purse didn't ring, she suggested we try Les's number."

"That explains her calls," Les said, "the ones you thought were so suspicious." He was relieved to see that Gaitano had been only fishing.

When Marcia heard this she glared at Gaitano. It was finally dawning on her that the police had been monitoring her phone and Bev's.

"What time did you board the ferry?"

"We were on the 9:15," she snapped.

"That makes sense," said Les. "When you acquired my signal this morning they were still on the island."

"We should have had your signal the entire time if there was battery.

On the night of the crash, you said you never turned it off, so who in the hell did and why? It doesn't sound like you did, Mrs. McKee."

"It was me," came a little girl's voice. All eyes turned to Breanna, who'd been listening from the top of the stairs. "I shut it off when I found it on the deck because the battery was getting low. I thought it was my mom's."

"Bree," said Marcia. "I didn't realize you were listening. This is really a matter for the adults, but do you remember what you did with it after you found it on the deck?"

"I put it in your purse."

Les shot a glare at the detective as if Gaitano should be ashamed of his suspicions.

Marcia looked up at her daughter. "Can you wait for me in your room, Bree? We're almost done here."

But Gaitano wasn't finished. Glancing at Les, he said, "Ask her how long she and her friend were taking pictures yesterday? When they were using the phone for their games or whatever, how long did they leave it on?"

Marcia looked at Les as if to signal she'd had enough.

"Bree," said Les, "you can answer him if you're able."

"I don't know . . . maybe an hour. The battery was about to die so we turned it off."

"Thank you, honey," he said, nodding permission for her to scurry off.

"One more thing. Ask her if she or her friend have seen it today."

"No, sir," Breanna responded without further prodding.

Les beamed with pride as his daughter went up to her room. "Where does that leave us, Rick?"

"With just one choice. We'll fly up there in the morning and search for it in your cabin. I'd leave now except I'm interviewing witnesses and I'll need to requisition a plane. Meanwhile, if you don't mind, I'd like to search for it in your van." Gaitano looked at Les and added, "I'll get another warrant if I have to."

The detective turned to Marcia. "Where is Mrs. Wells and how much access has she had to the phone since you realized it was your husband's?"

Les grimaced inwardly at the question.

"What are you getting at?" she asked edgily. "I just dropped them off."

"Was she in a position to remove it from your purse?"

"Why ask me that?" She shifted her weight defiantly. "Why would she want it? Is she some kind of suspect? You don't think she had anything to do with this, do you?"

"As a matter of fact, Mrs. Wells has become a person of interest in our investigation."

"What?" she exclaimed. "That's ridiculous. You can't be serious." *Do something, Les,* she pleaded with her eyes.

"Ma'am, I didn't say she was a suspect. I said she was a person of interest. We don't believe these deaths were accidental and we've uncovered evidence to back that up—which I can't divulge. As you know, she had a lot to gain from her husband's death and almost nothing to gain if he'd lived long enough to divorce her."

"Nonsense," retorted Les. "Beverly and Byron were inches from reconciling. She was devastated by his death. She still loved him, but she would've come out just fine if they'd divorced."

"Come on, Les. We both know she'd signed a killer prenup—*with* the benefit of her able counsel I might add. Jim Van Owen, the Prosecutor, tells me it would have stood in court, mainly because she had you telling her not to sign it before the wedding.

"The divorce meant her end," Gaitano continued. "Even if she'd kept him as a husband, the golden goose was dead—fired and disgraced. Nobody would touch him. He was washed up. Beverly knew he was selling secrets and probably headed for prison. To her he was worth everything dead and almost nothing alive."

Les felt a wrenching in his gut. Gaitano was probably right about the prenup, though he doubted he'd asked the prosecutor for a legal opinion on a matter of family law. He was name-dropping.

"Do you have any other suspects or persons of interest?" Marcia asked, this time more subdued.

"Of course," replied Gaitano. "And we're going to check out every one. This hasn't even been ruled a homicide for sure. The F.A.A. is conducting its own investigation—looking at the fuel tanks. My suspicions may fizzle if we get up to your cabin and find your husband's phone where you say you left it. But Mrs. McKee, I don't want to trouble myself if you already know it isn't there. I have to ask you again whether you think she might have taken it from your purse?"

"She absolutely did not, Detective. She would have no reason. Are you calling me a liar?"

Les looked at Gaitano. He pitied any man who fell victim to Marcia's wrath.

"Not at all. I'm suggesting she might have borrowed it for a while, maybe to view its contents in the privacy of her home. If she texts or emails or uploads any of those images anywhere, we'll know."

Gaitano let loose a grin that was almost evil. "I'm concerned because I want to preserve its chain of custody. God forbid she should try and delete any pictures. We're talking about material evidence that's been missing for more than a week."

Les was aware he was laying bait, suggesting they warn Bev not to delete them if she had them. The cops would be sticking to her like glue for the next few days. He couldn't imagine why she'd take his phone. Yet there was something strange about the way she'd invited herself over, just to be there when Gaitano came by, maybe to give him the wrong phone. Whether she'd intended to or not, she'd thrown their investigation off-track by a week.

He was wondering if she had his gun as well. But he'd searched for both on the morning she came over. They were missing before she got there.

Gaitano continued as if reading his mind. "Your husband said somebody broke in here on the night of the crash, looking for his pictures."

Marcia shot Les a panicked glance. "You never told me that."

"I don't know for sure," he broke in. "There were reporters on our property. One of them convinced our neighbor to come in looking for a camera or digital media."

Marcia looked away angrily.

Gaitano seemed to shrug it off as he ended their conversation. "My instincts tell me we'll find a goose egg at the cabin. Come on, Les, let's have a look in the family van." Gaitano stood to leave. "I guess I won't be needing this." He handed Marcia her phone. "There's no evidence on here. But I'd like to see that gun you pointed at your neighbor," he told Les. "Any problem with that?"

"What?" Marcia was clearly horrified.

"I can explain," Les said hastily. "You can search my van, Detective. Anything more and you'll have to get that warrant. Your boys are done here for today."

Gaitano waved them off the deck. "Nothing inside today, gentleman. You can head back down to the crime scene for now."

Les looked back at Marcia as she stood in the doorway motionless, dark as a shadow.

CHAPTER FOURTEEN

On the ride back to Les's office, neither of them spoke until Gaitano finally remarked, "You know this happened to her before."

"What does that mean?" he asked, deciding to play along.

"Her first husband died mysteriously, fourteen and a half years ago. I think you two were friends."

"I knew of him," said Les, trying to sound nonchalant. "He was the star of our college football team."

"Yep, Northwestern. His senior year was one of their better seasons. No bowl game, but at least it got him in the pros. Very strange how he died."

"Cocaine overdose."

"Really? I heard it was pain pills. A star athlete on pain pills . . . maybe . . . but cocaine sounds even more out of place. Did you know how much insurance she collected on a policy that was set to expire just a few weeks later?"

Les knew, but he shook his head.

"Half a million. Pretty good for a twenty-four-year-old third stringer, huh? At the end of the month in which he died, that policy was going to be history. It was strictly a player benefit."

"Rick, Marcia and I pretty much lost touch with her after college, and I never knew that much about her first marriage."

"Weren't you two an item at one point?"

"We dated briefly," Les said coolly.

"So what do you know about her second marriage?"

Gaitano had just rolled doubles. If Les had been wired to a polygraph he would have blown the sensors through the roof.

"I handled her divorce."

"Have you heard from Victor since his club burned down?"

For a moment he felt sure he was going to be arrested, but the statute of limitations had run. "Nobody has heard from him in years," he managed.

"Is he still in New Orleans?"

"Last I knew."

"Say, wasn't Sonny Lile your expert on that case?"

"Yeah."

"Sonny Lile . . . he was before my time. Kinda shady, don't you think?"

"I don't know, I still use him. He does okay work for me. Twenty years on the force."

"Arson. Yep. A real pro when it comes to fires. Say, isn't he the guy you've had snooping around the crash site over the past few days? What's that about?"

"I'll be suing the balloonists for Wrongful Death. At least one of the other families has filed already."

"Has he turned up anything?"

"I wouldn't know. We haven't spoken since I got back."

"Any reason you sent him out there at night? I sure hope he wasn't tampering. It's still an active crime scene, you know."

"I don't tell him how to do his job, Detective."

"You can still call me Rick. It's okay. And I agree with you, he needs no one's help. We both know if he can't find the evidence to support his theory, he'll invent it."

Les had entered an outer space-like vacuum, where no one could hear him scream. Gaitano was all over him.

"Too bad about his cancer coming back."

Sonny had battled with melanoma years before, but as far as Les knew it was in remission. "I don't know what you're talking about."

"He hasn't told you? His melanoma's back."

"He does the odd investigation for me, Rick. We aren't that close. Why does this matter to you?"

"Look, McKee," Gaitano began. They were nearing Les's office and he was eager to reach his point. "You're pretty clean or I wouldn't be telling you this. But the truth is I don't trust your client and if I were you, I'd start using a private eye who isn't known to all of Seattle law enforcement as a blood-sucking scumbag and a legal whore. You can do better."

"I don't know whether you've still got a hard-on for your client or what, but you've certainly got a beautiful wife and daughter. So before you warn her about my investigation, you should check her alibi. She would have been late to that recital even if we hadn't notified her in-laws about the crash. They all should've left by the time we called."

Les felt dizzy and nauseous.

"I'm just telling you to watch your step. Obviously I can't stop you from talking to her, but don't interfere with my investigation, especially for her sake. She's not worth it. In fact, if I find that you've been fucking with me about your pictures, I'll have you charged with obstructing an investigation so fast you won't have time to kiss your law career good-bye. *Capiche?*"

"Where do you suggest we meet?" Les asked.

"At the Kenmore Air Harbor—8:00 a.m. sharp. The department keeps a plane there. I'll be waiting."

He stepped from the car and pulled himself together. His nerves were frayed, though he hoped it didn't show. Gaitano was watching. As he entered his office, a short dark figure rose to greet him. *Now what?* he wondered, as the wiry frame drew near.

CHAPTER FIFTEEN

Sonny extended his scarred right hand. "Long time no see, Les. Out for a drive? We had an appointment, or did you forget? Peggy must not have told you. I'm on the clock, you know. What could the cops want that's more important?"

"I assume you've heard about my video?"

"Are you kidding? It's the talk of the town. Did you really film her ex going up in smoke? And then you gave them an empty camera while the real deal's gone missing? What are the odds of that? I didn't even know you lived in Kirkland."

"We just moved, and yeah, they think it's strange. Come on back and I'll tell you all about it."

Once they were alone behind closed doors, Les relaxed. He invited his companion to sit down and offered him a cup of coffee. "Sonny, a detective named Gaitano has been assigned to this case and he's an asshole. Do you know him?"

He nodded. "Homicide. Three years. Trying to make a name for himself, that's all. One of those fucking college types, more ambition than smarts. Nothing to worry about."

Les tried not to chuckle. Sonny was definitely a self-made man. "Well, he thinks Beverly did it. And he's got me scared because he's looking at New Orleans and Victor. Somebody told him that you were my expert on that case. He says the department is onto you, whatever that means. He's asking lots of questions, some of which make me think he may have talked to Victor."

"Les, do you honestly think Victor Garving would stir up trouble for us after eleven fucking years? For what conceivable reason?"

Les shook his head and let him continue. Sonny was never informed of Victor's blackmail a year after the fire.

"They've been pitching this kinda shit around about me since I retired. We were all a little crazy back then. I've cleaned up my act. Besides, the Garving case is so old it farts dust. I'll bet Gaitano didn't tell you anything he didn't get straight from the public record. You can't let this greenhorn get to you."

It was the closest to an admission about the arson he'd heard from Sonny.

"And they don't have a thing on your client, 'cause there's nothing to be had. I've still got friends in the department who are talking out of school. Gaitano is pumping you with 'what-ifs' just to scare the living shit out of you. Their only hope is that you'll go off and do something stupid, so they can bootstrap themselves from nothing. They've got zero on this case and they don't even know where to start."

"He says he's got evidence of a homicide," said Les.

"Did he say what it is?"

"No, he said he couldn't."

"Yeah, well I know what it is and personally I think it's bullshit. The crime lab claims to have detected traces of nitroglycerin inside the remains of Byron's obliterated flight jacket. I guess the balloonists issue heavy jackets to their passengers 'cause it can get pretty cold up there in April. They think that his was booby-trapped. Doesn't that sound crazy?"

"I thought a fuel tank exploded."

"It did," he replied. "But now they're claiming it was a secondary explosion. They say that without a primary explosion or prolonged exposure to heat, a sealed tank can't just rupture and explode like that. They think the heat from the burner destabilized the compound sewn into Byron's jacket. It exploded, killed him, and ruptured the fuel tank closest to where he stood. A chain reaction. He was messed up way worse than the others."

"Why do you say it's crazy?"

"For starters, any compound with a nitro glycerin base would be too damn unstable. You couldn't easily place it inside the lining of someone's jacket. It would probably go off before they were airborne." He laughed softly and shook his head.

"Hell, I had a case where this CAT driver at a construction site placed a box of blasting caps underneath the seat of his pickup, for a short drive back to the job shack. Blew himself to fucking kingdom come as soon as he hit a chuckhole! Byron could have detonated just by putting on that jacket, but not with enough explosive force to rupture a sealed tank. There were four tanks in that gondola, one in each corner. The other three just went sailing down to earth."

"I agree, it sounds far-fetched."

"The question is what made this one blow a hole through its top? Somebody would've had to climb on board with a stick of dynamite to tear open a metal tank like that. And a blast that big would've ruptured all four tanks."

"How hard would it be to hide a bomb?" asked Les.

"Tucked away in the corner of that little basket, are you kidding? They're like sardines up there. No, the tank ruptured out its fitting where the valve is housed."

"What does that mean?"

"It means it ruptured from within. They keep them under pressure—a hundred to a hundred fifty pounds per square inch. If the fitting comes loose it can fly off and kill somebody, just from the internal pressure. And if there's a flame nearby it would ignite and POW!"

"What if the bomb was inside the tank?"

"I don't think so, Les. They keep dozens of tanks on site and they swap them out before each flight. How could the killers know which one the pilot's gonna pull for any given flight? Plus there would be signs of tampering. And how would you time it to go off? Unless they had a Kamikaze on board. I guess one of them was Japanese." He grinned as Les shook his head. Sonny was as blunt as he was politically incorrect.

"Suppose they used a timer but the pilot touches down ahead of schedule. Everybody walks off and it blows up on the ground, with nobody inside. It's not like a car bomb that ignites when you crank the engine. The best they've been able to come up with so far is that the heat from the burner destabilized the compound in Byron's jacket. I call it their *tourist-turned-suicide-bomber* theory.

"Jesus, Jimmy Kimmel was closer to the truth than the friggin' government and they've had a team of federal dicks on their hands and knees for a goddamn week!"

"Why, what did Jimmy Kimmel say?"

"He blamed it on the lawyers who died, due to an excess of hot air. Said they came along to save on fuel. One was backup in case the other got laryngitis. Everything was fine until they started arguing about their bill."

This time Les had to crack a smile.

"Listen, Les, I can prove what happened. I've been out there and I've got the goods on that fuel tank. After Peggy called, I decided to rent a cherry picker. It was more like a goddamn crane. The feds weren't about to let me out there in broad daylight, so I went back at night. They've taped it off but nobody's guarding it, which makes it a free world in my book.

"I hoisted myself up to where that tree caught fire. Some of the branches were still coated with a liquid propane residue. I'm telling you that some live unspent fuel was escaping from that tank before it blew."

"I thought propane was a colorless gas."

"It stores as a liquid under its own vapor pressure. It can linger for days in liquid form. Here, check this out." He handed Les a data sheet from the Industrial Gas Division of Air Products and Chemicals, Inc. It was entitled, "Propane—Unusual Fire and Explosion Hazards."

Propane gas vapors are dense and can collect and remain in low spots even after the source of the gas has been eliminated. THERE EXISTS AN IMMEDIATE FIRE AND EXPLOSION HAZARD WHEN THE CONCENTRATION OF PROPANE IN THE ATMOSPHERE EXCEEDS THE LOWER FLAMMABLE LIMIT (2.1 % BY VOLUME).

"You may wanna keep that," Sonny said as Les moved to hand him back the sheet.

"I don't get it, Sonny."

"Too much internal pressure, or maybe the seal was faulty. Eventually the feds will have to let us look at all four tanks. And here's another angle. The propane itself may have been too volatile. I sent some of the residue I found to a petroleum lab and they're having trouble with the chemistry."

"You mean not all propane is propane?" he asked, feeling way beyond his depth.

"No more than regular is the same as premium at the pump. It's pretty complex but it's all in there." He handed Les the rest of his file.

"Its technical name is Dimethyl Methane. Natural gas contains about six percent propane, though it can be refined from petroleum sources too. The name itself is derived from propyl combined with methane. Its chemical formula is C_3H_8, meaning it has a single isomer. But the stuff I sent to the lab is showing too many saturated hydrocarbons."

"You've lost me."

"Propane has to be refined correctly, Les. This stuff may have been closer to butane. Or maybe it got contaminated with liquid hydrogen."

"So we can sue both the refinery and the distributor?"

"Who knows? I hope so 'cause the balloonists have a lousy million bucks in coverage. It was their final flight, as in they're going under. So hurry up and file that lawsuit because we need to impound the remaining tanks in their hangar. I need to test the chemistry from their latest batch of fuel."

"You don't think the cops can prove foul play?"

"Nothing solid, though they've sure got motives poppin' up like weeds. In fact, don't flatter yourself by thinking your client is all that high up on their list. Why do you think they assigned her a low-level rookie like Gaitano?"

"Why, who else do you suspect?"

"Are you joking? There's no end to the speculation. Most think it was a case of corporate panic, at Digitron or VVG. Either one of those big boys might have been going down for the count if Wells and Nakamura were pulling up stakes with their patents.

"Now it's even racial. The Japanese press claims the crash was Occidental not accidental. They say they've uncovered a murder plot at Digitron and maintain the 'round-eyes' did it. Then there's the A.T.F.—the red, white and blue of Waco, Texas. They claim they have evidence pointing to an Oriental plot—that VVG wanted to knock off their own Mr. Naka-whatever.

"Gaitano is one of ten detectives assigned to this full time. And in all seriousness, Les, either one of those lawyers could've been the target. They're covering this from every angle and right now it's looking like a goddamn Rubik's Cube."

"Sonny, what if I told you that when I was in Kyoto, I stumbled on a murder theory of my own?"

"Not you, too," he quipped. "I'm sorry, Les. Maybe I'm missing something. Have you suddenly become a damn cop? Or did you hire me because you want to sue somebody? Do you have any idea how much this case is worth, considering the cargo? Well it's not worth shit if they were murdered. So let the cops follow their leads. You and I should stick to good old-fashioned tort theories. The state will never get past reasonable doubt, which means you'll end up settling on a product's liability claim for a small fortune.

"Which brings me to your video. We've got to find it, 'cause insurance defense is going to claim there was a fire on board prior to the explosion. That's what normally causes these tanks to blow. If they're right, then we've got problems. Strictly pilot error. Everybody knows that even short-term exposure to heat can raise the pressure in all four tanks until one of them finally pops. Problem is, there's nothing but charred remains to sift through. We've got nothing to prove there wasn't a fire on board before it blew."

"My video," Les said. "You've got my video. Plus I saw it, remember? There was no fire. The only thing I saw was that they clipped a tree."

"Right," said Sonny. "How about two explosions? Did somebody go *poof* before the big bang happened? 'Cause that's what they're saying."

"It was a single massive explosion."

"Did they hit the tree first or after it blew?"

"They hit it first."

"Then your video may prove it, Les. The impact could've jarred the fitting loose on the tank that blew. Was their burner firing when they hit the tree?"

"I think so."

"Has Gaitano asked you this?"

"No, he just wants to see my video."

"Maybe. Or maybe they know what happened. Your missing pictures may be nothing more than an excuse to pump you full of their half-baked theories. They don't really care about the truth, Les. This case is too big, meaning they're under too much pressure to find a killer. They operate from a bias that accidents don't happen, not to rich people."

"Well my phone's about to surface. They've been tracking its signal. It was with my wife the entire time, just off. She turned it on this weekend, but then she left it at the cabin or they'd have it now. I'm going there with Gaitano in the morning."

"Ah, the cabin," Sonny sighed. On a few occasions when Sonny did work for a client who couldn't pay, Les had loaned him their cabin in exchange for his services. "So, what's the problem?"

"Gaitano seems to think that Beverly might have taken it from Marcia. She was with her when Marcia discovered that my phone was in her purse. A little later it disappeared. They've been tapping her phone, so maybe they know she has it. They're worried she might tamper with the evidence. He swears it won't be there in the morning. Then he'll start searching through her house."

"Let him. Why in the world would she take it?"

"I don't know. Maybe she felt awkward asking to see the pictures, or maybe she's worried they'll be leaked to the media and she'll be watching it on TV. Can you imagine if her little girl saw that?"

"Did you film anything besides the crash?" he asked intently.

"No. And what I got of the crash is probably sketchy."

"Then if she has it, why would she keep it a secret?"

"I'm worried she's not thinking straight. If she texts or emails any pictures to herself they'll know, or if she turns it on. And they can tell if anything's been deleted."

"Let me guess. Because you don't want her fingerprints on this, you'd like me to check her computer or her phone to see if she sent something to herself. Les, doesn't that make you the one who's tampering?"

"I'd like to know if it's at the cabin and whether it looks like she tried to hide it. If so, can you leave it in the open for us to find? And check it to see if anything's been deleted or sent. I'm not suggesting you change or cover up a thing."

"Les, why are you constantly looking out for her? If you're worried about her, pick up the phone and ask her. Suppose she has it. How would that change anything?"

"I don't want to accuse her of hiding evidence unless I have something more than Gaitano's bullshit to go on. I don't want to upset her. But if it turns out she's done something funny, I want her to come clean before it's too late and she tries to deny it. That's what any good lawyer would do, you know, keep the client from lying before it's too late."

"A good lawyer would confront her with it."

"She doesn't know they're watching her and Gaitano said I shouldn't warn her. They're waiting for her to screw up. He's probably getting a warrant for her house as we speak, or he would've gone straight for the cabin. If his suspicions hold up, her reasons won't matter. He'll be on her like a bloodhound. And it'll be you and me next.

"Here," he said as he handed the key to Sonny. "Marcia has a spare. I certainly can't warn her if they're listening. But you could stop by her house in Bellevue on your way out of town. If she has it then get it from her and take it back to the cabin."

"They're probably staking your cabin out," said Sonny. "Have you considered that? They didn't go today because they're waiting for somebody to show tonight, either looking for it or to put it back. They're playing you. They'll probably be watching both of us tonight and for sure they're watching her."

"Since when has a stakeout scared you off?"

"I'm good, Les, but not that good. They'll have the fucking East Precinct at your cabin. They've probably been inside already, they just can't admit it until they've obtained a warrant or entered with your permission."

"Then should we call it off?" he asked, uncertainly.

"It's a moot point, boss, 'cause Beverly's not involved. Gaitano has you paranoid all of a sudden, just because he knows about Victor. They haven't ruled this a homicide and I have my doubts about their theory."

"You think the nitro thing is fabricated?"

"Where do you suppose I learned to do it?"

Sonny's unexpected comment made him sick. He was in too deep and Sonny was letting him know.

"Listen, I'll stop by her house. If she's there, we'll have a chat. If she's not, I'll have a look. The cops are probably tailing her, which means they won't be at her house if she's not home. Since you don't want to alarm her, have Marcia summon her to the local Starbucks. I can be in and out before she finishes her latte. If I find your phone or any pictures on her computer, I'll wait until she comes back and let her know she's in over her head. I'll make sure she doesn't fuck with evidence and I'll help her come up with an explanation for why she's been acting weird."

"Marcia wouldn't lie for me or help divert her," said Les. "I'll have Peggy call and ask her to come sign some papers." He felt uneasy but he didn't know what else to do. "If the cops see you at her house or on the island, it'll be a giveaway."

"Don't worry about me, Les. I need her address in Bellevue. It's just her and the kid, correct?"

"Marcia said her sister will be coming to stay with her next week, but for now it's only those two. Should I have Peggy call her just to see if she's home?"

"No calls from your office, Les, or from your cell. Use mine instead. I have one that can't be traced. If she answers, hang up, don't leave a message. Her line is tapped and so is yours."

He reached Beverly's machine, then tried her cell with no success. He wondered if she was ever home. "No answer," he told Sonny.

"I'll head over. And keep that phone. I've got another one just like it. Turn yours off and leave it off. If I find something at either place I'll call you on mine. If you don't hear from me in the next forty minutes, it means her place was clean and I'm on my way to Friday Harbor.

"It'll be obvious if she tried to hide it. I've got chargers and a lead-lined bag. I can power it up without emitting any signal to see if anything's been deleted or sent. I'll wipe her prints. Don't worry, I won't take any chances. I'll abort if I think I might be seen."

"Wow. A man with gadgets," Les said, relieved.

"You're paying for them. Speaking of, we need to discuss my fee."

"Sonny, I've always paid."

"I know, but this won't be at my regular rate. I haven't pulled this kinda shit for you or anybody else since New Orleans. It's dangerous—especially getting inside if either place is being watched. For that I'm going to charge you extra."

Great, he thought. He knew he'd have to go along with it, especially with Sonny letting loose about New Orleans.

"I've been at that crash site for a week."

"Don't worry, you'll get paid, as soon as I get your bill." He'd figure out a way.

CHAPTER SIXTEEN

Les awoke feeling the tension he'd been battling through the night. He was waiting for a call from Sonny that never came. He dressed quickly and left the house. Slogging through early-morning traffic he made a few business calls on Sonny's phone. As he pulled into the Air Harbor, a single white float-plane bobbed beside the dock, its prop already turning. The image of MLK, the county seal, was emblazoned on the door, above the words, Official Use Only. Gaitano waved impatiently from his seat next to the pilot.

"I'm not late, am I?" Les asked as he seated himself behind the pilot.

"McKee, I'm so pissed at you I could spit fire." He looked it too.

"Why? What's happened?"

"You can act like you don't know, but I'll get to the bottom of this. If you've been involved in a cover-up or made so much as a fucking phone call, so help me I'll throw your ass in the slammer and get you disbarred myself."

"Whoa, Rick, go back three spaces and tell me what's happened."

Gaitano eyed him suspiciously.

"There was a break-in at your cabin. Your phone, if it was ever there, well it isn't now. Somebody got in by smashing a window. We need you to tell us what's missing, but right now it looks like a few electronics and some booze."

"This is unbelievable. Is there a chance it was random?"

"Maybe. More likely it was staged to look random. Four other cabins near yours were hit as well. The entire crime spree looks like it lasted forty minutes." Gaitano was clearly ready to explode.

"This makes no sense. Do you think it's related to my phone?"

"I can't believe I was so stupid!"

Les stared at him agape. Gaitano, normally cool and unruffled, was losing it. "I'm not following," he said, trying not to sound nervous.

Gaitano struggled to raise his voice above the engine. "I spoke to the San Juan County Sheriff yesterday. He sent a deputy to check on your cabin. He said he couldn't see any phone just by looking through the windows. I asked them to get a warrant yesterday, but there are only two judges in San Juan County and on Mondays they both sit in Island County."

Les looked at him, then glanced away without speaking. He wondered what made Gaitano think they had probable cause to search his cabin.

"He convinced me to wait until this morning when I could enter with your permission. They promised me they'd watch it until I got there. I knew I should've sent my men! Last night a fire broke out on the island about 4:00 a.m. A barn was destroyed and the rancher's house was threatened. It took every volunteer fireman and piece of equipment they had, not to mention the deputy who was keeping an eye on your cabin. He was gone for ninety minutes . . . when the break-ins occurred."

Les kept quiet. He was thinking of Sonny, who was supposed to find the phone, not take it. Perhaps he'd been followed. Or maybe the killers had learned about his phone through a leak on Gaitano's end. Either way, it was gone, as Gaitano had predicted. He deeply regretted involving Sonny.

"At least we know you filmed something the killers don't want us to see. And the fire? That sounds like Sonny. Wouldn't you agree?"

"Don't be ridiculous," Les replied.

"Didn't I tell you to stay away from him? Now they tell me he was sitting in your lobby, while I was with you in the parking lot, giving you a lecture."

"I told you, Rick. He's been working on the crash since I left for Japan. You don't have a thing on him."

"Did you warn him we'd be following him?"

"No, why would you even ask me that?"

"Because as soon as he left your office he gave us the slip, and he hasn't been home all night. Doesn't that seem odd?"

"Only if you're into wild speculation," said Les, masking his panic. "Where is this going?"

"I think you sent him there to beat us to your phone, which was hidden somewhere in the cabin by your client, not left there by your wife. I think your wife's the only innocent party in this little cast. He managed to ditch us but he found a uniform on watch. He couldn't get in, so he started a fire across the island, then broke into several cabins just to make yours look random. This reads Sonny Lile in neon lights."

Les stared at Gaitano. His mind had switched to turbo drive, and the noisy, bumpy plane ride wasn't helping. "Detective, if I'm under suspicion then read me my rights and stop talking to me about this case until I get a lawyer. You're on a wild goose chase and you know it. Why are we even going if my phone's not there? Why would I tell you about my pictures if I was trying to keep them from you?"

"That's just it, counselor. We learned about the pictures from your neighbor, the one you aimed a gun at before inviting her to have some wine." He raised his eyebrow, as if privy to some sexual exploit of Les's.

"You couldn't deny it because we knew. She said you bragged about them at first, then tried to deny you'd taken any. And about your phone being on the island. Your wife let us in on that. I bet you swapped them yourself and told your client to give me Marcia's phone instead of yours."

Asshole, Les thought. His neighbor, the lush, had no doubt exaggerated their encounter, but Gaitano was embellishing the story. Les was used to this kind of fact manipulation. He faced it weekly on the family law motions calendar, or the *perjury calendar* as he preferred to call it. Here was Gaitano, not much different than the sleaziest opposing counsel—twisting facts beyond recognition and nimbly overstepping the truth to reach a foregone destination. He decided to keep quiet. In the end, the truth devoured men like this.

"Anyway," the cop continued, "we need you to go through your cabin and tell us what's missing. I brought a real camera for your insurance claim, since your camera phone won't be doing us any good. Which reminds me, you've been a little lax about your follow-up with insurance."

"What does that mean?"

"Didn't you call 911 on the night of the crash to report that your van was broken into?"

"Oh, that. Marcia had it fixed."

"You were supposed to file a police report and an insurance claim. Did you just forget?"

"I've been busy."

"And why did you clam up so fast when I asked you about a prowler being in your house that night? You told your neighbor but not your wife? I think you owe me some explanations, McKee. And while we're at it, I trust you've got a permit for that gun?"

"I do," he said. With another crippling flash, he remembered about his gun. Marcia hadn't found it or she would have used it on him by now. Maybe he should just turn himself in.

"Somebody was in my house," he offered. "Maybe a reporter. Ginny had no problem walking in while I was gone. Did she tell you that?"

"She told me lots, Les, like how fast you took off after the explosion."

"Bullshit," he shot back. "We were late for the recital."

Gaitano cut him off with a dismissive wave. "How about Fosse, the *Dateline* reporter? He said he heard you instruct your assistant to cancel our appointment. He was there when your wife brought you the phone—he said you were with her long enough to view its contents before leaving for your flight. Did you take it to Japan?"

"That guy doesn't know squat," Les protested.

"He says you threw him out, like you threw your neighbor out when she asked to see your pictures."

"He's a vulture."

"No shit. But did he break into your van on the night of the murders, before the story even broke? And do reporters rip off TVs and stereos, or break into cars and cabins in search of a story? Les, we've got a killer on our hands. Somebody who would ice four innocent people just to divert the attention from Wells and Nakamura." He paused long enough to make him sweat. "You're hiding something. Did you delete the pictures?"

"Absolutely not."

"How about Sonny? Was he there last night?"

"I have no idea." The half lie slipped without a thought, as the sand beneath his feet gave way.

"Did you send him there ahead of us? There's no point in lying, Les. As soon as the sheriff's deputy discovered the break-ins, he did a little videotaping of his own. He went straight to the ferry terminal and recorded every car that boarded for the 6:30 a.m. sailing. He had a roadblock up by the 8:05 and we've now got roadblocks in Anacortes and Sydney, B.C. We're checking every car and walk-on coming to or leaving San Juan Island. We're going to find whoever did this. I've got my men searching for an abandoned car or the stolen goods. The culprits may still be on the island. I'll call in the National Guard if I have to and start searching house by house."

Les said nothing as he stared out the window. If Sonny was there, he was headed for a trap. Maybe he'd been and left. Maybe the phone was still in Les's cabin. It was possible Sonny hadn't even gone. He tried to keep his focus on the scenery. Friday Harbor, the county seat, lay north in Puget Sound, just south of the international border. It was his favorite getaway. Whidbey Island passed beneath them as the San Juan chain came into view. San Juan was the largest of the four main islands, serviced by the ferries. Each was visible in the distance.

It was a breathtaking view he would never tire of, even under circumstances like these. The pristine coastlines, dotted with rustic cabins, made it easier to sit in tense silence.

Two San Juan County patrol cars were waiting for them when they landed. The suspense was grinding away at Les. Ten minutes later they were standing inside his cabin, photographing the broken glass on the floor—with no sign of his phone. A small flat-screen had been pulled from the wall and his liquor cabinet was empty. The thieves hadn't even bothered taking an older computer he had surplused from his office.

The uniforms had combed his place with no sign of prints. Maybe they'd found his phone and weren't telling him. He wouldn't know until he talked to Sonny. They were there just long enough to inventory and clean up the mess, seal the door, and meet with the San Juan uniform while he wrote out his report. Gaitano was busy meeting with his team. Another local deputy handed him a flash drive with pictures of every vehicle that had boarded for the early sailing. There were no leads and the road blocks had turned up nothing. Gaitano instructed his subordinates to step up their search.

By 9:30 a.m. they were back in the air. The drone of the De Haviland's turboprop was the only challenge to the silence in the cabin. Finally Gaitano spoke. "This may turn out to be the biggest manhunt in years."

Les remained silent. He was thinking that Gaitano's arrogance betrayed his youth.

"Detective?" The pilot handed Gaitano a headset. "It's for you."

"Gaitano," the detective barked. He paused. Whatever he was hearing made his face darken. "Crap. Are you certain it was him? . . . was he driving his Acura? How did he get off the boat in Anacortes?"

Les was flooded with relief.

"Well, run the plates on every one. I suppose he could've parked it on another island. No, keep 'em up. And keep up with the searches. I'm sure he's our man, but he may have had some help. The stolen goods are bound to turn up somewhere. Yes, of course—bring him in. I want to know where in the hell he was last night." Gaitano returned the headset to the pilot.

"Sounds like Sonny came home," said Les.

Gaitano looked annoyed. "Yeah, but not until three hours after the first sailing." He was holding up his flash drive. "That's about how long it would take him to get back. If his Acura shows up on this jump drive, Les, then we're going to nail him. He was there and you know it. You know he's been working for her since her first divorce, right?"

Les's temporary relief was fast slipping away.

CHAPTER SEVENTEEN

The seaplane landed with barely a splash on the northern tip of Lake Washington. Gaitano was sullen as they parted company, but Les hardly noticed. He was thinking about the break-ins. Whoever wanted his pictures might also mean him harm, thanks to his antics in Japan. They might be cowards but they were also thugs.

He needed to secure his remaining evidence. After returning several calls, he collected Byron's most damning files and headed for his bank. He rented a large safe-deposit box for the discs and the most sensitive of his papers. The rest of his many boxes could be stowed in the back of his attic.

He returned to his office at 2:30 p.m. While he was checking email, a "new client" notice appeared, generated from his website. It meant one of two things: either someone was inquiring about a new client consult, or Sonny was signaling him to pick up a message. Sonny preferred this to email, which he claimed was not secure. They communicated through an offshore message board using a secure server service that was nearly impossible to trace. He didn't bother checking to see if the client inquiry was legitimate, but went directly to the site. His heart began to race as he waited for Sonny's message to open:

> Les—I just spent two unpleasant hours with Gaitano. No worries—I wasn't there. Still, I need to tell you where I was and what has surfaced. It's urgent. They can't know we met. Take the 6:15 to Bainbridge. Walk on and proceed to town on foot. Make sure you're not followed. I'll be waiting for you at the Harbour Pub. —Sonny

—› | ‹—

The ferry docked at Eagle Harbor at 7:02 p.m. Les stood with the other foot passengers as they lowered the walkway ramp. He let them pass while watching for the slightest turn of a head. As the last man off the boat, he exited the covered walkway and approached the terminal. He saw Sonny waiting near a taxi stand. He was confused. Was this a change of plans or was Sonny simply confirming for himself that Les had not been followed?

He walked past him without making eye contact and stuck to their plan. The Harbour Pub, Sonny's favorite watering hole outside of Seattle, was a fifteen-minute walk along idyllic Eagle Harbor. As usual it was filled with happy patrons. Les was seated at the bar for several minutes before Sonny finally tapped him on the shoulder. He'd shaved and his hair was clean. He motioned Les to join him at a booth.

"This is risky," said Les. "Gaitano thinks I sent you there to steal it, not put it back. If they knew we were meeting . . ."

"Relax," said Sonny. "He knows it wasn't me. In fact they're not even following me anymore. I have no idea what went down last night, but I'm starting to think that you're in danger. You've stumbled into some serious shit, but that's not why we're here."

He'd never seen him look so somber. "Did you get inside her house?"

"Not until this morning, after she left to take her kid to school. Gaitano had a couple dicks watching her all night. I waited but I couldn't make my move until they all left. Les, I didn't find anything inside."

"Then what is it?"

"It's about some old shit that both of us stumbled into a few years back." He moved a folded paper across the table, keeping his hand on top. "She wasn't home when I got there, but those dicks were. They weren't following her, Les. They were waiting for somebody to break in, probably you or me. They must really think she has your phone, so that's why I decided to stick around.

"About an hour later her mail carrier showed up. His truck was blocking their sightline so I strolled up the driveway next to hers, like I was picking up my mail—only I grabbed hers instead, just to have a look." Sonny removed his hand while Les took the paper. As he picked it up, he froze wild-eyed.

"What's the matter?" Sonny asked, alarmed.

"I could swear I heard a camera," he said, trying not to look around. "Did you hear it?"

Sonny turned his head sharply. "Stay cool, I'll be right back." He was gone before Les could react and returned a minute later.

"Nobody's watching us, Les. You're too damn jumpy."

"Sorry," Les said, as he finished unfolding the letter. "Where's its envelope?"

"In my car. There was no return address, but look who signed off at the bottom."

As Les skipped to the end where Victor Garving had typed his name, his face grew pale and his stomach churned.

April 17

Dear Bevy,

Surprise! Guess who's coming to Seattle? A detective you know would like to interview me. He says it's about you, McKee, and Sonny. He thinks the three of you are up to your old tricks again. Only this time he says it's six counts of murder.

I might see fit to no-show if you could see fit to pay me back the rest of my $500K (what your lawyer stole). Act fast Bevy, otherwise I'll see you on the 26th. Have Sonny bring the dough. He'll know how to find me.

Victor

Les sat staring at the letter in agonizing silence.

"What in the hell does he mean, 'the rest of his 500K'?" asked Sonny.

He hesitated. "I never told you, Sonny, but Victor showed up in my office about a year after the divorce. He knew Bev had married Byron and he was trying to extort a hundred grand—or he said he'd confess to the arson and turn her in. He was scamming us I'm sure, but he said the loan sharks were after him and he was broke. He said jail was looking pretty attractive. I guess now he's come to collect the rest of his half million."

"You mean she paid him a hundred grand?" Sonny looked skeptical. "Just like that?"

"She did it without even telling me."

"Great. So of course he thinks he gets the rest, especially if she's a suspect in her husband's death."

Les nodded. "I'd forgotten about him, really. The statute of limitations has run on that."

"So what? He can spill his guts about you to the Bar, or try and get my license pulled. We could both go down for this, not to mention we're smack in the middle of a murder investigation, including her. This is bad, Les. I wish you'd told me he was into blackmail. I could've gone back down there and roughed him up. Now he thinks he owns her every time her name appears in the fucking paper. Considering what she's worth I guess she's lucky he's not asking for more, the bastard."

"What, are you saying she should pay him off? She might not pass go on it this time around. She doesn't have a license to protect like you and me. Her divorce is ancient news."

"She's a suspect, Les. Suppose he convinces Gaitano that she played a part in torching his club for the insurance? They'll figure she could kill for the insurance too. She has to pay him something, at least enough to keep him quiet until they break the case. That sleazeball. Somebody ought to kill him, that's what needs to happen."

"I'll pretend I didn't hear that."

"Are we ever going to shake him, Les? He's like smoke on meat, and I don't appreciate him throwing my name around like that. He has no idea who he's dealing with. I've worked hard to rebuild my reputation."

Not too hard, Les thought. "So what do you propose?"

"Can you raise four-hundred grand by Friday? 'Cause that's when he says he's flying out here."

"No way."

"I didn't think so."

"She can't either. Byron's estate will be tied up for months, maybe years."

"When are you going to tell her?"

"I'm not sure. She's leaving with Marcia in the morning for the coast. It's spring break and they're taking the girls. She doesn't know they're following her and listening to her calls. Maybe I should go over there tonight on business."

"You're the lawyer, Les. Come up with something."

His torment wrenched another notch. The fact that Sonny suggested paying Victor off, or worse yet *killing* him, was the ultimate confession that he'd committed the decade-old arson.

"With her help I could raise maybe a hundred grand at most," he sighed, hating every syllable. "It was enough to shut him up the last time. Tell him he needs to disappear for thirty days if he expects to see his next installment. By then we can free up some of Byron's dough. Tell him he can expect a hundred grand every thirty days for the next three months, assuming he vanishes. That should buy us enough time for the cops to find their killers. Then they'll lose interest in him."

"We don't have much choice, Les. Not now. You're doing this for her. A hundred grand is play money to Bev."

"Sonny, have you done work for her since New Orleans? Gaitano was asking."

"Les, I don't even like the lady. That would be your department. I work for you, not your clients. What was he getting at?"

"I don't know. I thought maybe she'd asked you to check up on Byron. You know, to see if he was cheating on her."

"Gaitano's done a damn good job of making you doubt everybody, Les. I think I count for more than that. So how soon do I leave for New Orleans?"

"Sorry. As soon as I raise the dough. Tomorrow afternoon. I don't want Victor talking to Gaitano again if we can stop it."

"Can you make it a hundred and *ten* grand, Les? I've got to get paid. And I'll need your credit card number for my flight."

"You drive a hard bargain, Sonny."

Sonny looked away just for a second as Les remembered about his cancer.

"Hey, but you're worth the big bucks." He hesitated a moment before continuing. "Is it true what Gaitano told me, about your cancer coming back?"

"How does he know that?" he demanded. "Is nothing sacred?" He sighed deeply and looked away. "It's true. But my doc isn't ready to say how long I've got. Hell, maybe another year."

"I'm sorry," Les said quietly. "Have you told your wife?"

He shook his head. "I promised myself I wouldn't burden her with that if it came back. I've got no life insurance. Can't qualify. That's why I need this job and why I'm willing to take some risks if the price is right. I need to leave her something.

"As far as finding Victor, I heard he left New Orleans after Katrina. But I'll call you on Friday and let you know whether I've located him or if I know where he is. He might try calling you if I haven't found him. If so, get his address and phone."

"Who do you think broke in last night?"

"Did you get a look at the other cabins?"

"No, why?"

"I've probably gone mad, Les, but what if it's not the phone or the pictures they want? Maybe the cops staged it so they could get inside your cabin, then sit back and watch what you and your client do next. If your phone was there they probably have it."

"Somebody broke in. Cops don't do that sort of thing."

"Gaitano said the intruders smashed a window. But you were there to see it, right?"

"Yes," said Les.

"I'm just not picturing a smashed window. I'm guessing it was more like a single pane from your back door, cut diagonally so that only half a pane's worth of glass was on the floor."

"How did you know that?"

"Every cop I know can get inside like that, then blame it on the local hood. If you were going to mistrust anyone, Les, my money would be on Gaitano."

"Do cops steal booze and TVs in the name of their investigation?" As he spoke, he caught himself staring at the scar on Sonny's hand. He wondered when he'd burned it—before or after he'd retired. Sonny followed his gaze and casually dropped his hand below the table.

"If it wasn't the cops, then we're left with only one conclusion. Gaitano's right and there's a killer on the loose. They knew as soon as you did that your phone was at the cabin. Tell me again what happened in Japan. Your family may be in danger. I hate to say it but you're the one who asked."

Sonny's words sank in like a dagger. *Marcia and Breanna were in danger.* He pushed his anxieties aside and focused on bringing Sonny up to date on everything, including the evidence he was keeping at the bank. "So what would you do?" he finally asked.

"Bring everything to Gaitano."

"I'm a suspect. What if he won't believe me, or if the killers try to silence me for talking? At the very least I'm headed for witness protection. Wells and Nakamura were playing with fire, but I can't prove that Sugiyama and Yamamoto had them killed. They probably have my phone, so maybe I should just keep quiet."

"He'll believe you, Les. You've got those files and emails. Give me a couple days to settle things with Victor. I'll call you when it's done."

"Do you need this?" He handed over Sonny's phone.

"Keep it. That's how I'll call you. I've got another one, remember? I keep them under phony names. Victor is the only landmine we need to worry about. Once I've hushed him, take everything you've got to Gaitano on Monday morning. But Les, if something should happen to you while I'm gone—not that it will—who else knows about those files?"

"No one but you, Sonny."

CHAPTER EIGHTEEN

Back on the ferry he was fighting an anxiety attack, and losing. He needed to speak with Bev. He had to tell her about Victor's reappearance and that Byron's lawsuit for Wrongful Termination was a sham. He was a corporate spy and Beverly was a suspect in his murder. She was under surveillance by the police and maybe by her husband's killers.

At least she could take comfort in the fact that he was beside her on the sinking ship. The killers had bugged his home and office. They were assuming he knew more than he did. He was behind on filing Byron's probate and he still needed to prepare a complaint for Wrongful Death, even if the balloonists were innocent. He was in debt and his client wasn't paying, though somehow he needed to raise $110,000 for her over the next sixteen hours. He would be forced to raid his client trust account. Of course he would quickly replace the funds, but he was fast becoming an outlaw himself. And why? He wasn't sure he knew.

He almost wished the ferry would turn around, or sink, but as luck would have it, they docked. Fearful of wire taps he drove straight to her house. She was gone, of course, so he left her a note beneath the handle of her brass door knocker:

> Beverly: Something's come up re Byron's estate. We need to talk before you leave with Marcia. I'll be in my office by 7:00 a.m. Please stop by. It's urgent. —Les

It was after ten by the time he got home. Breanna was in bed and Marcia was buried in laundry. He hated himself for neglecting his family and it pained him to see how his preoccupations were affecting his wife.

"Where have you been and why didn't you call?"

"I think they've tapped our phones."

"I doubt that, Les, but so what? You have nothing to hide. Did they find your phone? You should've called me. Who cares if they listen in? They were there. I've been worried sick."

He proceeded to explain the saga of their cabin, leaving out as many disturbing details as he could, but his whitewash didn't hold.

"Les, I'm scared. You've got to withdraw from all her cases. Whoever killed Byron knew as soon as we did that your phone was at the cabin. Can't you see that you're putting us in danger?"

If she knew the half.

"What took you so long?"

"I was meeting with Sonny about the crash. He seems to think we've still got a case for Wrongful Death."

"Couldn't that have waited? Besides, if they were murdered, Les, then how could you even consider suing the balloonists? They were victims too."

"Yes, but she's a suspect. She needs to join the other families, at least until the coroner rules it a homicide."

"That's ridiculous. But I can see where this is headed. You're involved in her defense, aren't you? I forbid it. She needs a defense attorney. Have you spoken with her tonight?"

"No, not at all."

"You didn't go over to her house?"

"No, why?"

Her chilly look clued him in. "Because she called about a note you left. She's on her way here now. Les, tell me what's going on. Why did you lie to me just now about not going to her house?"

"Because I knew it would upset you. I'm sorry, honey. You're right. I should've told you. I need her to sign a power of attorney in connection with Byron's probate, that's all. My note asked her to come by my office in the morning."

"Why not call her instead of going there?"

"Because her phones are tapped like ours. There's nothing going on, Marsh, so don't start in. It only upsets you."

"Of course it upsets me. I think you want to be with her, like before. You were lying then and you're lying now." Her eyes filled with tears. Hurt and confusion wracked her delicate body as he reached out and held her tightly.

"I'm sorry," he murmured. "I'll find her another lawyer, I promise." But his words rang hollow, even to him.

Marcia was still in his arms when the doorbell rang. She dried her eyes as she greeted Beverly and Tiff.

"Hi," she said as pleasantly as she could. "Les, Beverly and Tiff will be spending the night so we can get an early start. Can you help carry in their things?"

Before he could respond they were off to the kitchen. "He just needs you to sign some form," he overheard her say.

The idea for a power of attorney had occurred to him on the ferry. Perhaps he could sell some of Byron's stock in Beverly's absence. That way he could pay Victor off without alarming her just yet. Once things died down he'd tell her everything.

As he helped them pack the van, he caught snippets of Beverly's reaction to the news about their cabin. "My God, why would someone steal it? It's been so hard to realize he died like that, but to think he was murdered." She started to cry.

Marcia said nothing, but as he peered in he saw her holding Beverly. Their relationship had thawed. Feeling like an outsider, he decided to slip off to bed, but he was only faking sleep when Marcia finally joined him. He continued to lie there motionless, until her breathing was deep and regular.

Then quietly, one centimeter at a time, he crept from his bed. He prayed he'd meet her in the hallway like before. But no such luck. Carefully he shut the door so Marcia wouldn't hear him open hers.

There she was—sound asleep. He would have to wake her. In the moonlight that fell across her gentle form, he saw that her covers were pulled back to her waist. She was wearing her crème-colored nightgown which was undone just enough to reveal the generous curves of her perfect body. Her heart-shaped lips were still. Part of him wanted to crawl in bed with her.

As he reached out gently to touch her arm, he heard his bedroom door. Marcia was up. He was terrified, feeling like a prisoner of war about to be exposed by the tower light. He knelt to the floor and lay prostrate beside her bed, praying he wouldn't be discovered. If there was a God, Les hoped he would take pity on his predicament.

The hall light came on. He heard Marcia open Beverly's door. Light rushed in. She cracked it just enough to satisfy herself he was not inside. Then she gently closed it and headed down the stairs.

His conscience tormenting him, he drew in a breath and opened Beverly's door as quietly as he could. Marcia was downstairs so he headed for the master bathroom. As she came back up, he flushed the water works, knowing full well he was wasting water.

"Where were you?" she asked as they met near the bed.

"I thought I heard Breanna cry, but she seems to be okay. What's the matter? Can't you sleep?"

"I woke up and you were gone."

"Why did you shut our door?" she asked, sounding suspicious.

"I thought she was crying and I didn't want her to wake you. Come on." He guided her back to bed. He tried to cuddle her, but not with her head against his pounding chest.

Thank you, he prayed silently to a God he didn't deserve. He hoped she hadn't noticed that Beverly's door was still ajar as she headed back up the stairs. He wanted to pray some more but he already knew the answer: "Les, you need to get out of the lying business!" Just a few more days, he thought. Then never again. But those words troubled him as he'd made that pledge before.

CHAPTER NINETEEN

He woke with an adrenaline hangover. He'd slept but he hadn't rested. Depression anchored him to the bed while fear urged him to rise. He didn't want to wait around for the morning's doubleheader: Beverly's bare shoulder and Marcia's cold one. Perhaps if he slipped out early he could still find her and have a private word.

"Where are you going?" Marcia asked as he slid out of bed.

"I need to go in early."

She was wide awake. "You mean you're not even going to see us off?"

"I'll kiss her good-bye," he said, referring to Breanna.

"Who, Beverly?"

Her words stung him to the core. He dressed quickly. As he headed downstairs, he noticed Beverly's door was closed. Pulling out of his driveway he saw two detectives parked up the street. They'd probably been sitting there all night, though they didn't follow him as he drove away.

Back in his office, he surveyed the damage caused by his recent absenteeism. His practice survived on volume, yet he'd hardly returned a call in the ten days since Byron's death. His office was at a standstill, his paralegals in disrepair, yet all the same he left again at ten o' clock for an appointment with his banker.

"I'll be back by noon," he said to Janie. "I've got a client meeting." He raised his briefcase while walking by her, as if to prove he wasn't lying.

The McKees had only ten thousand dollars remaining on their line of credit, but he couldn't risk touching it as Marcia watched it closely. Nor could he borrow against their new house without her signature. So he took out a loan against his practice for $50,000, the maximum his banker would allow on just his signature. He withdrew the remaining $60,000 from his client trust account. He was holding over $700,000 for various clients, mostly house sale proceeds in cases where the parties had not yet agreed on how to divide their liquid assets.

He returned to his office two hours later, briefcase in hand, as if everything was fine. But inside was a cache of a hundred thousand dollars—all in hundred dollar bills. Sonny was waiting for him in the lobby. As they stepped inside his sanctuary, he handed him a separate envelope with ten thousand cash, bills he actually counted before he left. Sonny hadn't shaved and the unlit cigarette was back dangling from his lips.

"I sure hope this makes him go away," sighed Les.

"It'll work," said Sonny with confidence. "I'll be back on Saturday."

He felt nauseous as he handed the briefcase to Sonny. So it had come to this—placing his trust in a man he'd never really trusted. As Sonny strode across the lobby, Les turned to the next order of business, replacing sixty thousand dollars in client funds he'd temporarily "borrowed." If it was discovered, even after he put it back, he would be disbarred. The money wasn't his to misuse.

He didn't have a clue where to begin in the process of selling Byron's stock. What he knew about their assets was limited to the scant financial discovery documents from the divorce. Byron had no broker. He'd received his stock certificates directly from Digitron and had never sold any shares except to pay attorney fees to Milton James. At least that's what he'd claimed in his deposition.

At 1:00 p.m. he asked his own broker, Jeremy Blaine, to initiate a sale of Byron's stock based on the power of attorney he'd obtained from Beverly the night before.

At 2:00 p.m. Jeremy called him back. "Les, I've come across something rather strange. It turns out Byron owns only 52,000 shares of Digitron. At just under $115 a share that's not even six million dollars. They're telling me he sold the rest."

"What?" Les exclaimed. "You've got to be joking. He had over 435,000 shares, Jeremy! This isn't possible." His mouth was dry.

"Turns out he's been selling his stock off at the rate of about 9,000 shares a week since he got fired."

"That's impossible. There's a restraining order that prevented him from selling any assets during their divorce."

"Well, I'm telling you it happened. He's been using a broker over at Smith Levinson and keeping his transactions to under a million dollars a week. Any more and somebody would've heard about it, due to S.E.C. requirements. He knew exactly what he was doing."

"I still don't buy it, Jeremy."

"I'm not saying the money's gone, Les. The cash was wired from Fidelity to Smith Levinson, and from there it was probably reinvested. It sounds to me like he was simply ducking out of Digitron. He must not have been too confident about getting his job back. Either that or he had some reason to think their stock is going to plummet."

"Who's his broker? Have you spoken to him?" He was trying to sound collected.

"I have a friend at Smith Levinson who could get in trouble for telling me this, but the broker's name is Dwight Bonadelli. He's a hot shot. I've heard of him, though I didn't know he was at Smith Levinson.

"I guess he hasn't been there long. Changed firms a year ago, bringing some new client with him that he'd picked up over the summer. Word around the water cooler was *fifty million* to invest. They made him a VP. I guess it wasn't too hard to figure out who his mystery client was."

"But Jeremy," said Les, "Digitron must've known that Byron was selling stock. Why didn't they cry foul?"

"You're the lawyer, Les. You tell me."

Byron was one of their largest shareholders, so of course they'd want him out. But they were keeping his evacuation a secret until trial, when they'd reveal it as further proof of his plan to cheat on his employer. They knew Beverly would've stopped it had she known.

Les finally broke the silence. "Didn't Fidelity realize we had an order against this kind of thing?"

"Again, you're the lawyer, but we both know a restraining order is enforceable only as against the parties to the divorce. Neither Fidelity nor Digitron was restrained from letting Byron sell his stock—if he chose to violate the order."

The comment hurt. Les could have named Digitron and/or their designated brokerage house as parties to the divorce. Such a move would have conferred jurisdiction on the court to restrain both employee and employer from the unauthorized sale of stock. At the very least he could have put them on notice. Unlike Byron, Digitron and Fidelity would've honored such an order.

Arguably he'd committed malpractice. With a stab he recalled Farrago's speech at the Kyoto depositions: "You just cost your client fifty million. I'm sure your malpractice limits aren't worth a fraction of that, you moron."

At least there was an order. Perhaps it was enough to meet the legal standard. But was it entered? Milton had promised to sign and enter it, though he couldn't remember whether he'd received a confirming letter. He wanted to hang up and rush to his file.

"Les, are you still there?"

"Yeah, I'm here. I can't believe this, Jeremy. Can we at least sell some of what's left?"

"No. I'm afraid I've got more bad news. Before he died, Byron left explicit instructions with Fidelity that no one but Bonadelli could liquidate his stock."

"Byron is dead. Assuming his broker had a power of attorney isn't valid any more. Don't they know that?"

"They know that, Les, but until an order issues out of probate, Fidelity isn't going to let you touch his stock. There's no way. He comes from money and they're not about to risk getting sued for prematurely liquidating his estate, especially if his wife is a suspect in his death. What's that about?"

"It's bunk. Now listen, I disagree with whoever you spoke to at Fidelity. Half that stock is hers. We're a community property state, remember? She can sell her half any time she pleases."

"Les, they tell me it was his separate property, due to the prenup she signed. They say they can't sort it out and that it has to pass through probate. It's going to take an army of you guys to pick through this. I'm just telling you, there's no way we can sell his stock right now, power of attorney or not. It might take a year to unwind this mess."

"Can I have his broker's name and number?"

"Yes, but you can't say it came from me. It's Dwight Bonadelli. My buddy says he's on vacation for twelve more days."

"Of course he is. Give me the number. I'll get somebody else to look into this for me." Trying to suppress his anger, he dialed Smith Levinson, where it seemed that nobody at the firm was covering for Bonadelli. After several transfers, he finally managed to make an appointment with Bonadelli's immediate superior, another Vice President named William Grady, for 9:00 a.m. the following day.

After hanging up, he pulled Beverly's divorce file to confirm whether or not the restraining order had been entered. A copy of it was in his file, but the signature lines for Milton James and the judge were blank. James had promised to sign and enter it, a common practice between attorneys, though standard protocol would also dictate that James email him back, to confirm the date of entry and the name of the signing judge. He could find no such email or letter in the file. How could he have forgotten to follow up?

It was still possible the order had been entered. It wouldn't bring back the money—if the money was even missing—but it might mean the difference between *guilty* or *not guilty* in the largest malpractice claim ever filed in King County.

He phoned the office of Milton James. He'd been meaning to ask them for Byron's divorce file anyway, though he encountered stiff resistance this time around. He chose not to argue but simply told them he was on his way, demanding that they print everything they had on Byron's case, including any codicils or wills.

As he raced across the floating bridge, his mind was overheating. If not for the concrete barrier between his shiny black Saab and Lake Washington, he might've considered drowning all his troubles. It had just begun to rain and driving on the floating bridge in a heavy Seattle downpour could make a person feel submerged already.

The forecasters had announced the late arrival of Seattle's April showers. They normally appeared in early March and ran through February of the following year. He thought about the propane at the crash site and how it was washing off the branches.

The early rush-hour traffic was a nightmare. It was 3:50 p.m. by the time he arrived at James's office. He sat down in the lobby to examine Milton's files. He opened the folder containing hard copies sent by mail or messenger and immediately saw his order sitting loose inside, signed by him alone. His heart sank.

Milton's failure to enter it had been intentional, he was sure, but Les hadn't followed through to confirm its status. In a lesser case such an error might have been overlooked, but not where the adverse party had exclusive access to fifty million dollars.

His fate was now in the hands an unknown broker named Dwight

Bonadelli. He hoped Bonadelli had wisely reinvested the missing money. The good news was finding no sign of a second will in James's files. The bad news would be finding nothing for his client to inherit.

Les returned to a darkened house, but the emptiness inside was a relief. He couldn't have faced his family and he wondered if he could ever face Beverly again. She was his client and he'd failed her. He couldn't fathom how he'd screwed up. He'd never been served with so much as a bar grievance, let alone a summons and complaint for malpractice. It would devastate his career. His insurance limits were a million—*the same as the balloonists'.* He shook his head at the irony.

Milton's divorce file filled five more boxes. He decided to spend the night poring over every page. He was searching for a memo, a note, any shred of evidence to confirm that James's failure to enter the restraining order had been deliberate. He noticed Byron had been living off a line of credit too, just like Beverly (not to mention Les and Marcia). It seemed no one in this cast had a regular paycheck. Byron had paid $76,000 in attorney fees for the divorce so far, and owed James another $25,000. He was cash poor and seemed to have little financial sense. Apart from his 401K and about $300,000 in IRAs, he had not diversified. He and Beverly owned their house and their vehicles, but the rest of their vast estate was all tied up in Digitron.

The more he read the angrier he became. Sitting in front of him were the financial documents connected to the divorce that he'd repeatedly requested and which James had failed to produce. Byron claimed he'd left his records in the house when he moved out, though Beverly could never find them. He now knew why.

A paralegal in James's office had been paying Byron's bills and balancing his check register for him. She kept a folder of receipts and invoices, including a VISA statement that had arrived that day. He'd been warned the bills were piling up but assured them he was on top of probating the estate. If only it were true.

His curiosity was piqued as he began reviewing Byron's charges—over $75,000 in March alone. Running down the list he quickly spotted the solitary culprit and whistled low: $59,895 to Tiffany & Company on March 22. He turned and thumbed through the stack of receipts until he found the one from Tiffany's. It was a diamond ring: round, two-carat brilliant, ideal cut; VVS in clarity, D in color; half-bezel set in platinum. *What have I unearthed?* he thought.

The rest of Byron's credit card statement read like a diary of his final days, right up until he died. His last charge was to FOLLOW THE SUN for $1,500.00 on Sunday the thirteenth. Working backwards, he saw that Byron had paid $254.20 for brunch at a Kirkland hotel on the morning of the crash (probably no tip). He'd paid the same hotel $288.91 for a room the night before. Someone else must have picked up their tab on Saturday, as the next charge back was to Yoshi's Teriyaki on Friday the eleventh. But it was the charge before Yoshi's that captured his attention: Exotic Rentals in Bellevue for $524.77.

Perhaps Byron wanted to impress Nakamura by driving him around Seattle in a Lamborghini or a Hummer. But who returned it? He would check it out tomorrow.

CHAPTER TWENTY

Les was fifteen minutes early as he stepped onto the opulent 38th floor of Smith Levinson's Seattle office. The receptionist eyed him warily as if she'd been warned about his coming. She spoke in hushed tones through the phone and in short order William Grady appeared. Razor-thin, polished to a dark gleam and on full alert, Grady led Les across the lobby to the firm's all-window grand conference room, overlooking Elliott Bay, Century Link Stadium and Safeco Field. In the distance the Olympic Mountains shimmered with a fresh coat of spring snow through a temporary respite from the clouds. Seeing Bainbridge Island and a ferry in the distance he thought of Sonny, who by now was in New Orleans. But Sonny couldn't help him when it came to the blundered order.

Two men rose to greet him as they entered—Gordon Thomas, chairman of the board and Drew Parris, in-house counsel. Grady invited the awkward threesome to sit down.

"Why don't you start, Mr. McKee, by telling us why you're here." It was Thomas, whose hair was grayer than the others.

"As you know, Beverly Wells is my client," Les began. "This firm represented her deceased husband and therefore her. She wants me to find out how you could have allowed a broker name Bonadelli to sell off nearly forty-four million dollars' worth of her husband's Digitron stock despite a restraining order that strictly forbade it.

Thomas sat up in his chair and belted out his response. "Our attorneys tell us there was no such order, Mr. McKee. Mr. Wells was perfectly free, therefore, to hire our firm to buy and sell securities for him at his good pleasure. You'd better think twice before suggesting we've done something wrong. Perhaps you wish there had been such an order, because I'm told your failure to procure it was severe malpractice on your part. But don't try and heap your problems onto us."

"If you think I'm here to cover my ass, gentlemen, then you're mistaken," Les said flatly. "That restraining order was drafted by me and delivered to the attorney for Byron Wells. It certainly wasn't my fault that I was misled into believing it was entered.

"What I'm really here to learn is what your firm did with all that money, once you sold the stock. It belongs to my client now and as soon as you tell me where it is, she'd like to reinvest it with someone else."

"Mr. McKee," Thomas asked, "how did you learn of Dwight Bonadelli? His relationship with Mr. Wells was confidential. We have concerns about security."

"I couldn't tell you that."

"Then I'm afraid we can't tell you much, either," Thomas replied. "Mr. Bonadelli left on April 12 for a three-week vacation. You can talk with him yourself when he returns." He stood to leave.

"Oh, I won't have to wait that long," retorted Les. "I'm sure you'll get his smart ass back here the minute I file in federal court for your firm's embezzlement of forty-four million dollars. You'll be reading about it on tomorrow's front page."

The lawyer, Parris, took over. "Mr. McKee, there's no need for brash threats. Your vulnerability in this matter is much greater than ours. You know that. I don't think for a minute that you're about to go public with your blunder. Right now we need each other to piece together exactly what has happened."

Les ignored him. "Will somebody tell me what has happened and why you're all so goddamn pale? Where is Bonadelli? He didn't disappear with the money, did he?"

"Not at all," Thomas spoke up hastily. "He's taking a few weeks off in Mexico. He's due back here on the fifth."

"So what's the problem?" Les asked. "*Show me the money.*"

"Your assumption that it was carefully reinvested by Mr. Bonadelli is accurate—to a point," said Thomas. "It appears that under a General Power of Attorney from Byron Wells, Mr. Bonadelli liquidated $43,878,316.48 in various stocks, bonds and mutual funds over the course of seventy-two hours, starting on April 8. From there the money was wired to an account at the Lexington Bank of the Cayman Islands in the name of Byron Wells. We've checked and we believe the funds were withdrawn by Mr. Wells himself on April 11, two days before he died. We didn't learn about this until last week. The money it would seem, is gone."

"That's bullshit!" Les erupted. "Forty-four million invested with this firm was withdrawn in cash and you think you're ever going to see this joker Bonadelli again?" He sunk down in his chair feeling like he was about to collapse.

Thomas spoke carefully. "I didn't say Mr. Bonadelli withdrew the cash. We believe it was withdrawn on April 11 by Mr. Wells himself."

"And when were you planning to notify my client?"

"We've been trying to contact Mr. Bonadelli," said Thomas. "We've hired several private investigators, who are looking for him now, in Mexico and in the Caribbean."

Les was incredulous.

"I may not be a securities lawyer, gentlemen, but there's no fucking way a stockbroker can liquidate forty-four million dollars in client funds without somebody crying foul."

"This was not Mr. Bonadelli's idea, Mr. McKee." This time it was Grady who spoke.

"Mr. Wells's Digitron stock was sold over a ten-month period at no more than one million dollars' worth per week. It was diversified from there into several highly liquid investment vehicles. Mr. Wells had obviously been positioning his assets to allow for their immediate liquidation in the future. He'd been plotting this course for nearly a year. Mr. Bonadelli was simply carrying out his wishes."

"I see," said Les, still reeling. "And did Mr. Wells arrange to get himself murdered on the thirteenth of April—two days after he pulled out all his money?"

"Murdered?" asked Grady. "The police haven't declared this a homicide, have they?"

"So you think it's a coincidence that Wells withdrew his life's fortune on a Friday, then wound up dead on Sunday? Where's the money if he wasn't murdered? I don't think you guys have tracked it yet, or we wouldn't be here, would we?"

"No, the money hasn't surfaced," said Thomas, with resignation. "We've got a few questions for Mr. Bonadelli. And so does the Securities Exchange

Commission. We've learned he's been under investigation in New York for several months now, due to the mysterious pattern of his Digitron stock sales. The feds were waiting for him to sell off the last six million before they made their move. They alerted us ahead of schedule when they heard about the crash. We didn't even know where he'd wired the money at first. It took us several days to trace it to the Cayman Islands."

"Are you saying the authorities know about this?" asked Les.

"I didn't say that. I said the S.E.C. has approached us about Bonadelli. If he doesn't return on May 5, then we expect to receive a mountain of subpoenas. That's when the news of the missing cash will go public."

"So we have twelve days to find forty-four million dollars," injected Les. "How certain are you that Byron flew to Georgetown and withdrew the cash himself? He was pretty accustomed to having others do his leg work."

"Not very," Parris answered. "We should know more soon. The bank claims to have a signed authorization for the withdrawal bearing Mr. Wells's signature. But the physical description they gave us of the man who came into the bank sounds more like Mr. Bonadelli."

"So where was Bonadelli on the eleventh?" asked Les. "I thought you said his vacation didn't start until the twelfth. And wouldn't the bank have to report such a withdrawal? Do they even have that kind of cash?"

"Mr. Bonadelli left for Mexico a day early," said Grady. "It's possible he flew to Georgetown instead, to retrieve the cash for Mr. Wells. U.S. law mandates reporting cash withdrawals of $10,000 or more, but in the Caymans it's both possible and legal to quietly withdraw this kind of cash in a single day."

"Then of course he withdrew it instead of Byron." Les sat up straight and glanced at each of the others. "And he didn't bring it back unless he's into smuggling. Even in big bills, a coffin couldn't hide that kind of cash. Does somebody have to paint you numbskulls a fucking picture? Do you have any idea where in Mexico he's hiding—excuse me, staying?"

"No," said Grady, "but that doesn't mean—"

"Is he married? What about his family?"

"He's gay and single."

Parris took a stab. "Maybe Byron flew to Georgetown or maybe Dwight went there for him. Either way, we have no evidence to suggest that Dwight did anything illegal. Maybe Byron gave the cash to Nakamura at their secret little meeting."

"And it's just as likely," said Les, "that Dwight was part of a murder plot. Maybe Byron didn't even know his assets were being liquidated. Who is Bonadelli anyway?"

"One of our best," said Grady, who clearly had the most to lose if things went bad. "We ran him through a thorough background check."

"How long has he been here?"

"A year."

"So you don't know shit."

"He was with Merrill Lynch before us and he passed their background check."

"You mentioned the bank can't say which of them withdrew the cash. Do they look alike?"

"Actually they do bear some resemblance," offered Grady, as he handed Les a photo. From a distance Bonadelli appeared to be about the same age, height and hair color as Byron.

"Not a lot to distinguish them by phone," observed Grady. "We emailed this photo to the bank along with a photo of Mr. Wells. That's when the bank said that maybe it was Dwight. To be sure we've sent an investigator to Georgetown with more pictures, and to examine the withdrawal form. I guess it's possible it was forged."

"Can a broker rip off his client that easily?"

"Our brokers aren't supposed to accept general powers of attorney from a client," said Parris. "Only special powers are allowed for the sale and purchase of securities through wired funds. A general power of attorney would be unusual."

"How about illegal? I'm sure young Dwight was supposed to register it. You're in deep shit and I think you know it," Les said and fell silent as he realized their screw-up was worse than his.

"If Bonadelli is clean," he began after a moment, "then where's the cash? I think it's fair to say that Nakamura didn't leave town with any of it, though they did send him to Kyoto in a coffin."

"No, but his bodyguard is missing," Grady offered. "The Japanese authorities seem to think he had something to do with his boss's death. For all we know, *he* got away with all the money."

"So you're conceding it was murder," said Les. "What else have your investigators found? Did Byron have any other accounts, here or abroad?

Have you searched his condo or his car for the cash? How am I supposed to believe you haven't found it and split it up among yourselves?"

"I'm getting tired of this," Thomas said. He rose and motioned to the others.

"Hold it," Parris told Thomas. "Mr. McKee isn't serious." Turning to Les he said, "Actually the investigation we're conducting has been entirely legal. There are no indications the money has made its way into any financial institution worldwide. As for where Mr. Wells might've hidden his cash, we're not about to break into his condo in the name of Smith Levinson. We assume the police have searched it. Maybe they're sitting on the money."

Les thought of Gaitano. Now there was a cop who couldn't be trusted.

"As you were quick to point out," said Grady, "Mrs. Wells is now the beneficiary of her husband's estate. She can give you access to his condo. There isn't a stone we should leave unturned over the next twelve days. Speaking of which, we'd still like to know how you learned the identity of our broker."

"Whoever told me doesn't know about the money. Can you imagine what this city will be like once word leaks out that forty-four million in cold hard cash is on the loose?"

"Can you get inside his condo?" Grady asked.

Les thought back to the key he'd seen in James's file. "So I'm supposed to help you gentlemen get your asses out of the sling?"

"It's not just our asses, counselor." It was Thomas again and this time he closed his file.

CHAPTER TWENTY-ONE

Les emerged from Smith Levinson at 10:05 and headed for Beverly's bank. He'd given up on trying to salvage his trust account through the sale of Byron's stock, so he decided to borrow what he needed from Beverly's line of credit. As he filled out the forms without her knowledge, he thought of Bonadelli.

Her HELOC had thirty-five thousand dollars in available credit, which forced him to access the last ten thousand on his own line of credit and obtain a cash advance on three of his credit cards for the remaining fifteen thousand dollars. By 1:00 p.m. he had the sixty thousand dollars he needed to replenish his trust account. Both Les and Beverly were now mortgaged to the hilt.

He was able to catch up on other matters over the following thirty-two hours. He was alone in his office at 8:52 p.m. on Friday when Sonny's cell phone suddenly rang.

"Les, this is Sonny. I'm in New Orleans."

"Any luck with Victor?"

"Absolutely. This afternoon—and none too soon. They'd booked him on a flight that leaves tomorrow. He wasn't very happy about getting just a quarter of his dough, but he took it like you said and surrendered his ticket in return."

"Has he changed much since you saw him last?"

"Shaved his fucking mutton chops, that's about it. He still wears those bracelets. And he's aged something awful."

"So what's he going to tell Gaitano?"

"Zip. He promised to disappear as long as I show up at noon on the twenty-fifth of May with his next installment. He says the deal's off if I'm as much as an hour late. So far he swears he hasn't given them a thing."

"Do you believe him?"

"What can I say, Les? He's pond scum. But I think we can keep him quiet for a few more months. We gotta hope the cops can find their killers soon. I'd sure like to throw him off a levy. What in the hell did she ever see in him?"

"What did she see in Byron?" echoed Les.

"That's easy. His money. And now she has it."

"Maybe not, Sonny." He related the story of Byron's disappearing fortune.

"Les, there's no way that Byron took that cash. Didn't you say he worshipped his money?"

"Yeah, which is why he'd been scheming for a year to sneak it out from under her nose."

"That's my point. He probably did have his broker unload him into liquid funds. But he would never have pulled the plug with six million dollars left at Digitron. He had six more weeks to go, which means they murdered him down the stretch. You said Nakamura was on the verge of going public. Somebody decided to shut them down and you can bet his broker played a role. You said he started cashing out on April 8?"

"Yes, and he was liquid by the eleventh. Nakamura would have been exposed at his deposition on the seventeenth."

"Well, the broker didn't keep it. Maybe he's missing because they killed him. The money is probably with Sugiyama, helping him to finance his ultimate defection. Didn't your Kyoto lawyer say that Nakamura's money men were tied in with the mob?"

"Sonny, the bank in Georgetown told Smith Levinson that Byron signed for his own withdrawal. And even if Bonadelli went there and got the money for him, suppose he smuggled it back and gave it all to Byron?"

"If you're right, Les, then I should have no problem finding him on vacation."

"The brokerage firm has a team of private dicks in Mexico and the Caymans. They've been on his trail for days without any luck so far."

"That's because they don't know what they're doing," Sonny said modestly. "Look, I'm halfway down there on your nickel as it is. Why don't I take a week and go to Mexico for you?"

"Sonny, I couldn't possibly—"

"Les, it'll cost your client a small fortune. There's no way around it. But what are we talking about? That money's all but gone and your career is next. Hell, if you had cancer like me it wouldn't matter. But this is your life. If I find her dough, you can pay me double and she won't even feel it. I'll keep charging my expenses on your card. She'll pay you back. Hell, the six million he left at Digitron is more than you could've gotten her in the divorce."

"What if Bonadelli is dead?"

"Trust me, I'll sniff him out. Let's hope he's only hiding. If so, he can lead us to the killers."

"I guess it's worth a try. But Sonny, don't bankrupt me. I maxed out my cards to replenish my trust account. For the next couple days you'll have to get by on that ten grand. I'll wire you another five on Monday. We're ahead of the cops on this and maybe we can break it for them. But don't do anything stupid."

"No worries, man, I'll take a short flight to Georgetown in the morning. The banks will be closed but maybe I can pick up on his trail. From there I'll go to Mexico, then back to Georgetown when the bank opens on Monday. You'll need to wire me more dough. Tell Beverly to pay off your credit cards, she's got plenty of dough so remind her of that. I'll call you on Sunday to confirm whether she's on board. And hey, Les. *Hasta la vista.*"

The line went dead.

CHAPTER TWENTY-TWO

Les sat in silence, his head in his hands. The sickening thought of Byron's missing fortune prevented him from working. He fingered the key to Byron's condo. Surely the cops had been there. But would it be a crime for him to have a look as well—for inventory purposes? Byron's condo was now an asset of the estate, and Les was the estate's attorney, at least in theory.

He'd never been to Byron's condo and wouldn't have known how to find it if he hadn't come across the address in James's file. As it turned out, the condo was in Kings Gate, Unit 22, just a few miles away. Les arrived at 9:55 p.m. No one had followed him, though to be safe he parked several buildings down and walked. It was dark and quiet as he padded up the stairs. The key turned and he was in before he knew it. His gloves bore witness to his new career outside the law.

Plainly stated, Byron's condo was a dump. For a multi-millionaire seeking custody of his daughter, he certainly boasted an extensive collection of IKEA. Scattered throughout were half-packed cardboard boxes. Someone had begun the process of gathering up his things. A collector's edition Monopoly board, game unfinished, was sitting on the table next to an empty bucket of Kentucky Fried. A single yellow game card lay face down in the center of the board, so he turned it over:

From sale of stock you get $45.

He grimaced, hoping it was not an omen. Someone had scribbled a series of numbers on the underside of the card:

$$44/2=22/2=11; \ 44+22+11=77$$

He slipped it in his pocket and drew closer to the oversized game box for a better look. Something seemed out of place. He lifted the currency container and discovered a treasure trove underneath. It was the Galileo—half Bluetooth, half alien techno-wear, thin and light, made mostly of high-grade plastic. It looked nothing like VVG's more bulky HMD. Thinking there must be a transmitter, he examined a wristwatch that was sitting in the box. Its crystal was black. He touched the crown and it came to life. At the same moment a green light appeared on the left end piece of the Galileo, and another from inside the box where he noticed a pair of fabric gloves with embedded sensors. He removed his gloves and put the new ones on. He touched a lighted button on each wrist as his fingertips began to glow.

The Galileo fit snugly over his eye sockets and was comfortable. He could see easily through the lens as the clear glass visor allowed for normal vision. He adjusted the mic and inserted the earphones. With his left index finger he depressed the button on the end piece as the Galileo sprung to life. The familiar, dazzling colors of Digitron's "Horizon OS" logo consumed his field of vision with brilliant clarity. It was as if he'd stepped inside an IMAX screen.

As he moved his head from side to side, his field of vision changed. A slide along the right end piece adjusted his field of vision from forty degrees to three hundred and sixty degrees immersion. The brightly colored Digitron logo was prompting him for Byron's password.

By directing his focus through the lens, he could still see the room in which he stood. He pressed the button again and the translucent visor switched to jet black opaque. He now saw *only* the "Horizon OS" logo, as if suspended in outer space. Another touch to his temple and the Galileo fell silent, except for the glow of the button itself. It was still communicating with the watch, which he slipped into his pocket.

Wearing the gloves and the Galileo, he continued moving through Byron's condo. His fingertips glowed as he started looking for the cash. He entered Tiffany's room, which looked innocent and girlish, and noticed a picture of Breanna on her dresser. He entered the third bedroom, which had been converted to an office, with three large servers and two separate scanner/printers. Discs, papers and research files cluttered all three desks. A two-foot length of broomstick sat beside the keyboard next to a desk fan. He picked-up a DVD that read: *Euroglider* in DirectX 11.

He booted up one of the servers and started rifling through the mess on

Byron's desk. He came across an envelope containing five flash drives and several pages of stapled notes. Each flash drive was labeled "GC Quantum." When the monitor came to life, he could tell the server was communicating with the watch, which started vibrating in his pocket.

He was abruptly startled from his trance by a hard metal thump outside the condo. He hurried to the window and peered out. A squad car was there and the uniform was standing in front of it, pointing a flashlight up at Les. "Somebody's in there," the man yelled.

He shot a glance at the door, which he'd locked. Above the threshold he saw a red light blinking in the shadows. *A silent alarm!* He cursed under his breath, ducked, and crawled back into the makeshift office to grab the drives and notes. He could hear the uniform hot-footing it up the stairs. The officer began knocking and calling "police" as Les crawled toward the sliding glass door and balcony in the back. Quickly he stepped outside. Twenty feet below a miniature lawn beckoned him, sloping sharply down to a grove of dogwoods.

With a pang he remembered the server was still on. But by the time he went back in and pulled the plug, a second cop would be waiting on the lawn to escort him to Gaitano. Another door slammed, so in desperation he took the plunge. Landing hard he rolled violently down the hill. His right ankle bent sharply the wrong way. *Why am I doing this?* he thought. *I have a legal right to be here.*

He came to a rolling stop in tall grasses at the bottom of the steep slope. His ankle burned with pain though he managed to hobble toward the trees, soaking wet and lumbering like a wounded bear. Behind him a voice shouted from the balcony, "Chuck, around back. Hurry!"

He glanced over his shoulder. The cop on the balcony was shining his flashlight at Les. He ran faster, clenching his teeth against the pain. More condos emerged from the other side of the trees, close to a covered parking space. He turned again and saw the beam of a second flashlight in the distance, jerking up and down in a running pattern. He couldn't proceed another step, so down he went beneath the nearest car.

"I think he's in here," yelled a voice from the trees.

Cramped beneath the greasy underside of a Volvo SUV, he couldn't hear whether there was any reply, but moments later he heard footsteps approaching. His head was locked in position. He heard the cop just a few cars away, walking up and down the rows, then finally receding.

Cautiously, he squeezed out from under his hiding place and found his bearings in the dark. His Saab was parked two buildings down. He managed to reach it as two more squad cars pulled into the neighboring lot. He threw off his jacket and glanced in the mirror at his oil-stained face. He was still wearing the Galileo and his fingertips were glowing. He felt a little like the masked avenger.

White-knuckling the wheel, he drove away. As he exited the faux gates of the complex, two more squad cars passed him, their blue lights flashing. Through his rearview mirror he saw them setting up to block the exit as he turned onto the main arterial. Reaching for his jacket he felt the outline of Byron's flash drives. He removed the Galileo to confirm it wasn't damaged, then smiled.

CHAPTER TWENTY-THREE

On Saturday morning he woke in searing pain. His ankle was badly sprained, though fortunately he had nowhere else to be. Wincing, he hobbled to his computer and inserted one flash drive after another until he struck the mother lode. The drives contained what was essentially Byron's diary, documenting two years of his tireless work with Nakamura.

After spending most of the morning at his computer, he was finally piecing it together. The GC Quantum in its first iteration was designed for cell compatibility via USB 3.1 (10 gigabits per second). It possessed an advanced multi-core processor and on-board memory, capable of amplifying cell signals to the bandwidth required for VVG server downloads at speeds of one gigabyte per second. In its second iteration, already in production, the GC Quantum was being re-engineered for on-board integration with smartwatches like Samsung's Galaxy Gear 2.

In a word, the GC Quantum was intended to supplant the VVViron and the glasses would become the IMAX of the future. Palm-sized smartphones, endlessly vying for largest screen, would soon go the way of the chunky VGA monitor. The next generation iPhone would be smaller than a key fob, tucked in the pocket or worn around the neck. Its screen replacement would become the user's entire field of vision (or FoV) beamed directly onto the human retina via the high-resolution Galileo. Its reflective light, versus glowing light, was easier on eye strain. Consumers would one day wear it, whether in use or not, and customize it as so much stylish eyewear.

Nakamura's HMD contained embedded gyroscopes and accelerometers for 360-degree head tracking in an immersive VR and 3D FoV, or in multiple FoVs or screens. The Galileo could push graphic content at 240Hz with 1080P resolution. *Oculus Rift*, the industry's leading HMD, displayed at 720P. One touch to the right end piece and a player's spoken words would appear as text in one or more of the FoVs.

In his diary Byron referred to the VV Viron as a "useless paperweight." The latest consoles, Digitron's Xterminator and Microsoft's XBox One, would soon be passing from the scene. So why force Nakamura to break away? Why not keep him, join the future and open the Vortex to 4G networks? Clearly VVG would have done so had they known about the portable Galileo.

He found the reason for VVG's foot-dragging further down in Byron's diary. It seemed there were missing links to Nakamura's chip, namely the complex server software still required to push cloud-based graphic computing through 4G LTE networks. Digitron possessed this technology, but was refusing to license it to VVG for anything less than ten times the amount showing on the dice.

Digitron had become VVG's fiercest competitor in the space and so VVG refused to pay their price, given that they stood to make as much or more *without* the GC Quantum as with it. Survival for VVG hinged on winning the Quantum patent and then burying it.

By co-opting Byron as a silent partner, Nakamura had acquired the missing links from Digitron by means of subterfuge and theft. Unfortunately, Byron had not been much of a silent partner. The relentless press coverage connecting him to Nakamura had spelled disaster. Even though INTERACT was prepared to take on VVG over patent rights to the GC Quantum, if Digitron could expose the stolen "missing links," then those patent rights would likely perish in the womb.

Had Nakamura succeeded in breaking-free, VVG would have been forced to convert its entire VR division to a Quantum format or disappear from the corporate landscape faster than Atari. Les found Byron gloating in his diary over a federal court's "net neutrality" ruling in January that declined to recognize the cable giants, backbone of the Internet, as a public utility. The ruling meant the ISPs could soon start charging VVG a hefty surtax for hogging cable bandwidth through the Vortex. But by switching his pipeline to the telephone carriers, Nakamura's gamble was about to pay INTERACT in multiples of millions. Perhaps Nakamura had warned

VVG to convert, but the company was too invested in its 256-megabit bus. VVG was using him to win the patent just so they could kill it.

The Quantum, or the *Game Changer* as Nakamura loved to call it, was the perfect companion to the Galileo, making both devices fully portable. Already, stories were surfacing of young adults gaming inside the Vortex for days on end, surfacing from their attached HMDs or HD flat-screens only long enough to service their bodily functions. But as Byron put it, the Quantum-infused Galileo would unleash an even greater power of addiction:

> This is the total visual vortex—the cerebral cortex receiving real time images beamed directly to the eyes, anywhere, anytime, as VFR (virtual freaking reality).

The impact of VRD extended far beyond video games. HDTV, the single-greatest Japanese technology investment since Word War II, as well as its amplified offspring, UHD, would soon be obsolete. The techno-hungry world was about to experience a forward leap in visual spectography like none before.

There were dramatic applications for VRD: battlefield intelligence, video-assisted surgery, even medical hope for the vision-impaired. Galileo's infrared transmissions could be adjusted by an ophthalmologist to compensate for almost any visual impairment. And when the Galileo was not in use, its visor could be fitted with prescription glass. The Galileo was as much a medical device as an HDTV replacement.

A spreadsheet on Les's screen compared video clarity among the various visual platforms currently on the market: VHS: 250 x 333 lines; Digital Video (or DV): 500 x 666 lines; Super VGA: 768 x 1024 lines; HDTV (or Blu-ray): 2000 x 3000 lines; VRD: 3000 x 4000 lines. "Lines" were strings of pixels or individual projections on a screen. At 3000 x 4000 strings of pixels, an image could be projected on the human retina five times clearer and more brilliant than 50 millimeter IMAX. Les had seen it for himself, if but for a few intoxicating moments in Byron's condo.

How had they done it? He was gratified to find the answer. According to Byron's diary, Nakamura began his quest for immersive screen replacement by experimenting with infrared technology in the late 2000s—initially as the assistant director of the Fujitsu Research Institute in Tokyo, and later as a visiting professor at Tokai University. His focus before that had been on stereoscopic imaging and three dimensional graphics using display technology such as LED (light emitting diode) or LCD (liquid crystal display). Ironically those two platforms were also Byron's claim to fame.

But VRD differed in its use of infrared scanners, akin to bar code readers. Throughout his diary Byron kept mentioning a company called Retina Vision, a Seattle startup developing VRD. Somehow Wells and Nakamura had acquired RV's schematic for a full-color prototype of the Galileo. Thanks to the acquisition Wells and Nakamura were estimating less than a year until mass production could begin in U.S. markets. A comment from Byron near the end of his diary seemed to summarize it best: "Akira predicts INTERACT will become the INTEL of VR."

But with the Galileo a year from market, their challenge was how to delay the GC Quantum. If Nakamura held back any longer he would risk a buried patent. VVG was pressing hard for him to complete the patent process.

As before, Dietrich's name did not appear. Was he in danger or was he uninvolved? Les could not let it go. He tucked the Galileo, the watch, and the gloves inside his jacket then limped to his car in search of answers.

CHAPTER TWENTY-FOUR

The Snohomish airport, surrounded by dairies and farmland, was modest and unassuming. Two dozen private planes lined the primitive tarmac. There were hangars for forty more. A sign directed him to FOLLOW THE SUN—Hot Air Balloons. Nobody was in the office so he rang the bell and waited.

A voice in the back yelled, "Just a minute." A young man of eighteen or nineteen years appeared. He introduced himself as Aaron Grey.

"Hi, Aaron. I'm Les McKee, an attorney. I suppose you've been talking to your share of lawyers and police."

"Yeah, my dad was killed," he answered bleakly.

"I'm sorry," Les said softly. "My client was married to Byron Wells."

"Our lawyer said you might be coming. We're not supposed to talk to anybody about the crash."

"I'm not here about the crash. I need to know whether you saw anyone accompanying the four paying customers who died. Did anyone come with them who didn't get on board?"

"My mom's been over that with the police. I wasn't here that day and I really shouldn't talk to you."

"That's okay. Is she here?"

"She's running errands. We're closing. I suppose you'll be suing too?" He looked pathetic and Les felt sorry for him.

"Actually, we think it was caused by a defective tank. If so, you and your mom should file with us."

"It wasn't pilot error, I can tell you that. And there was nothing wrong with that balloon. It worked for me on Saturday morning and again that afternoon."

"It would help if I could see your records and talk with whoever was working the front desk."

"That would be my dad, who's dead. My mom drives the chase car on Sundays. She was the first one on the scene. We had a guy named Dirk who drove the van. He was there too, but he's quit." Aaron frowned. "What does our passenger log have to do with the fuel tank?"

"Well, in order to sue the manufacturer or the distributor I've got to prove there was no bomb. I'm sure you've been reading the papers."

"Yeah," he said. He pulled out the flight log and turned to April 13, the last page with any entries. "They paid with a credit card." Aaron showed the receipt to Les. It matched Byron's statement from the Bank of Vermont and bore his signature. He noted they'd made reservations for *seven*, including crew. "Have the police seen this?"

"Yeah, they copied everything."

"Did Dirk notice anything suspicious?"

"No, he was in the hangar, working on our other balloon."

"Why weren't you flying both balloons?"

"We add the second one in May."

"How about your mom? Did she see anything?"

"You'll have to ask her."

"No problem. I'll call her. But can you tell me why it was reserved for seven people, when only six got on board?"

"I don't know. We get no-shows, or maybe they booked it full so they could have it to themselves. Otherwise we take walk-ons if there's room."

"Thanks, Aaron." Les did not leave his card. He had no business talking to the boy without the permission of his lawyer. Feeling no closer to the truth, he headed toward his car.

As he was pulling away he saw it streaking past him—the yellow Corvette, sixtieth anniversary model. It had to be Aaron's mother. She would have witnessed the crash and perhaps she could confirm whether they hit the tree before or after the explosion.

He whipped into reverse, in hopes of catching her before she reached her son and learned he was a lawyer. She might refuse to talk with him if she knew. He honked and waved as she emerged from her Corvette. He recognized her slim figure and cropped blond hair from the day of the crash.

"Mrs. Grey, I'm Leslie McKee. I live just above the crash site. I'm the guy who supposedly filmed it, only now we can't seem to find my camera."

"I read about you," she said warily. Her eyes were empty and she wore her grief like a disfigurement. "How can I help you?"

"I'm sorry about your husband."

"Thank you," she murmured. Fresh pain darkened her face. "He wasn't supposed to go that day."

"What do you mean?"

"Normally we use a single pilot, but he decided to tag along for fun." She wiped away a tear and visibly composed herself. "What can I do for you, Mr. McKee?"

"Well, the police have been asking me about the crash. It's a little hard to remember exactly what I saw. I think you and I might have been the only witnesses."

"Pardon me?" She looked as if he'd said something cruel.

"Your car. I'm sorry, your son said you were driving the chase car that afternoon. I thought I saw it on the service road by my house, just before the crash."

They were standing close to each other, talking above the whine of a small plane that was headed toward the runway.

"Yes, I was driving, but I never saw the crash," she said.

He was confused. "Are you saying you just weren't looking when it happened?"

"No," she answered with concern. "I'm saying I'd meant to be there sooner, but we couldn't start the car after Jon called me on his cell to say where they were landing. It was out of gas and it took us a while to refuel."

"So you didn't arrive until after they'd crashed?"

She started to cry. "I was driving as fast as I could when I saw the smoke from less than a mile away. I knew they were dead. Why are you asking me this?"

"The police think there were two explosions," he said, "which suggests a bomb. But that's not what I saw, so I was wondering what they've said to you, that's all. I know this must be hard. I'm sorry—"

She interrupted. "That's okay. Charlie and Jon were careful pilots so I do think it was a bomb. In fact, they've found traces of a bomb. But I was too far away to see what happened."

He saw Aaron walking toward them and quickly confessed. "Mrs.

Grey, as you may know, I'm also representing one of the other widows. She's the only one who hasn't sued, mainly because we can find no evidence of pilot error. But I'm skeptical of all the bomb-talk too. I have an expert who's examined the fuel tank and he claims it was defective. I need to share this with your lawyers."

She nodded and handed him her attorney's card. He was covering his ass. If challenged, he could say that as soon as learned they were represented, he'd asked for their lawyer's name so as to proceed through proper channels.

He turned toward his car as if to leave, then went back. "Can I ask you one more question?"

"Sure."

"That afternoon, who accompanied the paying passengers, or did they leave their car behind?"

"I didn't pay them much attention. Charlie dealt with that. The police have asked me this a hundred times. Someone drove them here because they didn't leave their car. After they landed, Dirk was going to take them in our van to the winery for a tour. I guess they'd arranged for a ride from there."

So the bodyguard was in town, he thought.

"Was the man who drove them Asian?"

"I'm not sure. One of them was, but I think he's the one who died. They were out of here pretty fast. It took another thirty minutes before we were go for launch."

"You said *they*. Did more than one man drive away?"

"There could have been two, I don't remember."

"Were they driving a fancy car?"

"It was a black sedan."

He thought it was probably Byron's Mercedes. "Okay, thanks," he said.

"Are you okay?" she asked

"It's just a sprain."

He limped away, feeling sorry that he would have to sue her.

CHAPTER TWENTY-FIVE

Les worked backwards through Byron's final hours. He drove to the Hotel St. James in Kirkland, where he learned from the maître d' that five or six men, not four, had dined that morning and that two of them were Asian. "Have the police been here?" he inquired politely.

The maître d' shook his head.

His next stop was Exotic Rentals in Bellevue. Byron had paid the weekend rate and picked up his rental a full day prior to Nakamura's arrival. They were getting ready to close, so Les asked for a quick minute with the manager. He was introduced to a pleasant looking athletic man whose nametag read, "Ramone."

"Ramone, I'm Les McKee." The two shook hands. "I'm the attorney for the estate of Byron Wells. He was killed in that balloon crash that's been on the news."

"Oh yeah, the guy from Digitron."

"Have the police been here?" he asked. Ramone shook his head. "Well," he continued, pulling out Byron's VISA statement. "One of my tasks in closing an estate is to determine which of the deceased's creditors have valid claims and which do not. Mr. Wells's final statement shows a charge he made to Exotic Rentals just two days before he died, though nobody seems to recall seeing him in a rental car that weekend. Would you have the paperwork on this?"

"Sure," he said. "Let me look it up for you." He was back in minutes with a printed receipt. "Here it is. I remember it was rented by his wife."

"His wife?" He examined the rental slip. Sure enough, Beverly's name

134 | MICHAEL W. BUGNI

and driver's license number appeared on top. "Do you have a copy of the contract she signed?"

"Right here," he said, as he handed it to Les.

He glanced at it and froze. "So she . . . rented a Corvette. What color?"

"Yellow. Come on, I'll show it to you."

Ramone led him to the lot, and there it was—a dead ringer for Mrs. Grey's Corvette.

His hand shook as he wrote down its Washington plate: 688 CKA. "Can you tell me what she looked like?"

"Sure. Attractive. Thin. Long blond hair. Early 30s."

He recalled that Mrs. Grey, the chase car driver, wore her blond hair short. A sickening rush ran through his gut as it became apparent why Beverly cut her hair.

"Did she come with anyone or did she say why she was renting it?"

"She was alone. She said she was headed down the coast. I remember because it was the last nice weekend we've had around here."

Les smiled back. "That's right. Were you here when she returned it?"

"Actually no, but I heard about it later. It was kind a weird. I guess she dropped it off before we closed, but without checking in or anything. She left the keys under the floor mat, but nobody saw her."

"What time was that, do you know?"

"Must have been around six, 'cause that's when we close on Sundays."

"Was there anything wrong with how she turned it in?"

"Not really. People do it. It was in good shape and fueled. She paid in advance and she brought it back on time, so we recycled it like normal. Is there a problem?"

"No," he said. "She probably charged it on his VISA by mistake. They were separated, and we couldn't figure out why he would rent a car, that's all."

"I figured she was getting divorced," said Ramone.

"That's interesting. Why?"

"Well, she mentioned she'd been looking all over for this particular model, 'cause her boyfriend has a thing for classic yellow Vettes."

Trying to seem unaffected he swallowed hard, gulping down a sharp stab of jealousy, laced with revulsion. Dazed, he headed to his car, his mind on overload.

CHAPTER TWENTY-SIX

Driving from Exotic Rentals, his emotions continued to reel as he tried to confront the truth about his client. He recalled her tear-streaked face on the night of Byron's death and how she'd professed her love for him. Could she really be a killer?

He drove aimlessly, half-veering off the road until reason began replacing fear. If she were the killer then she wouldn't have rented it using Byron's VISA. She wasn't stupid. She was framed. Someone had set her up and it was only a matter of time until the police came knocking. But how could someone trick her into renting it? And why would she return it just minutes after the crash?

If only he hadn't lost his phone. His picture of the Corvette would prove her innocence or guilt. How had Ramone put it? Something about her boyfriend having a thing for classic yellow Vettes. It hadn't bothered him that she was married, especially considering her choices. But the thought of Beverly making love to a real man was more than he could bear. Didn't Marcia say that she'd gone shopping with a girlfriend?

If Sugiyama was the killer, then Beverly was his patsy. She'd need a lot more than pocket change to defend herself. Without access to Byron's money, she'd be forced to file against Les, so his malpractice carrier could fund her defense. He felt both rejected and threatened by her now.

I deserve it, he thought grimly.

His thoughts jumped to the next morning. Spring break was over and Marcia, Beverly and the girls were due back. It was time for him to speak frankly with the widow, or was she a heartless and murdering cheater?

He was waiting for a call from Sonny, who by now was somewhere in

Mexico, tracking Bonadelli. In two more days he'd be going to Gaitano with everything he had.

He pulled into his garage at 10:30 p.m. A sharp pain shot up his leg as he hobbled to the house. It was dark and empty. Standing alone he found himself missing Marcia so much it ached. He wondered if she felt the same.

Switching on the kitchen light, he gaped in horror. His kitchen was in shambles. Several drawers were opened and upturned, their contents strewn about the floor. Most of the cupboards had been cleared. He made a path through the debris as he wandered through his ransacked living room. He moved upstairs to his den, snapped from his trance-like state and rushed to survey the damage. The disks, all of them, were gone, along with Byron's notes. A post-it was stuck to his monitor with a typed message:

Keep digging and folks keep dying
Ditto Dietrich
Get out now Les this is over your head

His gun was missing when he needed it most. He searched his house with a baseball bat instead. They'd found his boxes in the attic and all of them were gone. Should he call Gaitano ahead of schedule? His narrow escape from the Kirkland police the night before was still too fresh. Besides, the most important items missing were things he'd stolen from Byron's condo. At least he still had the Galileo and its accessories.

He needed to speak with Dietrich, who was apparently on the killer's trail like Les. Could he risk it? Farrago would insist on being present. He thought about the files he'd secured at his bank and realized with a stab that he'd left his key to the safe deposit box sitting in his desk.

Frantically he searched for it, but it was gone, along with the registration card revealing both the location of his bank and the number of his box. The killers had access to every scrap of evidence he'd gathered. But his bank would be closed until Monday. He would alert Gaitano, so the police could set a trap.

By the time his family arrived on Sunday afternoon his house was back to normal. While searching its perimeter, he'd discovered an amateur transmitter attached to his phone line on the outside of his house. It looked like a hack job, not the work of the police. He would call in the morning and have his entire house and office swept for bugs.

As Breanna came clamoring through the door, he picked her up and spun her through the air.

"Daddy," she shouted, "I found seashells!"

With a hug he set her down. She unfolded her paper towel with great care. While he admired her loot, she gave him another warm embrace. "I missed you," she said, kissing his cheek.

"Likewise, kiddo," he said happily. Her innocent smile and trusting gaze made him wish he could spend more time with her. He thought about the Greys and their small balloon company. They were as blameless as his daughter and he'd sooner resign than sue them.

Once Breanna was snugly tucked in bed, Marcia spoke to him for the first time since she got home.

"Have you found her another lawyer?"

"Honey, you've got no idea how things are blowing up," he started to explain, but her glazed expression made him stop. She didn't care about his troubles. She hadn't even asked him why he was limping. It occurred to him that she no longer loved him. Their house felt like a funeral parlor.

"I can't just drop her," he said carefully. "She's my client and I have a responsibility to her." He paused. "The truth is, I have to file another lawsuit on her behalf. I just learned that Byron's stockbroker may have bankrupted their estate before the crash."

"Another lawsuit?" Her dark eyes flashed dangerously. The revelation of Bonadelli's forty-four million dollar embezzlement hadn't even registered in her mind.

"I won't stand by and let you endanger our family any longer. You can choose between her or me. I'm serious."

"For God's sake, Marsh," he snapped, "I'm not taking any more bullshit from you about Beverly *this* and Beverly *that*. You can believe what you want and refuse to support me if you must. But I have to do this. It's my job and it's my duty. Somebody has to tell her that Byron was murdered and that she's a suspect. In fact I should tell her tonight."

"So that's what it's about," she thundered. "We haven't been back two hours and you want to be with her? You haven't spent two minutes with your family. If you go, Les, don't bother coming home."

A cold chill hung in the air as Marcia composed herself. "Can't you see what's happening to you?"

"It's too late," he whispered. "I can't stop now." He rose and hobbled to the door.

CHAPTER TWENTY-SEVEN

Tapping the knocker of Beverly's grand entrance, he heard her delicate footsteps cross the foyer. The door opened and there she stood. It was an odd sensation to see her for what she was. A cipher.

"Beverly," he said, his voice lowered, "I'm here because we need to talk."

"Of course," she said, looking concerned. "Come in and sit down. Let me introduce you to my sister."

"Not here," he whispered. "I think your house is bugged. I'll explain later. Listen, can she look after Tiff for a few minutes while we take a ride?"

"Of course, Leslie, just let me get my sweater."

As they walked to the car, the moonlight revealed her pale blue eyes sparkling in the night.

"Leslie, what happened to your ankle?" she asked.

"I'll tell you all about it."

As they drove toward the prominent outline of Cougar Mountain, he glanced periodically in his rearview mirror, satisfying himself that they weren't being followed.

"Beverly," he began, "I'm sure you've figured out by now that Byron's death was not an accident." He pulled into a car park overlooking the Sammamish Plateau and looked over at her.

She visibly tensed. "I've thought about it," she said slowly, "but I'm not ready to face it yet."

"You have to," he said. "The police are all over this case and things are turning up that will hit the papers soon."

Her face was the color of bone. "Like what?" she asked.

"Evidence that someone placed an explosive compound in Byron's flight jacket. The police think he was the target of a contract murder."

She looked out the window as her eyes filled with tears.

Without hesitating, he began to lie. "Byron's killers want my phone more than the cops. They've tapped my landline and probably yours, which is why we're here. No one can know this, but my mom called me this morning. She reminded me that on the night of the crash I emailed her pictures of our new house. Beverly, the pictures I sent her included the ones from the crash. They're still on her computer."

Nervously she fingered a button on her blouse. "Have you told the police?" she asked.

"Are you kidding? The detective who's been hounding me for my pictures almost hopped a plane for Chicago when I told him. But my mom's in St. Paul with her sister for the weekend. She'll be home on Tuesday when she's going to send them back. The police are going there to remove her hard drive so they can establish chain of custody."

There. The trap was set. If Beverly was involved with the killers, there would be an attempt, and soon, to remove or destroy his mother's computer. Never mind that nothing was on it.

He would call her tonight and warn her to leave town for the next few days. She'd be in no danger if she left. In fact, Gaitano could set *two* traps for Byron's killers—one at his bank and the other in Chicago.

She turned from the window. "Is he the same detective who came to your house for the phone?"

"Gaitano—he's one of several assigned to Byron's case. He's convinced they're looking at a multiple homicide. The A.T.F. is still combing through the scene and they've brought in the F.B.I. I'm amazed they haven't questioned you. They've been following you."

"Why? Do they think I had something to do with this? You've got to be joking me, Leslie. Don't tell me they think I would do it for his money. Don't they know I've got money of my own? I never cared about his."

Not according to your divorce file, he thought.

"Beverly," he offered, "Snow White would be a suspect if she was in the middle of divorcing Byron Wells. You'd better accept that everyone will be looking your way until they find the men who did this."

"Was he really murdered, Leslie? By whom?"

"He was playing with fire, Bev. He had more enemies than Jimmy Hoffa."

"Marcia said you and Sonny were working on a products liability case. And I thought you said you were going to sue the balloonists, that others had already filed."

"That was last week—before the break-ins on the island. Even Sonny has changed his mind. And speaking of Sonny, he was just in New Orleans. We got a call from Victor."

"Victor? Leslie, what on earth does he want?"

"The police have been talking to him about your divorce and the fire at his club. They're even asking questions about Ty."

She put her hand over her mouth and looked away. She started to shake, then broke down crying. "That bastard," was all she managed. "I hate him, Leslie. Victor wants to see me dead. Broke and dead."

"Sonny met with him on Friday. He says it's going to cost you to keep him quiet. A hundred grand a month for the next four months. I already maxed your line of credit, thirty-five grand, plus seventy-five grand of my own money—a hundred thousand dollars for Victor's first installment, plus ten for Sonny's fee."

"Where did you get the other seventy-five?" she asked.

"First my trust account. Then bank loans and credit cards. I need to pay it back."

She paused again and shot him her special look. "Leslie, I don't know what to say. The money means nothing to me, truly. You know that. I would've given it back to him if he'd only asked. But the fact that you've risked so much . . ." She squeezed his hand.

Her touch was warm and soft, her perfume intoxicating. "Beverly, there's more. It's about Byron's money." He had never referred to it as Byron's money. "While you were gone, I uncovered something that's going to upset you. It turns out he'd been selling his stock since he got fired. There's only six million dollars' worth left and the rest is missing. It looks like his broker was in on it and may have embezzled most of Byron's holdings, converting it to cash just days before he died."

She took short, shallow breaths. She looked trapped and about to strike. "Don't tell me this, Leslie. I can't handle any more. I'm getting out of here," she choked, as she suddenly flung the car door open.

"Beverly, don't. Come back."

She'd run into a dense thicket. He could hear her crying in the distance. He tried walking after her.

"Get away from me!" she screamed.

After listening to her sob from afar, he returned to his car. She was out of control—at least his. He had no idea how long she'd be, so he sat and waited.

A full ten minutes later she returned. She had torn her blouse on a sharp branch and her mascara was smeared, but she had calmed herself. As she climbed back in she gave him a contrite look.

"I'm sorry." She seemed almost stoic. "I'm such an idiot. I'd convinced myself we were getting back together, but he was ripping me off the entire time. Why did he hate me so much?"

As he reached to embrace her, she broke down again in a rush of pain. He sat quietly, his arms wrapped around her as she sobbed, until there were no more tears to shed. She was as close as his own skin, and he felt certain she hadn't killed her husband. Slowly, like a fog descending on Puget Sound, a strange calm entered the car. So he decided to dive deeper into troubled waters.

"Beverly, I could've prevented him from selling it off. I trusted Milton to enter that order, but I should've entered it myself. It turns out it was never signed by the judge. I could have named Digitron as a party. They would have frozen his account."

She kept silent, her short golden hair pressed against his chest. The windows were fogging up, as they'd done some twenty years before. Only tonight he wanted her even more.

"Sonny's in the Caribbean as we speak, looking for Byron's broker, a guy named Bonadelli. Have you heard of him?"

"Byron shared almost nothing with me about his money," she said at last. "But he wouldn't have let anyone get that close." Her voice was low and sensual.

"Do you know more than you're telling me?" he asked.

"No," she said, settling back down on his chest. "I just know Byron. Nobody rips him off."

"He wasn't invincible, Bev. Somebody killed him. Whoever it was used professionals and they're not about to get caught. You know the best way for them to get away with it would be to frame a patsy. I think you're it."

"What do you mean, I'm *it*?"

Take this slowly, he told himself and inhaled. "Nobody knows this, but on the day of the crash I filmed a car near my house, minutes before the explosion. It was a carbon copy of the chase car the balloonists used, only on the day of the murder the real chase car had been disabled."

He paused to see if she was following.

"What does this have to do with me?" she asked.

"The car I filmed was a yellow Corvette. It was shadowing them."

She gasped, then turned on him with violence in her eyes. "Tell me the rest, Leslie, and don't bullshit me."

He handed her Byron's Visa statement. "Here. Take a look for yourself." As she studied it, he added, "They remember you at Exotic Rentals. They showed me your signature and explained how you dropped it off around six on Sunday—just twenty minutes after Byron was murdered." He paused dramatically.

"Leslie," she said as she struck him with her fist. "What are you trying to do to me?"

"Hold on, Beverly." He gripped her wrist tightly. "I said you were *framed*, not guilty. I'm the only one who knows, but why in the hell did you rent a yellow Corvette on the weekend he died? I'm trying to get ahead of this for you. If I found out, how much longer until the FBI is on your tail?"

She tore up the Visa statement.

"The company has records, Bev. I think you've got some explaining to do."

"Leslie, you knew I'd gone shopping with a friend of mine to Cannon Beach. Her family owns a place there. Renting the car was her idea. She said she'd looked all over for it. I offered to pay if she could find one, so she got on the Internet and found this place in Bellevue. I picked it up for us on Friday. I charged it on his card because the bastard didn't even pay his child support. We were late getting back, so she dropped me at Byron's parents' before returning it for me."

"Why were you late getting back?"

"Because of her," she said with resignation.

"This was no coincidence, Bev. Who is she? You realize she was helping the killers to set you up. If she's a friend then you have to go to her tonight. She has to tell you who put her up to this. Both of you could be in danger."

"I guess," she said, as she wrapped her knuckles on the window and looked away.

"Whose idea was this little getaway?"

"Hers . . . of course."

"Beverly, who is she? Do I know her?"

"No, and I'm not going to tell you her name, at least not tonight. I can't believe this is happening to me." She started to cry again.

He tried to comfort her, but it wasn't the same. What he really wanted was to touch and hold her. Little had changed since their college days.

"How could I let this happen?" she sobbed, seemingly to herself.

"She's no friend, I can tell you that. She's connected to Byron's killers. Maybe they paid her, though she could end up dead for what she knows."

"I should've known," she murmured.

"The manager at Exotic Rentals said you were renting it for your boyfriend." Les thought he saw her flinch.

"I went with a girlfriend, Leslie. I've never said anything to anyone about a boyfriend. I don't have a boyfriend."

"How about Byron, was he seeing someone?"

"Not that I know of. Why do you ask?"

"Take another look at that Visa statement you just tore up. He paid almost $60,000 for a diamond ring at Tiffany's, just three weeks before he died."

"That's not possible," she said as she reached for the statement and stared at it intently. She gasped then started crying. "Leslie, what is going on?"

"You must have known he'd been working with Nakamura for going on two years."

"I swear, he left me totally in the dark."

"It was happening under your nose. He didn't care about his options because he was planning to lose at trial."

"Bastard."

"Did he mention a video device called the *Galileo*?"

"Not that I remember," she said. "What is it?"

He activated the watch and removed the Galileo. "Have you seen this? Do you know what it does?" He studied her for some hint of recognition, but there was none.

"I saw David wearing those," she said, as she examined the glowing button. "What are they for?"

"*Dietrich*? Are you sure? His lawyer swears he's not involved. So far I haven't found anything that connects him to the case."

"He's a jerk," she almost whispered, as she gently rubbed her cheek against his shoulder. She took the watch and put her arm across his waist, her hand resting very close to his lap.

His mind started spinning. "What about these?" he asked, showing her the gloves.

She tried one on, navigating it around her giant ring and pressing the power button on her wrist as if she'd done it before. Her fingertips were glowing green inside the car.

"I've never seen them, Leslie. Where did you get them?" She cradled his face with his chin in the palm of her glowing hand, staring intently into his eyes. "You know more than you're telling me, don't you?"

"I wish," he responded, his face just inches from hers. "I wish I knew what they were up to. I wonder how much Dietrich knows?"

"If Byron was cheating then so was David."

"If so, then the killers may be after him. Your girlfriend, whoever she is, can tell us who they are. The police have got to know this, Bev, or more people could die. I'm going to Gaitano in the morning and I think you should come with me."

She didn't seem to be listening. She drew closer as if something else was on her mind. Her fingers rested lightly on his thigh and her cool lips briefly caressed his cheek. His arousal was suddenly no secret.

"I can find out who you were with," he said nervously, gently moving her hand away, "I'll ask Marcia as soon as I get home."

"Tomorrow, Leslie. I'll go with you to Gaitano in the morning and help in any way I can. You've got to trust me. It's going to be just fine." She kissed him on the lips then pressed in gently as they were suddenly locked in a slow but probing kiss. He couldn't have let go of her even if she'd tried to pull away.

With an effortlessness that took him by surprise, he tasted her familiar breath inside his mouth. It was warm and sweet as she started kissing him with her tongue. Her scent was dancing inside his head.

She paused and gazed at him. Her soft eyes asked if he wanted more. "I remember this," she whispered. "I've thought about it more than you could know."

In silent response, he stroked her cheek. She carefully removed the glove and tossed it with the other one to the floor. Their second kiss was intimate and long. Despite two decades he felt twenty again as he slipped into her abyss.

Her hand made its way inside his zipper. She moaned, so pleased with what she'd found. As she turned toward him, her other hand found its way to the watch, which she deactivated and slipped inside her purse, along with the Galileo, before turning herself almost directly on his lap.

He was back in her dorm room, only this was better. He'd forgotten how bold and aggressive she was. As he paused to make eye contact, she adjusted his seat for him to make more room. What he saw was her desire, kept hidden from him for decades. He could sense there would be no turning back. Their next embrace became more intense, with a depth of passion he hadn't known. They both knew what they wanted. The front of her blouse was open. His restless hand had started to caress her when his judgment finally started screaming at him to stop. Yet her pleasure kept him going.

In twenty years Les had expanded and cars had shrunk, but for the moment that was good. As they paused, their breathing let him know that years of repressed desire were finally pouring out. He hadn't seen it coming. In fact he'd often wondered if she'd kept a single feeling for him. The dam had burst and her emotions were real. They'd been through more together than many spouses, yet he'd not so much as touched her face in all that time.

He wanted her whether it made sense or not. Some dark part of him reasoned that he'd earned the privilege. He longed to show her what he'd learned in all those years. But another part of him turned away, disgusted.

The sound of a cell phone pierced the air and they both sat bolt upright.

He caught sight of her bare chest and started groping like a man on fire, but not for her. "My phone," he muttered, fumbling beneath his seat. "I've got Sonny's phone in here." He was sorely tempted to throw it out the window.

"Sonny? Is that you?" he managed, finally grabbing it on the fifth ring.

"Hey, Les. I didn't wake you, did I?"

"Just a second." He looked at her, then away as he tried to slow his breathing. "Where are you? What time is it there?"

"Eight Bells and all is well," he said. "I'm in Georgetown, waiting for the bank to open in the morning. I'm already onto your friend, the broker."

"Good work. What have you got so far?"

"He was here on the eleventh. It's possible he was posing as Byron. I think he went back to the states. I've traced him as far as Tennessee where he seems to have disappeared. I ran into one of the private dicks working for Smith Levinson. They think he ended up in Cancun. They've got a man there looking for him now. I've booked a flight that leaves here in ten hours, as soon as I finish at the bank."

"What time did you say it was?"

Sonny hesitated. "One-thirty in the morning."

"Do you think you've got a chance? You're sixteen days behind him."

"It's worth a try, Les. I'll call you tomorrow from Cancun about 10:00 p.m. your time. Have you had a chance to talk with her?"

Les glanced at Beverly. "Yeah, Sonny. She's been great. I'll have Peggy wire you that five grand in the morning. Just tell me where."

"I'll email her with instructions from Cancun. I don't care who sees it since it looks like I'm down here doing Gaitano's job for him anyway."

"Good. We'll talk tomorrow night."

"Keep your fingers crossed, Les. I'm glad things went well with her."

He smiled to himself as he hung up, turning off the phone.

"I take it money's his god?"

"Always has been. Same as Byron. We've got tons of red tape to cut before we can sell the stock that Byron left. Can you come up with five grand on your own to tie him over?"

"Leslie, I'll bring you fifty grand, tomorrow," she smiled and began to kiss him once again. She stopped just long enough to whisper, "I was awake when you came in my room the other night. I thought you were going to climb in bed with me." They kissed again as he felt his life spiraling headlong from its ledge. Their kissing slowed but grew intense as each accepted where they were headed. She started nibbling on his ear and whispering endearments.

He was drunk with her.

She whispered to him playfully, "So let's recap what's been going on while I was gone. You're saying his options are a lost cause and that most of his actual shares are gone because you dropped the ball. You're not suing the balloonists, but you've uncovered enough on me to send me to the chamber. I'd say you're doing a helluva job as my attorney."

Her words were cutting but their sting was dulled immediately as she giggled, then softly kissed his ear while her fingers stroked his chest. The sheer pleasure of it was holding him down, but so was his fear. She owned him and she was letting him know it.

"Beverly," he whispered, "Where can we finish this?"

"Les, I really don't think I can wait for that," she moaned and grabbed his hand. Her cell phone rang out shrilly and she sat up and removed it from her purse to see who was calling. "Oh my God, it's Marcia."

He took the phone from her. "Hello?"

"It's almost eleven, Les," Marcia's voice crackled. "Where are you two? I just woke Bev's sister, and she said you drove off together. Put her on the phone."

He looked at Beverly. She was buttoning her blouse and looked horribly ashamed. "Marcia, you're out of line," he said. "I was just dropping her off and I'll be home in twenty minutes." He ended the call without waiting for her reply.

Seconds later the phone rang again.

"I'll talk to her," said Beverly, who took the phone before he could wave her off. "Marcia, this is Bev. It isn't what you think." After a long silence, she lowered the phone. "She hung up on me."

He was about to turn it off when it rang again. "Yes, Marcia," he said. He listened, then simply said, "Okay. If that's what you want."

She looked at him inquisitively.

"She told me not to bother coming home."

"I'm sorry, Leslie. This is my fault. I can't believe I let it happen."

"I'm to blame," he said. "Not you. I've wanted you for as long as I can remember. I should be ashamed of myself, but I sit and think about you almost every day. Why do you think I took that crazy insurance case for Victor? So don't apologize. This wasn't your fault. I'm the one apologizing. I've put you through too much tonight and I don't know what came over me. Whatever we think we're doing, we can't." He turned over the ignition as she clung to him.

"You literally saved me from Victor," she said. "He would have killed me if it hadn't been for you." She looked at him with renewed longing, but reality was in the way.

"Now I'm the one he's after," said Les. "They can't nail any of us for his arson, but he can nail me if he cooks up some story for the Bar Association to swallow whole. There's no statute of limitations on getting disbarred."

"Victor said there was no statute of limitations for Ty, either."

He nearly drove off the road.

"I mean the fire," she said quickly, trying to correct her slip. "Victor said there was no statute of limitations for the fire. But that's not true, is it, Leslie?"

Ice was forming in his veins. What if Victor had been blackmailing her for killing Tyler Pruitt? No wonder she paid him off so fast. Indeed there was no statute of limitations for murder, not in any state. Victor knew she was a killer. And Les had just finished purchasing his silence.

He couldn't dodge the grotesque truth any longer. She had tripped when her guard was down, revealing her corrupted soul. She was a ruthless destroyer of anyone or anything that stood in her way, and tonight she'd ruined his marriage.

"What's wrong?" she asked him quietly.

"Nothing." As he turned onto the main road, he glimpsed her newly cropped hair, glinting like fool's gold in the shimmering moonlight. He didn't have to ask her why she cut it. He thought again of the chase car driver and her murdered husband, Charlie.

They drove to Beverly's house in silence.

"Leslie," she said as she climbed out of his car. "I'll bring the money by your office in the morning. Okay? Then we'll go together to the police."

"Fine," he sighed and drove away. In the rearview mirror he watched her slowly merge into the dark night.

CHAPTER TWENTY-EIGHT

When Les arrived at work, unshaven and wearing Sunday's clothes, he noticed two patrol cars parked out front. *Something doesn't feel right,* he told himself. He limped into a veritable morgue. Every eye was on him.

Peggy stared him down, her face betraying the gravity of the moment. "Les, what have you done?" she seemed to say.

Gaitano was waiting for him on the lobby sofa, looking smug. "Where have you been all night, counselor?"

"What's this about?" he demanded.

"We had hoped to do this at your house, but your wife couldn't tell us where you were." He rose and reached for his cuffs with a flourish.

Les saw what was coming and felt at once indignant and mortified. Peggy gasped while Janie looked away. The rest of the office fell deathly still.

"I'm afraid I have to take you in for questioning."

"Why, what have I done? Am I being charged with something?" His voice rose against his will.

"Not yet," Gaitano replied, "but we need to find out what you know about the murder of Victor Garving."

"What?" he exclaimed. He felt lightheaded. His legs nearly gave way. He jerked his arm from Gaitano in defiance, which he found was a mistake. Two officers wrestled his hands behind his back as cold steel dug into his wrists.

"Victor Garving died around midnight in New Orleans, in a fire. New Orleans PD is searching for Sonny Lile as we speak. You shouldn't have booked his flight to New Orleans with your credit card."

"That doesn't prove anything. May I have two minutes with my office manager? It's about calling my attorney."

Gaitano nodded, as Les hobbled back with Peggy to her desk.

"Victor Garving?" she whispered. "That was years ago."

"There's nothing to it, Peg. Don't worry. They could've asked me to come down for questioning, but this way they get to make the papers. They think Beverly killed Byron and that I'm protecting her. This whole thing is crazy."

Speaking in a low voice, he brought her up to speed on recent events. "Sonny will be emailing you this morning," he said. "Reply and ask him if he's heard about Victor being dead. Tell him to get back here. He'll need some money, so go ahead and wire him five grand. He'll tell you where. Beverly will be coming by to pay off her bill and replenish her trust account. Use the money to pay off my credit cards and my line of credit. I need to zero out my balances. Here, the cards are in my wallet. The info on my HELOC is in my household file.

"And call Kim Hanson. Get him down to the courthouse for my bail hearing this afternoon."

While he spoke she seemed to focus on his whiskers. When he'd finished, she nodded tersely and asked, "What about Mrs. McKee?"

"Of course. Call her and tell her what's happened. It'll look better if she posts my bail instead of you. Kim can help her with all of that." He was interrupted as an officer appeared at each arm. While he was being manhandled toward the door, several uniforms arrived.

Gaitano waved a warrant as they fanned out to search his office. He held the door for Les and his escorts. "Nasty sprain, McKee. Did you get that jumping off a balcony on Friday night?"

Les said nothing but remained stoic as he was escorted out.

"I get wearing Batman gloves, but the mask and all? Seriously? We know you have the phone," Gaitano said.

As the back door of the squad car closed, it jogged his memory about the stolen key to his safe deposit box. He'd meant to be waiting at the bank with Gaitano when it opened at ten. Then a worse thought smacked him. *His mother! The trap he'd set for Beverly.* Someone had to warn her. He used his arms to feel for the contents of his jacket. *Where was the Galileo?*

"Turn around," he pleaded with the driver as they pulled from the curb. "It's urgent. I've got speak with Gaitano, just for a second."

The cop ignored him and kept driving. "You'll have plenty of time to tell your story."

He stared back in hopeless agony through the smudged glass of the window. Despair and nausea were overtaking him. Victor Garving was dead. He wondered how Beverly would take the news—or had she helped to make the news? It was all too coincidental. Was Sonny really working for her? Were they setting him up for Victor's murder?

That, he thought, was doubtful. Sonny wouldn't screw this up by leaving so much as a whiff of his involvement. Gaitano said it was a fire, not a murder. Gaitano could not be trusted.

Despite the fact that this latest twist had landed him in jail like a common thief, he was strangely relieved. Victor Garving was dead. His blackmailing days were over. Les needn't worry about raising the next $300,000 to buy his silence. Maybe it was Sonny's doing after all.

CHAPTER TWENTY-NINE

Les had dabbled enough in criminal defense to know what was coming next. It would take them several hours to book him through. He was left to wait in a ten-foot by ten-foot holding cell with a dozen others, who were on their way either in or out for everything from shoplifting to gang-banging.

At 2:20 p.m. a pair of officers escorted him through a corridor three blocks long, suspended ten stories above downtown Seattle. The mammoth skywalk connecting King County's jail to its courthouse could be seen from the surface streets for blocks. It was sterile, foreboding and dimly lit. His walk was long and lonely.

Bail hearings were held at 2:30 p.m. He waited with a group of detainees on a bench seat until his case was finally called. Defendants with private attorneys went first, before the public defender for the day took over. As he entered the courtroom, he could see the press waiting en masse behind their glass-encased gallery. The lawyer who stood waiting to represent him was not Kim Hanson.

"I'm Darryl Streich. I work for Kim. He's out of town until tomorrow. I'm being told they want to put you on States Avenue."

"What's that?" he asked.

"They want the judge to deny you bail."

"That's ridiculous," he said, in a whisper loud enough for the judge to overhear. "There's no probable cause to hold me."

"Counsel for Mr. McKee?" asked the judge, satisfying herself that lawyer and client had been properly introduced.

He cursed his luck. Dana Sullivan, a former family law attorney with whom he'd often clashed. She was new to the bench and she despised him. He didn't stand a chance with her.

"We're ready to proceed, Your Honor," said Streich.

"As a preliminary matter, counsel, the media has asked permission to film your client. Do you have any objection?"

The reporters and cameramen perked up behind the glass.

"I object, Your Honor. My client hasn't been charged with anything yet and he has a law practice to protect."

"Very well," said Judge Sullivan. "The press may film Mr. McKee and his counsel from the back, but to the neck and shoulders only. Case number?"

The prosecutor for the day took over.

"State versus Leslie Wayne McKee, held for investigation of conspiracy to commit arson and murder. Mr. McKee is also being held for a pending extradition to Orleans Parish, Louisiana, on the charge of accomplice to murder in the first decree. The King County complaint number is 14-1-64561-3 SEA. The State requests the court to deny bail, Your Honor, given the extreme nature of the crime and the high probability that this defendant will attempt to flee prosecution."

"Your Honor," Les's lawyer began. "I've submitted eight declarations from professionals in the community, attesting to the fact that Mr. McKee is a respected attorney and a property owner who would never flee prosecution. To deny him bail would be absurd."

"Your Honor," said the prosecutor, "We've checked with the defendant's wife. She says her husband no longer lives with her. She won't post bail nor offer any community assets as security against his flight. In fact, she just discovered that over the past few days her husband borrowed seventy-five thousand dollars using the couple's credit, though the whereabouts of the money is still a mystery.

"The primary suspect in this matter, Peter Sonny Lile, left the state on Wednesday using airline tickets charged to Mr. McKee's credit card. Mr. Lile's present whereabouts are unknown though he's believed to have fled the country. Mr. McKee has no home to return to, Your Honor, and given the seriousness of the allegations against him we're concerned he'll disappear, the same as Mr. Lile."

Every reporter in the room was scribbling madly, as Judge Sullivan had her day. "The court is prepared to rule. Bail will be set at five-hundred thousand dollars. As Mr. McKee is no doubt aware, the State must charge him or let him go within seventy-two hours. If charges are filed we'll have another hearing on Thursday. By then he will have had a chance to speak with his wife. If she's ready to take him back, I'll consider reducing his bail. Next matter, please."

As Les was led from the courtroom in handcuffs and leg-irons, shame enveloped him like his faded orange county-issued coveralls. As he was escorted from the courtroom he stopped and turned toward the bench.

"Judge Sullivan." The courtroom fell silent as the judge looked over at him. "I need sixty seconds to write something down for my attorney. It's urgent."

"Very well," she replied with a quizzical look.

The guard removed his cuffs as his attorney handed him a yellow pad and pen. Les wrote quickly, his hand shaking. As he gave the note to Kim's associate, he whispered, "This is for my mother in Chicago—for her eyes and yours only. Keep calling her until you get through and read it verbatim. Tell her she must leave her apartment at once, that it's a matter of life and death."

At 4:00 p.m. he was shoved in a cell with four beds and twice as many inmates. The air was ripe with body odor. None of his cellmates looked his way as he sat down on the hard edge of a bunk. At 4:40 p.m. a guard appeared.

"Visitor for Leslie McKee."

He rose, strangely elated, and followed the guard to the visitation block. She sat waiting for him, in her designer heels and handbag. She smiled slightly, with sympathy in her eyes as he sat down. Just the sight of her made his blood run hot.

They each picked up a phone. Behind her graffiti had taken over on the walls like blackberry vines.

"Leslie," she began in a rush of words, "I've been trying to get in here since noon. I couldn't believe it when Peggy told me Victor is dead. And they think Sonny was involved?"

"Sonny wasn't in New Orleans last night, remember?"

"Are you all right?" she asked.

"They set my bail at half a million dollars, and Marcia is telling me to piss off. That means I'm stuck here until they get around to questioning me. Three days max."

"I'm terrified, Leslie. Why would anyone kill Victor?"

She seemed sincere, but he was way past trusting appearances.

"I haven't slept," she said. "I came by your office with the money and I was going to tell you everything."

"Save it, Beverly. I don't want to hear your confession."

"I didn't kill him," she insisted. "Victor did. Ty and I were separated at the time, and Victor and I were having an affair. He knew Ty had been cut for using steroids, and he knew about the insurance. He'd been supplying him with various pills." She bit her lip, as a single tear rolled down her cheek. She was saying what he'd hoped to hear, whether it was believable or not.

"Victor and I were with him on the night he died. He'd taken me on a delivery to some party where Ty and a bunch of football players were present. It was true about the steroids. Victor supplied them for several players. Anyway, he saw me with Victor and later that night he overdosed. I blamed myself. But it wasn't until weeks later, when I tried to leave Victor, that he said he'd whipped up a toxic combination of pills for Ty. They were in preseason and he'd been drinking and using cocaine that night.

"The police were investigating because of Ty's insurance and because we were separated at the time. He said if I left him, he'd put evidence in their hands that I did it for the money. I was pregnant with his child, though no one knew. I was twenty-six and addicted to drugs. I'd just lost my husband. I thought I was going crazy and that maybe I had caused his overdose. I was scared to death, but I swear I've never killed anyone."

He noticed that the inmate in the next cubicle over appeared to be listening to their animated conversation. That was all he needed—a jailhouse snitch. "Calm down, Beverly. Tell me how Victor could get away with blackmailing you if you were innocent and he was guilty?"

"I tried to break it off, but he was worried I might say too much when the police came to question me. He said if I turned on him he'd convince them we did it together. When I told him I was pregnant, he promised we'd get married, as soon as we were in the clear."

"Pregnant?"

"I terminated," she cried. "Because of the drugs. Leslie, I've never told this to anyone."

Her pain was visible, tears streaming down her face.

"He brought it up again when I filed for divorce. But he backed off when you agreed to take his case. That's what I meant when I said you saved my life."

"And when you paid him the hundred grand?"

"He said there was no statute of limitations if Ty's case was reopened. Now he's dead, and I'm glad. I hope Sonny did it."

He motioned her to keep it down. "Beverly," he whispered, "they're looking at both of us for Victor's murder, along with Sonny the minute he steps off that plane. Watch what you say and who you talk to. Sonny didn't do this. Did Peggy say if she heard from him this morning?"

She nodded. "She got an email from him while I was there. She was discreet. She left and wired him the money, along with a telegram asking him to call her back. Isn't he supposed to call you tonight?"

"Yes, but only if you can get his phone. It's still in my car which is parked at my office. Peggy has the keys. Get the Galileo and the other things I showed you. Bring it to Kim Hanson. He's agreed to act as my attorney."

"Okay," she said uncertainly. "Oh, and Peggy called Marcia, but she said she isn't coming."

"Great," he said glumly.

"I feel awful about last night," she offered. I'm to blame, Leslie. I guess I'm sorry it ever happened."

"I'm not," he said. Just looking at her made him forget everything he knew about right and wrong. If it hadn't been for the wire and glass between them, he'd have taken her in his arms. Exerting his will power, he changed the subject.

"Beverly," he said, "the day Byron died, I saw the woman who was driving the real chase car. She had your same build and she's got short blond hair. Why did you cut your hair on the weekend of the crash?"

She appeared uncomfortable with his question. "My friend. We got our hair styled while we were in Cannon Beach. It was her idea."

"This isn't adding up," he said. "You do whatever this evil woman says? Yet you won't even tell me who she is? Can't you see why I'm losing faith in you? If you want me to believe you, give me her name so I can check her out. Are you blind? If she set you up then she knows who killed them."

"Leslie, I talked to her this morning. She's knows I'm onto her. I've never seen anyone so terrified. I don't know who they are or what they've said or done to her, but she's freaking out. I'm not sure she realized what they were doing. You're right—she knows who they are, but she says she had no idea it had to do with Byron's accident. She's still going to vouch for me, that I was with her for the weekend. She's my alibi, Leslie. She's on my side.

"However they got her to do it, I guess it seemed harmless enough at the time—a trip down the coast in a fancy car and a couple haircuts. Getting me back late. I think they're blackmailing her over something she says she can't tell anyone.

"So if you start questioning her, or if she helps me before my case goes to the jury, she says they're going to kill her. She literally begged me not to give you her name. It's strange. She admits she helped them yet she's my only alibi. I promised her I wouldn't expose her unless I have to. You told me they don't even know about this yet. What if they never make the connections?"

"Beverly, she's lying. If she was blackmailed into doing this, you would have some idea why. She was paid by professionals to assist them in framing you," he whispered urgently. "She'll be dead and the killers will be back in Japan by the time your case goes to trial. Then where's your alibi? Or what if she decides to deny it just to save her skin, or disappears like Byron's broker?"

"Do what you must, Leslie, but I gave her my word. I know it sounds crazy, but she swears she didn't know what she was doing. Now she's scared to death."

"Did she tell you who they are?"

She shook her head.

"Marcia will tell me who she is. I'm going to ask her just as soon as they let me make a call. You promised we'd be going to Gaitano and I'm still waiting for my chance."

He thought of his files at the bank. Could he trust her? Probably not, but he had nowhere else to turn. "Can you deliver a message for me to Kim?"

"What is it?"

"I've been keeping papers in a safe-deposit box at First Interstate in Kirkland. Someone stole the key from my house while you and Marcia were on break. The bank is closed by now, but in the morning when they open, he needs to put Gaitano on high alert. The killers will try and use my key to nab those papers. If I'm wrong, or if Kim can get there first, have him bring them to my interview. If the bank needs a release he can bring one here for me to sign. They'll have to make another key for him. Tell him the killers are coming for those papers and that Gaitano should set a trap."

She nodded, looking perplexed. "I could put my house up for your bail."

"Thanks, but that wouldn't look too good. Besides, I've got nowhere to go. I've been thrown out, remember?"

"I remember," she said as she rose to leave. "I'll be back, Leslie."

And I'll be here, he thought dismally.

CHAPTER THIRTY

He awoke on Tuesday to the sound of clanging bars and angry voices. He'd tossed and turned on his rock-hard mattress with little sleep. He could hear the sound of showers.

He picked at his tasteless breakfast and waited for his turn at the morning paper. This was not how he'd imagined making headlines. In bold type on the bottom half of the front page the caption read:

> Ex-Husband of Digitron Widow Found Dead
> in New Orleans. Widow's Lawyer Held for Questioning.

With state and federal authorities still perplexed over the fiery death of Digitron's Byron Wells and five others on April 13, the case took an even more bizarre twist yesterday in New Orleans. Police were seeking to question Victor Garving, the ex-husband of Wells's estranged wife Beverly. Before they could locate him, firefighters discovered his charred body in the smoky remains of an apartment fire, where he resided near the French Quarter. Following the issuance of a warrant here, it was discovered that Mrs. Wells's divorce attorney, Leslie McKee, purchased airline tickets for his investigator, Peter "Sonny" Lile, to visit New Orleans last Wednesday. Lile, a former detective for the Seattle arson squad, missed his return flight on Saturday and is still at large. McKee was arrested and is being held in the King County jail for questioning. His bail was set at $500,000.

The article went on to say that the apartment fire broke out at midnight in New Orleans. Adjusting for the time zone, that meant it happened thirty minutes before Sonny called him from the Caymans. Garving was the only victim in a fire of "suspicious nature," apparently started by a propane stove. Although the aging complex was nearly destroyed, the remaining occupants escaped unharmed.

In a related article the police had arrested an unnamed suspect in connection with the San Juan break-ins and fire. This was news to Les. Apparently Sonny was not their man on San Juan Island.

Setting down the paper, he realized his law career was over, along with his marriage. The sound of jangling keys cut off his thoughts. The guard announced his lawyer's arrival. Les followed him to a barren, concrete room. Kim Hanson, his long-time colleague and friend, rose to shake his hand.

"Hey Kim, man am I relieved to see you."

"Maybe not for long, Les. You and I go back too far for me not to tell you what an idiot you've become. I can't comprehend why you've been talking to this detective, when you knew damn well you were a suspect. Did you even go to law school?"

"I told him to read me my rights if he thought I was a suspect."

"And then kept right on talking? Brilliant."

"Kim, I'm innocent. They've got zero proof."

"You haven't worked with some of the juries I've empaneled. I have a singular role here, Les, and it's to forbid you from saying one more goddamn word to them."

"I wish I could take your advice, Kim, but I'm in too deep. The fact that I can break this case for them does not make me an accomplice."

"I'm listening," said Kim. "Meaning I'm polite enough to let you finish before I conclude for certain that you're delusional."

"Do you know when it's happening?"

"I'm guessing Thursday, because they're still searching for Sonny Lile. Gaitano is gloating over the fact that Judge Sullivan tore up your get-out-of-jail card. He says two detectives from NOPD are flying here tomorrow. If they can reach a consensus on charging you, here or in Louisiana, they'll do it by Thursday. You'll be held for extradition, so this is way too serious for you to consider talking."

"She did, but there's a problem. I went there this morning and they told me they closed it out last week."

"Damn it, Kim, that's impossible! I've been there once—to open it. Those files prove everything."

"Les, did you go back and add Sonny as an authorized signer with full access rights?"

He nodded, disgusted with his own stupidity. "I trusted him, in case something happened to me. And I told him where I kept the key."

"Well he closed it on the day he left for New Orleans."

"Why would he do that?" He pounded his fist on the table.

"There's more. Gaitano says you denied sending Sonny to San Juan Island on the night your cabin was prowled. But they photographed every car on the early sailing and ran the plates. One was registered to a lowlife with a record from Seattle, a loser named Shawn Byers. They questioned him and he admitted he was there—claimed he was camping. On a rainy Monday? A real Boy Scout, this guy.

"They let him go but they kept an eye on him. Somebody connected to the investigation seemed to think he was a former perp of Sonny's. A few days later they pulled him over, decided he was high, and found some pot in his car. I know, it's legal, but you still can't drive under the influence, so they arrested him."

"Let me guess," said Les. "They cut him a deal to make him talk."

Kim nodded. "He confessed he was there with Sonny. He said they split up so Sonny could create a diversion—the fire. He admitted to raiding five cabins including yours. He said they dumped everything off a pier. In exchange for a plea deal he offered to show them which pier. They flew up with divers on Saturday and recovered almost everything. Your stuff was in the water too, so they had to tell your wife."

"I can imagine how that went," said Les. "I guess I should be glad I'm here."

"This looks bad, Les. Byers will testify that Sonny told him they were doing this in your employ."

"So why not arrest me sooner?"

"Because by anyone's account he makes a pathetic witness, plus what he says Sonny said is hearsay. That's why they're hot to question Sonny.

They've had a warrant out for him since they picked up Byers on Friday, but of course they never thought to look for him in New Orleans. They'd been asking NOPD to track down Victor Garving for questioning."

"Wait," Les said. "Sonny told me Gaitano had already spoken with Victor and was flying him here for an interview."

"I don't believe it. Gaitano said NOPD couldn't find him until he turned up dead."

He thought back to Victor's blackmail letter, the one he intercepted from Beverly's mail. It was a fake.

"Anyway," Kim continued, "with Victor dead and Sonny missing, they got a warrant for your credit card records."

"A judge found probable cause for that? He could feel the walls closing in. "I've been set up," he finally sighed. "Sonny was lying to Byers and he was lying to me. I didn't order any break-ins. I told him my phone might be there, but I had no idea he'd go and steal it. Who in God's name is he working for, Kim?"

"Gaitano thinks he's working for your client. But he thinks you may be in on it too. In fact, he thinks she's more than just your client. Why in the world would you send Sonny to New Orleans with seventy-five thousand in cash?"

Wait until they learn it was a hundred and ten grand, and that I got the rest when I tapped her line of credit. He thought for a moment, then answered, "I sent him because Gaitano had accused my client of killing her first husband, Ty Pruitt. I wanted Sonny to find out what Victor knew about that, if anything."

"And for that he needed seventy-five grand?"

"No. That was for something else. Fasten your seat belt, Kim, but a missing broker named Dwight Bonadelli managed to embezzle forty-four million dollars from Byron Wells just days before he died. No one knows this yet. He's somewhere in Mexico as we speak, and Sonny went to find him on my nickel. The money was to cover his expenses and to bring him current on some other matters. He left New Orleans a day before the fire. Someone must have followed him there, because I spoke with him myself from the Cayman Islands on Sunday night."

"Seventy-five grand sounds like hush money, Les. Look, either you're scamming me or you've been scammed. San Juan County has filed arson and burglary charges on Sonny Lile. And the New Orleans D.A. is about to charge him with murder one. He's wanted in two states, and as soon as you tell Gaitano about this missing broker, they'll be hunting him down in Mexico. Do you really think he's going to help you once they find him?"

Les wilted as the gravity of the moment finally descended. "I've got nothing to hide, Kim. I'll do whatever it takes to show them I've been set up. I was planning to spill my guts on the morning that fucker arrested me. It's his own fault he lost three critical days by making me sit in here and rot."

"He won't buy it, Les. You've become a laughingstock. He told me about a certain nightclub fire eleven years ago, and the lawsuit you filed on behalf of Victor Garving. He says Sonny was your expert and that he probably torched the club. He thinks with Beverly in the news, that Victor was blackmailing you three, so you let Sonny go down there and settle an old score."

"That's bullshit," said Les. Looking at Kim, he experienced what it must be like for one of his own clients, once he'd written them off as lying. "The insurance company agreed it wasn't arson."

"The problem is who you hang with, Les. Even Sonny's friends call him a sleazeball. And Beverly—what does it say about her that you're spending seventy-five grand of your own money to check up on her story? How did you get involved with these people? They make you look like scum."

"Kim," he pleaded, "humor me for a second and assume I'm innocent. What do they have? I sent my investigator to New Orleans with a return ticket for Saturday. Big deal. Victor died on Sunday. Sonny was onto his next assignment by then. He wasn't even in New Orleans. And who cares if some low-life pothead says that Sonny says I sent them to the Island on a crime spree? It's hearsay and it's bullshit."

"But when they find Sonny?" queried Kim. "It won't be hearsay then, will it?"

"If Sonny's guilty, and from what you're saying he clearly is, well, they're never going to find him. But if they do, he'll rat on whoever hired him. It wasn't me."

"So exactly how much are you going to spill on Thursday? You do realize, I hope, that you can't violate your client's privilege."

"Did you tell them about my missing files?"

"No. I didn't feel like bringing up evidence that doesn't exist. Plus that frickin' bank box is just another tie between you and Sonny."

Les sighed. "There was email in there between Wells and Nakamura that showed who was behind the crash. The rest of what I had, boxes worth, was stolen from my house on Saturday. We can recreate some of it from the digital files of Byron's lawyer and I've got pictures to prove what a mess they made of my house, searching for my files. They taped a death threat to my computer."

"Who is they, Les?"

"I've got two more leads, either of which could break this open. The cops aren't even close. But until I pursue them, Kim, I shouldn't tell you any more."

"Which means you aren't really going to spill on Thursday. If you're not ready to kiss and tell, Les, then you shouldn't talk at all."

"We both know they don't think I'm guilty. They're trying to scare me so I'll rat-out my client. And maybe I will, by giving them evidence that isn't privileged, but not until I've satisfied myself she's really guilty. Right now it's just as likely she's the patsy."

"If you tease them, Les, it's like defying them to charge you, so they can hold you. An obstruction charge at least. Gaitano claims he's got slam-dunk probable cause with Byers' story. So don't go asking for trouble, especially if you've got nothing to hide."

"I'll tell them why I sent Sonny to New Orleans and I'll clue them in about the missing forty-four million. That should take the heat off me for a while."

"Fair enough. So what about your leads?"

"Actually, I could use your help with them. The first is David Dietrich. I think he knows a lot, and that his life may be in danger. He could spill once I tell him what I know, but there's a lawsuit pending. I'd have to go through his lawyer, Mike Farrago."

"I know Farrago," said Kim, rolling his eyes.

"Well he and I are on shitty terms. So maybe you could call him. Get him to let me talk to his client. Tell him it's urgent and that I won't discuss the Digitron case. My preference would be to meet alone with Dietrich, but if Farrago has to be there, fine.

"Dietrich knows who did this, Kim. Find out what you can about him. Maybe he'll team up with me. The sooner we go to Gaitano with something solid the better. Try for a dinner meeting on Thursday night—as soon as I get out. Oh, and I might need to borrow a little cash."

"I'll do some checking on him and I'll call Farrago, though he'll probably say no. Maybe I can be your go-between, should you see fit to fill me in. It sounds like you know way more than you're letting on."

"Right, and look where it got me. For your sake, Kim, I'm gonna keep you out of it. I owe you just for coming."

"Les, you'd do the same. Now what about your other lead?"

"She's Beverly's alibi, but I need to find her. Beverly won't tell me who she is, but Marcia would know. Beverly went road-tripping with her on the weekend Byron died. Get her name and phone number for me if you can."

"Your client is unwilling to name her alibi?"

"My client is starting to lose it."

"I think you've crept out with her on the ledge, that you've convinced yourself the Titanic will never sink."

"I almost forgot. Did your associate get through to my mom?"

"Yes and you'll be happy to know he refuses to tell me what that was about."

"Good. One more thing. Ask Marcia to find a manila envelope at the bottom of my sock drawer. It's got the pictures of our ransacked house, the death note, and a listening device they attached to our phone line. Bring it all on Thursday."

"Anything else?"

"The Galileo."

"Come again?"

"It's a virtual reality headset. It looks like robot glasses. Did Beverly say anything about it? She was supposed to give it to you because we need to show it to Gaitano."

"I don't know what you're talking about."

"Forget it," he sighed, his voice trailing off. "Can you ask Marcia to come see me?"

"I'll ask, but honestly, Les, it's a long shot."

CHAPTER THIRTY-ONE

Tuesday faded into Wednesday as he felt life ebbing from his body. Most of the inmates slept, like animals at the zoo. But he could hardly close his eyes, and when he did, fiery, yellow-splashed nightmares rocked his sleep.

When it was finally his turn to scan the morning *Times*, he was relieved to see no mention of his name. Near the bottom of the front page, however, a seemingly unrelated article grabbed his eye.

> Virtual Retinal Display comes of age
> Your retina becomes IMAX screen with latest 'reality'

> Two leading University of Washington computer technologists and a Seattle-based start-up company called Retina-Vision have made huge strides this year in reducing the footprint required for beaming electronic images directly onto the human retina, obviating the need for a video screen. Retina-Vision is the exclusive licensee of a breakthrough HMD equipped with two million micro mirrors, accelerometers, scanners and a gyroscope.

The name, Retina-Vision, had surfaced in Byron's files. According to the article the retinal technology had its genesis at the University of Washington's "Human Interface Technology Lab." The article mentioned neither Wells nor Nakamura. He read on:

> Digitron, a supporter of the lab, has expressed interest in funding further R & D on immersive VRD. The technology will be the

primary topic at tomorrow's meeting in Seattle of the Virtual Worlds Consortium.

Nakamura had planned to unveil his prototype at the Consortium. It was a strange sensation, a story big enough to make headlines, yet Nakamura was years ahead of Retina-Vision, whose research and plans he'd stolen.

"McKee?"

He looked up from the *Times*.

"Let's go." It was the guard again. They were almost pals. He led him through a steel labyrinth to the visitation block.

Behind the glass and wire Beverly looked as trapped as he felt. "I meant to come yesterday," she apologized, "but I couldn't get here. How are you and have you seen Kim?"

"I'm okay," he said wearily. "He was here. Has Gaitano brought you in?"

"No, but they're following me, just like you said. Are they going to arrest me?"

"They could."

"Will you be getting out tomorrow?"

"Hopefully, once they finish with me. Kim says they're trying to find Sonny. Did he call you on Monday night?"

"Yes. Peggy gave me your keys and Sonny's phone was in your car. I guess they'd searched it, but they didn't take his phone. I did and Sonny called it at 10:00 p.m., just like he promised.

"I said you wanted me to take his call. After a long pause he asked me where you were. I told him you'd been arrested for Victor's murder. He sounded like he didn't believe me. I asked him if he was still in Mexico and he said yes.

"I said he's wanted for questioning and he should get back here right away. He said he wasn't sure he could do that, because he was close to recovering the money. I asked him what that meant—it's my money after all—but he just hung up.

"He didn't ask me how Victor died or why you'd been arrested. It just sounded like he wasn't coming back. It was clear he didn't want to talk to me."

"At least he called. Did he say whether he got the money?"

"Yes. He actually thanked me for it."

"Good. We'll have a paper trail to prove he was in Cancun, not New Orleans."

"For all we know he was in New Orleans when he called you on Sunday. He probably flew to Cancun just to get the money. I bet he's got Victor's hundred grand as well."

"It was a hundred and ten grand."

"Not to change the subject, Leslie, but I have a message for you," she said, lowering her voice. "From David."

He raised an eyebrow. "Really. What is it?"

"He's willing to meet with you, though his lawyer said no way. He's agreed to do it discreetly. Tomorrow night. He said it's urgent because he's leaving the country, possibly for good. He'd like you to drive out to the Quinault Lodge on the Olympic Peninsula. He's been staying there because he says it's not safe for him in Seattle. He said to come at eight, that he's made reservations at the Lodge."

"What did you tell him?"

"That I'd pass it along. Leslie, do you have to go? I don't trust him."

"I thought he and Byron were bosom buddies."

"The firing and the lawsuit made them enemies. David blamed Byron for getting him in trouble."

"Weren't they in on this together? You must have some idea. You said if one was cheating so was the other."

"I didn't know there was a conspiracy," she answered. "Byron never talked to me about his work, remember?"

"What about that video device I showed you in my car? And the gloves. Did you look for them?"

"Yes. I found Sonny's phone, but the other things were gone. What do they have to do with this?"

"I'm not sure. Gaitano must have them. I need to talk with Dietrich. Let him know I'm coming."

"Leslie, can I go with you?" Her open hand pressed against the glass. "I'm going crazy. I need to be with you. I haven't stopped thinking about the other night."

She said even more in the charged silence that followed. "I have an idea," she offered. "Let me go ahead of you. I'll pay for adjoining cabins at the Kalaloch Lodge, which is just up the road from Lake Quinault. You probably won't finish with David until ten or so, which means you have to spend the night."

His pulse quickened. "What if the cops follow you?"

"I'll make sure they don't, and I'll check us in using made-up names."

He knew he should get up and walk away. But where? Her soft voice and her gaze anchored him as powerfully as the shackles he'd worn to court. "What names will you make up?" he asked, sounding like a fool, even to himself. "You'd need a phony credit card to reserve two cabins."

"I've got it covered. I'll reserve yours under Daniel Wallace."

He nodded, half-drunk with anticipation.

"What are you telling Marcia?" she asked.

He looked at her and noticed she still wore her ring. His was gone, but only because they'd confiscated it when they booked him. "She threw me out, remember? She's probably filed for divorce by now." All these years he'd sworn it wouldn't happen. Not to him. But it was happening. At this very moment she was probably holed up in the office of one of his most hated adversaries. The truth was, he wasn't sure he cared.

CHAPTER THIRTY-TWO

No sooner had she departed than the guard reappeared. "Keep your seat, McKee. Your wife is on her way."

"Maybe she posted my bail," he answered hopefully.

"Nope, just visiting," he grunted and left.

As she entered the cubicle, her dusky-rose complexion looked sallow under fluorescent light. Her lavender eyes were red-rimmed and puffy with dark circles.

"Hello, Marsh," he said quietly. She was silent. Her tears spoke for her.

Finally she stammered, "I can't believe this, Les. I just can't believe it. Detective Gaitano says you're going to be charged with Victor's murder."

"Marsh, I'm innocent."

She looked at him as if they were meeting for the first time.

"Do you want to know something terrible?" she said. "I don't believe you."

As she nervously ran her hands through her hair, he noticed she'd removed her ring. He thought he caught a glimpse of the old woman she would one day become.

"They arrested the man who broke into our cabin. Gaitano says you set that up. He says you sent Sonny to get the phone as soon as you realized it was there. He says it makes you an accessory to Byron's murder. You and Beverly were going to run off with all that money, weren't you?" she said tonelessly.

"Never," he told her. "I tried to explain this to you on Sunday night—"

She waved him away dismissively. "Don't bother denying it," she said. "You've probably been fucking her since the day she left Victor."

"That's bullshit."

"Les, your mother called," she continued without looking at him. "She was hysterical."

Fear stabbed him. "Is she all right?"

"Yes. After she got your bizarre warning she left and she's been staying with a friend. And thank God for that. Someone broke into her apartment last night, now she's too scared to go home, so she's not even certain what they took. Les, how did you know that was going to happen?"

Her words crashed all around him, like sheets of glass. "Beverly," he answered, as if in a trance. "She's behind the murders. She thought I'd sent my pictures to Mom."

"You're working with her, Les. She took your phone from my purse and left it at the cabin, so Sonny could get it. You sent him to Chicago, to get those pictures from your mom. And he went to New Orleans, to kill Victor for you and Bev.

"They know he called her on Monday night. They know Peggy wired him more money. Then you have the gall to send some awful message to her through a perfect stranger, to flee for her life so Sonny could get inside? You're very sick, Les."

"Marsh, the message I sent her said to have the police set up surveillance."

"Right. And the Chicago police are going to listen to some little old lady, who received a secondhand coded message from her son, who's in jail on murder charges? Have you gone mad? You and Beverly needed her to leave the house. You're up to your neck in this."

"You're wrong, sweetheart. You've got to believe me. I'm going to Gaitano. He's going to nail her and then you'll see. I had nothing to do with this."

"Do you think I'm stupid?" she asked incredulously. "I saw her leaving here just now. I suppose she came to confess?"

He tried to look her in the eye, to convince her he wasn't lying. But she refused to meet his gaze.

"Your mother wants me to bring Breanna and stay with her someplace safe. I'll be flying out this afternoon."

"Marsh, you're making a huge mistake. We need to talk." His head was pounding with images of Beverly—smiling, sobbing, and throwing her head back in gloating laughter at the havoc she'd wreaked.

"You're a liar and a manipulator," she said without pleasure. "Maybe it helps you as a lawyer, but I didn't marry a lawyer."

"Marsh," he said desperately, "I never slept with her."

"And I'm the Queen of England," she replied evenly. "I leave in a couple hours. Breanna will be staying with my parents until Saturday. If you get out by then you can say good-bye to her before my dad brings her to Chicago. But do yourself a favor, don't even try talking to my parents."

"Why, what have you told them?"

"Everything. That you maxed out our credit cards and borrowed another sixty thousand dollars while we were on break. They want me to get Bree away from you, Les. They're going to get me the best divorce attorney they can find, a much better one than you."

"Maybe it's best."

"So you're glad we're through?"

"I'm glad you'll both be safe and away from here."

"I'm sure you are."

He knew she despised him and he could hardly blame her. He was starting to despise himself. "Marsh, believe me, I don't want you to leave me. I only want you safe. We'll settle this once I get out and prove to you I'm innocent. How are you getting to the airport?"

Reluctantly, she answered, her reserve a reflection of her pain. "My dad is taking me. Why?"

"Maybe you should drive yourself and leave the van at the airport. I'll arrange to get it once I'm released. That way your parents won't have to deal with me. I'm probably the last person they want to see right now."

"That's true," she said bitterly. "Fine, I'll leave it somewhere on the third floor. Good luck finding it."

As she rose to leave, he asked her quickly, "Did you give that envelope to Kim?"

She nodded.

"Then you saw what they did to our house while you were gone. That's what I was trying to warn you about, but you threw me out before I got a chance."

"I didn't open it," she said impatiently. "Don't you get it, Les? I'm not playing your cruel games any more. Good-bye."

"Wait," he begged. "Did Kim ask you about Beverly's friend—the one she drove down the coast with?"

"Supposedly drove," she said. "Her name is Monica Taylor. She lives near Overlake in the Pine Brook Apartments. She was not involved. This little fiasco seems to be a private party. Just you and Beverly. And to hell with the rest of us."

CHAPTER THIRTY-THREE

On Thursday morning he was escorted once again through the suspended skyway, down to the fifth floor of the King County Courthouse and into the Prosecutor's Office. He was deposited into an interview room where Kim sat waiting for him.

"Did you get a chance to call Farrago?" Les spoke in a low voice, drawing close to Kim.

"Yeah, and he said to stay the hell away from his client, that if you try anything he'll go straight to the Bar on you."

Les sighed. "Did you find anything on Dietrich?"

Kim handed him a printed dossier. He scanned it quickly until an item caught his eye.

```
Previous employment:
University of Washington, Human Interface
Technology Lab
```

Dietrich must have given them the schematics for the VRD. The picture was suddenly clearer—*3,000 lines x 4,000 lines clearer.* The Galileo came from Dietrich!

"Good morning everyone!" It was Gaitano, who hadn't bothered knocking. At his side was another familiar face, Amy Gifford, King County's most tenacious prosecutor. There were no detectives from New Orleans, though Les assumed they were behind the glass.

"Can I ask something?"

"Later," said Gaitano. "Why did you send Sonny Lile to New Orleans?"

"I wanted him to find out whether Victor had an opinion on your theory that Beverly might have killed her first husband," he answered promptly. He was saying it so often it was starting to sound like the truth.

"Bullshit," said Gaitano. "If you thought she'd murdered number one, you had to figure number two was in on it with her. In fact, she gave number two the insurance money, so he wasn't about to cop. Try a different explanation."

"When they divorced, Victor was blackmailing her, though she never told me why. All these years later you got me thinking that maybe it was Tyler Pruitt. If Victor was blackmailing her, then maybe he wasn't involved. I thought Sonny should at least ask him for me. And apparently he confessed. He told Sonny she loaded Tyler up with pain pills when he was drunk and high.

"Sonny left New Orleans after that—a day before the fire. He called me from the Cayman Islands on Sunday. If he was going to kill him, he wouldn't have left you clues—like tickets charged to me. He went to *talk*, not kill."

"How'd he find him?"

"Same way you did, I guess."

"Pardon?" asked Gaitano, looking up from his notes.

"On Sunday, he said you'd talked to Victor and you were going to fly him here."

"Wait a minute, counselor. I've never spoken to Victor Garving."

It was as Les had feared—Victor's blackmail letter was Sonny's fraud. He hadn't even been to Beverly's mailbox. He and Byers went straight to the island to get the phone. He was working for the killers. The blackmail letter was his way of tricking Les into sending him to New Orleans. He wondered if Beverly had put him up to it.

"Let's back up because I'm confused," Gaitano said, though Les found that unlikely. "You're saying you honestly believe your client murdered Tyler Pruitt?"

"Well, it's based on double-hearsay, but before you locked me up, I was going to confront her with it." It was his veiled offer to wear a wire in exchange for immunity from prosecution.

"She's visited you twice," he remarked.

"We didn't discuss Ty Pruitt. Plus whatever we discussed is privileged,

I'm still her lawyer." He would give them nothing more against his client until they dealt. He was already begging for a malpractice claim from her.

"You've got to be joking," Gaitano scoffed. "Now you're covering for her, after you just finished telling us she's a killer?"

"I didn't say that," he answered, backtracking. "Victor did."

"Was Sonny working for her?" asked Gaitano.

"It's possible. Though it's just as likely that someone followed Sonny to New Orleans, to kill Victor after he left town."

"You mean they were framing Sonny . . . and you?"

"Exactly."

"Who besides your client would want to murder Victor?"

"Whoever killed Byron wants to pin it on Beverly or me by having Victor turn up dead."

"They couldn't frame you for killing Victor unless they knew your history—that you've got a reason to want him dead. When we question Mrs. Wells, will she admit that Victor was blackmailing the three of you for helping him commit an arson? That would give you motive, right?"

"She's liable to claim anything if she learns I've incriminated her."

"Why would Sonny lie and tell you I'd spoken with Victor?"

"Search me," said Les.

"None of this adds up, counselor. How about this instead? Sonny convinced you that we were flying Victor here. It's not true, but you believed him. So to shut him up about the arson you sent Sonny down to purchase his silence, but he killed him instead. And now he's disappeared, to spend your seventy-five grand on a beach somewhere before he dies."

Les was mildly impressed. For once Gaitano had earned his cocky smile. "Sonny left here on a three-week assignment," he said patiently. "New Orleans was just a whistle-stop. The money was intended to finance his work in Mexico. He was going to be hiring several colleagues."

Gaitano ignored the bait. "You say he called you on Sunday night. What time?"

"About ten thirty, our time."

"Did he say anything about Victor being dead?"

"No, he said he was in the Caymans and about to leave for Mexico. My assistant wired five thousand dollars to him in Cancun on the morning you arrested me. We have the records to prove it. And he's called me since from there."

"How would you know that?" fired Gaitano. "You've been in the clink since Monday."

"Beverly took his call but he denied any knowledge of Victor's death."

"Did she relate this to you during one of her recent jail visits?"

He froze. If he revealed anything she told him while he was in jail, he'd be waiving her attorney-client privilege. It would mean they could compel him to testify about everything she'd said. He had malpracticed once again.

"No, she didn't," he lied.

"Then what makes you say he called her on Monday from Cancun?"

"She told Mr. Hanson, who related it to me."

Kim nearly spit out the coffee he was sipping.

"Is that true, Mr. Hanson?" Gaitano asked.

"Yes, it's true," he replied as he shot Les a look of cold fury. Gaitano's restless gaze returned to Les.

"How did Mrs. Wells happen to have your phone?"

"She got it from my car because I was expecting Sonny's call."

"Why didn't your wife take Sonny's call?"

"My wife is not involved in this. She thinks I'm having an affair with Mrs. Wells."

"Are you?"

"No," he said defiantly.

"I see," Gaitano said with a smirk. "Does your wife think Beverly killed her husband?"

"I'm sure you would know better what she thinks, since the two of you are on such good terms."

Gaitano gave him a withering look. "Why in the hell did you send Sonny to Mexico and the Caribbean?" He was suddenly sniffing at the bait.

"It'll be on the front page of every paper starting Monday—when a stockbroker named Dwight Bonadelli fails to return from the Mexican Riviera." He filled them in on the missing broker.

When he'd finished, Amy Gifford exhaled dramatically and turned to Gaitano with a look of bewilderment. "Forty-four million was taken from the community chest, just days before these murders—and your department doesn't even know about it yet?" She peered over the rims of her reading glasses at Les. "Do tell," she said.

He ran it down, from Bonadelli to the Japanese, and as he did he started to relax. He was no longer on the hot seat. Neither was Beverly, he realized.

With each question and answer, he was increasingly uncertain about her guilt. Somehow she was involved, but this was bigger than her. She deserved a chance to explain the break-in at his mother's apartment. He was starting to regret his lies and implications about Ty Pruitt.

"Are we close to wrapping this up, Detective?" asked Kim.

"We have a little more," replied Gaitano. "Pursuant to a search warrant, I have a print-out of your client's calendar." Turning to Les, he reached in his briefcase and produced a hard-copy version. "I'd like you to explain an entry you made in January."

He leaned over and observed where he'd typed *DOA 4/13* on the January screen, along with other notes.

"This is where I keep dates and notes to myself," he said. "I didn't make this entry in January, if that's what you're implying. I typed it on April 14. DOA means Date of Accident."

"I know what it means, counselor, but there are no entries for February or March." He had to admit, this would not look good to a jury.

Gaitano continued. "We have a recording of your call to 911. You told the dispatcher there were six men on board. We've been out to your house, Les. There's no way you could have seen them that clearly."

"Yes there is," he insisted. "They passed right over and I was zooming in on them."

"That brings me to another point. Your neighbor, Ms. Dwyer, says she never saw a camera phone. She says whatever it was, you were pointing it at the balloon. She described it as a small device with a blinking light. Like a detonator."

"Or a camera phone."

"She was standing in her kitchen with the window open and she claims she distinctly heard you say 'perfect,' right before the blast. The F.A.A. has recovered the remains of a receiver-detonator that came from inside the tank."

"What happened to your nitro theory?" he asked.

"How'd you hear about that?"

"I guess Sonny was good for something." He'd started to wonder if Sonny had told him anything that was true.

"This is my interview," said Gaitano, "not yours, but I'll indulge you enough to say that we're not quite sure what to make of the lab results on the nitro. We're convinced the detonation occurred inside the tank."

"So you think I detonated it with my phone? How absurd."

"Really? We think you sent Sonny to San Juan Island to destroy the phone, or the detonator, or whatever it was. Maybe there never were any pictures. Maybe that was your cover story when your neighbor spotted you with the device."

"That's bullshit," Les charged. "My phone was blinking because it was recording. We both know my neighbor's got a drinking problem, now I'm starting to worry about you. Have you forgotten you were tracking my signal?"

"Cell phones and detonators can be one and the same, Les. Your neighbor will testify quite soberly that you were acting strange that afternoon, that you couldn't get out of there fast enough once she saw you. Then you came sneaking back that night without your wife and almost shot her when she asked to see your pictures. She says when she asked you if she could see your phone, you tossed it aside and ordered her out."

"It was a phone, detective, identical to my wife's. We bought them on the same day."

"I'm not so sure." Gaitano smiled wryly. "They make an app for just about everything these days. You know our divers never found it."

"Kim tells me you recovered *some* of my stolen goods in the water. My phone is probably with the killers."

"I'm the one smelling bullshit, McKee. What in the hell are these?" he asked, holding up the wired gloves he'd taken from Les's Saab.

"They're virtual reality controllers."

"Where did you get them? Was it the night you contaminated a crime scene in Kirkland? I need to know about them. They've got embedded sensors and a transmitter-receiver. They're evidence, maybe related to detonating the bomb. So why were they in your car?"

"I could probably explain how they fit in if I thought you were listening." Les figured Gaitano had the Galileo and smartwatch and knew more than he was letting on.

"I can't get my mind around the coincidence of you filming her ex's murder. Do you expect us to believe you didn't know he was in that gondola?"

"I had no idea."

"Yet minutes later you were on the phone to her."

"We've covered that."

"We didn't notify his parents for another hour."

"His father said you called them shortly after six. Are you saying it was later?"

"Again, *my* interview," Gaitano said, "but yes, it was much later—almost 7:00 by the time we called, meaning they were all late to the recital.

"On April 21, shortly after I dropped you at your office, you called her again using Sonny's phone. What was that about?"

"We figured you were tapping my phones, so Sonny gave me his. He claimed it was secure."

"Not with me sitting in your parking lot. I picked up the signal before it hit the tower, which we then traced to his phony account. After that, his phone was on our radar. The call was suspect, Les, since he went straight to Friday Harbor from your office. It proves you were acting in concert with her, even if she wasn't home to take your call."

"You should be working for the NSA, but it doesn't prove he went to San Juan Island."

"Certainly you've read about our witness? His story is enough for us to charge you with obstruction and with conspiracy to commit arson and burglary. Accessory to murder may be next. Don't you think it's time to cooperate?"

His heart was hammering against his ribcage. He wanted to tell them that she'd rented the Corvette, but he couldn't risk giving them any more. He'd sold her down the river as it was, and what if she was innocent?

"Mr. McKee, would you like to confer with Mr. Hanson?"

"That won't be necessary, Detective. I've told you all I know. Shawn Byers is full of shit, and what he claims Sonny said is hearsay. Not a word of it would get to a jury."

"Do you have any idea why the killers want your pictures, seemingly as much or more than me?"

"Maybe." He was suddenly ready to take the plunge. "I photographed a yellow Corvette by my house, just moments before the crash. It was shadowing the balloon. I assumed it was the chase car, but I've since learned the chase car was disabled and didn't arrive until after the crash. I think the person with the detonator was in the car I filmed, waiting for them to land. Maybe my photo can be enlarged or enhanced."

He knew it would be days until they stumbled on Beverly's rented

Corvette, enough time for him to confront her about the burglary in Chicago. She was the only one he'd told.

"That's helpful," Gaitano offered, though curiously he didn't follow up. "Anything else?"

He glanced furtively at the clock. "That's all," he replied, masking his rush to leave.

"Can I assume you'll be withdrawing as her lawyer?"

"Yes, but it won't take effect for ten more days."

"Can you manage to stay out of trouble until then?" It was his first hint that charges would not be filed—at least not today. Les said nothing as Gaitano stood to leave.

"Don't leave town, is that understood? And one more thing. Will you submit to a polygraph?"

"Absolutely," he replied, before Kim could wave him off.

He leaned forward as Kim whispered quietly in his ear. "No way, Les."

"I'll be fine," he whispered back.

"How about 9:30 tomorrow morning?" asked Gaitano. "We have some guests from New Orleans who'd like to attend."

He considered his appointment with Dietrich and his all-nighter with Beverly. "Not to insult your guests, but I've been in here since Monday," he replied. "Can you at least give me until tomorrow afternoon?"

"First floor. Two o'clock," said Gifford.

"Great," said Les, "Can I leave now?"

"Not yet." Gifford reached in her briefcase as she spoke. "This is a judge-issued subpoena for your phone, the one with the pictures, an affidavit of probable cause, and a criminal complaint for *Obstruction of a Criminal Investigation*. I have a warrant for your arrest, but I'll hold off serving it so you can bring us the phone on your own, tomorrow, when you come here for your polygraph."

"What?" protested Kim, studying the papers. "The court can't issue a subpoena if you haven't filed charges."

Les looked on, shocked and confused.

"Looks to me like the Court just did," said Gifford. "We can file the charges if you'd like. We thought he could use the next twenty-four hours to bring it to us without forcing our hand."

"Read the affidavit," Gaitano added. "We had detectives follow Sonny Lile to a hush-hush meeting with McKee on April 22, on Bainbridge Island.

They photographed him handing the phone to McKee, one day after the break-ins. In exchange, McKee gave him a check."

Kim looked at Les as if to ask, "Is this true?"

"He can't deny it," Gaitano said cagily, as if reading Kim's mind. "Have a look for yourself." Gaitano handed him two black and white photographs, taken from inside the Harbour Pub. The first showed Sonny, handing Les what was clearly a phone. The second showed them exchanging what looked like a folded letter or possibly a check. Les recalled the unmistakable click of the analog camera during one of these exchanges.

"We were meeting about Sonny's next assignment," Les said. "He was leaving in the morning and, yes, he loaned me his phone—the one you traced—it was still in my car when you searched it. I'm sure you left it there to see if he would call me on it. Detective, if he led your men to Bainbridge then it proves he was trying to set me up."

"Save it for the polygraph, McKee. You just finished telling us he gave you his phone on April 21. This phone was yours. You went from there to Beverly's and she ended up at your house all night."

"What does it mean?" Les asked Kim, while scanning the papers.

"It means they think you or your client have the phone. You're now under a subpoena and if you don't turn it over to them tomorrow, they're going to file criminal charges and ask the Court to find you in contempt. If the judge agrees he can hold without a conviction until you purge your contempt, meaning you can't bail out."

"You're in contempt," said Gifford. "At least you will be by tomorrow afternoon. But don't worry, we'll let you go as soon as we get the phone. And don't even think about deleting any pictures."

"And if I don't have it?"

"Then we'll hold you here until she turns it in." Gifford did not look up. She was correcting the times on several copies as she handed Kim a hearing notice for criminal contempt. "Consider yourself served. The hearing will be at 4:00 p.m., right after his polygraph."

"You'll be there, Mr. Hanson?" asked Gaitano.

"Yes," said Kim sharply. As they filed out, he shot a fiery glance at Les. "I expect to see you in my office first thing in the morning."

Before Les could collect himself, Kim handed him a couple hundred bucks to help him get up and running, then stormed out ahead of all the others.

CHAPTER THIRTY FOUR

He was released shortly after 3:00 p.m. Traveling on foot and by bus, he eluded the cops who were on his tail. He eventually hailed a cab for the airport. He couldn't risk picking up the Saab from his office as they'd be watching it, waiting for him to surface.

Once at Sea-Tac he started searching for Marcia's van. Frustration turned to fatigue as he walked almost the entire third floor. When he finally found it, he was glad to see she'd left her parking ticket on the dash. He placed it under the seat, then convinced the attendant he'd lost it. To his surprise, she let him have free parking.

He drove first to Exotic Rentals. "Remember me?" he asked the manager.

"Of course," said Ramone. "I read about you. Did you really get arrested?"

"For questioning. Listen, about that Corvette, I need to know if someone other than Mrs. Wells reserved it?"

"I don't think so," he said. "When she called, she said she'd looked all over for it—"

"I know. But how can you be sure it was her who called?"

"I guess I'm not. But she reminded me about the call."

"Did she mention a friend of hers, Monica Taylor?"

"No, she said something about her boyfriend, remember?"

"Yeah, I remember." He wanted to punch him for his help. "Thanks for your time."

His next stop was the Pine Brook Apartments. As he approached the complex, he rolled his eyes at the irony of its name. Developers, forever compelled to invoke the name of whatever natural wonder they destroyed. He searched the directory for her name then rang her doorbell and waited. The door opened just a crack.

"Monica?" he asked.

She nodded. From what little he could see, she looked short but athletic, with shoulder-length black hair.

"I'm Les McKee, Beverly's lawyer. I need to ask you a few quick questions."

She shrank back. "Leave me alone."

As she started to close the door, he inserted quickly, "I can serve you with a subpoena if you'd prefer." He rang the bell again.

"Go away, or I'll call the police," she shouted.

Resigned, he turned, though he'd learned something. Her hair was long and wavy. Beverly had lied to him about their dual haircuts in a Cannon Beach salon.

He drove from there around the southern tip of Puget Sound, in strict defiance of Gaitano's order to "stay in town." Just beyond the capitol rotunda in Olympia, he turned west on Highway 12 and continued past Aberdeen, then took Highway 101 to Lake Quinault. The Olympic National Park, North America's largest temperate rain forest, rose in emerald splendor before him. And snuggled deep in the heart of the mammoth weald was the historic lodge on Lake Quinault.

It was almost 8:00 p.m. when he arrived. The sun had set and dusk was settling in. He recognized Dietrich's silver BMW from the night outside the elder Wells's house. He parked further up the road, at a small general store across from the lodge. As he approached on foot, Dietrich opened the door before he knocked.

"I saw you coming," he said as Les stepped in.

"Thanks for agreeing to this," said Les. The two shook hands. "Does Farrago know I'm here?"

"Are you kidding? He'd blow a vessel. I'm going behind his back since you agreed not to discuss the Digitron case. But before we chat, one thing."

He reached out as Les stepped back, half-expecting a right hook. Instead Dietrich flashed a thin-lipped smile. "I need to see if you're wearing a wire. I don't trust anyone."

"Suit yourself," he replied, raising his arms enough for Dietrich to frisk him.

"Satisfied?" asked Les. "I'm clean. So let's get some dinner already. After three days of taxpayer-funded meals, I'm starving."

"Later," a taciturn Dietrich answered. He sat down on the couch and fingered the bling in his ear, glaring at Les expectantly. "So?"

Les took a seat across from him, starkly aware that his hunger pangs would have to wait.

CHAPTER THIRTY-FIVE

Les was hesitant to begin.

"What," said Dietrich flatly, "you wanna roll to see who goes first?"

"For starters," Les began, "I know what's going on. Wells and Nakamura were jumping ship—leaving VVG and Digitron with the Quantum chip. They were starting INTERACT. Several VVG directors were in on it with them—the ones we deposed in Kyoto. But the inner circle was furious with Byron over press leaks in Seattle. You weren't too happy with him either, since his big mouth got you fired. But it seems he *wanted* to get canned. He was out to ruin Beverly in their divorce."

Past Dietrich's broad shoulder he thought he glimpsed some movement in the trees, just outside the room. When he looked again the dark branches were still. The entire setting felt surreal, like he'd stepped into a trap.

"Anyway," he continued, "Whoever killed them wants you dead as well. You were in on this with them up to your eyeballs, or should I say your retinas. I know about your work at the UW. You stole the specs for the VRD, then the three of you perfected it in record time. Nakamura was going to reveal his Galileo today, as a matter of fact, at the Virtual Worlds Consortium in Seattle.

"But when the press connected him to Byron, the others got scared and wanted to cut you two from the team. They wanted to wait another year, as it would've been too obvious how they'd obtained the source code they needed and the VRD. Nakamura disagreed. He was under too much pressure to break away, to prevent VVG from killing his patent. He voted to stick with the plan and forge ahead. So he and Wells were murdered. And you're next—unless we stop them."

"You're laughable," said Dietrich. "You have no idea who killed them. But you're right about my being next. In fact I'd be dead by now if it weren't for you."

"Come again?"

"Your pictures. I know where they are. And they're the only reason I'm still alive. I overheard you telling Fred about your video that night. I knew if I could get my hands on it, even if it turned out that you filmed nothing, then I could blackmail them into leaving me alone.

"And now the word is out. They've been warned that if any harm should come my way, then your pictures will be going to the cops. But if they leave me be, their secret will stay safe."

"So you broke into my car?"

"You must have figured out that your registration was missing."

"Yes." Goose bumps rose on his arms. No one, not even Marcia, knew about his missing registration, which bore their new address.

"This is nuts. You know who's trying to kill you, yet you're keeping it from the cops? How did you get my phone? I assume you were the one who broke into my cabin?"

Dietrich smiled darkly. "She gave it to me."

Les looked at Dietrich as his mind started reeling.

"I was in your house that night. I arrived before you did with your daughter. In fact, I barely beat you. You were supposed to report the car prowl and wait for the cops. I'm pretty sure you would've killed me if your neighbor hadn't shown up when she did. I never pegged you as a gun owner, Les. Anyway, I didn't find your camera, and I was about to leave for the ballet instructor's house when I overheard your conversation with Ginny Dwyer.

"I could've sworn you told Fred it was a video camera, but then you flashed a cell phone at her. At least you could've checked it for the pictures. That would've spared me from taking it after you went upstairs to check on your little girl. I didn't think to look at it either until later that night.

"At first I thought you'd screwed up and forgot to push record, or maybe you were lying. So I had Beverly put it back. We decided there were no pictures—until she told me how your wife stumbled on them at the bottom of her purse."

"So you broke into my cabin?"

"Wrong again," he shook his head. "Beverly took it from Marcia while they were packing up to leave. Sonny came for it that night, but he was too late. Can you believe your own investigator is working for the killers?"

"Why is she helping you?"

"Let's just say we have a special friendship."

A jealous pang gripped him again despite the fact that Dietrich was gay.

"She knew if I could get my hands on your pictures, before any copies leaked, it might just keep me breathing."

"She said you're leaving the country. Why, if you think my pictures can keep you safe?"

"Because you sent a fucking copy to your mother, that's why. My leverage disappears the minute your pictures go in circulation. The killers will learn you didn't film shit. Plus they're digital, they can be manipulated until nobody can say for sure what was or wasn't on the originals. VVG has the means to put fucking Danica Patrick behind the wheel of that Corvette.

"But Les, do you really think she'd help me steal it if she was in on Byron's murder? If your pictures were evidence against her, she would have deleted them. She's freaking out that someone tried to set her up, but she's got an alibi if the cops get close. If anything, those pictures will prove she's innocent when they surface. They're safe with me and I can still use them to clear her if it comes to that."

"Interesting" said Les, who wasn't buying it. "It's a good thing I was able to warn off my mom. Sonny never found them because they're on her phone, not her computer, and she's not even in Chicago at the moment. She's going to forward them to Gaitano, so we'll know soon enough what they prove or don't."

"I've seen them, Les. They don't prove anything. Everybody is guessing and the killers are scared shitless. For Christ's sake they had Sonny break into your cabin while a cop was standing watch."

"I'm pretty sure I filmed the bomber. They can enlarge the pictures and trace the car if not the driver."

"She told me how the pilot's wife didn't make it to the scene. Nice investigation, Les."

"Did she tell you she was in the car I filmed?"

"She explained how Monica suggested the rental and the haircuts for their trip, but it wasn't Beverly behind the wheel."

"How can you be sure if you haven't traced the plates?"

"Okay, I'll admit, you filmed a Corvette that wasn't the balloonists'.

I can't read the license plate and I'm a software engineer. But let's say the technology exists to enlarge it and fill in the gaps. If the police track the killers with your picture, they'll know I released your phone—and I'll be dead. Trust me, it wasn't your girlfriend."

"Fuck you," said Les. He was livid. "You're out of time. You should come forward now. Help me solve this and they'll put you in witness protection."

"Sorry, Les. They'll have to crack it without me. I'm sure your mom will help them, but it can't be me. Sad thing is, we both know you're lying. You were trying to entrap your client with bad intelligence about your mom. You sent nothing to her or she would have sent it back."

"I'll tell Gaitano you have my phone."

"If you make trouble for me, McKee, I'll deny this conversation happened. But I won't deny the meeting. In fact I'll tell Farrago how you tracked me down and hassled me for information, then lied to the police about what I said. He promised me you could be disbarred for pursuing me like this."

"Are you and Beverly lovers?"

"Don't be ridiculous. She's not my type. But we're friends and all the more so since she left that spineless bastard."

"I thought that you and he were friends."

"That's none of your business. I wasn't working with him or Nakamura, I can tell you that. And I didn't steal source code from Digitron or hardware specs from the UW. I got dragged into this because he'd convinced himself I was fucking his wife. She cheated on him plenty, but not with me."

Nor me, he thought, obsessing again about his enigmatic client.

"What did he think would happen? He couldn't satisfy her. She was way too much woman for him. You're in over your head, McKee. That stunt you pulled in Japan may have cost me my job. She didn't ask you to do that for her. Things were going fine until you took over. Digitron was going to settle and take me back, but not now."

"Byron's case was a sham."

"I was not involved with him, goddamn it."

"You can tell Farrago I'm getting out. I'm not representing her anymore."

"Oh really? Why not?"

"Because I can prove she was in on this. I can prove it was her behind the wheel. I know the license number of the car she rented. If it matches the picture on my phone then she's busted. If you have my pictures, Dave, then let's check it out."

"I told you I need certain software."

"Well download it and confirm for me if the license plate was Washington 688 CKA. If it was then she's your hit man. You don't know her. Sonny planted the bomb and she set it off. They needed someone to shadow the balloon until it got close enough to the trees and she's a dead ringer for the pilot's wife." He studied Dietrich intently, hoping for a reaction.

"The conspirators at VVG put a contract out on Byron, Akira and you. Sonny and Beverly were with them. Fleeing the country isn't going to keep you safe."

"No way," said Dietrich. "I don't believe you, but to satisfy your morbid obsession I'll enlarge the image and prove you wrong. You aren't thinking straight. If she was in on it then she wouldn't have given me the phone. She would have deleted the pictures and ditched it."

"You haven't convinced me she would do anything for you," said Les. "I think you're lying about how you got the phone."

"Oh yeah, how do you think I got these?" He pulled the Galileo and the smartwatch from his jacket. "She lifted them from you the other night."

He stared at the Galileo in a state of shock. "That doesn't make her innocent. Her story about renting a Corvette double, and returning it by stealth, minutes after the crash—no jury will ever buy it. Dave, if she killed Byron and Akira, what's stopping her from killing you?"

"She says they blackmailed Monica." Dietrich slipped the Galileo back inside his jacket. "But Monica is her alibi. As long as they stick to the truth—that they were driving home when Byron died, and that renting the Corvette was Monica's idea—then the prosecutor won't ever get to a jury."

"Beverly is lying. I just came from Monica's apartment. She's got long hair. And the rental agency told me that Beverly reserved the Vette, not Monica."

"You're really into this," said Dietrich, grinning in disbelief, "though it's not clear to me who you're rooting for. She's not going to be happy when I tell her this. She let me know how you screwed up. She could end your career with a lawsuit, but for some reason she thinks you're working hard for her. It'll look bad if you drop her now.

"Besides, I don't think they'll even let you drop a case so close to trial. You need to get back on board and fight like hell for her husband's reputation—so I can get my job back."

"His case is a joke and you're leaving town."

"You know nothing about me or my plans. But you'd better relieve your mother of those copies on her phone, or your misjudgments could place her in harm's way. Make sure you look at them before you assume she's guilty. She's not and I expect you to stick with her case. Let me choose when and how the cops end up with your exculpatory photos. Your disloyalty is jeopardizing my future. And hers. I'll have her sue you pronto, and trust me, she'll do it."

"I'd have to get more out of staying on her case than her promise not to sue me."

"Such as?"

"Such as something solid I can take to the cops. They're about to file charges against me for Victor Garving's murder. It will force me to turn on her if I think she's guilty. So print an enlargement of the license plate I filmed. I want to know who was driving that Corvette if it wasn't her. That's if you care about her. I'm not about to take the fall while she walks."

"So you're admitting you sent no copies to your mom. I have your phone, remember? If you'd emailed or texted any pictures, it would have recorded the transmission. But just to humor you I'll compare the plate you filmed with the one on the car she rented. Here's the deal. If the plate you filmed was anything but—"

"688-CKA," Les offered.

He wrote it down. "Then it means it wasn't her. I'll confirm it for you, but you'll have to trust me. If I'm right and she's innocent, then stay on as her counsel and stop throwing her under the bus. I won't be giving up that phone unless it becomes a matter of her acquittal."

"What I *can* tell you, McKee, is that these murders had nothing to do Sugiyama or VVG, but everything to do with Bonadelli. Follow the missing forty-four million and it will lead you directly to your killers."

"Who told you about Bonadelli?"

"I'm not saying any more until I see what you do with the Digitron case—starting tomorrow. Practice law like a good attorney and stop talking to Gaitano. He's messing with your mind so you'll turn on your client. And pardon me for saying this, but his plan is working."

Les said nothing, though he had to admit he kept handing Beverly to Gaitano.

Dietrich glanced at his watch. "Okay, I think we can finish this in a more public setting, over a dinner and some Washington wine."

The two men stepped outside for a stroll along the boardwalk. They'd proceeded several paces from Dietrich's room when he stopped. "Wait. I forgot my wallet." Les stood and waited while Dietrich retreated to his room. He was inserting his keycard when Les heard a branch snap in the nearby woods. Peering into the black forest he saw movement seventy-five feet away, the murky outline of a dark figure standing behind a tree, drawing a rifle to his shoulder. He watched as the gunman took aim at Dietrich. "LOOK OUT!" he screamed, as a shot rang out splintering the door next to Dietrich.

Dietrich dove hard behind his parked car. The door to his room opened slightly from the force of the bullet. Les was completely exposed but hit the ground as well. He heard the shooter chamber a second round as the next shot completely shattered the back window of Dietrich's car.

As the shooter started chambering a third round, Les scrambled to the door and dove inside the room. Dietrich was crouched behind his car, afraid to make a move. But there was no third shot.

"Are you hit?" he shouted from inside.

"No. I'm coming."

He scampered from the hall to make room for Dietrich as the noise of screeching tires sounded from the road. But as Dietrich came barreling through the door, a second assailant, appearing just outside the room, shot him at point-blank range. He fell headlong into the hall and landed face down on the carpet. As Les dove around a corner, he managed to glimpse another bright flash from the barrel of a handgun, as a second bullet struck Dietrich directly in the back, then a third shot at even closer range. He cowered by the bed, waiting for his turn to be gunned down.

But nothing happened. He listened as the second shooter turned and ran. The next sound came from Dietrich, moaning and gasping desperately for air.

"McKee," he mumbled almost inaudibly. Gambling that the worst had passed, he scrambled to Dietrich's side. His body was half in the room, making it impossible to close the door. Blood was pouring from his wounds and a pool was forming on the carpet.

Dietrich was dying. Blood was trickling down the corner of his mouth. He was trying to tell Les something in the faintest gasp. He put his ear next to Dietrich's mouth.

"Get the phone," he managed.

"What?" said Les, touching him gently. There was nothing more he could do. He did not want this man's blood on his hands.

"The phone," Dietrich wheezed. "It's . . . it's under the bed . . . in my briefcase. Get it before she does. And take it all."

Blood now gurgled in his throat as he struggled to speak.

"Who is *she*?" he whispered. A dying declaration was an exception to the hearsay rule. "Do you mean Beverly?" It was too late. His stare went blank and his breathing stopped.

Les rose, his hands and clothing unwillingly stained with fresh blood. He wiped off as much as he could using a motel towel. Searching beneath the bed, he pulled out a briefcase, opened it and found his phone. Overcome with panic, he shoved it in his pocket. He'd seen a sniper who fired from the trees and a second shooter from point-blank range. Although they'd fled, either of them could be waiting for him outside. Dietrich had been their target, though they must have known that Les was present.

He thought of his van parked up the street. He couldn't afford to be found here. Farrago and his Bar complaint would be the least of Les's worries. He'd be looking at Murder One. Again. Maybe that was the killers' plan. He had his phone. There was a large white envelope in the briefcase. "Take it all . . . before she does," had been Dietrich's final words.

Reaching into Dietrich's jacket, he removed the Galileo and the smartwatch and tossed them in the briefcase. He used the towel to wipe the blood from the bottom of his shoes and wiped down anything he'd touched with a fresh towel.

He heard footsteps and a voice outside, then a scream further down the walk. Careful not to touch a thing, he grabbed the briefcase, stuffed the used towels inside, and left through the sliding glass door that faced the lake. It was black outside and the trees were thick.

The second shooter stood in the darkness and watched from the shadows as Les made his hasty retreat, then darted in and out of the room through the same glass door that faced the lake.

CHAPTER THIRTY-SIX

Stumbling blindly through the forest he reached his van. He heard a commotion gathering at the lodge. He tossed Dietrich's briefcase in the back and drove past a small group of horrified onlookers gathering cautiously near Dietrich's room. He would repark at the airport and take a cab back to his office. Marcia's parking stub would prove that her van had not been driven since her departure.

As he approached the junction with Highway 101, he debated whether or not to keep his next appointment. It was risky, but perhaps she was in danger. Didn't he owe her a chance to explain about his mom, before he released the phone? As he turned west, he glanced at his rearview mirror and saw the lights of a patrol car coming from the south, getting ready to turn in the direction from which he'd come.

His mind was frozen on the scene in Dietrich's room. Would they be able to make his bloody footprints? What had he touched and what was in the envelope? He decided to pull over and park off the road behind some trees. No sooner had he doused his lights than a highway patrolman came screaming past him, this time from the west.

He thought about his pictures, but if he turned his phone on to check them out, Gaitano would know. He could see Gaitano's men descending by helicopter within minutes of his signal pinging the nearest tower.

Sonny said something about a lead-lined bag, so he'd be forced to improvise once he advanced his newfound token to the motel. He opened the briefcase and removed the envelope. Inside he found three airline tickets to St. Petersburg, Russia. There were three passports, each with a tourist visa.

He opened the first. Inside was a photo of Dietrich, traveling as Daniel Wallace, *the name Beverly said to use when checking-in.* In the next passport he found her photo and saw that she'd be traveling as Julie Wallace. The third passport was Tiffany's.

According to their itinerary, the threesome was scheduled to depart from Vancouver, B.C. in two days, on Saturday, May 3rd. They would be traveling as a family, though he wondered if he'd find Beverly murdered in her motel room next.

He removed a medium-sized envelope, unsealed and addressed to Mike Farrago. It was marked "confidential – hand delivered." He removed a check for fifteen thousand dollars and a letter from Dietrich to his lawyer.

> Mike:
>
> Keep this phone safe pending further notice. I got it from McKee at our meeting. He claims it incriminates his client—that the license plate will prove she was at the scene. He says he can't turn her in, so he wants me to say I got it by some other means.
>
> I'm no longer safe in Seattle, even if we win. Here's a check for your time—and more. Run up their fees, then throw in the towel when I fail to show for trial.
>
> He might be right about her, so check it out. If something happens to me, give this to the cops. Otherwise hold it as insurance and wait for further word.
>
> —D.D.

The letter was another fake, intended to deceive Farrago as to how Dietrich had obtained the phone. Les sighed. He guessed he was the resident patsy. Dietrich had nearly convinced him she was innocent, yet in his letter he revealed his doubts. Then why cover for her and agree to flee with her to Russia?

The night and the fog were closing in. Reality was a fleeting illusion and illusion was a way of life.

CHAPTER THIRTY-SEVEN

He skimmed the crest of the ocean highway as he left the massive confines of the rain forest. Soon he was speeding beside crashing waves and sandy beaches. The Kalaloch Lodge emerged abruptly as the winding road came home to rest beside the shore. Almost by surprise, he found himself at the water's edge. At least the night and the sea were bigger than his troubles.

The lodge held only a restaurant and a lobby. Tiny seaside cabins were spread across a shallow bluff, overlooking the beach. The horizon was black, though he could hear and smell the brine and taste the salty presence of the ocean. As the moonlight flashed white across the rumbling tide he noticed blood on his jacket.

He scanned the cabins for any sign of danger. For now at least, the park-like hideaway seemed peaceful. He spotted her Lexus and instinctively parked a hundred yards away. Along the way to Lake Quinalt he'd purchased a change of clothes, in the event he spent the night. Dressing quickly, he shoved his bloody garments in Dietrich's briefcase. He pocketed the smartwatch and the Galileo as he back-tracked to the lobby.

"Are you holding a room for Daniel Wallace?" he inquired at the desk, reluctant to use the name himself.

"Here's your key," she said, smiling faintly. "Your sister has checked into the adjoining cabin."

It was 9:30 p.m. as he stepped lightly past her cabin, where he noticed her lights were on. Without warning he was startled by the crack of a metallic pop, sounding from beneath her car. Touching the hood, he realized it was warm.

Noiselessly he slipped into his cabin and chained the door. It was black inside. The door connecting his cabin to hers was locked. As luck would have it, his kitchenette came equipped with a small microwave. He would power up his phone inside and trust that its walls were dense enough to contain the signal. As he opened the door to the microwave, its internal light cast a faint glow across the room.

His phone came to life, fully charged. Seconds later he was looking at his pictures: the video clip, the still of the Corvette, two wide-angle shots of the gondola, a close-up of the passengers, and the final moving sequence as it burst into flames. All of it was exactly as he remembered.

His high-angle shot of the Corvette was centered on its grill as it approached his house. It was just starting to turn as the road wound down. He enlarged the image as far as the phone allowed. The silhouetted driver was a short-haired female whose head was turned in the direction of the balloon. The tinted glass obscured her face and the license plate was too grainy to read. He wanted the truth so badly he considered removing the phone to search for signal, just long enough to find and download a software app that could magnify and enhance the image.

"Leslie, is that you?"

He looked up when he heard her panicked voice. She had entered through the patio which she must have unlocked when she checked in. One of the thin straps of her filmy negligée had fallen from her creamy shoulders. She was barefoot, her ring was gone, and she looked ravishing—though sex was hardly on his mind.

He must have looked foolish to her, standing in the dark kitchenette with his arms inside a microwave. He closed its door, leaving the phone inside. The internal light went out, leaving only moon beams from the patio door to backlight her shapely form.

"What are you doing?"

"It's not your concern."

"Oh my God, is that your phone?"

"What do you think?"

"Goddamn it, Leslie, how did you get it?" She stormed across the room, unlocked the connecting door and went inside her cabin. "He swore he gave me the only copy," she seethed as she returned. She was clutching her robe though she didn't bother to put it on. In her other hand she was holding up a flash drive.

"What's that?" he asked, stepping toward her.

"You know the killers changed the picture on your phone. But David made a copy before they did, and gave it to me for safekeeping." Her breathing was labored. "That lying bastard."

"Beverly, he's dead. He was gunned down by a pair of assassins outside his room tonight, at the end of our meeting."

"Show me what's in there," she said, pointing to the microwave.

"It's my phone. I need to turn it off before I take it out or they might pick up the signal." He removed his phone as he powered it down and propped it on the counter. Beverly gasped in shock, yet she hadn't flinched at the news of Dietrich's murder.

"What's on the flash drive?" he asked.

"Give it to me," she interrupted. "He swore to me that Sugiyama had it."

"Calm down, Bev."

"Give me the phone!" She dropped her robe as he found himself staring at the barrel of his missing .44.

CHAPTER THIRTY EIGHT

"Beverly, for God's sake put that down."

Adrenaline pumping, he reached for the knob at the bottom of a table lamp as the light came on. She stood there, arm raised, his gun trembling in her hand. She squinted faintly at the light.

In that unexpected moment it was clear. It was the second time he'd seen his gun that night. "You killed him, didn't you?"

Neither of them breathed for the next few seconds.

"You set me up to meet with him, then you killed him. And you used my gun to do it. I'll bet three rounds are missing from the clip . . . because they're in his body."

Without lowering her aim she took her eyes off Les, glanced at the gun, then raised her chin defiantly. "Of course I did," she replied. "And when I tell you why you're going to applaud me."

"I don't think so, Bev." He took a seat. Her barely covered body looked inviting behind the menacing .44, but in reality he was terrified for his life. He took the phone in his hand.

"Give it to me or I'll kill you."

He made no move to comply. "It makes me sick to know that you were in on this."

"I wasn't. Your fucking pictures, the ones on that phone, have been altered. David gave it to Sugiyama, and he had his people change the license plate to match the car I rented. David showed me how they did it, so he could blackmail me with it."

"Nice try."

"Why did he give it to you? Did he tell you I was in on this?"

"Quite the opposite," replied Les, looking past her to the gleaming, jagged surf. "He wanted me to believe you were Sugiyama's patsy. But it's pretty clear you killed them," he said matter of factly. "You were helping Sugiyama."

"I didn't kill anyone," she insisted. "Until tonight. I don't even know Sugiyama. Did he tell you the Japanese arranged the murders?" She began to weep, her bare shoulders shaking. "He was lying, Leslie. He killed them all, including Victor. David and Sonny are pure evil."

"He said you two were lovers."

"I hardly think so. He's gay. We were friends—until he dragged me into this. On Monday after we talked at the jail, he said I had no choice but to leave with him."

"The two of you framed me for Victor's murder."

"I had nothing to do with Victor's murder. I didn't even know Sonny was in New Orleans, or that he was working for David. I killed David because he deserved it."

Her eyes were wild, her voice like broken glass. She was capable of anything and he feared it was only a matter of time until she pulled the trigger again.

"So you weren't sleeping with him?" he prodded.

"No. We wanted Byron to think we were. My marriage was a disaster, Leslie. I was trying to make him jealous . . . for once in his pathetic life. Instead he got even. First he got David fired. Then he divorced me. That bastard."

"You were there the day he died, just like you were there when Tyler died."

"I was nowhere near it, Leslie. I was driving back from Cannon Beach with David. I had no idea he was going to have Byron killed while we were gone, or that he was framing me."

"So now it's you and Dietrich in Cannon Beach?"

"The trip was his idea. He was trying to flaunt our supposed affair in Byron's face with a weekend getaway. I think he realized he was losing me. He suggested I get Monica to cover for me with Byron's parents. He wanted me to rent that car and rendezvous with him on Saturday for our trip. He asked to cut my hair, that it was an erotic thing for him. She lowered the gun and wiped the tears from her cheek. I'll admit I wanted him to want me. The way Byron did once. I guess I have that effect on gay men."

"Beverly," said Les, "In the name of decency please put on your robe."
She complied, without letting go of the gun. "If Dietrich framed you, then
why did he try so hard to convince me that you were innocent?"

"No one was supposed to know he framed me. He claimed Sugiyama
made him do it. It was their backup plan if the cops got close. It was supposed
to look like an accident, because the bomb was supposedly untraceable. He
said he was sorry they messed up and that he would help me leave the
country."

"And fly to Russia."

"Jesus!" she exclaimed. "He gave you the tickets, didn't he? I need them,
Leslie. At least the tickets and the passports. I looked all over his room for
those."

"You're not going anywhere, Beverly."

"And you think you're going to stop me?" She raised the gun again.

"You were in on this from the start."

"No I wasn't!" she shouted. "After Byron got David fired and filed for
divorce, I'll admit we talked about killing him. He deserved it, or at least
I thought so at the time. But I would never have followed through. It was
David who went on about it and kept planning. It was all he ever talked
about." Shivering, she clutched her robe.

"Byron knew I loved him. We were seeing each other again. We might
have reconciled if David hadn't killed him." She started to sob. "He claimed
it was Sugiyama, but I know better. He wanted to run INTERACT for
Sugiyama."

"If you're innocent, then why would you agree to flee the country
with him?"

"I was lying about that, just to get these copies." She held up the flash
drive. She lowered the gun and snatched a tissue from the table to wipe her
tear-streaked face.

He remained motionless. "You might want to start from the beginning."

She paused, tied her robe, then took a seat across from him. The gun
was getting heavy so she set it on the table, but her finger was still on the
trigger.

"About a year ago he came onto me, which was totally confusing. I knew
he was gay. He said, 'Let's mess with Byron.' I was lonely and miserable so
I thought, why not? After all, he deserved it." Her words fell away as she

looked at the gun. Sitting in a shadow, darkness carved her face in half. For the first time he was seeing her for what she was.

"David wanted his revenge more than I did. We never had sex, but we let Byron make assumptions. It was wrong, I know. But instead of getting jealous he ignored us. And the more time I spent with David, the more I started to have feelings for him."

"Did anyone else know about your affair—if you can call it that?"

"No, it took place mostly at the house, practically in front of Byron. He was too busy playing with his computers and board games to care if we were flirting."

"What about Byron and Nakamura? You must have known what they were up to. You keep mentioning Sugiyama, which is a name you didn't get from me."

"Yes, I knew about them. I got him to come clean with me a year ago in May. He swore me to secrecy. But I told David and that's when he said he could help them with his research at the UW. The VRD. He said it could complete the picture for them and that he could get it. They had millions to work with so I forced them to include David. I told Byron I'd go to the police if he didn't."

"You sound like Victor. So you're admitting that Dietrich was part of INTERACT?"

"Yes, though he'd managed to fool his lawyer. Byron's lawyer knew everything. In fact, Milton was going to leave private practice and become their corporate counsel. They had raised close to half a billion dollars. It was going to be so huge."

"What went wrong?"

"Byron. He was furious that I'd blackmailed him into including David. So as soon as he got his hands on the VRD he started planning how to dump us. He gave David a lousy million bucks and told him to fuck off. He said if he caused any trouble he'd go to jail for stealing the VRD. Then he decided to leak that bogus story about David selling source code. It was actually Byron who stole the code."

"Did Byron admit to tipping off the press?"

"No. He acted like he was outraged and promised David they would file suit together. David should never have been fired."

"But why did Byron get himself fired?"

"He didn't care. You called it, Leslie. He was going to leave and forfeit his options in the end. He said their stock was going to plummet."

"Then why file suit with Dietrich?"

"He wasn't helping him," she replied. "He was screwing me. He filed suit so he could stay unemployed during our divorce. He knew David would have to back him, even though he was guilty.

"He planned to lose—then appeal. He wasn't going to jump ship for INTERACT until after the divorce. He was going to leave David hanging on the appeal."

"That's a peach of a man you fell in love with, Bev. Did Dietrich know this? Why not go to the police?"

"Because he'd already testified that Byron was innocent. He couldn't very well change his story."

"Did Bryon admit to any of this?"

"No, but I suspected. Toward the end we started talking, once I convinced him I never slept with David. He started coming clean, but the Oregon trip was bothering him."

"That's a good point. Why would you run off with Dietrich for the weekend if you were trying to reconcile with Byron?"

"I don't know what I was doing." She was crying again, though her hand was on the gun. He considered grabbing it but thought better of the plan. So he sat, intent on hearing the rest of her sordid story.

"Why kill six people? Why not just kill Byron and Akira?"

"It would have been too obvious. He claimed Sugiyama ordered the hit, but I think he did this on his own. He's an opportunist. He killed them so he could replace them."

"Was Byron afraid of Sugiyama?"

"He knew that Sugiyama and Yamamoto were upset with him, but he didn't think it would come to violence. David was in touch with them so maybe he offered to take care of it for them. But really I think he did it on his own. He's ruthless."

"Was ruthless," said Les. "Before you shot him."

"I'm not sorry. He killed my husband and he tried to frame me for it. I figured it out on Sunday when you told me about the Corvette. He was going to get away with it."

"Did you try confronting him?"

"Yes, on the night you dropped me off. It was the first time we'd spoken since Byron's funeral, because he said we couldn't be seen together. That's when he tried to pin the blame on Sugiyama. He told me about the altered phone and said they were planning to double-cross him too. He said both of us would have to leave and that if I'd promise to go with him he'd let me have the copies that prove I'm innocent."

"I'm not following."

"Leslie, when I removed your phone from Marcia's purse, I had no idea what was on there, except you'd filmed the crash. I never bothered looking at the pictures because I didn't want her to see me with it. I just knew from the day of Byron's funeral that David was desperate for your phone. He said we were being framed and that your pictures would prove us innocent."

Les sat in silence while she dried her eyes and blew her nose.

"On Sunday he admitted the real reason he wanted your phone was so his bosses could frame me with it. He told me how they'd made him arrange our trip, and the rental. That was supposed to be the extent of it. Then you showed up with your fucking camera. Thanks, Leslie. He said they were going to kill him if he didn't bring them the phone, so they could make it match.

"Leslie, your pictures proved I wasn't there, but now they prove I was. He said he got the last laugh because he made a copy of it before he let them have it. That way we could prove they changed it."

She held up her flash drive again.

"That's why I agreed to leave with him—to get these copies. I didn't believe him about Sugiyama. Now I'm sure he was lying."

"But why Russia of all places?"

"I guess fugitives can disappear from there."

"Did you look at the pictures on that drive?"

"Yes, but I can't read the license number. I don't even know the license number of the car I rented."

"So you put all your trust in a man you knew had framed you. None of this makes sense."

"It was supposed to look like an accident, Leslie. They weren't supposed to find any bomb. And nobody guessed you'd be standing there with your camera. He framed me so he could own me. He didn't know what I might do when I learned he'd killed my husband. And he had good reason. I wanted out before this happened."

"Then why let him blackmail you? You could have gone to the police. In fact you promised me we'd go."

"I told him I didn't care about his flash drive. Your mom's copies would clear me. He laughed and said he'd take care of that. He knew I couldn't go to the police. I had no proof and I'm a suspect. That's when I knew I had to kill him. But I didn't kill anyone else, I swear."

"Right—like you couldn't stop thinking about anyone else but me."

"Oh my God you're jealous. Is that what this is about? I swear you're the only man I've touched since Byron left."

"Save it, Beverly." He tried to ignore her bare legs and delicate ankles. "Did Dietrich order Victor's hit?"

"Probably, though he denied it. He said Sonny was working for Sugiyama, that killing Victor was part of their plan to set me up. He did say that Victor's death was the final straw. It meant we had to leave. Things were getting out of hand and I didn't stand a chance if I stayed."

"He told me you helped him steal what you thought was my phone on the night of the crash."

"That's a lie, Leslie. On the night of the crash he returned to the Wellses after we got back from the morgue. He took me aside, with this wild look in his eyes, and told me it was a murder and that we were being framed. He said he'd heard you tell Fred about filming it and he didn't want it getting out until he could see your pictures. He said he'd been to your house and had taken your phone, but there weren't any pictures on it. He asked me to put it back and find out what camera you used. He wanted me to go get Marcia's camcorder from Melissa Peters."

"So you brought Marcia's phone back and gave it to Gaitano? Is that when you took my gun?"

"David took your gun. He was in your house when you were upstairs with Breanna. Then he asked me to put it back, along with Marcia's phone. But I kept the gun. You're too absentminded to be considered a responsible gun owner, Leslie."

"Why did you give Marcia's phone to the police?"

"I don't know. I guess I saw no harm in throwing them off the trail for a few days."

"Beverly, you killed your friend in cold blood tonight, and you used my gun to do it. The more you lie to me, the more I know you've been in on this from the start. I'm the only patsy. Why did you tell me to check in here as

Daniel Wallace? That's Dietrich's alias. You were planning to kill him and make it look like me, by using my gun and by having me check in as him just thirty miles away."

He searched her icy blue eyes for answers. "Sonny was helping you back there in the woods, wasn't he? I saw him take two shots. He's been working for you the entire time."

"Leslie," she cried. "The meeting with David was your idea. I told him it was because you thought his life might be in danger. He said, 'good, then let's prove it to him, by letting him witness an attempt on my life.' It was staged to fool you and the police. To throw you off course. He wouldn't be a suspect if he was a target. It was going to be his excuse for disappearing. He had no idea I was going to be there too, to make it really happen.

"I agreed to get you to the meeting because I saw it as my chance to kill him. The police would think it was someone else. He'd already given me a credit card that matched our passports. We were going to use it during our first few days out of the country. I used it to reserve these rooms and that's why I had you check in with that name."

"Did you plan on confessing to me?"

"Of course not. You figured it out yourself. I had no idea you'd recognize your gun."

"So what did you think would happen here, after setting me up to watch him die?" He gestured to her costume, courtesy of Victoria Secret. "What made you think I would even show?"

"I don't know," she said blankly. "I certainly didn't think you'd be coming with the doctored phone and my travel papers. Now give them to me, or David might not be the only one I shoot. You know I'm capable."

Outside, the wind blew off the ocean, rattling the windows in their sockets.

"I'm walking out of here," he said, "and I'm going to the police. That was our agreement."

"No, you're not! You're still my lawyer and what I've told you here is privileged. You can't ever testify against me."

"I didn't say I was going to testify, but I'm under a valid subpoena to surrender my phone. It's evidence, and if I don't turn it in tomorrow they're going to lock me up until I do."

"Leslie, you didn't even have it until tonight. You weren't ever supposed to get it back. He swore I had the only copies and that the phone incriminating me was with Sugiyama. You know, he recorded your meeting—to prove he could convince you I was innocent."

Les sat in stunned silence. *The meeting was recorded?* He should have searched Dietrich's room more thoroughly. The police would find the tape and it would prove that he had been there. He'd be suspect number one in Dietrich's murder, especially since he fled.

"Beverly, if you knew he was recording it, you should have removed the tape. You don't want the cops finding it. If they ask me why I was there, I'll have to tell them what I know."

"What makes you think I didn't?" she fired back. "You were out of there so fast. He had it in his shirt pocket." She held up a miniature recording device as Les's blood turned to Freon. "If you can't accept I'm innocent," she continued, "then trade me this recording for your phone. I want the phone, the tickets and the passports."

"This isn't Monopoly, Bev. If that's a recording of our meeting then you should listen to it first. He didn't let you off the hook. In fact the cops would love to hear what's on there and you'd be insane to turn it over."

Maybe she was insane. The last time they were alone she'd been greedily running her tongue down his bare chest. Now she was threatening to puncture it with bullets.

"Les, you need it because it proves you weren't the shooter. Otherwise they'll charge you with his murder. They'll trace the bullets to your gun."

He met her strange look with a level gaze. "I'm no closer to the truth than when I walked in here," he said. "All I know is that I finally have my phone and I'm going to cooperate like we agreed. I won't be telling secrets, I'll be honoring a subpoena.

"The crime lab can tell if the pictures on here were altered. You don't know whether anything Dietrich said was true. You don't know what's on that drive, you don't even know what license plate I filmed. If you're innocent, then all you have to do is tell the truth. I've told my last lie for you. I can't believe I once thought you were worth protecting."

"Leslie, the pictures on that phone will crucify me. I know that much because he showed me." Her voice was edging to hysteria. "They changed the number and now I'm screwed."

"You've got an alibi. Or at least you did until you shot him. Monica must have seen you leave with Dietrich, and there must be others who saw you two in Cannon Beach."

"There aren't," she said. "He was adamant that no one could see us together because of the Digitron case. He even cut my hair for me."

"Wouldn't there be motel records?"

"We stayed at a cottage owned by Monica's parents."

"Why would you drop the car off just minutes after the crash, then vanish from the agency without a trace?"

"It wasn't me," she protested. "He made sure we were late getting back. He dropped me at Monica's so she could drive me to the Wellses. He promised to return the car without letting anyone see him."

She looked out at the beach longingly, as if she wanted to walk out into the jet black waves and never return. "I have to get out of here," she pleaded, "with Tiffany. Give me the passports and the visas at least. That's all I ask."

"You're going to live in Russia?"

"What choice do I have? We'll be starting out from there. I'm innocent, goddamn it!"

"No, you're not," he said, as he slipped the phone into his pocket. "Dietrich didn't give me this until after you shot him. He knew it was you. Before you killed him he was planning to leave it with Farrago, for safekeeping, in case something happened to him. Clearly he didn't trust you and neither do I. He wrote a letter to Farrago that said you were possibly involved. I can show it to you if you'd like. You know my mom's apartment was broken into yesterday. Someone tried to steal the pictures I sent her."

"Sonny must have done that," she protested. "I had nothing to do with it."

"You were the only one I told. If you thought her copies would prove your innocence then you wouldn't have told Dietrich about them . . . so he could go and destroy them."

"That's not how it happened," she pleaded. "I told him about them because I wanted him to think I didn't need his help. I told him her copies were all I needed. I was scared and confused, but I swear I'm *innocent*. Leslie?"

He looked at her coldly. "You've been lying to me since I took your case. The other night when we were in my car and you came on to me, it was a sham."

"Leslie, what are you talking about?"

"You distracted me so you could take the Galileo."

"How can you accuse me of that?"

"Because it's true. How else did Dietrich end up with this?" He removed the VRD from his pocket so she could see he had it.

"Bev, you'll have to kill me if you want to stop me. Can you do that?"

She looked at him with pure loathing. "Okay, so I took it. It wasn't yours to begin with. David said he'd been all through Byron's condo, he even tore up your house looking for it. He said it was the only thing linking him to VVG's conspiracy, and he didn't want it getting into the hands of the police. Quit being so high and mighty, Leslie. It's not like you're the innocent one."

"What does that mean?"

"You know exactly what it means. You extorted half a million dollars from Victor in my divorce. And you took that insurance case you knew was bogus. I never asked you to do any of that for me. And trust me, I'll be telling Gaitano the whole story."

"The whole story?" he asked. "That I did it because I loved you? That's the whole story, Bev. Besides, the statute of limitations has run on that. It's old news."

"So what? You'll be disbarred. And I'll be suing you for malpractice. Forty-four million dollars' worth."

"Beverly, the minute you sue me you'll be waiving your attorney-client privilege. It opens the door to everything you've told me here tonight. And a confession isn't hearsay. You can sue me and then collect your winnings from death row."

He had silenced her at last. Outside a driving rain began to fall in sheets. When she finally looked at him she seemed as young and guileless as the day they'd met in college.

"Why won't you believe me?" she whispered. "I'll go to jail. Or worse. And what about Tiffany? You can't do this to her, Leslie, she's already lost her father." She started sobbing uncontrollably.

"Thanks to her mother."

"Liar!" she shouted. The gun was suddenly up and trained on him by a trigger finger.

He rose with effort, as if twenty years were pulling him down. He reached in slow motion for the Galileo and walked toward the door without looking back. As he raised his hand to lift the chain from the lock, gunfire pierced his ear. He almost welcomed his own death. But she missed.

In the sinister silence that followed he feared she'd killed herself. He heard her move and wheeled around. She'd fired into the microwave and now the barrel of his gun was nudging at her temple.

He turned and left without a word.

PART TWO

CHAPTER THIRTY-NINE

Through his windshield the gray face of the King County Courthouse rose like a giant headstone. After fourteen years of practice, the sight of it still sent butterflies through his stomach, though today he was sure he'd retch. While the courthouse embodied justice, its silent guest was humanity's darkest side. On this occasion it represented pure evil. Nausea began rising from the pit of his belly. Distant horns blasted in the thick summer air as he waited for a parking spot to clear.

It was day five of Beverly's murder trial. Today, the State would call its star witness—former lawyer for the accused, Leslie Wayne McKee.

How things had changed in three short months. Prior to her arrest, he would have dismissed his butterflies, casually strolled into the courthouse, and confidently greeted several colleagues before reaching the sixth floor clerk's office. He would have conducted business on several matters in the hall, waiting to begin whatever hearing had brought him to the Family Law Department.

But he no longer practiced in Seattle. First it was the paparazzi. And after two network crime magazines had finished with him, his phone stopped ringing altogether. As her trial approached, the accusations, the editorials, and the epithets hit fever pitch. His entire staff, except for Peggy, had deserted him one by one. So had all his clients.

With Marcia gone, he didn't have the heart for divorce work anymore. By late June he'd removed himself and Peggy from a situation that had become intolerable. His new house went up for sale, but even then, tabloid reporters would pose as prospective buyers, hoping to film a teaser from his infamous deck. After closing his practice, he moved to San Juan Island and opened a storefront law office in picturesque Friday Harbor.

Marcia was substitute teaching in the Chicago suburb of Oak Park, and though she hadn't filed for divorce, they were barely speaking. He missed his wife and daughter so much that the ache in his heart had become a permanent fixture on his face.

His hand trembled as he parked the car and killed the engine. A block away, in the glare of the August sun, he saw the first reporters waiting. He hated the press, but at least he knew what to expect from them. He had no idea what awaited him in court.

Beverly had been in custody for exactly ninety-five days. The Washington State Constitution requires a defendant to be brought to trial within ninety days of charging, sixty days if in custody. Thanks to her fake passport and her attempt to flee the country, Beverly's bail had been denied. She wanted out and she wanted to make Amy Gifford pay for filing charges way too soon. Her attorney, Tag Berenson, had forced her case to trial in record time, with a single thirty-day continuance. They were banking on the fact that the State would be unprepared.

Since the day of her arrest in Vancouver, B.C., Les had been Monday-morning quarterbacking her defense by way of his daily fix in the *Seattle Times*. He'd agreed with her choice of Berenson, whose nickname "Tag" came from his legendary reputation for pinning his clients' crimes on someone else. But he doubted whether Tag could pull it off this time.

Allowing only three months' preparation between an arrest and a capital murder trial was an astonishing risk. On the positive side, it forced the State to place its bet entirely on a single, disputed point of proof: that Beverly's imposter rental, positively identified by its license plate, had been photographed at the scene of the crash.

The first reporters spotted Les and came running to his side. "Mr. McKee, the public has never seen your footage. Will it be shown in court today?"

"Were you offered immunity to testify against your client?"

"Do you expect to be sued?"

"Have either Bonadelli or Sonny Lile surfaced?"

He held up his hand and kept walking. Since witnesses were excluded from the courtroom until after they'd testified, he would be forced to withstand them in the hall until the bailiff came to get him. That could take all morning.

Mercifully, when he arrived on the ninth floor and tiptoed across the TV cables that covered the hallway, a uniformed officer escorted him to a private office next to chambers. Sitting down to wait, he picked up the front page of the *Times* and read the headline story.

DEFENDANT'S FORMER ATTORNEY TO TESTIFY IN MURDER TRIAL

Entering day five, the murder trial of cyber-heiress Beverly Wells has reached its climax almost as fast as the case itself has come to court. The defendant's former divorce attorney—turned state's witness—Leslie Wayne McKee, will take the stand mid-morning. Compelling an attorney to testify against his or her client is virtually unprecedented in Washington law, but in this case, McKee was a witness to the crash that killed his former client's husband and five others on April 13. Today the public is expected to get its first, long-awaited look at pictures and video taken by McKee as the alleged murders occurred – pictures the prosecution claims will establish the defendant's guilt. While McKee may be questioned about his pictures, the court has forbidden the State from attempting to invade the defendant's attorney-client privilege.

So far in the trial, the State appears to have established that the April 13 explosion aboard a commercial hot-air-balloon, carrying the defendant's husband and five others, originated from a radio-detonated plastic explosive inside a fuel tank. The chase car used by the balloonists, a bright yellow 60th Anniversary model Corvette, arrived late at the scene. Yet several witnesses saw an identical Corvette nearby at the time of the explosion. Various descriptions of the driver match the defendant.

Yesterday the courtroom was rocked by the revelation that the defendant had rented the same model and color of Corvette just days before the crash, which was returned, anonymously, 20 minutes after.

The State's first witness today will be an expert from the D.O.T., who is expected to testify that the driving time from the crash site to the rental agency is approximately 15 – 20 minutes in typical Sunday traffic. Armed with -

"Mr. McKee," the bailiff interrupted, "you've been called to the stand."

He looked up reluctantly. Cotton mouth seized him. His hands were cold and clammy. He hadn't laid eyes on her since he left her holding a gun to her temple, yet he'd be seeing her in seconds as she faced her accuser.

But he wasn't her accuser anymore. He'd given the police his damning evidence, but that was it. Thanks to a deal Kim Hanson made for him on the morning after Dietrich's murder, he couldn't be questioned as to how he'd recovered it due to attorney-client privilege.

As he stood, his mind flashed back to the night of Dietrich's murder in a series of images: losing Dietrich's briefcase in a dumpster south of Kalaloch, before driving to Seattle; the police, banging at the door to his office not fifteen minutes after he'd slipped in through the back. He'd slept there after they left, departing at 8:15 a.m. before Gaitano could return with another warrant. He'd taken refuge in the office of Kim Hanson, who was on the phone making deals for him until noon.

"Will the witness please come forward and raise his right hand." The judge's booming command snapped him from his trance-like state. It was the imperious but soothing voice of Judge Charles McGovern, a stout, commanding, and deeply religious man, who was uniformly respected by bench and bar alike. His skin was as black as his robe, accented only by the tufts of white in his perfectly trimmed beard.

"Leslie Wayne McKee, do you swear to tell the *truth?*" His eyes fixed on Les as he paused like a preacher. "The *whole* truth. And nothing *but* the truth." Then staccato, "So-help-you-God?"

Most of the other judges had dropped the name of God when swearing-in a witness. But not so Judge McGovern, or Saint Charles as he was called in private circles. Les could swear he heard a sister in the choir loft say, *Amen.*

"I do," he replied and then sat down.

The prosecutor, Amy Gifford, appeared from nowhere, as in a nightmare. She asked him to identify himself, then the questioning began.

"You were the defendant's divorce attorney on the day of her husband's death, correct?"

It was more of a statement than a question, to which he softly answered, "Yes." He'd been avoiding Beverly, but now he turned and met her chilly gaze, as remorse squeezed its fingers around his throat. Flanked by her lawyers, she seemed like the innocent patsy he now judged her to be.

"And you represented her in two other cases. There was her first divorce, from Victor Garving, and then the Garving's lawsuit against their insurance company, in which there were allegations of insurance fraud. Is that correct?"

Again her question was technically a statement. She was leading him, but Tag let it go. She was also teetering on the edge of Judge McGovern's wrath. He'd issued a stern pretrial ruling that Les could not be questioned about any particulars with respect to this or any other case he'd handled for the defendant. To Saint Charles, the attorney-client privilege was as sacred as the priest and penitent privilege.

He paused long enough to let the judge's blood simmer to a boil. Berenson stood ready to pounce on her next question if she went further. Then he answered, "Yes."

Sensing she was about to be trampled by the judge, Gifford reluctantly left the past alone. "Weren't you also a witness to the April 13 crash, which occurred just below your house, as we see in the photographs mounted next to the jury?"

"Yes," he said. He was getting good at this.

"In fact, you were recording and photographing the balloon in question with your camera phone when it exploded."

Again he answered, "yes."

From there she grilled him forwards and backwards as to the saga of his missing phone. Most of his answers were single word affirmative. She was continuing to lead him as if she'd surgically implanted a ring in his nose, yet Berenson was not objecting. With surprising speed she reached the end of her examination.

"Handing you what's been tagged as State's Exhibit 74, for identification, can you please identify this object?"

"That's my phone. The one I used to film the crash."

"The one that went missing for a time?"

"Yes."

"Yet somehow you managed to turn it over to the police, pursuant to a subpoena, on May 2nd of this year, correct?"

"Yes."

"And showing you Exhibit 75, can you please identify the contents of this envelope?"

"Two passports, visas and airline tickets for Beverly Wells and her daughter Tiffany. I turned them over to you on May 2nd as well."

"No further questions, Your Honor. The State offers Exhibits 74 and 75."

"No objection," Tag announced.

"Exhibits 74 and 75 are admitted," Saint Charles responded.

Amy looked visibly surprised and relieved that her exhibits, the heart of her case, had been admitted without objection. Smugly she continued.

"The State is ready to show the jury the pictures and footage from the witness's phone, Your Honor, just as soon as Mr. Berenson finishes with his cross."

As she returned to counsel table, Les almost felt sorry for her. She'd made the mistake of her career back on May 2nd. She'd believed Kim when he told her that Les would sooner rot in jail than incriminate his client by revealing how he'd regained his phone.

"The phone is all you need," Kim told Amy. "How he got it is attorney-client privilege. He's not going to let you have it unless you sign a stipulation that says he can't be questioned at her trial as to how he got it."

"One condition," she replied, clearly desperate to have the phone. "Her defense counsel and the court must both be willing to accept the following jury instruction: Quote. The State was not allowed to examine Leslie Wayne McKee as to how he recovered his missing phone due to Attorney-Client Privilege. Close quote.

"If her lawyer or the judge reject such an instruction, then we can ask him on the stand as to how he got the phone. If he wants to assert her privilege at that time he can, but he'll have to do it in front of the jury, in which case we'll let the court decide."

"Deal," said Kim. "But your right to question him, assuming your instruction is ultimately rejected, will arise only at the time of trial. Until then, no more arrests and no more interrogations of my client. Charge him with something if you want, but he's done talking. And this time he's going to follow my advice."

"Deal," she answered back. And that was that.

Now she was going to pay.

The judge asked, "Any cross-examination of this witness, Mr. Berenson?"

Tag rose from counsel table. He looked like polished steel in his raw silk suit of charcoal gray. Les had been to his office the week before, where Tag entrusted him with a preview of their defense. It was more of a request on Beverly's behalf, which would profoundly shape the course of her entire trial. Tag revealed they had no plans to mention David Dietrich as part of their case-in-chief.

Amy Gifford could not have been prepared for what was about to happen. She'd assumed Les had recovered his phone from Beverly, which explained why he wouldn't tell them how he got it. She'd assumed that Tag wouldn't ask, because if Les revealed through Tag that Beverly gave him the phone, it would nullify their stipulation and open the door for her on redirect. She was content to let the jury reach its own conclusion as to how and why his phone had disappeared for twenty-three days. She must have been surprised that Tag was cross-examining him at all.

"To repeat what you told the jury, Mr. McKee, from the moment you stopped filming on April 13, until you flew to Friday Harbor with Detective Gaitano nine days later, you never once viewed the pictures or the footage on your phone?"

"No sir, I did not."

"And you never transferred those pictures to another phone or computer. You never deleted or altered or emailed them in any way?"

"No sir, I did not."

"As it turns out, on April 14, thanks to your daughter, the phone ended up at the bottom your wife's purse for several days. Is that correct?"

"Yes." As an adverse witness, Tag could lead him all he wanted.

"Your wife thought it was hers, but later discovered it was yours?"

"It went from me, to the deck, to my daughter, who turned it off, to Marcia's purse. Once she turned it on, she realized it was mine."

"Then do we know how it came to be that your wife returned with your daughter from San Juan Island, yet the phone was left behind?"

"Objection, Your Honor. Not covered in direct and it calls for hearsay."

"Sustained."

"In any event, upon making that discovery, you and Detective Gaitano chartered a plane and went back to your cabin almost immediately to retrieve it, correct?"

"Yes, that's what I testified to on direct."

"But when you got there you didn't find it. Your cabin had been burglarized just hours before your arrival, is that correct?"

"There were signs of forced entry and my phone wasn't there."

"Then how were you able to turn it over to the police on May 2nd, along with the passports and plane tickets you've identified?"

Amy Gifford sat bolt upright. Tag was opening a door for her that her poorly conceived stipulation had once shut—only she didn't realize what was about to walk through it.

"As I left my house for my office on the morning of May 2nd, I discovered a manila envelope on my front step, with my phone and those travel papers inside."

"That's it, just sitting there on your porch?"

"Yes, with no note or anything else to indicate who left it."

"And you're certain it was this same phone, Exhibit 74?"

"Yes."

"Thank you, Mr. McKee. I have nothing further."

"Very well," said Judge McGovern. "Does the state wish to redirect?" There was an unnerving silence in the courtroom.

"We agreed not to question this witness, Your Honor, on chain of custody issues. But counsel has opened the door."

"I object, Your Honor." Tag was up and roaring. "That's not how the stipulation reads."

"Sustained."

"But Your Honor, I think it's important for the jury to understand why—"

"Objection, Your Honor. The stipulation states on its face that the issue she's about to delve into can't be argued to the jury until the time of closing."

"Counsel is correct. The objection is sustained. I will admonish the State to comply with its pretrial stipulation. You made this deal, Ms. Gifford. Now I'm going to hold you to it. I'll ask you once again. Does the State have any redirect of Mr. McKee?"

She looked like she'd been clobbered by a train. The stipulation had prevented her, not the defense, from pursuing chain of custody with Les. If she tried to work around it, without asking Les to violate his client's privilege, he would only reinforce his unbelievable explanation on redirect. So she decided to leave his tall tale hanging with the jury.

"None, Your Honor."

"Very well. The court will stand at recess while the Bailiff prepares the equipment we need to view the contents of this witness's camera phone."

Les was mobbed by reporters during the break. Several uniformed officers had to restore order in the hallway.

"What deal was the judge referring to?"

"Were you given immunity from prosecution? If so, why didn't you incriminate your former client?"

He walked briskly to his car, wondering whether he'd redeemed himself. Only time would tell. With a single, hopefully believable lie, in which he made no mention of David Dietrich, Les had done all he could to deliver what she needed most—reasonable doubt.

His testimony would provide her digital images expert with the backdrop he needed. Nelson Bennett could now persuade the jury that during the nineteen days his phone went missing, the image of the Corvette had been remastered by the real killers to superimpose the license plate number from her rental.

Without a clean chain of custody his phone was worthless evidence, subject to any number of Hollywood special effects. He'd given the jury a basis for reasonable doubt, without introducing Beverly's motive for killing David Dietrich. As he turned the ignition, he caught himself smiling in the mirror.

CHAPTER FORTY

Stepping back inside the courtroom, he hoped this time that he'd be noticed. Now in day fourteen, Beverly's trial was galloping toward its finish. The press was manic with anticipation. The defense had two key witnesses left to call, then Beverly herself might take the stand.

Today he was a spectator, which required an early arrival. The reporters were setting up in the hall as he grabbed a front-row seat. He wanted the jury to know he was back, to sense that he was firmly in her camp, offering her moral support.

She would need it. Though things had been going well for her so far, a massive chasm remained. How was she going to explain having rented that Corvette? And there were other concerns. He had his doubts about her overall strategy and worried it was flawed—and that he was the cause.

Her decision to leave David Dietrich out of her defense had been telegraphed to her by Les himself, on the day after Dietrich's murder. Amy Gifford had waived his polygraph in exchange for the phone when he handed her the travel papers as a bonus, but only the ones for Beverly and her daughter. For reasons he himself did not yet fully understand, he withheld the passport, the ticket, and the visa for David Dietrich.

Owing to that decision, no one had linked Dietrich to Beverly's escape plans with her daughter. The authorities had discovered the purchase of a third ticket in the airline records for a Daniel Wallace, but no one had been able to figure out who he was or if he even existed. The passports were fake. There was no official record of any real Daniel Wallace—just the purchase of a ticket in his name, using her phony credit card, for a seat next to Beverly and Tiff.

After Les's passport revelation, it became public knowledge that she'd planned to flee. Phony passports? A flight from Vancouver to St. Petersburg? Those facts became the basis for denying her bail, which in turn forced her case to trial quickly. But how could she explain these papers to the jury without bringing Dietrich's name into her story? Dietrich was her husband's killer. He'd framed her and he'd blackmailed her into leaving with him. But if she brought him in she'd also be handing the State a perfect motive for his murder.

Beverly claimed she had copies of the undoctored pictures on a jump drive from Dietrich. But without introducing him to her story, she had no way to explain the drive or its exculpatory pictures. Dietrich probably lied to her about its contents or it would have surfaced. Les thought she must have decided that implicating Dietrich would only help them to convict her of his murder.

Les had come to believe that Dietrich, not Sugiyama, was the mastermind behind the sabotaged balloon. He'd tricked her into renting the Corvette so he could own her. And after his plans went bad, he'd made arrangements for them to flee.

Beverly was facing six counts of capital murder, and Les felt it was high time for her defense to invoke the name of David Dietrich. But she feared exposure for the slaying she did commit more than she feared Amy Gifford's "hot air" case, which was rife with reasonable doubt. If she came clean about her relationship with Dietrich then she might lose the support she'd earned from Byron's parents. Ironically, her lack of any tie to Dietrich had been serving so far to bolster her defense.

Dietrich's gangland murder remained unsolved and was the hottest topic in all the blogs that were following her trial. The public was clamoring for the State to find his killer, though they couldn't seem to agree on exactly who the State should charge. Public opinion for the most part held that Dietrich had been gunned down by a pair of professional assassins. Many argued that his contract murder was proof of a larger conspiracy, much farther reaching than Beverly's marital woes. Many were declaring her the patsy.

He wondered if maybe that was why she killed him—to point public opinion away from her. That thought sent shivers down his spine. He wanted her to take the stand and crucify Dietrich for killing six people. He wanted her to tell the jury what she'd told him.

So far, the digitally altered license plate on Les's phone had seemed an easy sell for Beverly's expert. Videographer Nelson Bennett was nationally known for his expertise in digital image analysis. It was his unwavering opinion that the license number in the photo on Les's phone had been superimposed after it was taken.

Still, why had she rented a look-alike and returned it minutes after the crash? That question had to be hanging on every juror's mind. If she took the stand to explain it, her clouded past would be opened wide to relentless, damning scrutiny. She'd be cross-examined for days. Her first husband, dead from an overdose just days before losing his insurance? Her second husband, accused of torching their club for the insurance, later killed under equally suspicious circumstances? And what of all her ties to Sonny? He'd flown to New Orleans with an obscene amount of cash, a trip paid for by her attorney. None of this would come before the jury if she declined to take the stand.

Les glanced at his watch. With only ten minutes to go, a commotion seemed to be brewing in the hall. Reporters were darting in and out. Phones were sounding off like fire alarms. One reporter, mic in hand, was madly preparing for a satellite feed. He wanted desperately to know what was happening outside though he couldn't risk giving up his front row seat. So he waited, eyes trained on the doorway, searching for someone to snag. Something was definitely amiss. It was 9:00 a.m., but none of the attorneys were in court.

Les was checking his watch for the third time when Amy Gifford burst through the door, her entourage in tow. Tag followed close behind, holding the door for Beverly as the guard removed her cuffs. She seemed numb to the outside world. Before either lawyer sat down the bailiff cried, "All rise! King County Superior Court is now in session. The honorable Charles McGovern presiding."

"Be seated," Saint Charles boomed. "The State has a motion?"

"Your Honor," Gifford began. "The State has learned that an essential witness to our case, Peter Sonny Lile, was discovered dead this morning, by Interpol in Palma on the Island of Majorca. Apparently he died of natural causes two days ago in a cancer clinic there. He was using the alias of Felix Graham. His remains are still intact and we believe that critical evidence will soon be discovered from his personal effects. We're asking to recess the trial for a week."

A wave of emotion was sweeping over Les.

"You want the court to halt this trial so your office can go on a fishing expedition in the Mediterranean?"

"Not at all, Your Honor."

"What could you possibly hope to learn from this man's human remains?"

"His personal effects, Your Honor. It's too soon to say—"

"Mr. Berenson?"

"We object, Your Honor. We feel—"

"Say no more, counsel. Motion denied. Bring out the jury. Ms. Gifford, the defendant has a constitutional right to a speedy trial. Maybe you filed your case too soon, but the defendant is a single mother, and I'm quite certain she wants to finish this. Besides, if she takes the stand today, you'll have at least a week before you have to put on your rebuttal."

Whoa, if that isn't tipping his hat, Les thought. Not only was Judge McGovern letting Amy Gifford know what he thought of her case so far, but he was outright instructing Beverly that she'd be a fool to take the stand. Before Gifford could register her complaint, the door to the jury room swung open and in filed the guardians of Beverly's fate: nine women and three men. All somber. Several made eye contact with Les. They looked at Beverly, who sat motionless with her attorney.

Tag rose to his feet and smiled at each juror. "Good morning, Your Honor . . . members of the jury. The defense calls Monica Taylor to the stand."

Les sat up, as the bailiff retrieved Monica from the hall. While introducing herself to the jury as Beverly's long-time friend, she shot a nervous glance toward Les.

"Where were you on April 13 of this year, at approximately 6:00 p.m.?" Tag began.

"I had been with Beverly for the weekend," she said stiffly, as she tried to smile. "We were returning from a trip down the Oregon coast. At six o'clock on Sunday we were bringing back our rental car."

"We know," said Tag, as if speaking for the jury. "The Corvette. Is it true you dropped it off without even checking it in?"

"Yes, we were late getting Beverly to her in-laws. The car was clean and we'd gassed it up. So she let me out to retrieve my car from the parking lot while she dropped it off. We were in a hurry to get her home."

"What time did the two of you arrive at the Wellses' in your car?"

"About ten after six."

"Did you go inside?"

"Just to help her with her bags. I spoke briefly with Byron's parents."

"Were they in a hurry to get to the recital?"

"They were having trouble with Tiffany. She said she didn't want—"

"Objection. Hearsay," Gifford screeched.

"Sustained," replied the judge, sounding annoyed.

"Did you observe Tiffany to be in a defiant mood?"

"Yes."

"Objection. Now he's leading, Your Honor."

"Sustained," the judge barked again, waiting for Tag to get it right. "The jury will disregard the witness's last response."

"Ms. Taylor, did you observe whether Tiffany's behavior was making them late for the recital?"

"Yes . . . she wouldn't put her costume on."

"All right, and turning to Exhibit 80, which the State has shown the jury, I want you to assume that a Corvette with the same license plate number and color as the one you rented was photographed near the scene of the alleged murders at about five thirty-six that evening, which—if we're to believe that car was yours—would've given you and the defendant sufficient time to make it back to the rental agency by six."

"Mr. Berenson," Monica began, "at five thirty-six we were driving north on I-5, approaching South Center Mall. We were talking about where to gas up before proceeding on I-405 to Bellevue."

"Was Beverly with you for the entire weekend?"

"Absolutely."

"Why did you rent a Corvette identical to the chase car at FOLLOW THE SUN—Hot Air Balloons?"

"Well, we didn't know a thing about the company's car. We rented the Corvette because it was something on my bucket list. Neither of us had a clue what Byron was up to for the weekend."

"If it was your idea, then why didn't you pay for it?"

"Beverly wanted it be her treat. When I first suggested the idea, she offered to call around until she found one."

"Can anyone vouch for the two of you being in Cannon Beach?"

"I don't know. We didn't see anyone we knew, but we didn't try to hide ourselves."

"Did you charge your room on a credit card?"

"No. My parents own the cottage where we stayed."

"Why were you late getting back?"

"The time just got away from us. And the traffic didn't help. We knew the recital didn't start until seven."

"Thank you, Ms. Taylor," Tag said politely. Turning to Gifford with the air of an English butler, he said, "Your witness."

Les was cringing. It was far too rehearsed—and too damn tidy to be the truth. The judge cast a bewildered look at Gifford.

"No questions, Your Honor." She sounded almost apologetic, though Les figured it was the right move. She wasn't about to let this witness embellish her lies. She'd save her attack on Monica's credibility for closing argument.

"I'm sorry," Gifford said rather suddenly. "I do have a question for her, Your Honor."

"Proceed," beckoned the judge.

"Ms. Taylor, are you absolutely certain you accompanied Mrs. Wells to Cannon Beach that weekend?"

"Of course," she said, with a furtive look.

"Is it possible you never set foot inside the Corvette in question?"

"No," said Monica. "I was with her the entire time."

"Thank you," she said, with a smile that declared she knew better. "That's all."

Beverly's witness seemed to vanish from the courtroom as mysteriously as she'd appeared. Tag called Arlene Wells to the stand. The doors swung open and in walked Byron's mother.

"Mrs. Wells. On the afternoon of your son's death, where were you about the time the crash occurred?"

She looked frail and stricken. It wouldn't matter what she said, her presence on Beverly's behalf was all the testimony he needed.

"We were home, waiting for Beverly. We were having trouble with our granddaughter."

"What kind of trouble?"

"She was upset that her mom had left her with us for the weekend.

Beverly was late getting back, and Tiffany refused to get dressed for the recital without her."

"What time did Beverly arrive?"

"About six ten."

"Who dropped her off?"

"Monica. They'd spent the weekend together."

"Objection. Foundation."

"I guess you don't really know that for sure, do you?"

"Well, they drove off together on Friday and they returned together on Sunday. They had been planning the trip for weeks."

"Did Monica stay and visit?"

"A little."

"Did either of them say why they were late?"

"Objection. Hearsay," said Gifford, with a sardonic lilt.

"Sustained."

It suddenly dawned on Les what Tag was up to. He had baited the last objection by Gifford in order to startle the jury and put them on full alert for his final question.

"I withdraw the question, Your Honor. Mrs. Wells, do you have any reason to believe that Beverly might have been involved in your son's death?"

"Objection. Calls for speculation," Gifford interrupted.

"I'll allow it," Judge McGovern replied. The courtroom fell deathly still.

"She's innocent, that's all I know. It's preposterous to me or to my husband to think she had anything to do with this. It's completely absurd."

Tag stood silent then turned and sat. Judge McGovern let the stillness hang.

"Does the state wish to cross-examine?" he finally asked.

To Les's surprise, Gifford answered in the affirmative. "Mrs. Wells, what time did the police call your house that night, to notify you of your son's death?"

"About ten to seven."

Gifford tried not to look too smug as she moved in for the kill. "So let me get this straight. Beverly arrived at six ten, meaning she was there for forty minutes before the call. During that time you had no idea your son was dead, so why weren't all four of you on your way to the recital? Wasn't Tiffany supposed to dance in the opening routine at seven?"

"I'm not sure we were going, Ms. Gifford. Tiffany had not calmed down. In fact, things got worse after Monica left. Beverly couldn't get her to dress, either."

Gifford's forty-five dollar question had backfired and it was obvious she had no follow-up. "Thank you," she said, then sat down awkwardly.

Les pondered the depth of what had just occurred, realizing that both Monica and Byron's mother had just committed perjury. His own memory of that night was crystal clear—Beverly crying in the dining room and Tiffany resting in her lap, wearing her sequined ballet costume.

"Your next witness, Mr. Berenson?" asked the judge, as if summoning the grand finale.

"The defense rests, Your Honor."

CHAPTER FORTY ONE

It was August 29, the Friday of Labor Day weekend. The jury was in day five of its deliberations. Les was nursing an afternoon latte in the courthouse cafeteria. He no longer cared that the local pundits were calling him a groupie. He was determined to be there when they returned a verdict.

He was still in anguish for her sake that Tag never put her on the stand. He understood the reasons. Judge McGovern said it himself—she'd be on there for a week—long enough for the State to find more leads from Sonny Lile. In the eight days since Sonny turned up dead the authorities had been utterly tight-lipped as to what, if anything, they'd uncovered.

On day fifteen of her trial, the state called a single rebuttal witness, a digital videographer of their own. In flat contradiction to Nelson Bennett, the State's expert testified that following an equally involved analysis of Les's camera phone, he'd concluded that the image of the license plate had *not* been tampered with, or in any way superimposed. The license plate in Les's photo was the real deal.

A journalist from *48 Hours* stuck his head inside the cafeteria and yelled to Les. "You'd better get upstairs. The judge just called the lawyers in."

His nerves felt like the brittle strings of an attic piano as he climbed nine flights of stairs. In the hallway the commotion had subdued. Within minutes the cast had assembled.

"All rise. Court is now in session." The judge came in without the jury.

"Counsel. Be seated. I've called you in because the bailiff has given me a note from the jury forewoman. Quote. 'We do not understand attorney-client privilege. Would you please explain it to us?'

"I'm sending them back a note, which says that while I'm not permitted to comment on the instructions they've received so far, I will be expanding instruction number eighteen into two subparts. Subpart A, and this is new. Quote. 'Under Washington law an attorney cannot be compelled to testify as to the confidences or secrets of his or her client.' Subpart B, which is the instruction they already have. Quote. 'The State could not examine Leslie Wayne McKee as to how he recovered his missing phone, due to Attorney-Client Privilege.' Does either lawyer have an objection?"

In ironic unison both Gifford and Tag replied, "No, Your Honor." For Les, it was an ominous sign. It meant the jury was having trouble with his story. They were wondering why it was never challenged by the State. They wanted more details about how he found his phone, especially if its discovery was related in some way to his relationship with the accused. If he was protecting her, it meant she must be the one who took it.

"Then the court will stand at recess."

As the galley filed out the reporters converged on Les. He ignored them and ducked into the men's room until they disbursed. Then he left the courthouse for some peace and quiet in a nearby bar. He was ready for a drink. But no sooner had the bartender poured his first shot of Cuervo, than a local anchor appeared on the flat screen overhead as the word *verdict* flashed across the bottom.

"Turn that up," he urged.

"We'll be going live to the King County Courthouse where we understand the jury has reached a verdict in the murder trial of Beverly Wells. The lawyers are present, having arrived just minutes before, for the judge to read a question from the jury—"

"Damn it," he yelled. He left his half-full rocks glass and dropped a twenty on the bar. He sprinted across the street and waited in agony for his turn to pass through the courthouse metal detectors. He missed his turn as the elevator departed, so he climbed nine flights of stairs for the second time in twenty minutes. Reaching the ninth floor he could barely open the stairwell door. The hall was packed with onlookers. The courtroom had filled to capacity. He fought his way to get near the door, but there was no way he could get inside.

"Where's the jury?" he asked frantically.

"They just came in," said a stranger standing near him. His chest burned painfully as he panted desperately for air.

Suddenly the hallway grew still. A benevolent guard cracked the courtroom door just enough so he could make out the voice of the jury forewoman, reading from the verdict form.

"In the matter of the State of Washington vs. Beverly Wells, King County cause number 14-1-54932-3 SEA, we the jury, as to Count One of the charge, Murder in the First Degree, do hereby find the defendant, Beverly Wel—"

Inches from his ear, an onlooker coughed. He couldn't hear what was said. The courtroom erupted like Mt. St. Helens. The corridor was a madhouse of rushing reporters. Shouts rang out. A stampede ensued from the courtroom while the hallway onlookers held their ground. He was being knocked about, desperate to know what had just occurred. The forewoman was still reading the verdict in Count Two.

As if in slow motion, he saw a reporter come to the door, halt, make eye contact with a nearby cameraman, and draw a single finger across his neck. "Roll tape," he mouthed. He heard her cry, "No," repeatedly, in deep and painful sobs. His heart nearly failed him. Guilt made his legs give way. Propping himself against the wall, he heard the foreman reading, "As to Count Six—Guilty."

He wanted to rush in and comfort her, but he was lost in a sea of bodies. Gulping for air, and trying in vain to push through the mob, he watched her rise unsteadily, her captors on all sides as she left the courtroom. Long after she was gone, when the last news team had packed and left, he still stared at her empty chair—as if sheer need could summon her back.

PART THREE

CHAPTER FORTY TWO

Outside the cabin the winds off the strait were gathering force. Les set down his coffee cup and tried to focus on his bar review materials. Reuniting with his family would be easy, but leaving San Juan Island wouldn't. He felt at home among the hearty and eclectic: farmers and hippies, new age and old, city folk hiding from their crazy lives, and broken dreamers hiding from themselves. They marched to a drumbeat all their own, each as different as the next, yet enchantingly harmonious. Living among them had helped him find a rhythm. They didn't judge him. In fact, he'd become a legend of sorts among the brotherhood of the disenfranchised.

He'd managed to attract his share of clients, as long as he took whoever stepped inside his lobby. At least it was a living. But despite finding his place, he felt he had to leave. After several trips to Chicago, he knew he belonged with his wife and child in just one household.

He picked up a photo of Marcia and Bree. She was the love of his life but he had crushed her spirit. The humiliation was too great for her to return. She was closer to his mom than she was to her own parents. With Beverly in prison she was beginning to trust him again. So he'd suggested they start fresh, in *his* home town instead of hers. His next advance was to the bar exam in Illinois.

As darkness fell it began to snow, but he barely noticed. He kept thinking of Dietrich's words: *What I can tell you, McKee, is that these murders had nothing to do Sugiyama or VVG, but they had everything to do with Bonadelli. Follow the missing forty-four million and it will lead you directly to your killers.*

It was no surprise the missing millions never surfaced. Neither had

Bonadelli. The authorities never confirmed whether Bonadelli or Byron had pulled the cash, or what they did with it from there. Smith-Levinson, still bracing for a lawsuit from Byron's parents, was offering a million dollars to any bounty hunter who could find their missing broker.

Beverly was broke and barred from enforcing Byron's will or from receiving any of his life insurance. A slayer is barred by statute in all fifty states from inheriting or otherwise benefiting from her victim's estate. As long as her conviction stood, Smith Levinson and maybe even Les would be safe from claims by her.

The half million from her first divorce had been swallowed up in legal bills. Her claim to the house and the stock he left behind was knotted up in litigation, her assets set aside to settle lawsuits filed by the families of the other victims. A small portion of her estate had been placed in trust for Tiffany, who was being raised by Byron's parents. Beverly never saw a dime.

Thinking about the money, he removed an envelope he was keeping in his drawer. He remembered the day he found it, amidst a pile of office mail—his own billing envelope—bearing his address but without a stamp. At first he thought it was a payment. But instead of a check he found forty-four one dollar bills inside, clipped to a yellow Monopoly card, like the one he'd found in Byron's condo. *From sale of stock you get $45.* This one bore a handwritten note: *Les McKee—a day late and a dollar short.* He'd assumed it was sarcasm, pointing to the forty-four million he'd let vanish on his watch.

Byron's killers were on the loose and Beverly was on death row. He just wanted it to end. He'd lost everything and he was perfectly alone, with no one to share his grief, his guilt. Would Marcia ever share it? Could she really ever trust him? Would he ever trust himself? Tears welled as he realized there were no comforting answers to his questions.

The sound of the wind was beginning to rise above the drone of a TV program he wasn't even watching. His restless gaze settled on the files and newspaper clippings he'd been compiling since Dietrich's murder. For the hundredth time he started thumbing through the various articles and notes from her arrest and trial when the lights suddenly flickered and went out. The television died, followed by an immediate and bone chilling silence. He was filled with terror. These days it shadowed him everywhere. He lived in constant fear that Byron's killers would come for him. He half expected a henchman to appear, sent by Beverly from prison. All were frequent, unbidden guests in the dreams that plagued him nightly.

He sat frozen in his chair, listening for the intruders, but all he heard was the storm. The power was out. He ought to be used to it by now since storm-induced blackouts like this were frequent on the islands. During the winter months they could last for days. He rose to find a match. A gas lantern hung above the table for times like this. He lit it and kept thumbing through his files. By now the snow was falling hard and sticking. He built a hearty fire for the long, cold night ahead.

"GUILTY AS CHARGED" was the headline reaching up like a hand from the grave to grab him by the throat. His mind replayed Monica's testimony about renting the Corvette. They should have known it wouldn't work. Beverly was either guilty or she was framed. Pleading "coincidence" had been suicide. She should've nailed Dietrich. He should have given Gaitano Dietrich's passport and the Galileo. By holding onto them he had, in fact, been protecting himself. Since the day of her arrest, he'd been sending her an unspoken message: *Don't turn over Dietrich's recording and I won't give them his papers.* He didn't want the police connecting him to Dietrich's murder any more than she did.

The epilogue to Les's betrayal of his client had been written by Beverly's jury just four weeks after her verdict. The same twelve kangaroos who'd convicted her of murder on the basis of tainted evidence had also sentenced her to death by hanging. Once her appeals were exhausted she'd become the first female to be executed by the State of Washington since 1904. Though her case would be tied up in appeals for many years, one day it wouldn't matter that Les was holding key evidence connecting her to Dietrich's murder. Let them convict her of one more killing—she couldn't end up any deader.

It made him shudder, though not for her. At the end of the line she would have her revenge. Right before her execution she would quietly provide Gaitano with the tape of his meeting with Dietrich, then lead him to the murder weapon—his .44. The recording by itself could convince a jury, especially one like Beverly's, that Les had fired the fatal shots. And there would be no statute of limitations to protect him this time around.

Whoever was taunting him with bills and notes in his mail seemed to know the whereabouts of his gun. An email had appeared the same day he found the envelope with the forty-four ones. He'd almost deleted it as spam until the subject line caught his eye: *Find the 44.*

Further down in the body someone had typed the same string of numbers he'd found on the card in Byron's condo: 44/2=22/2=11;44+22+11=77. Whoever sent it seemed to know he'd been there, in Unit 22. It was as if they'd anticipated his arrival that night and were taunting him with it now. Only this time they'd added a sentence to the equation: *Your vanishing piece waits 7 by 7.*

Was it random or was it a clue as to the whereabouts of his gun, the one she'd used to murder Dietrich? He was getting used to pranks from his not-so-adoring public, many of whom were demanding answers about his role in the Digitron murders. The aftershock of his strange testimony had yet to settle down. The press was demanding a full investigation into his role in the Garving restaurant fire, the death of Victor Garving, and the disappearance and reappearance of his pictures from the crash. They wanted him to be charged with perjury at least, if not accessory to murder.

The "deal" Kim struck for him with Amy Gifford might have saved him from being effectively cross-examined during her trial, but it was still being criticized as one of the brashest examples of lawyer protectionism in King County's history. He kept waiting to be re-arrested.

He started feeling groggy as the cabin warmed. He moved closer to the fire and laid his head on the table, using his arms as a pillow. Slowly, he drifted into fitful, nightmare-ridden sleep.

The penetrating silence was broken by an unexpected noise. Startled, he jumped from his chair. *What happened?* He reached for his gun, a new .38, which he kept hidden in his desk. The power was still out and his fire was only coals. His gas lantern was still glowing.

He rose to look outside, then heard the noise again and realized it was the sound of an incoming text. Despite the power outage he had cell reception, at least for the moment. He picked up his phone and smiled when he saw it was from Breanna. For her tenth birthday Les and Marcia had purchased her a phone. It was two hours later in Chicago and Marcia had probably just tucked her in for the night.

Hi Daddy. Are you up?

Yep. How are you?

Fine. I made a new friend today, Abby. Wanna see her?

Sure.

Go on Instagram and look at my latest pictures.

How do I do that?

I put it on your phone, remember? Just click the app.

Okay. I'll text you back.

He hadn't used the app since returning from her party and he was delighted when it led him to her pictures. He smiled as he looked at her with her new friend. Through it all her smile kept him going. He scrolled back to the earlier pictures from her party, but noticed there were more, from before she got her phone.

Scrolling back to the start he was stunned to find a picture of Beverly with her arm around Marcia. The two were looking their best, smiling broadly, probably laughing with the girls—still friends. After Beverly's arrest they never spoke again. He doubted whether Beverly had anyone to talk to these days. As he thought about her, sitting alone in her barren cell, without her daughter, he was overcome with sadness and guilt.

The first picture in Bree's collection was one of Tiffany, playing near their beach. She must have snapped it on the weekend of Byron's funeral. She would have used his phone to do it.

You still there? He texted her back.

Yes.

I like Abby. She seems nice.

She's gonna be in my Girl Scout troop.

That's great! Honey, how did you load pictures onto Instagram from before you got your phone? I see Tiffany on there.

Those are from my Facebook page. I sent them to my phone.

But how did you get them off of my phone?

Transfer to the computer.

What computer?

At the cabin.

How did you do that?

Mommy had a cable. It came with her phone.

Where is it now? The cable?

I don't know.

He picked up his lantern and went over to the desk where he kept an old computer from his Kirkland office. He nearly jumped when he saw a white cable dangling from the USB port in the forward panel of the CPU.

I think I see it. Did you leave it in?
Maybe.
Did you transfer every picture from my phone or just the ones you wanted?
I don't know.
Okay. His heart was pounding. *When are you going to bed?*
Right now. I love you, daddy. I can't wait for Christmas!
Me too kiddo. Talk to you later.

The cabin was crowded with boxes he'd packed for the movers who were due on Saturday. The sale had closed but his buyers were letting him rent until the holidays. In three more days he would board a plane for Chicago.

But Les had something bigger on his mind. On the weekend before the break-ins, Bree and Tiffany had been playing with his phone and taking pictures. Apparently Bree had transferred them to this computer. His pictures from the crash—his *undoctored* pictures—might be on this computer. But as luck would have it, the power was out, possibly for days.

Earlier in the day he'd sold his car, which meant he'd be stranded at the cabin until Saturday, when he'd arranged for a ride into Seattle with his movers. He had to talk with someone. Gaitano? His thoughts turned to an email he'd received in early December. He dug out a printed copy from his file.

> Les: I've been thinking about your client and frankly I'm plagued by doubts. This article caught my eye and I'm wondering what you think. Direct line: 206-561-5431. I can meet you in Friday Harbor if you'd like. —Rick Gaitano

He'd printed the article from the November issue of *The Cybernetics Journal.* It debuted the latest technology advance from Germany—VRD and the GC Quantum. The signal enhancer was called *Das Pedal* and the VRD *Der Astronom,* but all the essential elements were there: multiplexing of cell channels to produce accelerated graphics, delivered through Virtual Retina Display. The VRD looked eerily similar to the Galileo he still had in his possession.

It was an intriguing article, but why had Gaitano sent it? Neither VRD nor the Quantum Chip had come to the light in Beverly's trial. The gloves Gaitano had removed from his car were never introduced. And in three and a half months since her conviction, he'd read nothing more about the fate of Sugiyama, Yamamoto, or the other conspirators at VVG. They'd seemingly vanished from the scene.

VVG had released its second-generation VVViron in a move described as a *full retreat* into its bastion of proprietary hardware. Yet here it was in print: the portable world of Akira Nakamura. Somehow it had risen from the ashes, this time in Western Europe, only seven months removed from Nakamura's murder.

In the States, Google Glass was now available to the public, but in Germany, a whole new generation of VRD, or "smartglasses," was nearing full production as the continent's hottest cyber-gadget, certified safe by Germany's Medical Safety Board. *Der Astronom* was flooding the market a year ahead of Retina Vision's stateside version, still on track to begin its FDA trials that month.

Gaitano was obviously still on the killers' trail, but the article provided little help. The German start-up making its run on VVG was called *Sprung Technologies*. Perhaps Sugiyama gave them the stolen code, which was of little use to him without Nakamura's help. Sugiyama and his cronies were under too much scrutiny to try so soon themselves. Maybe they'd profited more by disbursing what they had onto the black market.

Not that Les cared. In fact he'd almost deleted Gaitano's email when he saw it, thinking it was a trap, but for some reason he'd printed it out. He trusted no one connected to the case, especially Gaitano. And he did not believe he was in the clear. Each day brought new fears that charges would be filed. He looked at his watch—it was almost 9:30 p.m. He was tired and cold, but he wouldn't be getting any sleep.

In refusing to believe his client, he'd destroyed her. She sat on death row, stripped of everything, including her only child. He looked again at Breanna's Instagram of Tiffany. There was no guile in little Tiff, yet her life had been forever ruined. No amount of money, not even a reversal of her mother's conviction, could ever make them whole. She would be traumatized for life.

In all of this, it seemed the only person who got perfect justice was David Dietrich. If Beverly hadn't taken matters into her own hands, he might have escaped to Russia without a scratch. Maybe hers was the only right course of action. In any case, her confession would remain his secret. He would never again betray her.

The winds were picking up. Several inches of snow had fallen with no end in sight, and Les was without a car. He would call Tag Berenson as soon as his office opened, but that was ten hours away. And what if he couldn't get through due to the storm? His cell phone might be dead by morning and he didn't trust his reception at the cabin, so he grabbed his flashlight, bundled up, and prepared to leave on foot. Friday Harbor was a two-and-a-half-mile walk. Maybe they'd have power in town.

The storm was fierce and the sun wouldn't rise for hours. He knew it was crazy, but he set out in the wind and snow.

CHAPTER FORTY-THREE

This was no postcard snowfall. The winds were biting and the heavy flakes felt more like teeth. His visibility was nonexistent. The island would be crippled for days. So far, at least a foot of snow had fallen as had several trees. The drifts were three feet deep in places and Les might not have made it in his car.

At about the point of no return he began to regret his choice, but he pushed ahead and managed to reach Friday Harbor by 10:30 p.m. His face felt numb. Nothing would be open at this hour except for a tavern or two and the night clerk at the local motel. They were operating on a generator and were almost full from locals seeking a good night's sleep with heat. He'd encountered no one on his way to town. He was frozen, wet and miserable, but they still had a room so he took it and stripped down for a long, hot shower.

His office, just two blocks away, had been cleaned out for several days. He'd closed his doors the week before and had farmed out all his cases. But his rent and phone were paid through December 31. If the lines were open in the morning he'd call Berenson using a landline from the privacy of his office. These days he rarely used his cell.

He labored into fitful, restless sleep, checking his watch throughout the night. In the morning he awoke to the sound of the motel's generator, still chugging away outside. Dawn had broken but the island was still without power. He picked up the phone in his room and was encouraged by the sound of dial tone. He had cell reception too, so he dressed and walked through snowdrifts to his empty office.

It was barren inside and he was all alone. He immediately thought of calling Marcia, to inform her of the night's events, though he reconsidered. His marriage could not afford another setback over the fate of Beverly Wells. The less enthusiasm he showed for Beverly, the better. At the moment he felt ecstatic for her as he sat in the cold and waited, praying the lines would stay open until he got through.

By 8:00 a.m. the winds had quieted and the snowfall was tapering off. It had been half a decade since Friday Harbor had seen a storm like this. The motel clerk was told it might be twenty-four hours until the island's meager electric company could begin restoring power.

Tag would know what to do. He dialed 411 from his cell for Berenson's number and discovered Tag's office was closed due to the storm. Next he tried Gaitano, almost hoping for no reply, but he got him after just one ring. "Gaitano," barked the voice on the other end.

"Detective Gaitano, this is Les McKee. I received your email, but that's not why I'm calling." He hesitated. He could hear Gaitano change positions in his seat. He was probably signaling for someone to pick up the other line or to start recording.

Here goes, he thought. "I can prove she's innocent. I found a copy of my pictures. On the weekend of Byron's funeral, my daughter and Bev's were playing with my phone at the cabin. Bree thought it was her mom's phone so she transferred the pictures they took onto an old computer from my office."

"I remember, they had it on for forty-seven minutes."

"What?"

"Your phone. Your daughter said she'd been playing with it until the battery almost died, the day before your wife realized it was yours, not hers."

"Right. Well last night I was texting with her. She has her own phone now and she uses it to upload pictures onto Instagram. I noticed a picture of Tiffany that she took using my phone when they were at the cabin. I asked her how she got it because you'd said no pictures were transmitted over the Internet from my phone. She said she transferred them to the computer at the cabin using a cable that came with the phone. From there she uploaded the ones she wanted to her Facebook page."

"Les, I've been on her Facebook page. I know the picture you're talking about. It never occurred to me how it got there. This is unbelievable. You've never checked her Facebook page?"

"I wouldn't know how."

"How is it she never told us that she transferred your pictures of the crash to that computer?"

"She doesn't know about this yet. I haven't said anything because I don't even know it happened."

"What do you mean?"

"Last night's storm knocked out the power. I can't boot that computer up."

"Son of a bitch, McKee. You and your fucking pictures. But if you're right, this is going to prove it."

"You mean prove her innocence?"

"Either way. Has anyone touched that computer since she uploaded her pictures to Facebook?"

"No. I use a tablet or a laptop now."

"This is unbelievable. I'm amazed Shawn Byers didn't throw your old computer off that pier, I guess no one steals them any more. I've got to get up there with a generator. How is it you're calling me from a landline."

"I walked into town and the lines are open."

"Get back to your cabin, McKee, and guard that computer with your life. If the power comes back, don't turn it on. I don't want your fingerprints anywhere near it. Just your daughter's. No more fucking with my chain of custody.

"Son of a bitch!" he heard him say, but not into the phone. It sounded like he threw something, then he charged back on the line. "This better not be some stunt to help your girlfriend."

"This is real, Detective. How do I know I can trust you not to screw it up?"

"Look," said Gaitano. "I've been taken off the case if you haven't heard, for asking too many questions. And with what I know I could serve up plenty of political heads on a silver platter if I wanted. Give me what I need and I might just do it. You trust me or you wouldn't have called."

"Your people don't know squat when it comes to video forensics. You used tainted evidence to convict her."

"We'll know soon enough. But you just identified one of the reasons I'm no longer on the case. That and one other screw-up I've uncovered. Let's just say the County wasn't so sure the photograph we used at trial was pristine."

Les recalled their expert's testimony and his knees went weak.

"I'm coming," he said. "Today."

"The ferries aren't in service."

"They will be by the afternoon. I could ask for a plane but I need to lay low on this until we're sure."

"What time should I look for you?"

"By seven. I'll catch the five thirty and bring a generator and the software we used at trial to enlarge and enhance the image."

"I'll be waiting."

"McKee?" Gaitano paused. "What do you know about your missing forty-four?"

CHAPTER FORTY FOUR

It's over, he thought. They found the weapon.

"I'm not sure what you mean, Detective," he said, straining to sound unaffected.

"I got an email that no one here can trace, about a missing forty-four, or maybe it said to find the forty-four. At first I thought it was referring to Byron's lost fortune, but maybe it was your gun. I remember this part though. It said, 'You had your chance with him in jail.'"

"I have no idea what you're talking about," Les said, while he felt himself getting sick.

"I'm looking at it now. The subject line says, quote: 'find the forty-four,' then further down there's a string of numbers that end with: 'you had your chance with him in jail.' Have you received any messages like this?"

"No," he lied. He wouldn't be surprised if Gaitano had been hacking his emails. "What are the numbers?" he asked.

"*Forty-four slash two equals twenty-two, slash two equals eleven, semicolon, forty-four plus twenty-two plus eleven equals seventy-seven.* It showed up three weeks ago. My IT guy says it's fucking untraceable—like nothing he's ever seen."

His mouth grew dry as he tried to lower his heart rate. "It means nothing to me, if that's what you're asking."

"We'll see. Don't talk to anyone until I get there."

→ | ←

Shortly before 7:00 p.m. Gaitano pulled up in a heavy-duty pickup belonging to the county, marked *K.C. B&O* for *Business & Operations*. The two didn't bother shaking hands as Les went out to help him haul in the generator. Gaitano grabbed a duffel bag and a bedroll. The cabin was still without power but Les had a nice fire waiting for Gaitano. Within minutes the generator was up and running with plenty of power for two lamps and his computer.

"Jesus, Mary and Joseph," Gaitano exclaimed as they pushed play on Les's video of the balloon. The first bit of footage ended and they were staring at his close-up of the Corvette. Without a word Gaitano inserted a disk and installed the required software. He started clicking slowly through the program as he isolated on the front grill of the Corvette. Reframe. Magnify. Condense . . . and again . . . then finally . . . *proof positive*. In the dim light and cold each could see his own breath, though no sounds emerged.

Gaitano carefully studied the blow-up. "Sonofabitch," he finally breathed.

"That's not her Corvette," said Les.

"I've got no service," Gaitano said while scowling at his phone.

"It's spotty here, but I've got two bars."

"Give it to me," he barked and took the phone. He dialed quickly and spoke to someone on the other end. "It's me. I'm using McKee's. Listen, I've got it. Washington 341-CKA. Find it."

Gaitano ended the call and returned to the pictures. Two wide angles. Then a close-up of the passengers. He hit *play* on the final sequence and waited for the moment of the explosion.

Les was trying to be helpful. "I've got movers com—"

"Shut up," Gaitano barked.

He hit *Stop*, then *Rewind*.

The explosion, thought Les. He's comparing it to what he remembers from the original.

But Gaitano rewound and froze on the frame just prior to the explosion, when Les had zoomed all the way in on the passengers. He recognized only Milton James and Byron, whose back was to the camera.

Gaitano worked with his software program for a long time, then enlarged the image as far as it would go. After what seemed like minutes he said, "I fucking can't believe this." He scrolled backwards to Les's final still, his semi-close-up of the gondola. After going through the same slow process of reframing and magnifying, he was zeroing in on Akira Nakamura.

Les peered at the enlargement, though the grainy, magnified image of a blurred Nakamura signaled nothing. Gaitano bowed his head in silence, his right thumb and middle finger massaging both his temples. After a long pause he looked at Les.

"I'm sorry. What about your movers?"

"I've sold this place and the movers will be here on Saturday. I was going to pull the hard drive on this tomorrow, drill a hole through it, and donate the rest of it to the high school. I wouldn't have bothered even turning it on. The transfer cable has been sitting here for months. I'm sure Bree's prints are on it."

Gaitano stared at Les for a long moment. "We cracked it," said Les. "We just proved she's innocent."

"Maybe. All we know is that she wasn't there."

"No way. No one frames a guilty party."

"I guess you're right," Gaitano conceded. "But we still don't have our killers."

Just then Les's phone rang. Gaitano picked it up and started taking notes. "Good work. We should've known. Okay, I'll be in touch." He turned to Les. "The person who detonated the bomb was a fifty-year-old African American woman from Spokane, named Alma Franklin," he reported without smiling.

Les was deadpan, waiting for Gaitano to explain.

"Meaning that about three and a half weeks after the murders, our Mrs. Franklin reported to the DOL that her Washington plates, 341 CKA, had been stolen from her car and replaced with randoms. Someone had swapped hers with a set of decommissioned, expired plates, though it took her almost a month until she noticed. Nothing came of it and the DOL sent her a set of new plates.

"The expired plates she found on her car are a dead end. But we know they were put there by whoever took hers. It means the killers were in Spokane before the murders, trying to steal a set of plates that were somewhat of a match to Beverly's. They had to know the plate number of the car she'd rented on the eleventh. They had very little time to find something close enough and get back to Seattle."

"Why Spokane?" asked Les.

"We just ran a check on whether any sixtieth anniversary Corvette was rented or stolen near Spokane on the weekend of the murders. And we found such a vehicle, yellow, registered to a rental company in Coeur d'Alene. We called them, they're still open, and their records show that this particular Corvette was rented on April 11 by a man named Felix Graham. He drove it five hundred fifty miles over three days and returned it on Monday the fourteenth."

"Sonny," said Les.

He nodded. "We knew he rigged the bomb but we didn't think it was him behind the wheel—in drag. Somehow he knew the license plate of the car she rented on Friday. Both Corvettes were rented on the same afternoon. As he drove back to Seattle through Spokane, he managed to track down a set of plates with at least the same three letters. He started out with Idaho plates, which he put back on when he returned it."

Gaitano smiled and reached for Les to shake his hand. "You're right, we broke it. But who hired Sonny? They must have known about his sordid history with you and Bev. You two were their patsies, which is why they had him murder Victor."

"Why didn't your team check every yellow Corvette rented or stolen within a day's drive of Seattle before you charged her?"

"Once we had your phone, we thought we knew which Corvette you'd filmed. We could have searched from here to Connecticut, but the name name Felix Graham wouldn't have meant a thing to us back then. Her trial was practically over by the time we learned of Sonny's alias."

"But if there was even a possibility that the picture on my phone was altered, you should've kept looking for other rented or stolen Corvettes."

"We didn't start to think it was tampered with until three weeks before her trial," he argued. "It's Tag's fault for bringing her to trial so goddamn fast. We asked for a continuance when we found Sonny, but he opposed it."

"Why did you call an expert in rebuttal if you didn't trust him?"

"The first one we consulted said there's really no way to prove when a digital image has been altered. He said it's too easy to swap the pixels in and out.

"Then Tag gave us Bennett's report. He approached it by analyzing the actual media on the phone. He maintained that by looking on the drive he could tell whether sufficient original pixels had been overlaid or deleted to render the image suspect. That's when we decided to get another opinion." Gaitano looked almost contrite.

"Meaning the next person you consulted agreed with Bennett?"

"Not my call," replied Gaitano. "Amy got a third opinion—the expert we finally used. Les, I haven't slept very well since then."

It had been a while since Gaitano had called him Les.

"Whoever altered the image did a first-rate job. And they had a lot to work with since Sonny had already matched the last three letters using Alma's plates."

"You assholes were required to inform her defense team if you had reservations."

"I disagree," he objected. "In the days of analog you could tell. But we were looking at digital media, trying to ascertain whether certain pixels had been created in a different instance than the originals. Reasonable minds can differ about this type of thing. We had competing experts, not witnesses of fact."

"You're a piece of work," Les fumed. "I assume the lab will be able to confirm that until you showed up here tonight, no one else has been on my computer? Bree's copy is all you need to prove she was framed. So what are you going to do about it?"

"We'll do the right thing, Les."

"Bullshit. Amy Gifford was prepared to send an innocent mother to the gallows."

"Hold on," said Gaitano. "You're preaching to the choir. I've been negotiating on your client's behalf all afternoon, as high up in Olympia as it goes. In fact, I told the governor to assume we'd find this. He said to assure you that if you cooperate, she'll be home by Christmas. And I'll be reassigned to Homicide.

"But if you keep jerking us around, McKee, the State can mount a challenge to the authenticity of your copy. We still have to account for six days between the crash and your daughter's transfer. And what if the tampering happened here?" He pointed to the computer. "Beverly had access to your phone and to this computer."

"Rick, my daughter made this copy before Sonny broke in and stole my phone. The incriminating image came after the break-in. This one is exculpatory."

"Okay, but she still rented that Corvette. And the exculpatory plates were stolen by Sonny Lile, which raises as many questions as it answers. We'll have to conduct another trial. And what if the jury convicts her again? Amy can take all the time she wants this time around to prepare for a second trial, while Beverly rots in prison."

"You just said she'll be home by Christmas."

"If you help us. Tell me why St. Petersburg."

"It's a fashion capital."

"Seriously. Possessing forged passports is a federal offense. And what about you? I guarantee more charges will be filed if you won't help. You have no idea how many times I've saved your ass."

"This is starting to feel like extortion."

"Not by me," he argued. "I'm just a messenger for their plan. It's the quickest way out for your client."

"Don't you think I'm cooperating? So tell me how this works."

Gaitano nodded and motioned them to sit closer to the fire. "They're sending a plane for us in the morning. Van Owen has scheduled a press conference for noon, where you'll be the star attraction. Berenson knows and he'll be there. Just tell the truth about how you found these copies. Explain how we cooperated with you as soon as you came forward. You can't reveal that we had doubts before we tried her—not to Berenson, not to anyone."

Les shrugged noncommittally. "And she gets out?"

"The governor has agreed to sign a pardon. It's a much faster process than conducting a new trial. Berenson wants the deal. It'll take a few days for the County to conduct its own analysis of your hard drive, then file a report with the Clemency Board. Strictly a formality."

"Rick, I wouldn't even know about your doubts if you hadn't told me."

"I'm being straight because I need your help. The killers are out there and I think you know who they are."

"I told you what I know."

"Like how you got your phone? You didn't know your pictures had been altered or you wouldn't have turned her in. Whoever gave you the phone was the person who framed her."

"I testified how I got it."

"Bullshit! Stop fucking with me. You knew we'd throw your ass in jail if you didn't give it to us. Dietrich wound up dead the day we let you out and you showed up the next day with your phone. He gave it to you, didn't he?"

Les struggled not to react. He stood up to get a beer. "I thought we already had a deal, Rick. You're not supposed to ask me how I got it—not then, not now. I was working in my office when your men showed up that night, a hundred and fifty miles from Dietrich. I went home and in the morning I found it on my porch, like I testified. I've wondered if it was related to his murder, but I have no proof of that."

"You're lying," said Gaitano. "It's okay for now. Eventually you'll come clean."

Les did not reply. He was beginning to think that involving Gaitano was a big mistake. It was going to be a long night.

CHAPTER FORTY-FIVE

"Here's what I think happened. As soon as we let you out of lockup you went straight to Beverly, because you knew she had your phone. You were tired of her antics and tired of sitting in jail."

"Would you like a beer or something?" asked Les.

"It turns out you were right—but not because she'd stolen it. She was being blackmailed with it by her husband's killers. They let her have it after altering the image. They were threatening to email us a copy if she didn't do exactly as they said. She was terrified she'd lose her daughter. In exchange for taking the fall, by leading us to the phone, they were promising to get her and Tiffany out of the country."

"Seriously, Rick. You need a beer."

"Fine, but I am being serious. You found her with the phone and you thought you had her dead to rights. She begged you to hear her out, but you were convinced she'd stolen it from you and that she was guilty. So you took it back and brought it to us. Now you can't live with yourself. Have I got it right so far?"

Les ignored the question.

"Those counterfeit passports cost somebody some big bucks to acquire. Whoever was blackmailing her had made some pretty impressive arrangements to get them out of the country, if she would let them pin the murders on her by leaving just enough clues behind to make us think she did it. They wanted to implicate her in Dietrich's murder, too."

Les felt sweat pouring from each armpit, despite the chilling cold. So they were onto her for killing Dietrich.

"We wouldn't know this, Les, if you hadn't given us her papers: Julie

Wallace and her daughter. The airline records show she'd booked a third ticket to St. Petersburg, for a man named Daniel Wallace. He doesn't exist, but someone calling herself Julie Wallace, and matching Beverly's description, paid for adjoining cabins on the afternoon of Dietrich's murder, just a few miles west of where he was gunned down. She used a phony credit card under the same name to reserve the rooms."

Gaitano was eying him like a wolf. Les wanted to kill the generator and run from the cabin, but he sat frozen to his chair. If he winced or reacted in any way, it was over. "I don't know what you're talking about," he said, shaking his head and trying to look mildly intrigued.

"I think you do. Beverly used her alias to pay for adjoining cabins just thirty miles west, on the afternoon of Dietrich's murder. One of those cabins was occupied by a woman fitting her description. The other was occupied by you, at least for forty minutes . . . until the gun went off."

"You've lost me, Detective," he replied evenly.

"The killers wanted Beverly to be staying close enough to the murder scene that after she fled, our investigation would eventually tie her to Dietrich's murder. She had no choice but to cooperate with them."

He paused while Les read the label on his beer.

"You two were having an affair. We know that. She was instructed to give you the doctored phone during your rendezvous at the Kalaloch Lodge. She let you in on her predicament and asked you not to turn her in until after she left the country."

Gaitano took a long draw from his beer.

"You were supposed to wait until she was gone before you gave us the phone. Maybe you freaked out when she said she was leaving. Or maybe you didn't believe her when she said she was being framed. You found her passports and her tickets and you took them. She tried to shoot you as you left. She didn't realize you were under a subpoena. You found her papers and you took them so we'd nab her at the airport in Vancouver."

"This is a one-sided conversation and I'm not on board."

"You were right, you know. She tried to leave the country by having those tickets reissued in their real names, using their real passports."

"You've gone nuts," said Les.

Gaitano smiled. "You mean about the affair? I don't think so," he laughed as he reached into a folder. Les wanted to crawl out of his skin as Gaitano handed him four night-vision photos showing Les and Beverly from a distance, half-undressed inside his car, locked in a passionate embrace. He was certain Gaitano had shown them to Marcia.

"I'd love to know what she told you on the night of Dietrich's murder. You two argued. A bullet—identical to the three we pulled from his body—was found embedded in a microwave in your cabin. Too bad it was too compressed to compare the riflings. Otherwise we could've charged her with Dietrich's murder. Whoever shot him gave her the same gun to use on you."

They found the bullet, he thought, as he felt the last shred of hope ebb away. The meeting was a setup and Bev would not be getting out of prison.

"I wonder how she got a .44? It's not like she was into guns. You never did show me yours—the one you drew on your neighbor. Now there's a lady who knows her guns. I pulled your registration, and sure enough you own a .44 Auto Mag. It's a classic, Les, so how come you never reported it as stolen?"

He declined to answer.

"Well, the gun that murdered Dietrich is bound to surface somewhere. I'm getting clues in my email, remember? Maybe you're afraid to cooperate because you know they used your gun. We know you didn't kill anybody, so why not tell me what you know?"

"Why would I hold back? I want you to find the killers."

"That's easy. You're protecting her. But you can't. The killers will come for her as soon as she gets out. She knows too much. Honestly I half-expected her to get snuffed inside. Her daughter may be in danger too. Maybe they've threatened your family. In fact, I remember the death threat they left you when they ransacked your house."

"That had to be Sugiyama and his henchmen," said Les. "Why hasn't anyone pursued him in all this time?"

"Because he's dead."

Feeling faint, he waited for the details.

"Kotaro Sugiyama died in a hit-and-run car crash while visiting Atlantic City five days ago. You'll be reading about it soon enough, though there's no proof it was a murder. And his partner, Takeo Yamamoto? He keeled over in Kyoto just last month, supposedly from a heart attack. Everyone is dying, Les. You've got to help me."

He hesitated before answering. He was in agony, wondering if they would turn around and charge her with Dietrich's murder, if only to prevent her from leaving the country once she got out.

"Look. I'll attend your press conference, but until I see that she's really free, and I can verify what you're saying about Sugiyama and Yamamoto, I'm not sure I trust you."

"Oh, she's getting out," replied Gaitano. "That was Van Owen on the line. He's crapping in his Armani because he can't get her out fast enough. Every blogger in Seattle wants him to resign, and they don't know the half. The killers are free and Van Owen knows his office colossally fucked up, which I just confirmed for him with my call. This will probably cost him the next election. He wants her steamrolled off death row like she owns the goddamn Pennsylvania Railroad."

"Is he going to admit any wrongdoing?"

"Wrongdoing is a strong word, Les. He prefers to say his DPA was overzealous. So the answer is no. And our conversation here—I'll deny it ever happened. Can't you see I'm trying to warn you that you and your client may be in danger once this breaks? The killers were banking on the gallows for her. If she's alive and talking then you're sitting ducks. They've knocked off ten people in eight months and they've already tried to kill you once."

"What are you talking about?"

"Come on, McKee. Don't sit here and lie to me. Do I look stupid? We know you were with Dietrich when they killed him, and dumb luck's the only reason you're still with us. Farrago told us about the meeting."

"You're fishing," Les muttered.

"Really? The clerk at Kalaloch isn't fishing. She identified you as checking in to the adjoining cabin, using *Daniel Wallace* as your alias, around 9:30 p.m. on the night of Dietrich's murder—less than an hour from when he was killed. And we've got a witness to his shooting, a guest who saw two men leave his room and head for the restaurant before the shots were fired. You scrambled back inside and ran out toward the lake. Have I got it right?"

Les shook his head in disagreement while Gaitano forged ahead. "I'd give my right arm to know what he told you that night. I suppose you've figured out that your friend Sonny was one of the assassins. He was gonna kill you, Les, his friend of fifteen years. I wanna know whose payroll he was on."

"What makes you say that Sonny shot Dietrich? I thought he left the country after killing Victor."

"He did. But once we found him dead in Spain, under the alias of Felix Graham, we were able to trace the rest of his travels. He was never in the Caymans. He went to Cancun just long enough to get the dough you wired him. Then he flew to Chicago to steal what he thought was a copy of the crash pictures from your mom. I'm sure you've figured that out by now."

"I have nothing figured out," said Les.

"He flew back here from Chicago and the next day Dietrich wound up dead. He was the third hit on Sonny's contract. He used a second shooter and they must've taken the ferry from Port Angeles to B.C. that night, because Sonny flew from Victoria to Portugal the next morning . . . didn't even say good-bye to his lovely wife, but she made out all right. We're pretty sure she's got a numbered account in Geneva with over four million U.S. dollars in it. So at least we know what happened to some of the missing forty-four."

"I wasn't there," said Les. "I was in my office."

"I know better. My point is that Sonny's bosses wanted you dead too. The bullets from that .44 were meant for you and Dietrich. They were going to kill you with your own gun, maybe stage it as a murder-suicide. But they failed, and you got away. They figured you were en route to warn your client. So they put the gun in her hands next, but she didn't have the heart to kill you."

"You like to speculate," said Les.

"Really? Then where's your .44? It must be in here somewhere. We know you purchased a .38 in June. Why would you do that if you own a .44 Handcannon?"

"Look, Rick, you seem to accept the fact that I had nothing to do with any murders, so let's just leave it there. I appreciate your integrity, I really do. And I'd like to thank you for spearheading her release."

"Les, whoever's sending clues knows where to find your .44. And they know you were with Dietrich when he died. They're trying to frame you for it, but that's okay. We know you didn't do it."

"I've been in the wrong place at the wrong time from day one, including tonight," Les said. "I'm tired of the badgering, so go work another angle. You're good at what you do and I'm glad you got your job back, but let's focus on how the County is going to release my client."

"It's simple. Van Owen will go public with your daughter's copy at noon tomorrow. But once it's out there, the killers will be coming for you because you know too much. I can help protect you and your family if you'll help me."

He felt apprehensive. Gaitano was groping with his theories, but it was becoming clear to Les that the multi-billion dollar conspiracy at VVG was very much alive. The mysterious deaths of Sugiyama and Yamamoto alarmed him greatly.

As if reading his mind, Gaitano pulled a magazine from his bag and asked, "What did you make of that article I sent?"

"At first I took it to mean that the Vortex conspirators gave Nakamura's technology to the Germans. But now you're telling me they're dead. You must think the impending implosion at VVG runs deeper than Sugiyama and Yamamoto."

"Sort of."

"Sort of? Look, Rick, I asked you up here to get an innocent woman out of prison. We both helped put her there, and either of us could have and should have stopped it sooner. We're on the same side, so what else aren't you telling me?"

"You won't believe me," he answered, sitting up. "And if you quote me I'll deny it."

CHAPTER FORTY-SIX

"Part of my arrangement with King County," he began, "is my agreement to keep their screw-ups out of this. I'm going for the killers, not the County. Besides, it's just a theory I can't prove. At least I couldn't until tonight."

He went back to the computer and focused on Les's semi-closeup of Akira Nakamura, while Les rose to stoke the fire. The wind outside was back to howling, but not as wildly as his soul. He still hadn't figured out where his "adversary-turned-ally" was headed.

"Okay," Gaitano said, peering at the grainy, high-contrast image on the screen. "We're looking at Nakamura here, correct?"

"I assume so."

"Have you seen his picture?"

"In the papers."

"This one?" He handed Les a snapshot. "Tell me if that's the same man in your video?"

"I can't be sure, but yes, it could be."

"How about this guy?" He handed him a snapshot of an Asian male who also appeared to be in his thirties. "Could this be the man you photographed?"

"It's possible, I guess. Why, who is he?"

"His name is Minoru Kawashima. He was Nakamura's bodyguard. He got the job because he looks like his boss. He often carried Nakamura's ID, and occasionally he would double for him at public events. The guy was that paranoid of getting bumped."

Les felt icier than the frigid winds outside. "Are you suggesting that Nakamura was not on board?"

"I'm damn near positive," replied Gaitano.

He looked again at the screen and photos. "But at Beverly's trial they said his corpse was identified with dental records."

"That's the other screw-up I referred to this morning. Worst piece of forensics I've ever seen. Granted, it was pure chaos that night. Six fried corpses and Nakamura's was the worst—burned beyond recognition. His dental records had to be flown here from Kyoto, but by the time they arrived, what remained of his corpse was on a cargo plane back to Japan. He was cremated without ever being identified."

Les was incredulous. "His body was never identified?"

"The wallet they found on the corpse had Nakamura's driver's license, his credit cards, even his plane ticket. I've seen them and I have no doubt they were authentic."

"Wait. He was burned to a crisp, yet his wallet survived?"

"Have you seen the crime scene photos?" Gaitano pulled out another black and white. "Unlike the others, Nakamura's head was practically blown off his shoulders. Remember the trace compound we found inside his jacket?"

Les glanced at the pictures then looked away. "But the corpse still had some teeth, which meant you had a duty to identify them. And what about his DNA? This is something you covered up. My God, the coroner lied under oath."

"There's more, Les. I don't think Byron was on board either."

"That's not possible. Marcia was at the morgue when they identified his body."

"Did she ever see it?"

"No, she stayed outside."

"Well, there wasn't much left of him either." He reached for another photo. "I trust you've got the stomach."

Les wasn't sure but he looked anyway. The corpse's face was burned to the bone and partially crushed by impact. At least a quarter of his skull was missing.

"The amazing thing is that his parents and his wife identified him. The Medical Examiner's report indicates a positive ID by multiple next of kin.

"All the victims, except for Nakamura, were positively identified by family."

"So let's exhume the body."

"I guess you missed his funeral. His parents had him cremated. They're supposedly good Catholics. No one else in that family has ever been cremated. They're raising his little girl, you know. It makes me think they know he's still alive."

"But if this isn't Byron," queried Les, pointing to the grisly photos, "then who is it?"

"Dwight Bonadelli. Who else?"

Suddenly it made sense.

"The way I see it," Gaitano continued, "is that somebody in Kyoto tipped them off and warned Nakamura not to get on that fucking balloon. The records show that seven passengers were supposed to make the flight, not six: the two lawyers, Wells, Nakamura, his bodyguard, the pilot, and Bonadelli, Byron's money man.

"The gondola holds a max of seven. Wells and Nakamura could have announced, just before launch, that they'd catch up with the others at the winery for lunch. Somehow they got the second pilot to fill one of the vacancies they'd created, then Byron gave his flight jacket to Bonadelli so he wouldn't get cold. Only he conveniently left his wallet in the pocket."

"That's so strange," Les said. The pilot's wife said she might have seen two men drive away."

"Really? She didn't tell us that. Anyway, the flight log said only six of seven got on board. We assumed, therefore, that just the bodyguard drove off. We suspected Bonadelli was in on it too, but we thought he was in Mexico at the time. I guess we don't really know what happened to the cash."

"The pilot's wife said her husband wasn't scheduled for that flight," Les said.

"She told us that as well. But it wasn't until after the trial that it hit me: once Wells and Nakamura bowed out, the second pilot must have decided to ride along. Had he stayed on the ground he could've told us who got on and who drove off. He was handling the desk that day."

"I've heard they can't confirm whether Nakamura's bodyguard was even in Seattle."

"It's the strangest thing. Homeland Security says he never went through customs, and the Japanese authorities are still looking for him. He's like a ghost, but we've learned he often traveled with false papers. He and Nakamura would sometimes take separate flights. Most people think he was here when he landed on free parking and drove away with all that money."

"What happened to Byron's car?"

"It ended up at his condo. We don't know how." Gaitano handed Les the rest of his crime scene photos. "None of the others were burned as bad. You know, enough of his teeth were missing, from what we thought was Nakamura's corpse, that a dental ID might not have been possible even if his records had arrived in time."

"Why not go back there and find the rest of his teeth?"

"They crashed on a turf farm, Les. Any body parts we didn't tag have presumably been rolled up and parceled out to developments from Kent to Marysville by now. Can you imagine mommy, when Fido tracks a molar inside the house, or a human jawbone, after digging in the brand new lawn?"

"Stop," said Les. "I get the point."

"I can't explain why Bonadelli wouldn't have his own ID—except he was supposed to be in Mexico. We know he flew to the Caymans with a withdrawal form signed by Byron, just to get the dough. Then he returned, though we have no idea how or if he smuggled in the cash."

"So my pictures are all you have?"

"Such as they are," he replied, pointing to the screen. "Nakamura turns his head to the camera just as you snapped this close-up. You weren't zoomed in enough. I suppose it could be either man. And Byron . . . well here, see for yourself." He clicked backwards to the wide-angle shots of the gondola and zeroed in on Byron's back.

"I've been through every frame of this a hundred times. It's my Zapruder film. Don't ask me why Byron had to be the one with his back to the camera. But this is the best we've got. It could be either guy."

Gaitano showed him photographs of Bonadelli.

"His broker, the doppelgänger. I'll bet Bonadelli had no idea what his client was up to. He smuggled or hid the cash for Byron somewhere, then Byron had him come along on their excursion.

"You're guessing."

"I was until tonight."

"How does Breanna's copy help? Except for the license plate it's the same as the original, right?"

"I was wondering when you'd ask." Gaitano reached in his briefcase and pulled out Les's phone. "I got this from the evidence locker."

He forwarded to the video sequence of the crash, using the phone's smaller screen. He froze on the last few frames before the explosion, then advanced them one frame at a time.

"Tell me what you see."

Les watched the now familiar sequence. As his camera zoomed all the way in on Nakamura, he drew closer for a better look, but the explosion came too fast.

"Let's use a bigger screen and take it very slow." He reached into his overnight bag and removed a laptop. After booting it up they followed the moving sequence once again. He went frame by frame until he froze on Nakamura's face.

"Blow it up," said Les. Gaitano complied. "What's that?" he asked, pointing to a line that ran horizontally across the screen, right through Nakamura's eyes.

"It's a static line, an audio distortion that degrades the image whenever there's high-frequency interference. You see lots of them when the balloon explodes, on both the original and your daughter's copy. But up until the explosion you see no such lines on your daughter's copy and only a few of them on the your phone, including the one running through his face."

"Are you saying it's been added?"

"Bingo."

CHAPTER FORTY-SEVEN

He turned to Breanna's copy where there was no static line at all. "You were zoomed in much closer at the end, but it's a moving picture. There's enough good data behind that static line that high-grade facial recognition software might just work."

"I'm not following," said Les.

"It has to do with pixels—literally the quantity of data collected by the media when the image is first laid down. As you enlarge the collected data, negative space gets created. The software uses algorithms to supply what it thinks is the missing data, based on the known data from the pixels surrounding the negative space. For example, your still of the Corvette was a lot closer, and the alpha-numeric image a lot easier to read, so the software was able to recreate the number leaving no room for debate. But when you snapped your still of Nakamura, you weren't zoomed in enough, meaning your image didn't capture enough data to allow the algorithms to guess or recreate his facial features.

"But your final moving sequence is much closer. So somebody removed the data on his face and replaced it with a static line instead. The data behind the line is gone, but not on your daughter's copy."

"Is it enough to make an ID?" asked Les.

"It's better than anything we've had to work with yet," Gaitano answered. "But as far as I'm concerned, the fact that somebody tried to conceal this—it's all the proof I need. Whoever gave your phone to the killers, so they could frame your client, didn't want them knowing who was on board . . . and who wasn't."

"So you're saying my pictures were doctored twice."

"Sonny was in a contract with Sugiyama and Yamamoto. His orders were to kill Nakamura, Wells and Dietrich. He started planning it as soon as his bosses received their intel on Nakamura's secret trip and the balloon excursion."

"I'm not following," said Les.

"Whatever amount they paid him, Sonny saw it as his chance for more. He was about to kill a man worth fifty million dollars, so he went to Byron, whom he'd known since Beverly's first divorce. Sonny was terminal and intent on bowing out of this world with flair. So he offered to turn Sugiyama's murder-for-hire into a chance for Wells and Nakamura to save their skins and their toys and vanish with their dough."

"I can see why they took you off this case," said Les.

"Think about it," Gaitano protested. "Byron was in deep shit in every possible direction, unless he was dead. He was certainly worth more dead than alive to Beverly, which made her the obvious patsy."

"Maybe," said Les. "If he faked his death it meant his options would vest, with no lawsuit and with no two-year wait."

"Exactly. He was hoping his parents could collect on his second fifty mill, which they are still trying to do. They have his daughter too. What do you think he's going to do to Beverly once he learns you've sprung her from prison?"

"So you're convinced he's alive," said Les.

"I am tonight. I think Sonny was working both sides of the equation. He helped the killers and he helped the targets . . . then he collected a fee from both."

"Your only proof is my daughter's copy."

"Why do you think Sonny was on such a mission to find your phone? It wasn't because you filmed the car, Les, it was because you filmed the cargo. He had to know if your pictures identified the victims. Once he saw you'd filmed the car, and not much of the victims, he realized the special effects team at VVG could alter the plate and make it match your client's rental. So instead of destroying your phone, he added the static line to conceal the bodyguard, then gave it to Sugiyama."

"You're assuming he knew how to tamper with it."

"He was resourceful enough to add a static line. It explains why he flew to Chicago in such a rush. Once he heard you'd sent a copy to your mom, he couldn't risk it getting into circulation. You were setting a trap for him, weren't you?"

"Yeah, and it might've worked if you hadn't arrested me when you did."

"Sorry about that, Les."

He watched silvery gusts of snow settle in the window frames. The moon looked flat and cold. "So the pictures I gave you were a total fraud," Les sighed. "I'm the reason she went down. I did this to her."

"Don't start," Gaitano said gruffly. "Two days after her arrest, we got the first of the anonymous email we can't seem to trace."

"And?"

Gaitano started clicking through his laptop until he arrived at an email from May 5. It read: *Here's what she doesn't want you to see.* Gaitano opened the attachment that came with it and showed Les the incriminating photos from the crash.

"We didn't get this from the killers. I think it came from Byron or his father."

"You mean I've been torturing myself for giving you the evidence that convicted her, yet you had a second copy?"

"We couldn't have used it. At least with your phone we had a plausible chain of custody. But Byron couldn't be sure we were going to get your phone and he wanted us to think she did it."

"But his parents were staunchly on her side."

"That was an illusion. They needed to win her trust so she wouldn't fight them over raising Tiffany if she want to prison. But behind the scenes they were making sure we charged her. Les, we could've convicted her without your phone."

Les raised his eyebrows, partly in disbelief, partly in anticipation.

"Her star witness lied about her alibi. We had a witness of our own who was prepared to blow Monica's story out of the water, though we never got to call her."

"Who was that?"

"A friend of Monica's, somebody who came forward when Monica first told her story. We know that Monica never went to Cannon Beach. Our witness saw her in Seattle on the weekend of the crash. Monica even bragged about covering for Beverly with Byron's parents, while Beverly was off gallivanting with her male companion."

"If Beverly was gallivanting, Rick, it doesn't matter who she was with . . . it's still an alibi."

"Not if she was lying to Monica. We don't know where she was that weekend. No one saw her in Cannon Beach and we've uncovered no trace of any boyfriend, except for you."

"What's your point?"

"My point is that we had Monica dead to rights. Perjury in spades. That by itself would have swung the jury, pictures or not. I think *Tag's* to blame for her conviction, putting on that kind of story."

Gaitano peered out the window. The sky was inky. "I still haven't solved it, Les. That's why I need your help."

"I'm not following."

"Why did Beverly let Monica pitch that cockamamie story? Tag was too smart for that. Who is she trying to protect? She was framed by someone and she's sheltering them. Did they threaten to kill her daughter? I think she told you who it is."

"No she didn't."

"You're lying. Who was her boyfriend?"

"So you agree it wasn't me."

"Why did you check in that night as Daniel Wallace? You weren't going to Russia with her, were you?"

He ignored the question. "Why not resurrect your witness and charge Monica with perjury?"

"We might," quipped Gaitano. "We tried to get her on the stand as part of our rebuttal, but Gifford blew it. Judge McGovern called it trial by ambush. I think he knew in his heart that she was innocent. He never liked our case and now he's going to go ballistic."

"What do you mean?" asked Les.

"I wasn't the lawyer on this," Gaitano said defensively. "Amy decided to sandbag Tag about our witness, and now Van Owen hates her for it. She was worried if she showed her cards to Berenson, Monica would change her story and they would come up with something else. So she held back on disclosing what we had until the end."

"You mean you had a witness you kept from Berenson until the end? That's misconduct. No wonder Saint Charles wouldn't let you put her on the stand."

"Our witness was cooperating, Les. She told the judge she'd just come forward, after reading about Monica's testimony in the paper. We thought the judge might let her in on that basis."

"On the basis that you lied about when she came forward? This makes me sick."

"Amy waited until Tag rested. She knew Monica had lied and couldn't change her story. She told Berenson it was over. She offered Beverly life in prison if she'd cooperate and reveal who else was behind the murders, but Beverly wouldn't talk. Berenson told us to fuck off. Can you believe it?"

"I never heard about this."

"It all took place in chambers," he replied. "Berenson had cajoled an informant from within the Prosecutor's office—a civil servant with a conscience—who signed an affidavit claiming that we knew about our witness all along."

"Which was true," insisted Les.

"I guess," Gaitano conceded. "But it was the word of a lowly staffer against the good graces of the County Prosecutor. Our witness was sticking by her story—that she'd just come forward."

"Let me guess," said Les. "Saint Charles didn't buy it."

"Not only that, he came damn close to declaring a mistrial and filing a Bar complaint against both Gifford and Van Owen. It could still happen if this matter advances to Saint Charles. The only thing stopping him at the time was that he'd pegged his jury to acquit your client. I still can't believe they found her guilty. Now that we know they got it wrong, I figure Judge McGovern will be going after Amy's license."

"Why didn't any of this come out?" asked Les.

"Both sides agreed to keep it quiet. Berenson certainly didn't want it coming out about our witness. My question, Les, is why in the hell did they lie in the first place if she had a real alibi? That's what made me so certain she was guilty. Why not tell us where she was, and who tricked her into renting that Corvette? Who is she protecting?"

"I don't know."

"She was falling for you, man. You were on your way to becoming husband four, so she must have told you something."

"I guess I should thank you for arresting me when you did and for charging her so fast. Husbands one through three are dead."

"One through two, Les. Husband three is still alive. We think he was cheating on her, or at least that he'd started seeing someone else after they split up. Did she tell you that?"

"Byron? A girlfriend? What's your proof?"

"He bought somebody a pricey diamond ring before he died. Any idea who that was for?"

Les shrugged and changed the subject. "How's it going to look if you let her out of prison, then start attacking her alibi with a perjury charge?"

"We won't have to cross that bridge if you'll just tell us who framed her. Whoever it was gave you the phone."

CHAPTER FORTY-EIGHT

"For the last time, Rick, I testified how I got it."

"You mean you committed perjury to protect your client, just like Monica. How about the gloves? Where did you get them?" Gaitano waived them in his face.

He laughed. "The last time you showed me those you thought I'd used them to detonate a bomb."

"And you were trying to convince me they were part of a super-secret virtual reality device that VVG was prepared to commit gangland murder for. Something you called the GC Quantum. It's back, Les, just read the *Cybernetics Journal*. Did you catch the name of the company behind it?"

"*Sprung Technologies,*" said Les.

"*Sprung* is German for leap."

Les gave him a curious stare.

"When I was a boy there was a TV show about a time traveler called *Quantum Leap*. I've been wondering whether *Sprung* Technologies and Byron's *Quantum* namesake are connected."

"If they're alive, Rick, they wouldn't be advertising."

"Obviously they can't resist a joke. Besides, you were the only one who used that term. Where did you get it?"

"From Milton's files."

"How about the gloves? I know two cops in Kirkland who swear they saw you running from Byron's condo with them and wearing an HMD like the one in this article, called *der Astronom.*"

Les winced inwardly. The Galileo was in his drawer, just feet from

Gaitano. Its current name, der Astronom, was compelling evidence that Nakamura was indeed back in the game. "I've helped you all I can," he said.

"Then you can have these back." Gaitano tossed the gloves to Les. "If that's the best you can do for me then I guess I'll be paddling up shit creek without my gloves."

"You've got my daughter's copy."

"For tonight. I suspect my higher-ups will go back in and superimpose the two static lines that were added to your phone. They don't want the press sniffing out their misidentification. They'll justify their cover-up in the name of their ongoing investigation."

"Are you suggesting they don't want you to find the killers?"

"Not at all. They want the killers. They're just not so interested in my theory about the victims. But I could change that with your help."

"You'll do just fine without me."

"I'm not going off half-cocked on this doppelgänger thing without more data. Given their resources, Wells and Nakamura can stay in hiding longer than Osama Bin Laden. You're my recognition software, Les, meaning you've got the surrounding pixels and the algorithms I need to fill the negative space. Help me and I'll be damned if I let them tamper with this copy. In this case the victims *are* the killers."

"Meaning they let six innocents get on board when they knew they were going to die?"

"It goes further," Gaitano answered. "Don't forget about the compound we found in the lining of their jackets."

"It wasn't even mentioned in the trial," Les said.

"As soon as the A.T.F. found trace C-4 and receiver fragments, they dropped the nitro theory like it never existed. But for Wells and Nakamura to pull this off, they needed Bonadelli and Kawashima to be maimed beyond all recognition. That's why those two took it the worst. When the bomb went off, the nitro in their jackets chain-reacted. I think Sonny planted it so as to render each man unidentifiable. Consumed, if you will."

Les shook his head. "I'm sure the M.E. took tissue samples before he turned their corpses over for cremation. There would be DNA."

"I think he did. But the testing on that would have set us back for months, and we didn't need it . . . we knew who our victims were, based on positive ID from next of kin."

"So test it now."

"I can't any find tissue samples in the evidence locker. They were probably the first things to go once I started asking questions. I can't prove it, Les, but I think I'm in the middle of a department cover-up."

"You can't let them bury the truth about their blunder. And you don't need me to expose it. I've got nothing to suggest that Wells and Nakamura weren't on board. But if you're right, it was a bomb within a bomb and your job is to bring them to justice." Les turned a log with an iron poker. Flames leaped as the fire crackled.

Gaitano tried a fresh approach. "Now that she can rightfully inherit her dead husband's fortune, she can sue you for malpractice, on account his fortune's missing. Your only defense may be to prove he's still alive."

Les warmed his hands by the fire. "That's reason enough for Byron to stay dead. She's got a much stronger case against Smith Levinson than she does against me, you know, *bank error in her favor*. But if Bonadelli did nothing wrong . . . if he was murdered and isn't in hiding, then she's got only me to sue."

"So we're both selling out the truth," Gaitano said.

Les stared long and hard into the fiery coals. "I take it you'll be spending the night? We should take turns keeping this fire going. I'll go with you tomorrow, Rick, but after that I'm done talking with you about the case."

"You're not a suspect, Les. In fact we knew you were innocent all along. The night you and Bev were steaming up your Saab? I was the one clicking snapshots. And when that call came in from Sonny, I was listening."

He frowned. "We weren't followed, so how did you find us?"

"When is it finally going to dawn on you that every fucking cell phone, including Sonny's, is a GPS."

"Fuckers. Every one of you."

"I had a warrant, so don't freak out. Sonny had just finished killing Victor when he called, but you thought he was in the Caymans. We both know why you sent him to New Orleans with all that cash. You were hoping to shut Victor up, not kill him."

Les stayed quiet.

"I loved those calls that came in from your wife. Talk about getting caught with your pants down." He laughed out loud. "I almost doubled over when she asked you if Beverly was there. You said you were about to drop her off, though I think you meant you were about to get her off."

Les glared at him. "So if you knew I was being framed, why did you arrest me the next morning and make me take a polygraph?"

"Victor's death was enough to haul you in for questioning. You volunteered for the polygraph."

"How can you be sure that Sonny set that fire in Victor's building?"

"He was good, Les. NOFD still can't say if that fire was deliberate. Sonny's dead so we may never know. The same goes for the fire on the island. But once we learned his alias, we knew he didn't leave New Orleans until Monday morning. Do you remember asking him what time it was in Georgetown?"

"Yeah. He said one thirty in the morning."

"He said, *Eight Bells and all is well*, remember that?"

"Yes."

"It's nautical, probably from his Navy days. It signals a shift change. He was trying to tell you in his own way that the saga of Victor Garving came to its end at midnight on April 28. Live by fire, die by fire. Did you know we came damn close to nabbing him in Cancun?"

"How so?"

"During that call he said he'd email your assistant in the morning with instructions for wiring him the dough. So we got another warrant, this time for any incoming email to your assistant. We knew as soon as she did where she'd be wiring the money. She acted fast, but we had Cancun PD dispatch a unit to the Western Union. Somehow he gave them the slip. I think he was a master of disguises."

"So you knew about the missing fortune when you brought me in for questioning?"

"I did, Amy didn't."

Douchebag, thought Les.

"Anyway, the deeper we drilled, Les, the more we could tell that you were clean and sniffing out answers all over town. You were looking for the truth, not hiding it. You lie like hell but you're okay. Now that you've closed your practice, I could use you in Homicide."

Les moved closer to the fire, but he still felt chilled. "What about Ty Pruitt?" he asked. "What if the New Orleans Cold Case Unit decides to reopen that investigation?"

"No proof," Gaitano answered. "Victor Garving is dead. Sonny Lile is dead. By the way, did Sonny really tell you that Victor ratted her out?"

Les didn't answer. It was a lie he'd perpetrated back when he was convinced of her guilt. Now he wanted to slither inside the fire.

"You were begging us to charge her, Les, he was NFL. Talk about a hit on a defenseless player, even Richard Sherman would have drawn a flag for that."

"I gave you hearsay."

"You were her lawyer and you told us she killed him."

"Because I thought so at the time."

"But now you don't?"

"No, I don't," he answered, tensing.

Gaitano was a two-edged sword, razor sharp, slicing the finest hairs on the back of Les's neck without breaking the surface of his skin. If he learned she had a motive for killing Dietrich, he would hunt her down like a wolf and plunk her back on death row.

So far he'd placed her, along with Les, just thirty miles from the scene of Dietrich's murder. He'd placed the murder weapon in her hands. But somehow she'd managed to leave no trace of her "affair" with David Dietrich. It helped that Dietrich's sexual orientation was common knowledge. Gaitano was clueless that she'd tried to get him to swing both ways.

Indeed there were no clues of Beverly's relationship with Dietrich, except for the passport in Les's desk. If Gaitano found it during the night, she would not be getting out. He couldn't hide it now, not with Gaitano rolling out his bedroll just inches from the desk. Why hadn't he thought to hide it sooner?

"Feel free to sleep in my room, Rick," he offered. "I'll stay here and keep this going."

"Too cold in there," Gaitano said. "I take it I can shut that generator off so we can get some sleep?" Moments later they were both bedding down, but Les knew he wouldn't sleep at all.

CHAPTER FORTY-NINE

Throughout the night Gaitano kept rising to feed the fire. Each time Les would close his eyes, but as soon as Gaitano moved away from the fire he'd look up to check on the detective. Still, it was more than Gaitano keeping him awake. He was in torment. Beverly was on death row for six murders she didn't commit, while VRD and the Quantum Chip were racing to market as if on schedule. Nakamura had obviously regained control of VVG's renegade investors. Was Byron alive as well?

As dawn rose feebly over mounds of snow, Les rolled up his sleeping bag and moved methodically through the morning in sober silence. Gaitano was sulking and Les was fighting demons in the caverns of his mind. There were answers just beyond his grasp. He managed to pack Dietrich's papers, the Galileo, and the smartwatch with his other belongings while Gaitano was distracted.

They drove to town. He looked back at Friday Harbor one last time as the float plane rose from the water and banked into the sun. His neighbor had offered to assist with the movers on Saturday, which meant that Les would not be back. Seated next to Gaitano he clutched his overnight bag with Dietrich's papers tucked inside.

The press conference was conducted on the first floor of the King County Courthouse. A throng of reporters had gathered by the time Les and Gaitano arrived. At precisely noon Prosecutor James Van Owen stepped to the podium. His receding hairline and graying sideburns looked more weathered than usual. Amy Gifford stood somberly by his side, along with Rick Gaitano. Les was one row back with Berenson, towering above the others. As Van Owen adjusted his microphone the crowd grew still.

"Yesterday," he began. The occasional camera clicked in the background. "Yesterday, the office of the Prosecutor was rocked with irrefutable new evidence in the murder conviction of Beverly Wells. Seattle attorney Les McKee has discovered and alerted us to heretofore unknown copies of his original pictures and video, which we have since confirmed to be genuine, and which fully persuade us that his client was framed for her husband's murder."

The crowd erupted with emotion as Van Owen struggled to continue. "Our investigation into the deaths of Byron Wells and five others on April 13 has been officially reopened."

The marble hallway of the majestic courthouse sounded more like the floor of the stock exchange. It took several failed attempts before Van Owen was able to complete his account of the mystery Corvette in Les's photo. At that point, the trial of Beverly Wells resumed, not before Judge McGovern, but before a skeptical press. The most shocking revelation was that Governor Campanello was prepared to sign a pardon, in fact, earlier in the day he'd signed an executive order staying all nine pending executions in the state, and banning any further use of the death penalty in capital cases.

Amy Gifford stepped forward to answer a final round of questions.

"Ms. Gifford," a reporter began. "How soon until we can see this new evidence?"

Gifford glanced at her notes. "The photographs and video are still being analyzed. The killers may have made other alterations to the images we introduced at trial, which we can now compare. We'll make everything available to the media a week from today."

Les listened to this announcement placidly as he knew what it probably meant. They needed time to conceal the bodyguard, just as Sonny had done. When the press was finished chewing up Amy Gifford, he stepped forward to confirm his story. To his surprise, he encountered scant criticism from his interrogators. They were after the prosecutor for his blunder. Many of them never thought she was guilty either.

After another twenty minutes of dodging hard questions, Van Owen announced there would be time for just one more. It was for Rick Gaitano from Joel Hastings, a reporter for *King 5 News*.

"The obvious question, Detective Gaitano, is who doctored the original pictures taken by McKee and then gave him back his phone? Sonny Lile had fled the country by the time the phone came back, so you must have other suspects. And please comment, if you will, on your alleged removal from the case. Have you been reinstated? And are you in fact pursuing rumors that Byron Wells and Akira Nakamura were not on board when the balloon exploded?"

The question made Les wince though Gaitano kept his cool, as a ghostly hush descended on the crowd.

"That's about three questions, Joel, but I'll do my best. I was not taken off the case. I was transferred into Fraud once we closed it. But I'm back in Homicide now that it's been reopened, due to my familiarity with the facts. We do have other suspects, though I can't comment on them now. As for the rumors you mentioned, we've heard them too and they're false. All six victims were positively identified by multiple next of kin or by dental records. DNA samples weren't required. So, no, we're not pursuing those rumors in any way, shape or form."

Once Gaitano finished, Van Owen turned toward the nearest service elevator. Gaitano offered to buy Les lunch, though he held back, bracing himself for a barrage of reporters who wanted more. As he scanned the nameless crowd, he spotted a familiar face. She was walking toward him with her deep-set eyes, heart-shaped mouth, and dark, shoulder-length hair. Questions were being fired at him from left and right, but he kept an eye on her as she struggled to make her way. "Ms. Taylor?"

"Here's my card," she said quickly, pressing it into his palm. "Call me—"

"Mr. McKee," a voice shot out. "You were once a suspect in the case before surrendering your phone. Now you claim the picture they used to convict your client was a fraud. How are we supposed to believe you didn't alter it yourself? And how do we know that your newest picture hasn't been tampered with as well? Apparently the experts can't agree on this sort of thing."

He shot an evil glance at the source of the insinuation then turned to look for Monica, but she was gone. As he slipped her card into his pocket, a nearby reporter looked on with interest.

Once the media disbanded, Les stayed behind and waited for Gaitano, who'd finally pressed him into having lunch with him and his Lieutenant.

What he thought was to be a cordial debriefing of the day's events turned out to be a last-ditch, tag-team ambush for information on David Dietrich. Sitting at the corner table of a greasy-spoon cafe near Pioneer Square, across from Lieutenant Omar, he felt more like he was trapped in the back office of a used car dealership after hours. Omar was the closer.

"A lot's come down today," he said, as Gaitano went to pay the bill. "We're not gonna rest until we break this fucker." As he spoke, his North Carolina drawl seeped across the table. "That goes for Dietrich's murder. So don't dig yourself a hole, counselor. We'll bury you in it. In fact, you won't be getting any chances after this. So who in the hell was Daniel Wallace? His name was on her credit card and her plane reservation. It wasn't you, was it?"

"No," he said.

"Was it Dietrich?"

"Lieutenant Omar, I have no idea."

"For your sake, I hope that's true."

Gaitano reappeared and the threesome strolled up the hill to the courthouse. Gaitano drove Les to the lobby of the Stouffer Madison. As they pulled to the curb he smiled at Les and said, "I guess this is it."

Les wasn't sure whether to be disappointed or relieved.

"It's never too late to change your mind," Gaitano offered. "So don't change your number."

"You mean this piece of shit?" asked Les, as he removed his cell phone from his pocket. "Here, you can have it." He tossed it on the dashboard of the cruiser. "The signal sucks and I misplace it constantly. Hell, those things are more trouble than they're worth."

"Les, I wish you'd reconsider. Neither of us slept last night. And while you were waiting on me to go to lunch, I was down in the evidence room again. I'm bothered by the passports and the airline tickets."

He removed the passports from a folder marked *State vs. Wells* and placed them on the police computer mounted between them. "I have to know how you got them. At trial, Berenson suggested they were forged by the killers—just like your picture of the Vette."

"You obviously don't believe him."

"Not the tickets. They're real. She tried to have them reissued in her real name. Take a look at the passport they found on Sonny Lile in Spain and tell me what you see. *Felix Graham*, remember?"

He handed it to Les. "It's a counterfeit, right?" he asked, expecting no reply. "Well after her trial we had them analyzed by the FBI back on Pennsylvania Avenue. The feds tell us the same ink and paper was used in all three. They were counterfeited together."

"So?" said Les. "You said Sonny's bosses were helping her leave the country. They would have procured Sonny's at the same time as hers, though you never brought it up. Showing the jury his phony passport would have supported her claim that she was framed."

"Not if Sonny was working for her, which is what we thought at the time. We learned about the ink and the paper after her conviction. And we learned something new last month. The CIA took a look at them for us, and they claim they're black market Russky. The best U.S. dollars can buy."

"So the killers had ties to spies. Sugiyama's henchmen could have procured them overseas—both Sonny's and Bev's. They wanted you to think she was about to flee."

"Excuse me, she *was* about to flee . . . to St. Petersburg. If these papers were a fiction, the killers wouldn't have her flying off to Russia. She doesn't even speak the language. Maybe she was leaving to be with Byron or maybe she was meeting him on the way. Maybe he was Daniel Wallace."

"You said he's in Germany if he's alive."

"Not exactly. I said he's running Sprung Technologies. After Germany reunited, the former East Germany became a pipeline for funneling Soviet black market secrets to the West. There's still a demand for KGB technology. St. Petersburg is the newest haven for foreign hackers and international cyber thieves. They're the ones who clobbered Target last Christmas. And I assume you've heard of Moonlight Maze?"

"The foreigners who cracked the Pentagon."

"They'd been in deeper than anyone before, and for more than a year before we discovered it. Moscow was their base, but it's since been moved to St. Petersburg—and their biggest customer for stolen and pirated technology is the Germans. I'll wager Wells and Nakamura are lying low somewhere in St. Pete's—and keeping an eye on Hanover. These days you can run a global enterprise from Siberia if you want."

"*Budem zdorovy,*" muttered Les, as he felt a chill sweep through his jacket.

"What's that?"

"Nothing," he said as he shook his head, picturing Byron with a vodka. "I think it means 'good day.' As in 'we're finished here.'"

With that, he undid his seatbelt. But Gaitano wasn't finished. "What if I told you his father has made two trips to Eastern Europe since the crash?"

"St. Petersburg?"

"No, but close. Helsinki and Gdansk. Strictly as a tourist, or so he told Uncle Sam. By himself? He's shown no prior interest in crossing the Atlantic."

"That doesn't prove anything," Les answered as he opened the door. "Everybody's flocking to Eastern Europe."

"He's there, Les. I can feel it. The State Department says his father has inquired about immigrating to Poland. His grandfather was a Pole named Ivan Velski. You know the court will make them give little Tiffany back to Bev, unless they disappear with her before she gets out of prison."

Gaitano studied him intently. "Did you find the passports with the phone, or was she keeping them someplace else?"

"*Don't*, Rick. I've told you all I can."

"I don't think you found them with the phone. Maybe the phone appeared outside your house, but not the passports or the tickets. You took them from her because you didn't want her to leave. If you'd waited another day she might have made it."

"This is intriguing," he said, as he stood to walk away. "But it doesn't involve me anymore. I wish you well. I'd love to be there when you solve it."

CHAPTER FIFTY

Gaitano sat in silence before driving off. Les was watching him from inside the lobby as his own mind took quantum leaps. That's why he'd ended it. He'd come too close to revealing the identity of Beverly's traveling companion. Was it possible they were both in on this with Byron? Until something went amiss?

Upstairs, standing in the shower, hot water pelted him as Gaitano's questions and speculations rushed through his mind. Wrapped in a towel, he dialed the number on Monica's business card.

Thirty minutes later he was downstairs in the lounge, waiting for her as she strolled in. "Thanks for meeting me," she said, her face half-hidden behind oversized sunglasses.

"How did you happen to be at the courthouse today?" he asked.

"Beverly asked me to come. She called me this morning from Purdy."

"They let her make calls from death row?"

Monica nodded. "She says everything's changed. They've promised her she'll be home by Christmas. She appreciates what you've done, Les. She asked me to thank you a thousand times."

"Let's sit over there," he suggested, pointing to an isolated table in the back, next to a synthetic olive tree. He didn't want anyone overhearing their conversation.

"I had no choice but to the tell the truth," he said, once they sat down. "You can tell her it was a picture of her smiling daughter that saved her life. I feel awful for implicating her. I don't think she can ever forgive me."

"You didn't have to come forward, Les. I think we both know the risks you were taking."

He wondered how much she knew.

Monica continued. "You lied for her about how you got the phone. It meant a lot. She understands why you turned her in, given what you thought at the time."

"You lied too," he said. "But you must have known the jury wouldn't buy it."

"We knew it was risky, but she couldn't admit that I never went to Cannon Beach. I'd committed to that story with Byron's parents before the crash. She wanted to stay consistent. Big mistake, I guess."

"Why not stick with the truth?" he asked.

"She couldn't bear the thought of Byron's parents knowing she'd been with David. Especially since she never really cheated. Tag thought there was a chance the jury might buy it, once they knew the picture on your phone was fake."

"Were Beverly and Dietrich lovers?"

"No. They had some kind of twisted need for each other, but it wasn't ever sexual."

He wondered if Monica knew that her friend's "twisted need" had turned to murder. "She must have known how risky it was, leaving Dietrich out of her defense."

She nodded. "Her hopes were lifted when you made that deal—not to say how you got the phone. I think it was the only thing that kept her going."

"But she lost."

"I know, but it gave her hope. Without you, she would've killed herself. She told me so. She asked me to tell you that you gave her what she needed— only she wanted more. She said you'd know what that meant."

Les was pretty sure that Monica knew as well. "Please tell her how thrilled I am she's getting out." He leaned farther across the table and said softly, "I don't plan on calling or writing her."

Monica's fingers lightly brushed his hand. "It's all good. She asked me to give you something I've been holding the entire time." She reached inside her purse and produced a digital recording device. It was the tape of his meeting with David Dietrich.

"She told me this was David's, but I haven't listened to it. She said maybe you'd have some things for her," she added, hopefully.

"As in papers?" he asked.

"She said you'd know what she meant."

"You know too," he challenged, this time speaking his mind.

"Maybe," she said, sipping her coffee.

"I don't have them here," he replied. "But I could get them for you before I leave. It's not something I'd risk putting in the mail."

"I've heard you're leaving on Sunday."

"Word travels fast. So, would you like to see me off? I think I could have her farewell gift for you by then."

Dietrich's passport and airline ticket were locked away upstairs, but he would listen to the recording first. Beverly might still have a copy. Monica studied him as if reading his every thought.

"She said to tell you, Les, that she never got a chance to copy any sound files from this device."

"Well, tell her I never got a chance to photocopy any of those papers either."

She smiled. "She said you were a good man."

She gazed at him for a moment and he blushed. "Now, where and when should we meet?"

He pulled his ticket out. Monica scribbled down the details as he read them softly: "United Airlines, Flight Sixty-Four, 12:31 p.m. Check the monitors to see which gate."

As she folded her notes she motioned to him with her big brown eyes to look behind him. He turned abruptly to face a stranger who said, "Excuse me, sir, are you Brian?"

"No," said Les, "wrong guy."

"Sorry," he said, then walked off to a distant table.

"Monica," Les said as he stood up. "Let's not plan on chatting at the airport. I'll hand you what you want as I board the plane. I won't get in line until they call row twenty."

"I'll be there," she said, though she looked as if she wanted to draw another card. "Les, you know how Beverly's been sued by the other victims? Is it possible those cases will be dropped?"

"Absolutely," he replied. "The lawyers were banking on her conviction sticking. If she didn't murder Byron, then she's not responsible for their deaths either."

"Thank God," she sighed. "Her house was about to be auctioned. Now at least she's got a chance at starting over, thanks to you. You've risked so much to make this happen."

"Not as much as you," he said. "They may still charge you with perjury—just to make you talk. Gaitano claims they have a witness who saw you in Seattle and not with Bev. I guess you bragged about being her alibi for the weekend."

"I know. Amy Gifford hid her from us until the end, but the judge saw through it and wouldn't let her take the stand."

"Who is she?" he asked.

"No one you know."

"Is she telling the truth?"

Monica nodded, looking worried and ashamed. "Do you think I'll go to jail?"

"They'll offer to deal with you if you talk."

"Never," she vowed defiantly. "I'll serve my sentence if I must, because I did lie under oath. Bev went to prison for something she never did."

"What did you think of the last question at the press conference today?" he asked.

"That Byron's still alive?" She rolled her eyes. "Those rumors have been bouncing through the blogs for months. But Bev went to the morgue and saw him with her own two eyes. She told me she'll never forget the look on his face, even though he was dead."

Les felt his internal organs turn to putty—rearranging themselves and leaking acid. He studied her and decided she believed her words. She didn't have a clue that Beverly had lied about what she saw that night in the county morgue. Les had seen the pictures—of Byron's nearly headless and thoroughly charred corpse.

CHAPTER FIFTY-ONE

The roar of a jumbo jet rattled the giant windows but no one seemed to notice. The holidays were fast approaching and the corridors at Sea-Tac were packed with harried travelers. The airport was almost back to normal after Wednesday's storm.

Les sat hunched over papers at an airport cafeteria. He'd been sitting there since 10:00 a.m. trying to devise a plan, but it wasn't easy. Since Wednesday he'd hardly slept. The audio recording was Dietrich's. It picked up almost every word of their secret meeting, right up until the fatal shots.

He no longer worried that Beverly might give a second copy to the cops. She wasn't blackmailing him with it. She was returning a favor. So he felt he owed it to her to do the same with Dietrich's papers. The night before he'd pulled them from his bag for one last look. He was putting them in order for the hand-off to Monica when he found it.

Folded in the jacket of Dietrich's airline ticket, and tucked behind his international flight coupons, was a half-page email from Byron, dated April 29—more than two weeks *after* the crash.

My David,
    We've arrived so this will be my only (I'm switching to the Vortex). I can't believe you let her charge it on my card and that McKee stumbled on the statement. Your ring was on there too. That statement will lead the cops to her so now we have to get her out.
    Give her the flash drive she thinks you made before she was framed. Tell her Sugiyama has the phone; that you're both being framed; and that you've got to flee together. The three of you will

leave on Saturday from Vancouver, using papers you'll get from
Sonny. Assuming she comes with you, imagine her surprise.

Leave the phone with Farrago. If she won't come then he can
turn her in and my parents can bring Tiff later. The German link is
strong—seven more months to market. Watch her. Love, Byron

Love, Byron? They were black hole words, sucking the light from the
cafeteria, or as Gaitano termed it, the negative space.

Byron and Dietrich had staged the crash. They used Sonny for their
pyrotechnics. Once Beverly was executed, or killed, Byron and Dietrich
would be Tiffany's parents. The expensive ring he'd purchased was for
Dietrich.

Byron had been liquidating his assets for a year, while Dietrich had
been seducing Bev. Perhaps there was no murder plot at VVG. Sugiyama
and Yamamoto were now the victims and the investors were back under
Nakamura's thumb.

Byron Wells, the master gamesman, the creator of illusions—from
his prenup, to embezzling his estate, to faking his own death. But it wasn't
enough. He had to have his daughter so he could raise her with his new
partner. She was the ultimate prize. He would've lost her in family court,
so he'd moved the contest to a more familiar grid—one of lies and grand
deception.

Had Tiffany disappeared without her mother, Interpol would have
started searching for a resurrected Byron. But Tiffany was meant to vanish
with her mother. The authorities would have focused their search on Bev—
and never would have found her. God only knows what Byron would have
done to her.

Les's pictures were the only snag. Byron's father told Dietrich about
them on the night of the crash, which meant the Wellses were in on it too.
Dietrich panicked, not just because Les had filmed the killer, but because
his pictures might prove who was and wasn't on that flight.

The mystery around his disappearing phone and its link to Beverly
brought the cops in sooner and much closer than expected. Byron couldn't
risk her arrest because she knew too much, or maybe he was concerned
about the trauma to his daughter. So he tried to get them out.

Gaitano might be wrong that staging their deaths was a rush job.
Beverly was framed in a rush, but maybe they had months to plan the

crash. The April 1 email from Nakamura, discovered on his flight to Kyoto, could have been a plant.

He wondered when the senior Wellses had first learned. Maybe they knew only that their son had been warned about a bomb, but by the time of the crash they were privy to his scheme. He replayed Gaitano's words: "In fact, they all should've left by the time we called." In truth they weren't going to the recital—and not because Tiffany threw a tantrum. They were waiting for the police to call.

Was Beverly waiting too? He couldn't shake Monica's final comment—that Beverly had no doubt about the corpse, due to the look on Byron's face. What face? Was she so sedated that her eyes betrayed her? Or did she know it wasn't him and lied? Is that why she'd begged him for the papers to fly to Russia? Is that why she still tried to leave for Russia on the day she was arrested?

Byron's email suggested she was clueless. But what if Byron was playing his lover against his wife when he sent that email? What if they both knew about his plan, but were keeping it from the other? What if Byron put her up to killing Dietrich?

Les started writing. His hand was moved as if by another force. He was composing a second email sent on April 29 from Byron . . . this one to Beverly:

My Bev,
   We've arrived so this will be my only (I'm switching to the Vortex). I can't believe he felt he needed to frame you and that McKee stumbled on the statement. I was going to surprise you with the ring. That statement will lead the cops to you so now we have to get you out.
   David has a plan but don't go for it unless he surrenders the flash drive he made before he framed you. If he refuses, I'll get it from him here and then I'll kill him. Or you could—at his meeting with McKee (the staged assassination). Why not make it real? If not then the three of you will leave on Saturday from Vancouver, using papers you'll get from David. Assuming he comes with you, imagine his surprise.
   He's lying about Sugiyama. Just get the drive. The German link is strong—seven more months to market. Watch him. Love, Byron

His mind was in a state of torment. *Was she in on it?* Was it possible Byron had her so duped that she believed they'd reconcile if she helped him fake his death? Had she seduced Dietrich to hatch a murder plot by suggesting he could run INTERACT as his reward? If so, was she playing Dietrich or was Dietrich playing her? Was she so blinded by Byron that she was prepared to take her secret to the gallows?

In the twisted reality only Byron could inhabit, both his lover and his wife had been vying for his affections. Did she realize he was going to betray her? Only Les knew that a second copy of the incriminating picture was emailed to Gaitano two days after her arrest—as a backup plan in case Les's phone failed to surface. That email couldn't have come from Dietrich, who was dead. It could only have come from Byron's parents or from Byron overseas.

Would Beverly reunite with Byron on her own, and bring Tiffany to him as soon as she got out? If so, she was headed for a trap. Assuming her decision to murder Dietrich was hers alone, Byron would soon have his revenge.

It was speculation. The only real evidence—Byron's email to Dietrich—suggested she was clueless. Dietrich's last words to Les were, "take it all, before she does." Was Dietrich afraid that Beverly would find Byron's email?

So here he was, paying his life-long poor tax to her when she didn't deserve it. Would her spell ever lift? He vowed it would, in fact, his life was about to change as soon as he stepped onto that plane.

Could he risk warning her? Maybe she knew and didn't want or need his help. Either way, he'd be signing his death warrant if he revealed what he knew. Let Gaitano break the case, or be consumed by it. If he could only believe in her innocence. But how? He had no confidence in anyone but himself and even that was waning.

She could have killed me but she didn't. He looked at his watch. Ten minutes to boarding. Time to execute his plan. He folded Byron's email, his list of questions, his notes, and the letter from Dietrich to Farrago. After folding each sheet four times, one way and then another, he carefully tore them along the folded lines, until he was looking at a pile of small squares. He moved them to the side and started writing on another sheet. This time he sketched a picture. Then along with several blank pages he tore them again into more small squares. Finally, one last sheet of paper.

Bev, I'm sorry. You begged me to believe you but I refused. I've never forgiven myself. Within two days of your arrest a second copy of the altered pictures arrived in Gaitano's email. He has no idea who sent them, but ask him if you don't believe me. Just be careful. I hope these papers show I'm not totally unforgivable. I still have feelings for you – feelings I can't face. –Les

He folded the note and slipped it along with Dietrich's passport and ticket into an envelope for her. On the outside he wrote, *Monica—please give this to her sealed.* He removed the contents. With five minutes until boarding, he scribbled a new sentence on the margin of the note and reinserted it with other papers. He sat motionless, his head in his hands, trying to decide. He'd done all he could. After this she was on her own. He too felt utterly alone.

CHAPTER FIFTY-TWO

But he was not alone.

A reporter named Marvin Foshaug was hot on his trail. He'd been eavesdropping during his brief exchange with Monica at Friday's press conference. He found it intriguing that the defendant's star witness was pursuing McKee, who'd testified for the State.

Foshaug had a contact in the police department who had intimated, strictly off the record, that the prosecutor had proof she never used, that Monica had lied for Beverly at trial. So when Monica's business card found its way into Les's palm, that smelled like a story.

Later that day he caught their act at the Stouffer Madison. He'd watched as she handed Les a cell phone. And by wandering over to their table at the appropriate time, he'd overheard their plan to meet at the airport on Sunday.

Now he sat pounding away on his lap tablet in a secluded corner of a Sea-Tac cafeteria. He'd been watching Les swill coffee and scrawl notes for going on two hours. It was plain to see the man was deeply troubled. Thank God he was finally looking at his watch.

Foshaug watched him tear the pages he'd been writing on into squares, then turn to clean sheets while he continued writing. Soon there were two piles of torn squares on the table. McKee folded and inserted a handwritten note, along with other papers, into an envelope, then jotted something on the outside. At one point he could have sworn he saw a passport. McKee took the papers out, put them back, then scribbled something else on his note, obviously conflicted.

Foshaug was eyeing the squares of paper, hoping against hope that

McKee would drop them in a waste bin. But instead he slipped one in each front pocket and took a seat beside Gate S-11. With his boarding pass in hand, he sat there like a slug until the third call announced that rows ten through twenty-four were boarding.

Foshaug scanned the concourse when suddenly there she was. She approached the gate, looking for McKee, though McKee did not look up. When she spotted him, she paused and stood there waiting. Foshaug watched as Les took his place in line.

That's when she made her move. It was over within seconds and without a single word exchanged between them. McKee gave her the envelope, then turned to board his flight.

Foshaug turned to follow Monica. She was almost running. He had to know what was in that envelope. Hot in pursuit, he turned one last time to confirm that McKee had boarded. He was three persons back from the attendant, who was checking passes. As he walked by a trash can, he reached into his pocket, pulled out the scraps of paper, and nonchalantly dropped them in.

Panic-stricken, Foshaug turned and scanned the crowd for Monica. She was about to disappear into the throng. He had to choose between her or those delectable bits of paper Les had deposited. *Damn it!* he thought. *I should've brought a partner.* But Foshaug was a bird of prey who hunted by himself. He had to act fast but it was *not* a decision he would make alone.

Fate would make it for him.

EPILOGUE

Monica walked briskly to the nearest Starbucks, where Rick Gaitano sat waiting for her.

"Here it is," she said excitedly.

The envelope was thick. Gaitano read Les's handwritten note to Beverly first. Then he opened a folded group of papers and examined several sheets of totally blank paper. He read the note again and puzzled over a sentence that McKee had crossed out: ~~I hope these papers show I'm not totally unforgivable.~~

"What papers for Christ's sake?" he said out loud. "Does he mean these blank pages?"

Les had scribbled a note to Monica in the margin: I'm sorry, Monica, she'll have to trust me.

"Damn it!" he swore. "That smart ass."

At the opposite end of the concourse, Foshaug was sitting in a bathroom stall, gingerly sifting through rotten apple cores, sticky yogurt cups and other miscellaneous trash. So far he'd recovered two dozen torn squares of paper, though most were blank. Still, the ones with Les's scribbles kept him working.

→ | ←

"Do we still have a deal?" Monica asked, disappointed.

Gaitano nodded. "This isn't your fault. He's wising up. I'll have an Illinois state trooper waiting for him at O'Hare with another warrant. Those papers are on him, whatever they are. Are you certain she didn't tell you what she was hoping to get?"

"No, he's the one who said it was papers. She just said he'd know what she wanted."

"Did she ever offer an opinion as to who killed Dietrich?"

"No."

"Did she ever accuse Dietrich of killing her husband?"

"No."

"I've been over that recording of your meeting with McKee. It's clear he knows that Dietrich got her to rent the Vette. Since Dietrich framed her, it gives her a motive for his murder. It's a shame McKee was her lawyer, I'd bet my career she confessed to him that night."

"Do I still give her his note?"

"Yeah," he replied. He didn't like the warning Les had slipped inside, but decided it didn't matter. *She'll lead me to Byron no matter who warns her not to go.*

"Detective?" she continued. "I expect you to keep your word. You can't let her know I tried to help you."

"Your secret is safe, Monica, as long as mine is too. She can't know I'm looking into her for Dietrich's murder. If you double-cross me, I can still have those perjury charges filed."

"Really? You'd have to subpoena Marcia McKee and she lives in Chicago. I don't think you want to do that."

Gaitano laughed out loud. "Are you kidding? She'd love to put you or Beverly back in jail. In fact I should call her now and ask her to nab those papers from her husband as he steps off the plane, or while he's bear-hugging his little girl at baggage claim."

Foshaug emerged from his stall and headed dejectedly for the parking garage. He should've followed Monica. He realized it now. All but one of the five pages he'd reconstructed were totally blank. On a single sheet of paper, McKee had written eight simple words to him.

Next time, asshole, try and be less conspicuous.

He'd sketched a hot-air balloon with a smiley face inside.

"Can't you bust him with that recording?" she asked. "I mean he was a witness to Dietrich's murder."

"Maybe," he replied. "Circumventing Farrago? Fleeing a crime scene? There's just one hitch. That tape would never reach a jury. It's inadmissible. Maybe I could get the Bar Association to punch his ticket, but he's gone inactive. Besides, if he knew you made a copy, then your secret would be out. Too bad, because you can hear Dietrich dying on that tape. He mumbled something to McKee before he passed. I just can't make it out."

"She never told me how she got it," Monica said.

"I can't believe you had it all this time. It might've helped had you told me sooner. Maybe we wouldn't have charged her, much less plunked her on death row. Dietrich is pretty convincing on there about her innocence. You must have some idea why she had you keep it secret, and why she was so eager to have you perpetuate that ridiculous story from the stand. Why is she protecting Dietrich? He framed her, at least he helped, and now he's dead."

"Les must have given her the tape, but why? She could have gotten him in trouble."

"He'd just witnessed a murder and he was on the run. Maybe he was afraid we'd hunt him down and find it on him. He was smart enough to realize that Dietrich would frisk him for a wire, so he must have concealed it some other way. I clock three minutes between the shots and when the device shuts off. I can't tell if McKee turned it off or if one of the shooters came back in and found it. But there's no way she was in on this with Sonny."

"You said she was thirty miles away at the time."

"McKee drove from the murder scene to meet her. They must have listened to it, then for some reason he let her have it. Or maybe she took it from him before she pulled the trigger. I keep wondering if she took a shot at him."

"Are you sure you want back on this case, Detective?"

"I never left it. By the way, do you think she would have reconciled with Byron?"

"Who knows? I think she held out hope."

"Did she ever tell you that he bought her a fancy ring before he died?"

"You mean a diamond?"

"Almost sixty grand."

"Really? Her wedding ring was the biggest rock I've seen."

"We took both rings from her when we arrested her in Canada. The new one was even bigger and brighter. Ask her to show it to you when she gets out. We have to give her both rings back."

"She was wearing double diamonds when she got arrested? That's weird."

"No. The new one was in her purse. The weird thing is that it was a man's wedding band."

As they walked toward the escalator Gaitano grabbed her sharply by the arm and moved her to the side. "See that bozo on the escalator, in the tweed jacket? His name is Foshaug and he's from the fucking *Times*. He's more obsessed with the case than me, which means he probably followed you here. Shit! Maybe you lost him, but he'll be waiting for you at the top of that escalator. If he sees me with you I'll have some explaining to do. Go on ahead. Just ignore him and go home. I'll call you later."

At twenty thousand feet and fifty miles to the east, Les observed the seatbelt light go off. As luck would have it, he'd drawn a seat next to a software geek who babbled on incessantly about how he programmed XML for Digitron—the whole time keyboarding on his tablet.

Les was expecting a search warrant at O'Hare, so perhaps the opportunity had just presented itself to offload the Galileo and the smartwatch that were hiding in the bag beneath his seat. Earlier he'd smashed Dietrich's recording device with a fire extinguisher in the hotel garage, scattering its remains in a nearby dumpster.

He was planning a visit to the head. His left front pocket was still bulging with torn squares of paper, the ones he couldn't let anyone see, along with Dietrich's passport and ticket. He would finish tearing everything into very small squares and flush it all down the airplane toilet, saying not one word to Marcia. He chuckled inwardly at the thought of Gaitano and his men sifting through the mucky sewage fluid of the 777's latrine.

Staring out at the vast emptiness beneath him, he thought of how little he really knew. She was as distant and unknowable as the clouds that drifted past him.

Maybe Byron's parents were the only ones who'd misidentified the corpse. Perhaps Beverly was in too much shock and grief—or too sedated to look that closely at the body she believed to be her husband's.

As for her phony passports, maybe she saw them simply as a means of escape. She knew what would happen to her if Les turned in his phone. It's possible she had no idea why Dietrich had chosen Russia for their destination.

He was content to let it go. To let her go. It was time, finally, to flush away the past. As he unfastened his seatbelt he noticed the geek beside him was inserting a demo DVD bearing a Sprung Technologies logo. *It was time to make his move.*

"What's that?" he asked, as a game entitled *EuroGlider* flashed across the screen.

"Virtual Reality," his seatmate answered. "My company's in a patent war with VVG since a federal judge ordered them to grant us public domain rights to the Vortex, even cell devices will soon get in.

"Sprung just released an HMD they claim will make video screens obsolete. It beams the image to your eyes, using blue-tooth from a cell. This is a demo of their flagship game, which you'll be able to play inside the Vortex, once all the appeals are concluded."

"You mean an HMD like this?" he asked, as he removed the Galileo from the bag beneath his seat.

"Holy shit! You know about this?" his seatmate exclaimed. "Those aren't even legal in the States. How did you get your hands on one?"

"Actually, I know the guys who made it."

"That's awesome. You know them? Dude, your friends are seriously nasty."

"I agree," he said. "Especially if you're into alternate realities and violence."

"Any chance I can try that sucker out?"

"Here, you can have it, along with the transmitter and the matching gloves." As he stood to find the lavatory he said, "You'll need a charger for them, which I don't have, but I'm sure you'll figure it out. Consider yourself the proud owner of the next generation in hand-eye coordination."

"This is un-freaking-believable." His seatmate was delighted.

"It's a prototype," Les said. "I'm not sure how to run it, but track that down and get those magic things to glow."

"Are you serious? This is off-the-chains. Thanks, man. And thank your friends for me the next time you see them."

"I might just do that," he replied, then he turned and headed down the aisle.

⤙ THE END ⤚

ACKNOWLEDGMENTS

I've been tinkering with *CONSUMED* since completing the original in 1994 (called *TWICE BURNED*). Les McKee was using a VHS camcorder in the day. I would like to acknowledge, as a group, dozens of friends and professional colleagues who have contributed immeasurably to its content and many re-writes over all that time.

I'm especially indebted to Jo Cripps, editor extraordinaire, who labored with me for months on perfecting the first re-write, back when collaboration meant dropping-off chapters of handwritten mark-ups at odd hours on one another's doorstep.

Many thanks to Melanie Austin for editing the final draft; to Margaret Fitzpatrick, for proof-reading it; and to Maureen Hoffmann for the wonderful cover art.

Most of all, thanks to each of my three children, who inspired me to write and revise until the finish line was crossed. And to Linda, my wife, my best friend, and my partner in crime (writing) – there simply are no words.

ABOUT THE AUTHOR

Michael W. Bugni is a Seattle lawyer of 30 years. He is married (once), the father of three and an avid enthusiast of all things Pacific Northwest. CONSUMED is his debut novel, an adventurous peek into the puzzling world of the family law attorney. For more, visit www.consumedthebook.com.

CONSUMED

money and power takin' you higher
up and up 'till you catch on fire

watch what's next better stay in-tune
get too close you will be consumed

divorce and scandal six men dead?
get out now Les this is over your head

just can't shake it, smoke on meat
rumors of an arson on Bourbon Street

virtue or virtual make your pick
'cause they're coming for you 'gonna
    make it stick

callin' you a liar fillin' you with dread?
get out now Les he is into your head

lots of dough but where's the money
cover your ass but don't trust Sonny

secret emails, corporate seizure
when will somebody get the picture?

find your gun or you'll end up dead
get out now Les you are over your head

it's a damned inferno and it feels
    like hell
you 'wanna come clean but your
    phone won't tell

rottin' in jail 'gonna get released?
they're playin' you man like a game
    board piece

fate and beauty takin' her to bed?
get out now Les she is into your head

CPSIA information can be obtained at www.ICGtesting.com
Printed in the USA
BVOW04s2229250314

348737BV00001B/3/P